Where the River Settles

-THE LOST PAGES-

HYMNS OF BLUE HOLLOW

BOOK 2

A novel by

Kemma Marshall

To the Ians in this world—
the men who wrap their arms around those they love,
shielding them with their bodies, minds, and spirits.
Who stand still in the storm so others can rest.
We love you.

Content Warnings

This story contains mature themes, including sexually explicit content, nudity, profanity, depictions of violence, and sensitive topics such as underage sexual assault from the victim's perspective. **Reader discretion is advised.**

Chapters marked with the symbol * contain **vivid, graphic sexual scenes.** These chapters are written with care, meant to reflect the depth of the characters' emotional and physical journey.

This book is a work of historical fiction that presents perspectives and events from the 1940s to offer an authentic account of the period. Some of the views and behaviors represented are not those of the author and are included to explore themes such as racism and the social attitudes of the era.

Playlist

Animal by *MILCK*
Thread by *Hunter Metts*
Someone To You by *Matt Hansen*
Sometimes by *Ashley Singh*
Control by *Zoe Wees*
More To This by *Marc Scibilia*
The River by *Hunter Metts*
Comatose by *Søen Ven*
Feel For Me-Live by *Foy Vancy, The Ulster Orchestra*
Cry by *Cigarettes After Sex*
Open by *Hunter Metts*
Hold Me Steady – Alt Version by *Valerie Broussard, Ronen*
Over Me by *Camylio*
Wild Horses by *Inland Sky*
Lovers to Strangers by *Chance Peña*
Oh What a Mess I'm In by *Hayden Calnin*
One More Dance by *d4vd*
Surrender *by Birdy*

Preface

This is the second book in the *Hymns of Blue Hollow* series and is part of *The Lost Pages*. It picks up at the end of **Chapter 43: Larkin** of *Hymns of Blue Hollow* (Book 1). This is not a standalone novel and assumes the reader is familiar with the events and characters of the first book. These pages unfold in the space between that chapter and **Chapter 44: Missing Pages.**

Some stories are left untold—not because they don't matter, but because they exist in the hidden spaces between chapters.

If you've walked this path before, you know where it leads. But now, you'll see the steps that were never written.

Chapter 1: Not Forgotten

Sunlight struck the windshield of Ian's old truck, scattering silvered reflections across the cracked surface of the dashboard. The blue Ford sat parked in front of Larkin's small red-brick police station, a silent witness to whatever reckoning lay ahead.

The building, squat and square, radiated the day's heat like an oven—thick, stifling, and draining.

Abram was perched on the worn wooden steps just outside, his hat tipped low, casting a slant of shadow over his face. He leaned forward, elbows on his knees, fingers restless, like he had a mind to jump up at any moment but resisted. They needed to wait—wait for word that they were free to leave, to go.

Inside the open passenger door, Esther sat on the edge of the truck seat, her fingers moving gently across Ian's brow. She held a handkerchief in her hand, dabbing, working at the thin line of dried blood that crossed his face. Her hands were careful but unsteady— her breath barely there, as if even breathing too loud might unravel her.

Ian braced a hand on the truck's frame, watching her with a patient intensity. He didn't flinch at the sting or pull away from her touch, simply letting her work. A slight tremor ran through her fingers as she focused on the task; a small frown pinched at her brow, as if she were tending to something delicate—breakable.

There was quiet around them, the kind of silence that follows when the world shifts in a way that can't be undone.

Ian's voice, when it came, was a murmur, meant for her alone. "I'm alright, Esther." His hand shifted, brushing against her shoulder.

But she said nothing, her lips tight, her eyes still wide. He could feel her worry—not just for him, but for everything that had happened earlier that afternoon. It clung to her, pulling her back into the moments she couldn't outrun. As if she were tearing through the fields, her feet striking the earth, the ground rushing beneath her— even as her body remained motionless.

Not sure if he should break the fragile peace between them, he gave in to the question that gnawed at him—rough-edged and restless.

"Esther... why did you go to Clive's house?"

Her hand stilled for the briefest second, but she didn't look up. Instead, her gaze dropped to the crumpled handkerchief in her lap, a guarded flicker crossing her face.

She opened her mouth as if to speak, then closed it just as quickly. Ian waited, the question hanging there between them, but she gave him nothing—only the faintest shake of her head, an answer buried in a place he couldn't reach.

Then came the rumble of an engine, breaking the quiet as it grew louder. Sheriff Ronell's police cruiser pulled up, tires dragging to a slow, deliberate stop against the unpaved road. Esther looked up, catching the sheriff's tired face through the dusty windshield. The day had harrowed his expression, carving new lines into his face— each one telling of something he wished he could forget.

Ronell stepped out, moving slowly, his shoulders bent with a kind of weary resignation. He gave a brief nod toward Abram on the steps, then turned to Ian with a somber look that said more than words could.

Ian took it as his cue and stepped away from Esther, meeting the sheriff halfway. His frame was stiff, every muscle drawn tight beneath his skin as Ronell began to speak, their voices low.

Esther watched them, clutching the bloodied handkerchief, her breath catching with each murmur that reached her ears. She could see Ian's face shift as he listened—as he swallowed, suppressing the ire beneath the surface, then worry, then something like acceptance settling into his features.

After a good ten minutes, he returned to the vehicle, his face cast in shadow as he leaned into the door, as if whatever had been discussed was now taken care of.

"Let's go home," he said, his voice calm as he offered a reassuring smile.

Esther nodded as she shifted back on the seat, making room for him.

He hesitated, then glanced toward the narrow cab.

"It's pretty tight in here," he murmured, reaching for her hand. "Why don't you sit on my lap, darlin'?"

She didn't protest, moving onto his knee. He liked that she didn't question him, just trusted him, her arms sliding easily around his neck.

Abram watched them from the driver's seat, a flicker of amusement crossing his face. With a gentle jolt, the Blue Ford pulled away, leaving Larkin behind. The remnants of something narrowly escaped trailed in their wake.

As they climbed the winding road toward the Old Reed Estate, Esther rested her head against Ian's hard shoulder, feeling his steady, even breath. She could feel the strength in his arms, as though he could hide her from all the shadows that haunted her, if only she'd let him.

The trees began closing in, hemming the road in shadow, the green foothills welcoming them back. Only then did she feel safe enough to speak, her voice low and frayed as she lifted her head.

"I was certain... certain Frank was gonna run right over me. End me fer sure," she murmured.

Ian's hand tightened on her waist, a gentle reassurance as he nodded. "Sheriff Ronell told me Frank confessed to killing Clive," he said, his tone careful, each word deliberate. "Shot him. I guess he was desperate."

Ian watched her, searching her face for an answer. After a beat, he asked, "Do you know why?"

Esther's hand stilled against his chest, her shoulders tense as she gave the slightest nod. She didn't offer anything more. Just a wall of silence.

Ian let the quiet settle again between them, his mind filling in the possibilities. He could see it in her eyes—she knew something, some type of truth, but whatever it was, she didn't want to share it.

The truck slowed as they turned up the drive toward Clarissa's house, the familiar shape of the old home coming into view, its walls bathed in the late afternoon light. Abram parked, and the engine sputtered to a stop, leaving only the sound of a gentle rustle through the trees carried on a warm breeze.

Ian helped Esther down from the passenger seat, taking her hand as he led her to the front doorway.

He was home. She was home. And what lay ahead was uncharted but was filled with possibility.

The storm of yesterday had spent itself, leaving them both standing—windblown, worn, but free.

Chapter 2: Indisposed

The old house creaked beneath a strong gust of springtime wind, pushing and pulling at its wooden frame. Esther tried to will peace into her body as she lay back in the bath, the tepid water soothing against her skin. She breathed in the familiar scent of lavender soap, a smell that seemed to belong to the house itself, especially that room.

She closed her eyes as she worked to release the world outside, but her body was her enemy—resisting her. Her hands trembled on the edge of the tub, knuckles clenched, as if they couldn't release.

The truth was, it was more than just what had occurred that day. It was something much more. Something she wished she could just rid herself of.

It was the thirst, the desperate ache for alcohol.

Withdrawal was coursing through her like a beast that refused to be ignored. It was subtle at moments but kept returning—sharper, more insidious—a deathly current beneath still water.

Believing she'd finally managed to calm herself, she remained inert—only for it to return out of nowhere, her breaths turning shallow again. Over and over, she sought to pace her body, as though she could stave off the storm brewing within her by keeping motionless.

She let herself sink beneath the water for a moment, holding her breath, letting the coolness press against her skin, muting the shaking in her hands.

When she surfaced, wiping water from her eyes, she blinked in surprise to find Ian standing in the open doorway, his frame leaning against the door jamb, his gaze softened with a hint of mischief.

"Well, look at this… seems you're a little indisposed," he murmured, a grin tugging at his lips. "You've been up here a while, just wanted to make sure you were all right. I knocked, but you didn't answer."

She raised a brow, looking up at him with a small, bemused smile. "Indisposed?" she asked, her tone cautious, unfamiliar with the word.

He leaned closer, his gaze holding hers as he clarified, "Naked, Esther."

Her eyes narrowed in playful warning, her lips quirking at the edges.

"Ya know yer gonna get caught in here with me," she teased, shifting slightly in the tub, her arms instinctively crossing over her chest.

Ian shut the door behind him, casting a quick, assured glance out the window before turning back to her with a grin.

"Nope. Clarissa's outside, busy with the wash."

With that, he eased himself down on the edge of the tub. His hand slipped casually into the water, fingers grazing hers just beneath the surface.

There was something about the way he was taking her in—her vulnerability, something she wasn't used to showing.

"I didn't know ya had such a wicked side," she murmured.

His grin widened as he leaned in closer, his face inches from hers, his breath warm against her skin.

"I've got a lot of sides," he replied, his voice a low murmur before he closed the space between them, pressing a soft kiss to her lips. The warmth of him melted away some of her tension as they lingered in the hush of a stolen moment.

"Ian," she said softly.

"Yes?" he replied, his eyes fixed on her.

"My water's getting cold."

"Yeah, it feels a little cool," he answered, not moving, his gaze holding hers, refusing to be hurried.

She gave him a small, amused sigh.

"I need to get out of the tub," she said, lifting her brows, expecting him to give her space. But Ian sat there, unmoving, his eyes smoldering as they lingered on her.

"Did ya really come in here just to see me nekkid?" she asked, a playful smirk pulling at her lips as she scooped a handful of water and sprinkled it over his arm.

He just laughed, taking it without flinching, holding his ground.

"Well, all right, then," she said, finally surrendering to his charm. "At least give me a hand up."

Ever the gentleman, Ian stood and offered his hand, his gaze steady as she summoned courage.

Slowly, she rose from the bath, exposing herself in her full glory. Her heart raced, her breath catching as she felt his eyes wash over her bare skin.

Water trickled down her glistening body. A slow, pleased grin spread across his face, satisfaction lingering in his gaze. It made her heart flutter, knowing she had shocked him with her boldness, liking it when she caught him off guard—though she was still completely uncomfortable.

Unable to resist touching her, he reached out, his hand settling on her arm as he took in her beauty, head to toe. A soft, awe-filled whisper escaped him, slipping out in his native tongue.

"Mein Gott, Esther, du bist so schön."

And beneath that, whispered more to himself, letting the words trail off, "Ich liebe dich..."

Esther's brows knitted gently as she looked up at him.

"What... what did ya just say to me?" she asked.

"I said... how beautiful you are."

But he lacked the courage to tell her what he had truly spoken. He hid the confession behind the comfort of a foreign tongue—words that conveyed more than just her beauty.

He wanted more than ever to say it here and now, to pull her close and speak the words plainly. But he cautioned himself—it would've been the wrong moment. Not when she stood there, bare, exposed, and cold.

She gave a small, nervous smile at his words as he reached for her, pulling her damp skin against him, his arms wrapping around her torso, enveloping her as though he never planned to let go.

"I'm all wet," she murmured.

"I don't care," he replied, his embrace tightening around her, as if to prove it.

Her body gave a soft shudder, one she couldn't control, and she whispered, "Ian, I'm kinda cold."

Without a word, he reached for a towel, wrapping it around her carefully, his hands gentle as they moved across her back. But as he held her, he felt it again, a tremor that went far beyond a chill—her breath was shallow, her body fragile against him.

He pulled back just enough to look at her.

"Are you all right?" he asked, sensing that the playful edge between them had faded.

Only then did he see it, the real vulnerability hidden in her eyes.

"I'm plumb give out," Esther mumbled. "Think I might need to lay down fer a bit."

He studied her, seeing the same weariness in her eyes that he'd seen after she had run from Clive in the rain days earlier. She looked spent, like something deep inside her had drained away, leaving her empty.

"Esther," he asked softly, "have you eaten anything today?"

She answered with a small shake of her head, her eyes not quite meeting his. "This mornin'," she replied, though she knew it wasn't exactly the truth. Her breakfast had left her stomach almost as quickly as she'd managed to get it down, nausea hitting her before she'd left for Larkin.

Ian drew the towel close around her, his hands lingering as he gently dried her off.

"Why don't you go get dressed," he suggested, "and I'll bring something up to your room." With that, he leaned down, pressing a tender, lingering kiss to the top of her head.

"Ya ain't gotta do that," she replied—though the way she clutched the towel indicated otherwise.

He walked her to her door and watched as she slipped inside, pulling it closed behind her.

He lingered for a moment, then turned and made his way down the stairs, his mind drifting back to what had happened in the bathroom. What had started as a playful excuse to sneak a peek of her in the tub had unfolded into something more—something intimate and unexpected.

He had thought for sure she'd toss him out the moment he poked his head in. But instead, she'd let him stay—only giving him a mild scolding.

A grin crept across his face—the kind a man didn't earn without seeing something he wasn't supposed to—her nude body still vivid in his mind.

The fridge door swung open as he reached in to grab some cold cuts, thinking he'd fix her something simple.

Just as he did, Clarissa pushed open the screen door, her arms wrapped around a large laundry basket.

Ian hurried over to hold it open, his expression easy as she stepped inside, her gaze catching on the gash on his forehead.

"They sure did a number on ya," she remarked, eyebrows raised in disapproval.

He shook it off, giving her a half-smile.

"Ah, Clarissa, it's a long story. Too long a story for right now." He paused, glancing up towards the direction of Esther's room.

"Do you think Mitzy would mind keeping Benjamin and Rebecca a bit longer? Esther's worn out. I'm taking her something to eat, then she'll likely nap for a while."

Clarissa nodded, her own concern flickering across her face. "That's a good idea. Ain't seen that girl eat more than a nibble these past couple days—got me worried."

Ian pulled a loaf of bread from under a towel and began slicing.

"You think she's alright?" he asked, his voice low. "She doesn't seem to have the same strength she used to."

Clarissa reached out, taking the bread from him as she started making a sandwich.

"Well, honey," she said with a sigh, "maybe more happened in them seven months than she's lettin' on. That kind of darkness... it takes its toll."

He listened, crossing his arms as her words settled over him. Clarissa moved to the icebox, pulling out a quart of milk, and he grabbed a glass from the cupboard. As she filled it, he spoke up, his tone hesitant.

"You don't think I'm... rushing her too fast, do you?" He realized he'd revealed more than he intended and tried to rephrase. "I mean... courting her—making my intentions clear."

Clarissa smiled, her eyes warm with reassurance. Handing him the plate and glass, she said, "No, I don't think so. That girl's had her eye on you since she first got here. If anythin', you'll help her find herself again. Just keep bein' sweet on her, honey."

Ian's smile deepened, feeling a bit of the weight lifted from his shoulders. "I don't know what I'd do without you, Clarissa," he said.

Her eyes twinkled with mischief as she gave him a pat on the back.

"Thought I was gonna have to break your tail out of that jail," she teased.

He laughed, shaking his head. "Wouldn't have surprised me if you had."

"Oh, I would've. They best not test me," she called after him as he headed toward the stairs, her chuckle trailing behind him.

Chapter 3: Painter Ghost

When Ian opened Esther's door, he found her lying on her bed, her body tucked against the wall, a pretty yellow knitted blanket curled around her shoulder. Her breaths came slow and steady, the kind of peaceful rhythm that spoke of deep sleep. Her long hair—still damp—flared out across her pillow like dark silk unraveling.

Setting down the food he'd brought, he sat beside her, gently rubbing her back, hating to bother her as he tried to wake her.

"Esther, I brought you something to eat," he said quietly. But she didn't stir, having fully surrendered to rest. He lingered, watching the calm that had overtaken her.

Days before, when he'd brought her home from Clive's, he hadn't dared curl up behind her—too restrained, too unsure. But now, everything had changed. They had been intimate, lain with each other, blurring the lines of propriety.

And earlier that day, when he had witnessed Frank's cruiser hurtling toward her, a visceral terror had registered in his gut. The traces of it still lingered—a reminder of what he'd only just found and how close he'd come to losing it.

That fear hadn't fully left him, and it had worn on him too, leaving a quiet, persistent longing—to feel her presence, her body close to his. So he let the desire take over. Just this once, he reasoned.

Feeling he'd given himself enough justification, Ian lay down, his long frame barely fitting, his feet hanging off the bed as he curled up behind her. His arm slipped gently around her waist as he pulled her close.

As his body molded against hers, he felt her sigh—a soft, contented sound, even as she slept—almost as if his presence offered her peace, a sanctuary in his arms.

Planning only to stay a short while, his own fatigue took over, and soon, he too drifted off, surrendering to the sweet comfort and warmth of her.

Hours later, Ian was startled awake by the sound of a familiar young voice.

"Papa... Papa, you need to wake up."

Blinking in the dim light, Ian found his son, Benjamin, standing at the bedside, looking at him with curious eyes.

"Aww, I'm up..." he mumbled, blinking as he shook off the fog of sleep. It took him a second to realize he was still lying behind Esther, his arm tucked around her. He quickly pulled back, sitting up and running a hand through his hair, scrambling for something—anything—to explain himself.

"Auntie said I needed to come wake y'all up for supper," Benjamin announced, seemingly unbothered by the situation.

Ian rubbed a hand over his face, glancing out the window to see the dark sky. "Well, I'm awake. Esther was... cold... so I was just keeping her warm."

He knew Benjamin was sharp, observant, and that he'd likely already made his own assessment, but to his relief, the boy simply shrugged.

"Tell Clarissa we'll be down in a bit," Ian said, trying to keep things simple. As Benjamin turned to leave, Ian wondered whether he should ask if Clarissa knew he was napping with Esther, but he decided against it, wanting to avoid any unnecessary explanations.

He pulled himself up, trying to tuck in his shirt as Benjamin paused at the doorway, glancing back with a question in his young eyes.

"Pa?" he asked.

"Yes, son?" Ian replied, bracing himself for what might come next.

"Do you and Esther kiss like Abram and Mitzy?"

Ian's face flushed with surprise, and his tone turned stern without meaning to. "Benjamin, don't ask questions like that."

Unfazed, Benjamin pressed on, his brow furrowing in childlike curiosity. "But why do girls like to be kissed so much?"

Ian let out a small laugh, though he quickly stifled it.

He moved toward the door, placing a guiding hand on Benjamin's shoulder and gently ushering him out. Once they were in the hallway, he leaned down to meet his son's inquisitive gaze.

"You'll figure that out one day, son," he said. "But for now, head downstairs. Tell Auntie Clarissa that I'm waking Esther up."

Benjamin gave him a look that was both bewildered and a little amused, as though he wasn't entirely sure what his father meant, but he nodded dutifully.

Ian watched Benjamin disappear down the stairs, then shook his head and turned back to where Esther lay. He wanted that warmth from earlier to linger just a little longer.

He slipped back onto the bed beside her, leaning close and whispering softly into her ear.

"Esther—it's time to get up," he said as his hand gently rubbed her back.

She stirred slightly, a low sound escaping her, almost a groan, as her hand rose to rub her shoulder. He could see the exhaustion etched in her movements, as if even the smallest action was too much.

"I know you're tired, but you need to eat something," he coaxed, hoping to rouse her gently.

"I can't... I ain't hungry," she replied, her voice soft and drawn, her words fading almost as soon as she spoke them.

"Come on, Esther," Ian said, pulling himself up and reaching down to turn her toward him. As she faced him, he noticed her pallor, the faint sheen of sweat across her brow.

"What's going on?" he asked, concerned. "Are you feeling unwell?" His mind worked through possibilities, wondering if her run through the field had taken more of a toll than he'd realized—maybe she had gotten overheated, perhaps even suffering from heat exhaustion.

He reached over, feeling her forehead with the back of his large hand, but she felt almost cool to the touch—no sign of a fever.

She forced a weak smile, shrugging as if to brush off his worry.

"Reckon I didn't sleep much last night," she offered, pushing herself up. But as she swung her legs over the side of the bed, her hands began to shake, and she moved quickly to sit on them, trying to hide the tremors.

He frowned, his heavy brows drawing lower.

"I really think you need to eat something," he insisted, reaching down to help her up. "You can go back to bed after."

She nodded reluctantly, putting on a small, forced smile as she took his hand, using it to steady herself.

But underneath, she could feel a storm raging, a raw, burning need clawing at her, whispering of the relief she'd find in a glass bottle.

The craving was a physical pain now, a ruthless ache that gripped her like a beast with claws sunk deep.

She wanted to cry, to let it all out, but she swallowed the feeling. Distraction would have to be enough.

"If ya think so," she said softly, trusting he was right, hoping that food might help restore her.

They made their way downstairs to the dining room. The table was set with the usual care but with a bit more elegance than normal, as though Clarissa had made a celebration of Ian's quick release.

The others were already seated, and Ian led Esther to their usual spots—seats Clarissa had strategically placed next to each other last year. Esther's place had stayed empty then, waiting for her to return.

As Ian helped scoot her chair in, Mitzy glanced over, catching his eye with a satisfied smile. She nudged Abram, who gave a slight nod, an amused look in his eye as he passed a large bowl of roasted potatoes.

Mitzy felt a little smug, having told Abram they'd end up together—no matter how much he'd disagreed. Ian and Esther were a pairing that felt natural... maybe even inevitable. And Ian, for all his good looks, had stayed a bachelor far too long, in her opinion.

Yes, Mitzy felt like she had maybe even played a small part in the matchmaking, always seeding the idea whenever given the opportunity. She'd known, even last year, that they were destined for one another—always catching them smiling at each other, passing playful, flirty words back and forth.

She'd never wasted an opportunity, telling Esther things like, "Look... Ian's taking his shirt off. He only does that when you're around." Mitzy smiled at the thought, remembering how Esther had turned bright red and begged her not to say something like that so loudly.

Ian barely had time to settle into his chair before Rebecca, having missed her father, got up and trotted over to him. Wrapping her arms around his neck, she clung to him, her small fingers brushing the gash on his forehead as she examined it.

"Did a panther get ya or somethin'?" she asked, her eyes wide.

Ian chuckled, hugging her and pulling her onto his lap for a moment.

"No, sweet girl. And I don't think there are any panthers in these mountains," he said.

Rebecca turned to Esther, seeking validation. "Oh yes, Pa, there is. Esther told us 'bout them before."

Esther's mouth curved into a faint smile as Ian shot her a playful, questioning look.

"No, I'm sure Esther wouldn't have told you any nonsense about black panthers roaming the hills, right?" he teased.

Benjamin joined in eagerly, grinning as he said, "She said there was one that cries like a baby to lure folks into the woods so it can eat 'em!"

Esther laughed, shaking her head. "That's not exactly what I said... well, not quite."

Ian raised a brow. "Maybe we should save those kinds of stories for later—when they're older and start thinking sneaking around in the dark is a good idea."

Abram leaned forward with a grin, adding his own flourish to the tale. "I've heard tell of that panther they call the Ghost Painter, roaming the ridges after dark, huntin' those that wander too far..."

Mitzy nudged him sharply, frowning. "Ya not helpin'," she scolded. "Don't you listen to him, young'uns—he doesn't know what he's talkin' 'bout."

Just then, Clarissa swept into the room with a bottle of her cherished blackberry wine in hand. Without a word, she made her way around the table, pouring portions for each of the adults.

As she passed behind Esther, Rebecca trailed close behind, letting out a playful growl, fingers curled like claws as if she were stalking her prey, drawing a giggle from Benjamin.

But strangely, Esther didn't laugh.

She didn't even smile.

Instead, she sat frozen, her expression shifting in a way that caught Ian's attention.

He recognized it—a quiet panic, raw and urgent.

Her eyes, locked in a trance-like state, were fixed on the glass of blackberry wine in front of her, its deep, rich color catching the light, almost taunting her.

Clarissa, unaware of the battle raging beneath Esther's calm exterior, had poured her a generous portion, the burgundy-colored liquid filling the glass more than halfway.

While the rest of the table buzzed with familiar chatter, Ian's focus stayed on Esther. Her face had tightened—lips pressed together—as if she were bracing herself.

Concerned, he kept watching, noting the way her gaze flicked to the wine glass, then away again, like it was something alive—something she feared.

She had never behaved this way before. It felt strange, and Clarissa's words from earlier echoed in his mind. Esther had changed.

His hand slipped beneath the table, reaching for hers, and as his fingers closed around hers, he felt it—her hand was cold, damp, and trembling with an unnatural shake that set off an alarm inside him.

Her grip tightened in his, almost instinctively, as she turned her gaze to his, a flicker of desperation mirrored in her eyes. It was a silent plea, and in an instant, he understood.

This was a beast he knew all too well, one he'd watched his father battle through in his youth—a battle that took years to win.

It was the same desperate longing, the same quiet agony he'd witnessed countless times, hidden behind the walls of a proud face.

But Ian could see Esther was trying—he could see that—fighting hard to resist the call of the drink that sat mere inches from her hand, battling while the rest of the room remained blissfully unaware of her struggle.

Without a word, Ian reached forward, his movements slow and deliberate, not wanting to draw attention.

His fingers wrapped around her glass, and with a subtle motion, he lifted it, pouring its contents into his own.

His eyes left hers only for a moment as he brought the filled glass to his lips and drank it down in a few gulps, the warmth of the blackberry wine washing over him.

Setting it down, he drew a steady breath, his chest rising and falling with the effort, as he looked back at her, meeting her gaze.

The relief in her expression was immediate, her shoulders sagging as her lips parted, and he could see the shimmer of unshed tears in her eyes. Her lower lip quivered, and she gave the faintest smile as she looked down at her plate, working to steady herself once more.

It had been so subtle, so quiet and unassuming, that it had gone entirely unnoticed as Clarissa continued passing dishes while Abram stayed caught up in a lighthearted debate with Mitzy.

They had no idea that, for Esther, that one small gesture had been nothing short of a rescue.

Ian reached for her hand again, giving her fingers a gentle squeeze and offering her what comfort he could.

With a soft smile, he nudged her plate a little closer, encouraging her to take a bite. She managed a small, shaky smile in return and lifted her fork, placing a piece of roast in her mouth, as though reclaiming a part of herself.

After dinner, Ian led Esther out onto the front porch, guiding her away from the crowd. As they walked toward the door, Rebecca tried to follow, her curious eyes wide, but Ian turned her around, ushering her back toward the table with his free hand.

"No, Rebecca," he said. "Go on now, help your aunt clear the table and do the dishes."

Benjamin, catching his father's intent, piped up with all the sincerity of a child. "They want to kiss out there."

"Oh my," Clarissa chuckled, gathering the children back toward the dining room.

She cast a smile in Ian's direction as he mouthed a quick, "Thank you," and she winked in return.

Once outside, Ian settled with Esther on the porch swing, reaching for the throw draped over the back and laying it across her lap. She leaned into him as he wrapped his arm around her shoulders, pulling her close.

The shaking grew more pronounced—a tremor running through her, her body revealing what she struggled to hide.

Ian knew he couldn't tiptoe around the problem any longer. If his fears were right, they needed to face them head-on—so he chose to be bold and ask her for the truth.

"Esther," he said softly, his voice careful. "How much did you drink at Clive's?"

His question sat there, not unheard, but not quickly answered, as Esther's body tensed.

A palpable fear rose within her, like the Black Painter itself was alive, watching her from the shadows.

With a warm hand, Ian turned her face toward his, seeking the same eyes he had made love to the night before—the eyes of the woman he cared so deeply for, wanting to convey it in the moment.

As if something had unlocked her voice, she spoke.

"Too much… way too much."

"Every day?" he asked, thinking of how easily she had drunk the whiskey in the barn—unafraid of the effect, familiar with the burn.

"I feel stupid, Ian," she said, pulling back slightly. She didn't want pity, nor did she want to be chastised for her choices—however reckless they had been.

"I did this to myself," she admitted, willing her hands to stop shaking.

With growing resolve, she turned to face him. Though her voice trembled, Esther vowed, "I ain't never gonna let these hands pick it up again."

She pushed herself up and crossed the porch, stepping down onto the wooden steps. Reaching the last one, she paused, staring out into the dark yard—like an abyss waiting beyond.

"I'll throw myself into the river 'fore I do," she said under her breath.

Not liking the direction of her words, Ian rose and followed. Taking a deep breath of the cool evening air, he turned, letting his own walls down, as if to meet her where she stood.

"I know I haven't told you much about my family, but my father's name is Wilhelm," Ian said, taking her hand as he led her farther out into the yard.

"Where we goin'?" She lightly resisted.

"Just a short walk—it's easier to talk while walking," he said.

Esther allowed him to lead her down the pebbled drive.

The same silken moonlight that had silhouetted them the night before now shone brightly as he guided her slowly down the lane, past the white fence.

"Growing up," Ian began, "everyone told me I looked just like my mother but that I had my father's personality. When I was young, I think I liked hearing it. But as I got older and saw the demons he faced… it started to bother me. One of those demons—well, it's the reason you don't see me drink much."

As they walked, Esther let him lead, feeling a strange relief in the steady movement of her feet. A light breeze wrapped around them, and the rhythmic sound of their steps against the ground dulled the shaking in her body—if only slightly.

Ian glanced over at her as he continued.

"Esther… my father had the same shakes in his hands. It took him a long time to fight through it, but he did." Ian paused, gauging her reaction, hoping she wouldn't be defensive.

"I don't need ya worryin' over me like that, Ian," she said, her tone sharp.

"I want to help you," he pleaded.

"My whole body's on fire… maybe ya could just put me out of my misery already," she said as she let out a bitter laugh and glanced sideways at him. "Maybe ya could just bring me some flowers on the hilltop and be done with it."

He halted, her words cutting through him painfully. He stopped in his tracks, gripping her arm to turn her toward him.

"Esther, stop talking like that. Don't say stupid nonsense like that. It isn't funny." His irritation flashed on his features.

"I had the hell scared out of me today—I thought…" He took a steadying breath. "I was sure I was about to watch Frank kill you."

His hands found her face, thumbs grazing her cheeks as he looked into her eyes, hoping to reach her through the desperation clouding them.

Not sure if the timing was right—almost certain it wasn't—but he wanted to say it anyway, to make her hear it, because keeping it unsaid felt like denying something that had already taken root—something that, the moment he named it, had become the driving force of his life.

Determined not to waste another second, he let the words go, surrendering them to her.

"I love you, Esther Primm," he said, searching for a reply in her moonlit eyes.

But it was like the sound had never left his mouth.

She stood there, unmoved, as though nothing had been said.

"Do you hear me?" he questioned her. "I love you."

He searched her eyes again, hoping to see some sign of recognition from his declaration.

Though he didn't expect her to relay the sentiment back to him—not just yet—it had lingered in him all day, waiting to share it with her.

A worry started to build in his normally confident demeanor, his chest tightening as he wondered if he had pushed things too fast.

Had he read her wrong, thinking his serious words might have frightened her?

Maybe she didn't want to hear them from him, despite liking his attention.

Instead of backing down, he doubled down, saying it one last time, softer, loosening his grip on her.

"I'm in love with you." The words left once more as an offering of his devotion, a rawness in his voice.

He was just a man, with a heart that could bleed as easily as hers, telling the woman he loved—her, giving her all the power over that heart and everything that it meant.

Finally, he saw a crack as a flicker softened her gaze, the cold shell slipping from her features. Her eyes swelled, tears spilling from the corners as his gaze held her.

His breath was heavy, and he stood firm in his truth.

"Ian…" she whispered, her voice barely there. She didn't say anything else, and he could see she was struggling to process his words, but he was certain they had made their mark as he had intended.

Then, without warning, she pulled back from him, pushing away as she stumbled toward the side of the dark road.

Doubling over, her whole body shook as she retched, her entire precious dinner lost.

She heaved over and over, though nothing else rose—only her chest. He leaned beside her, steadying her as best he could, holding her hair back with one hand.

When she was done, she staggered a few steps away, sinking to the ground in the grass, her knees pulled close to her chest. Ian watched her, then reached into his pocket, offering her his handkerchief.

"Here," he murmured softly. "Not quite the reaction I envisioned," he said playfully, but she didn't respond, only hanging her head lower.

Giving her time, he crouched beside her, his voice gentle. "Can you stand?"

She gave a slight nod, and he extended a hand, helping her to her feet. He waited a moment as she got her sea legs, remembering something his mother used to say to his father on nights like these.

"I think sleep's the only thing that'll fix this," he said. "I'm taking you back inside."

This time, she didn't resist as he led her back up the path toward the big house.

When they quietly slipped inside, the front room and hall were empty as distant sounds of dishes clattering and children laughing from the kitchen drifted toward them. Ian led her up the stairs, thankful they hadn't been noticed.

When they reached her bedroom, she sank down onto the bed, exhaustion etched across her face. Ian knelt down in front of her as she lay there.

"I'm going to leave my front door unlocked tonight," he said. "If you need me—please come get me. I wake easily."

Despite her fatigue, a small, mischievous smile tugged at her lips.

"What if the Ghost Painter slips into yer room instead of me?" she said as she gave him a sly look. "Or... maybe I'm the ghost."

He chuckled. "Well, I always knew you were part wildcat. Still got the bite marks from last summer to prove it." He rubbed his arm with a smirk.

Esther returned his smile, despite how crummy she felt.

He watched her close her eyes tightly, no longer resisting sleep's pull. When she had drifted off, he pressed a kiss to her forehead, then rose and slipped out of the room.

Downstairs, he found his children still gathered in the kitchen, lingering over a treat Clarissa had given them.

"All right, you two, time to get home and get some rest. You can do your studies tomorrow," he said, patting Benjamin on the back.

When the children had gone, Ian turned to Clarissa, his expression shifting. He took a step closer, keeping his voice low.

Wanting to prepare her and not wanting her to feel blamed, he said, "I want you to know, it isn't your fault. Please."

The seriousness in his tone stopped her in her tracks as he continued.

"Clarissa, we need to get the last of your blackberry wine put away, and any other spirits in the house. Remember when you said we didn't know what happened at Esther's cousin's place? Well... seems she hit the bottle pretty hard there."

A shocked expression passed over Clarissa's face as he continued.

"And I mean hard," he said, rubbing the back of his neck. "She's got the shakes, lost her dinner out on the road."

All the older woman could think about was how she had missed it, how she had thought something else was ailing her niece. She had even told Esther that she thought she was pregnant, not even considering this as a possibility.

"Sweet Jesus," she said.

"I don't want her to find a drop of it in the house," he said adamantly. "She's determined, but I don't want to make it any harder on her."

Clarissa nodded in agreement, even as her face fell, her eyes clouded with regret.

"Oh, Ian… I didn't know. And I filled her glass up at supper."

"It's not your fault, Clarissa," he quickly retorted.

"Can ya ever forgive me?" Her voice was a mixture of apology and worry as she gripped his shoulder.

He gave her a soft smile and placed a reassuring hand on hers.

"Only if you can forgive me for everything I've been up to lately, too," he replied, his tone half-serious, half-playful.

A small smile broke through Clarissa's worry as she squinted at him, something knowing in her expression.

"Not sure if I want to know what ya talkin' 'bout," she said as she continued. "But listen here, our girl's got an iron will when need be, Ian—she'll get through this. Folks got all sorts of reasons for drinkin' and not drinkin'. I reckon those young'uns of yours will give her more than enough reason to lick this."

He nodded, letting her hope settle over him. "I hope so, Clarissa. I pray she does."

Chapter 4: Ghosts in the River

Darkness had swallowed Esther whole as she drifted through a cavernous maze, untethered and lost. Desperate, she searched for an exit, her fingers trailing along the rough, wet walls as she turned down one stony tunnel after another—each leading to a dead end.

Then, without warning, the walls were gone.

She stood before the old moonshine still, nestled deep in the woods, a fire blazing too hot beneath it. Panic clutched at her chest as the flames surged, burning viciously, threatening to blow the delicate valve.

Esther dropped to her knees, yanking at the logs, but the fire only roared higher—licking at the hem of her dress. She watched in horror as it spread and crawled up her skirt, racing up to her waist.

In desperation, she ran down the hill toward the creek, plunging into the icy water. But somehow, the flames clung to her, dancing beneath the water's surface.

A familiar voice cut through her terror. Gran stood at the bank, her presence foreboding.

"You tryin' to steal from me?" Gran screamed, raising Pawdad's gun in the air and aiming it directly at her.

"Gran, it's me," Esther pleaded, reaching out, her voice catching.

Gran's face shifted, distorted, and then darkened into another familiar figure.

It was Clive. But not the Clive she had known in life—the bullet hole in his forehead marked him as the dead incarnation, though he seemed unbothered.

His laugh rang out, hollow and cruel, as his form quickly warped into something primal, his body contorting into the massive frame of a black bear.

The bear's teeth were ferocious, its eyes gleaming with malice, the bullet hole now in its chest, gaping and raw.

Panic overtook her as she turned and stumbled deeper into the river. Beside her, a deer stood in the shallows, a silent witness—its body trembling, its wide eyes mirroring the same fear that possessed her. She didn't question why it was there, only that they were fleeing together, prey hunted in unison.

The beast let out a deafening roar, the sound vibrating through her bones, as it stepped closer, its paws crashing against the water.

It lunged, sharp claws swiped through the air, raking along the deer's flank as it leapt. The animal let out a pained cry, stumbling but managing to scramble onto the far bank. Its dark coat now streaked with blood as it disappeared into the forest.

With a sudden, breathless gasp, Esther jolted upright, rising to a standing position in one fluid motion.

She was no longer in the creek or the woods—she was in her bedroom, the darkness of the night around her, the silence suffocating.

It had been a nightmare—a horrid nightmare. Her body was drenched in sweat, her heart pounding wildly, each beat echoing in her ears.

Her hands, her limbs, shook as an intrusive voice whispered inside her mind, clear and insistent, as if it had lodged itself deeply—"Just a sip… You have to have it, you need it."

Another voice followed, luring her in. "It'll soothe you, drown out the images of Clive, the bear, your nightmares. Help you forget everything…"

Without thinking, Esther rose and headed toward the staircase, her feet barely feeling the cold floor, as if she were sleepwalking.

Having descended the steps, she found herself on the ground floor, staring down a long, dark hallway. She wanted to resist, but it felt like a rope was cinched around her, tugging her toward the cellar stairs where Aunt Clarissa kept her liquor.

Escape was the only solution. She needed distance, air—she couldn't stay here, not with it under the same roof, not with the thing calling her by name.

The front door loomed ahead, a silent, shadowed escape. Barefoot and still in her dress from earlier, she slipped out into the night.

Cool, crisp night air swept over her, offering a fleeting relief that drew a gasp. Looking up, the stars blurred, their distant light unable to hold her attention—the ache returning without mercy.

"Dear God, please help me," she whispered, her voice a cry to anyone who might be listening.

Ian's voice from earlier drifted back, replaying in her mind. "Come and get me," he had told her before she fell asleep.

But it was late—she told herself, clinging to the guilt, to the fear that she had already pushed him too far. What if he didn't want her after seeing all this darkness inside her?

Her instinct was to run—run toward the hills. To keep running until she burned herself out, her body surrendering or giving in to the chaos of oblivion.

But then, an inexplicable warmth washed over her—like Ian's voice calling to her softly, urging her to come to him again.

She found herself at his door, her hand resting on the knob, shaking as she slowly turned it.

Half-dreaming, half-awake, she felt shadows closing in— Clive's laugh taunting her sanity, voices echoing around her. Her hand trembled on the knob, and out of desperation, she pushed it open, stepping slowly inside.

The smooth floor beneath her feet felt calming, drawing her into reality just long enough to whisper a name.

"Ian," she called out in a rough voice.

But the ghosts in her mind refused to be dismissed, growing louder in rebellion.

A sickening sound played in her mind—the deep, grunting moans of Clive, the way his voice dropped low as he had demanded things from her.

She felt herself slipping further, the sanctuary of Ian's home offering no protection. The demons had found her there anyway.

There was no escape, she thought, spinning as she searched for the exit.

Through the haze, she found the door and turned to leave, her mind pulling her into the night—toward the sound of water. A reverberating pounding. An ominous drum.

Her feet moved as if commanded by some other force, the river's sorcery overwhelming her—calling her—guiding her.

But just as she crossed the threshold, an arm wrapped firmly around her waist, reclaiming her, pulling her back inside.

Ian's breath came heavy and urgent as he held her, his arms a fortress around her trembling body.

His grip was strong, holding her tight with a steadiness, though his thoughts had been anything but.

Restless, he'd tossed in bed for hours, his mind unsettled as he debated whether he should rise and check on Esther.

Then he heard it—the faint creak of his door, followed by the softest whisper of his name. Thinking his imagination might be playing tricks on him, just the sounds of a house settling, he had lain in bed for a few seconds more.

Yet, his fear nagged at him as he gave in, wanting to put it to rest.

A chill ran through him as he made his way into the front room— just in time to see her moving slowly through the entrance, her gaze hollow, like a drifting entity, her steps listless, as if lost in another world.

"Esther," he whispered, careful not to wake his children. She didn't respond, trapped somewhere beyond reach.

As he held her from behind, he could feel her heart pounding, wild and frantic, as if it might leap from her chest at any moment. Her dress was drenched, clinging to her like she had lain in a tub, cold sweat chilling her body.

There was agony in her face as he turned her to face him. She wasn't alright—far from it.

"Let's go to my room," he said, gently ushering her inside and shutting the bedroom door behind him. The space was dark, and Ian moved to a lamp by his bed, turning it on, casting a soft glow over the walls.

"Sit down," he instructed, pointing toward the bed, but she didn't comply—remaining frozen in place.

He hurried to a tall, large wooden wardrobe, flinging the doors open as he searched the hung clothing, pulling out one of his soft, worn flannel shirts.

"Sorry... I... I saw a bear..." Esther murmured a fragmented apology, her words stumbling out.

As he turned back, her gaze was stuck on the wall, her eyes filled with shadows he could only guess at.

"Esther, let's get you comfortable," he said, turning her to him as he unbuttoned her dress. It slipped from her shoulders, pooling at her feet. Only then did he realize that she had never put on any undergarments after her bath. She had clearly been distracted even then.

There was a tenderness in his touch as he dressed her in his large shirt. Despite her swimming in it, he buttoned it gently, like wrapping her in a cloth embrace. A soft smile crept over his face as he rolled up the long sleeves.

"You look cute in my shirt," he said, but her eyes barely flickered in response.

Weary as she was, she still looked beautiful—her features softened in the dim light, her dark hair unruly from a sleepless night.

Ian addressed the bed covers, which had been thrown off in haste, making a comfortable spot for her in his bed.

"Let's lie down, try to see if we can get some rest," he said as he eased her down. He drew her close as he lay on his back, encouraging her to lay her head on his chest, her body in the crook of his arm.

Restless, she kept moving as he brushed her hair from her face, trying to settle her.

She started mumbling again, something about the river, her voice tinged with a feverish tone. He listened, her words slipping into talk of moonshining—the fire too high, the "Devil's cut." Her voice shook as she said, "Gran's gonna be angry."

Her hand curled over her ear, pressing tightly as if to hold back voices only she could hear.

When it wasn't enough, she moved his hand to her head, urging him to cover it as well, as though his touch alone could silence the haunting sounds.

And it did, as she smiled at him. A peaceful look fell over her features, as though Esther had come back to him.

Her breath slowed, and her body began to still. They lay there quietly for a while as she took in the relief, until she broke the silence.

"Ian," she whispered, "I wanna kiss ya."

She turned to face him better, still holding his hand to her ear— refusing to lose the protection of his touch.

He wasn't so sure it was a good idea, but how could he resist? What could it hurt? he thought to himself.

She leaned into him, her lips brushing his softly, moving tenderly against his, her warm breath mingling with his. A hint of shakiness still lingered in her movements, yet she wasn't rambling— she seemed present, if only for the kiss.

But a voice of reason in Ian's head told him to hold back. To be careful with her, unsure if she was still adrift.

Strangely uninhibited, Esther's hands traveled down his chest, her fingers tracing along his bare skin until they found the waistband of his boxers, drawing a gasp from him.

Ian quickly realized she held stronger intentions than he'd anticipated as she reached lower, moving her hand to his crotch, grasping him.

Carefully, he reached down, lifting her hand back to his chest, his own resting heavily on top of it, holding it in place. It took all his willpower to resist, to keep his body from following where his mind refused to let him go.

"Ya don't like me no more?" she asked, her voice tinged with hurt.

"Quite the opposite," he replied, his voice a low murmur.

"Why'd ya stop me then? Ya always changin' yer mind 'bout me," she mumbled, her legs shifting restlessly beneath the sheets.

"Not true," he said softly, knowing she wasn't in a state to reason with, though it didn't stop him from trying. "Don't you remember what I told you out on the road?"

Her expression grew slightly lost again, as if drifting from him, but he continued.

"Esther, I told you that I loved you." His words were tender, resolute.

"When you're feeling better," he added, "I'll remind you of what you were trying to do tonight. Don't worry—I'll happily give you the chance to finish what you've started. But for now, my dear... sleep."

Her eyes fluttered as her words turned into incoherent murmurs until she finally stilled, her breathing soft against his chest.

Just before sleep claimed her fully, she murmured something barely audible, "Do ya hear it? The river... it's whisperin'..."

Ian brushed a gentle hand over her ear, hoping it would soothe her as before, easing her toward peace.

His worry began to fade as her breathing grew softer, and finally, he felt her drift off. He lay awake for a while, listening to the night until he, too, eventually fell asleep.

Hours later, darkness still held its grip when a jolt of cold air struck Ian's bare back. He awoke instantly, the chill sharp as he reached down in the dark to pull the covers up, only to find them bunched at the bed's edge.

Fumbling in the blackness, he searched for Esther, wanting to cover her as well, but found only empty blankets.

A surge of panic hit him as he quickly flipped on the bedside lamp, scanning the room.

She was gone.

The bedroom door stood wide open, swaying slightly from a breeze.

Ian leapt from the bed, rushing into the main living area.

Just like his room, the front door was open—Esther nowhere in sight.

He raced back, hastily throwing on pants and boots, not bothering with a shirt, and bolted toward the door. His foot sliding on something on the ground, his heart pounding as he looked down to find the shirt he'd dressed her in—now discarded on the front porch.

All Ian could think about was finding her as he rushed toward Clarissa's house.

But as he neared the towering structure at the driveway's edge, a dark thought crept in—he worried he wouldn't find her there.

Reason was far from her mind—she was deep in withdrawal delirium. Her last mumbled words echoed through his mind—the river.

Her voice had been a strange mix of fear and surrender as she'd spoken of it.

"Oh God," he muttered as he bolted toward the upper orchard, his body moving with long, powerful strides, as if possessed.

He pushed through branches that clawed at him, racing past the budded trees.

The river, he knew, was swollen with mountain runoff, churning with dangerous force. He prayed she was safely asleep in her own bed, but his fear told him otherwise.

As he neared the river's wooded path, the moonlight that had guided him dimmed, now obscured by thick clouds. The trail narrowed, twisting into pockets of near-total darkness, forcing him to slow down, his mind tormented by frightening thoughts.

Worried he'd find her there, but equally afraid he wouldn't. Angry that he hadn't woken when she left, hadn't even felt her slip from his arms or the pull of the covers.

The sound of rushing water filled his ears now, louder and angrier as he reached the last bend.

In the fading moonlight, the river gleamed, a dark silver torrent.

Ian had already decided that if Esther wasn't there, he would comb his way down past the falls as he had last year. Despite the dangers, he was determined to make sure she hadn't been swept up, reminding himself that she was a good swimmer and might have survived.

An ever-increasing certainty built in his mind—one that knew she hadn't returned to the house, something he couldn't explain.

When he finally reached the riverbank, he quickly scanned the area. He saw nothing.

That was until he glanced upstream.

There, amidst the raging current, Esther's nude silhouette stood waist-deep in the rushing water, her pale skin glowing under the ghostly light.

She moved her hands as if searching for something beneath the surface.

"Esther!" he yelled, his call raw, but the river's roar swallowed it.

Without another thought, he plunged in, the icy water biting into his legs as he fought the current toward her.

The river was swift, but his resolve was stronger.

He kept calling her name, pushing through the wicked torrent as she slipped beneath the surface, his hands slashing through the water, desperate to catch hold of her.

When he finally reached her, he gripped her tightly, whipping her up from the water in one swift motion. Cradling her to his chest, he waded to shore with determination.

Her body was icy cold, limp, and as fragile as a ghost in his arms, carrying no warmth within it at all, her gaze vacant and unmoored.

On the shore, he tried to warm her with his own skin, but it wasn't enough. She felt as though she was slipping away.

"Please, Esther, you need to stay awake," he demanded, shaking her gently, realizing he had no time to search for the shirt he'd brought for her—lost somewhere in the shrubbery.

He knew he'd have to carry her as she was, her body bare.

Ian gathered her close, tight in his arms as he hurried up the path, dodging branches with his back as he shielded her as best he could.

"We're going to warm you up," he promised, his voice measured—words meant less for her comfort than to keep himself from unraveling.

He picked up pace as he moved through the orchard, knowing the layout by heart.

Briefly, he looked down at her face. It was so drained of color that, for a heartbeat, he feared she'd stopped breathing. He paused, leaning his ear in, listening close to her lips, relieved when he felt a faint breath.

Renewed, he pressed on until he reached Clarissa's back door.

Finding it locked, he stepped back a few feet and, with determination, kicked at it with his boot.

But the old door resisted.

With a fresh surge of iron will, Ian kicked at it again, harder this time, shattering the doorjamb as it swung open from the force.

Inside, he shouted, his voice echoing through the entire house—desperate, frantic.

"Clarissa! CLARISSA!"

He bolted for the stairs, taking them two at a time.

At the top, a startled Clarissa appeared, her eyes widening at the sight of Esther limp in his arms.

"Start the bath!" he commanded, breathless. "Make it hot!"

"What happened?" she asked, rushing toward the bathroom, as he followed close behind.

"I found her in the river. She's out of her mind."

"Sweet Lord," Clarissa muttered as she plugged the tub and filled it with steaming water.

"God, Clarissa, I can't do this," he choked out, shaking as he tried to rouse Esther, her head lolling back, lifeless in his arms.

"Does God hate me?" The words tore from him as tears filled his eyes.

"She's gonna be alright, Ian," Clarissa reassured him, her hand pressed to Esther's heart, though her own confidence wavered.

There was something about Clarissa that always brought down Ian's defenses. She had seen him through the hardest part of his life, and it felt like she was guiding him through another one, despite her own panic and fear.

"Put her in. It's warm enough now," Clarissa instructed.

Ian eased Esther's body into the water, and a small cry escaped her lips as she stirred.

"She'll be all right. Just needs to warm up a bit. This girl's from the hills—cold ain't no stranger to her." Clarissa's voice was soft but sure, wiping Esther's face with a warm washcloth.

"Where's her clothes at?" she asked, glancing at Ian as he knelt by the bath, watching as the water filled the tub.

"She stripped them off on my porch before heading to the river," he replied, almost numb.

"Oh my…" Clarissa paused for a moment, quickly putting her hands together to pray.

"Lord, we ask ya to help our girl here, bring her back to us once again. We ask ya for Your help. In His sweet name, Amen." Clarissa prayed with fervor, looking up to see Ian's expression, as though it had brought him a sliver of peace.

Just then, Esther's eyes flicked open.

"I heard her cryin'… she was cryin' in the river," Esther said as panic laced her voice.

"Who, honey?" Clarissa asked, as Ian just shook his head.

"Clarissa, she's not making sense," he murmured, resting his chin on the rim of the tub, glad to see her talking at least.

An irritated Esther turned to him. "I heard her, Ian. I heard Adeline," she whispered.

With that, Esther's eyes drifted closed, falling silent once more, her body sagging back into the warm water.

Clarissa looked at Ian, searching his face, knowing that the mention of Adeline's name—his loss—would always be a tender subject. But his gaze remained steady, focused on Esther.

"She's been like this all night," he said quietly. "Must be talking about the Painter Ghost." A long sigh escaped his lips as he continued watching her.

He thought about how everything had unfolded over the last couple of days. He was tired, both mentally and physically, but he knew that Esther's body had taken the brunt of it.

She had battled Clive, Frank, and now herself, all in the span of less than a week.

He said his own silent prayer, asking God to heal her, to give her the peace she needed to recover.

He only wanted more time with her, time to love her.

Chapter 5: The Light

Esther, warmed and bundled in blankets, had finally fallen into a deep rest. Though still worried, Clarissa offered to stay with her, assuring Ian she'd keep an eye on things so he could finally get some sleep.

But he refused to take the chance.

His mind hummed with a warning—if she stirred and bolted, Clarissa might not be quick enough to stop her.

Seeing the strain on the tall man's face, the older woman agreed, sensing that Ian had taken on a new kind of responsibility for her niece—the kind a partner claims, a silent vow.

Clarissa took his hand, her fingers rough and warm, and told him to take Esther into her own large bedroom.

"There's a big bed, and a lock on the door," she'd said, her voice practical. "You keep the key with you in the room."

The sun was beginning to rise, softening the edges of the world, when Ian tucked Esther tight into Clarissa's soft, down-feather bed. The sheets, smelling faintly of lavender and years of gentle use, cradled her as he pulled the covers up to her chin. He told Clarissa he'd return shortly, that he needed to grab dry clothes.

When he returned, he found Clarissa sitting beside her, her hand resting lightly on Esther's head as she brushed tendrils of hair aside. Clarissa quickly wiped at her swollen eyes, but Ian had already caught the redness there—the tears she hadn't meant for him to see.

In a whisper, she said, "She sure did give us a scare tonight."

"She sure did," he replied, easing himself down at the end of the bed.

"How many hours ya reckon you've slept these past couple nights?" Clarissa asked, her voice hushed.

Ian laughed lightly. "Not too many."

"Well…" she said as she climbed off the bed, smoothing the sheets as if tucking her own worries away.

"I'm gonna just pretend ya sittin' in that chair over yonder. But if ya find ya self curled up in the spot I just left, make sure ya put this key somewhere safe," she said.

A faint smile flickered on her lips as she handed him an old, iron skeleton key, its weight heavy and cool in his hand.

A little shocked at the open permission to lie near Esther, he gave her a small, grateful smile.

"That chair over there?"

"Yep," she said.

"You want me to go and sit in it right now?" he asked, his voice sincere but playful.

"Maybe until I leave, at least," she suggested.

Not hesitating, Ian moved to the chair, leaning back, his body already worn down to the bone. He watched as Clarissa left the room, the door whispering closed behind her.

He sat still for a few minutes, listening to the soft creaks of the house as it settled. When he was sure she wouldn't return, he stood, moved to the door, and locked it with the key she'd given him, tucking it high up on the door trim.

His eyes returned to Esther, her face peaceful, framed by the soft bedding.

Stripping down to his boxers, he slipped under the covers beside her, feeling the warmth of her body close to his. The room was quiet, save for the gentle sounds of her breathing. Rest finally found him, drawing him into a deep, dreamless sleep that held him tight.

Hours passed, with no movement from either of them. The day outside shifted, golden light spilling across the floor, but inside, time seemed to stand still.

Ian woke to a gentle stirring beside him, a warmth pressing against his shoulder. He opened his eyes to see Esther looking at him, her color restored as a soft smile appeared on her lips.

"Ian?" she asked, her voice a little drowsy.

"Hmm?" he replied, a smile of relief spreading across his face.

"What we doin' in Clarissa's bed?" She looked around the room, her eyes a bit puzzled, yet calm.

A seriousness settled in Ian's face as he searched for the right words, careful not to overwhelm her. If her memory wasn't filling in the details, he didn't want to be the one to alarm her.

"Do you remember anything from last night?" he asked gently.

She squinted, her eyes narrowing as if she were searching through fog. But her mind drew a blank, and all she could think about was food as her stomach let out a low growl.

"Not sure what ya talkin' 'bout," she said. "Does Aunt Clarissa know we're in here? She's gonna get mad."

Esther lifted the covers, eyes wide as she noticed Ian's state of undress.

"Real mad," she added.

He chuckled, pulling her closer, then paused as his face turned serious.

"Esther, you had a rough night. And yes, Clarissa knows. Don't worry. "

"I had me some crazy dreams," Esther said.

"Well, chances are, some of it wasn't a dream," he murmured, not wanting to say more than she was ready to hear. "Do you remember what I told you out on the road after dinner?" he asked, a hint of nerves in his voice, wondering if he'd have to say it all again—bracing himself for that, knowing how many times he had tried.

"I remember what ya said, Ian." She glanced down, voice soft with hesitation.

"That right? Are you sure we're talking about the same thing?" he teased. "Maybe I should just say it again, to make sure we're talking about the same thing."

He leaned in, his lips brushing against hers.

"I want you to hear it again, with a clear mind," he said. He kissed her once more, tender and lingering, then pulled back, waiting to see her reaction, feeling the words building within him.

Esther felt his gaze—warm and steady—holding hers, rooting her in place. He always had a way of looking into a person's eyes, like he could see past flesh and bone, straight to the soul.

And though she knew what he was about to say, she felt the gravity of it building. She didn't know how to respond, so she just breathed slowly, resisting the urge to close her eyes tightly, thinking it might come off as rude.

"Esther Primm," he began, his voice low, each word measured and drawn out. "I love you."

The words glided over her, washing her in their rawness, the meaning settling into places she hadn't known existed.

The only response she could muster—unable to speak—was to lean up and press her lips to his, holding them there, letting the silence say whatever it should.

She hoped he could feel the warmth in her, hoped he understood that she couldn't say those words.

One of Esther's deepest fears—one that clung to her tightly, fiercely—was that Clive had shattered that part of her, had defiled the word in her mind forever.

Oh, she could tell Clarissa or the children she loved them, but to say it to a man was different—it held weight, a kind of claim she wasn't sure she could ever declare.

But here, with Ian, a good man, the only man she wanted, he was giving her those words freely, hoping for them in return.

Yet, they were nowhere to be found, like they had been stolen from her mouth, erased from her language.

She pulled back, meeting his eyes. He didn't seem disappointed—if anything, his expression held peace, as though just saying the words was enough.

"I wonder what time it is," he murmured, his gaze drifting to the window, trying to read the light seeping in through the curtains.

"Not gonna lie, Ian, I'm real hungry," she said, her voice unguarded.

He smiled, her words a small reassurance that she was here and well.

"You think I can run down there in my shorts and grab something?" he said playfully, sitting up.

"No, Ian, don't," she said quickly. "Ya gonna get caught fer sure."

He chuckled, glancing down at himself as his brow creased in playful agreement. "You're probably right," he said, pulling on his pants and buttoning up his shirt. "But I'm kinda sad to be leaving Clarissa's comfy bed—with a pretty girl still lying in it."

"Oh, I'm gettin' up with ya," she said.

Ian walked over to the tall door, reaching up on the framed trim, his fingers finding the iron key he'd tucked away safely. Bringing it down, he unlocked the door with a soft click. As he turned back, he caught Esther watching him, still nestled in the bed, a curious expression on her face.

"Why ya lock us in here?" she asked, arching an eyebrow as she pushed back the covers and swung her legs over the side of the bed.

"Just bein' cautious," he replied. "Didn't want any panthers sneaking in."

She shook her head, rolling her eyes as she stood up, her bare feet padding softly across the floor to follow him into the hallway as he reached his hand out for hers.

They made their way downstairs, the house alive with the warm, late-afternoon hum of activity. The sounds of clinking dishes and low conversation drifted through the hall, mingling with the smell of freshly baked bread and something savory simmering on the stove.

As they stepped into the kitchen, Ian's children spotted them immediately.

Benjamin's face lit up as he ran over, tugging on Ian's pocket.

"Pa, ya been asleep all day," he called, his voice bright with the joy of seeing his father.

Rebecca enthusiastically ran over to Esther, wrapping her small arms tightly around her waist.

"Esther, look!" Rebecca said proudly as she held up a crinkled piece of paper.

On it was a drawing of a black cat with sharp teeth, a child's world captured in bright, bold strokes. Esther looked down, amused as she took in the artwork.

"It's beautiful," Esther replied as she held it up for Ian. "This what ya were worried 'bout?" she asked, shooting him a playful glare.

He studied the picture closely. "Yep, that's exactly what I was talking about," he said.

Clarissa turned toward them as she waved them over to the table. "Now, y'all sit yourselves down," she said, her voice warm but firm. "Ya need some vittles in ya—must be starvin'."

Esther moved to a chair, but before she could pull it out, Ian was there, pushing it back for her.

"Good to see ya hungry, honey. How much ya fixin' to want in yer bowl?" Clarissa asked as she picked up a ladle.

"I reckon I can eat as much as ya can give me," Esther answered.

It was music to Clarissa's ears. She smiled at Ian, her eyes full of relief. His expression reflected it back, something unspoken passing between them. Perhaps it was knowing more than one of their prayers had been answered.

Chapter 6: Sheriff

Sheriff Marty Ronell drove his police cruiser up the narrow road leading to the Old Reed Estate. There were multiple things on his agenda today. It had been a week since he'd been forced to pull the trigger on his deputy, Frank, and emotions had run raw in town as people learned of what the trusted lawman had done.

News of Clive's murder had grown more infamous by the day, gossip spreading as Marty tried to justify and explain it all. Most of Clive's parishioners now knew about his bootlegging—some of them had perhaps suspected it all along, but had conveniently turned a blind eye.

The ever-faithful members of the congregation, those who refused to believe Clive could ever do wrong, had even asked the sheriff if they could go help clean up his home, which Marty had denied. He knew Esther's clothes and belongings still remained there, and not wanting to tarnish her fragile reputation, he had gone himself, boxes in hand.

He had taken a life for his daughter, the daughter he had never claimed. And now, he had packed all of her belongings up, hiding the evidence of Clive's wickedness.

It wasn't easy—Marty struggled to keep the guilt from overwhelming him, still blaming himself for leaving her there and playing a part in her suffering.

Now, he found himself wanting to watch over her from a distance, measuring the people in her life the way a father would, even if she never knew the truth.

He wasn't rightly sure what kind of man Ian Huggler was, but he had been protective of Esther, and the sheriff could respect that about him, despite finding Esther half-dressed at his house.

The sheriff planned on having a little talk with him about that once he got up there, though it wasn't his main reason for visiting. The boxes in the back gave him an excuse for the trip, but he also hoped to get a better sense of what Esther might know. She was tied to the moonshining operation in his county, and while he didn't want to scare her, Vic Porter was still missing.

He'd heard through a local man that Vic had hooked up with a big supplier out of Jasper, and nothing had changed—the distribution not even missing a beat. The sheriff worried that it made Esther a target as well, glad she was at least out of town, not waltzing around on Main Street. Still, he wanted them to practice caution, keeping her away from hotspots and gossiping folk.

Local townspeople had asked him if he thought she had any involvement with Clive's sordid enterprise, and he had been sure to steer them clear of such thoughts. He had never filed a report about Grannie Primm's moonshine operation, nor did he ever plan to.

With Frank dead and Vic in the business, there was no one to connect Esther to the actual liquor production.

The Alcohol Tax Unit would never know her name if it were within his power to keep it from them.

The very thought unsettled him—an uneasy, persistent pull in his gut. His fear was that they might try to use her to get what they wanted, prying information from her without conscience or restraint and, in the process, painting a target on her back. Even worse—dragging her into a federal court as a bootlegging accomplice.

His plan was to tread carefully when it came to that. All he really wanted was to gauge how involved Frank had been—and whether there was anyone else local he should keep an eye on.

As the sheriff neared the estate, he spotted Ian off to the side of the road by an open, plowed field. The earth lay freshly turned, dark and rich, furrows stretching in neat lines toward the horizon. The scent of soil, earthy from recent work, drifted on the faint breeze.

Ian, dressed in a worn button-down shirt with the sleeves rolled up and dirt-streaked trousers, moved with the unhurried ease of a man who had clearly been working since sunrise. His dark boots were caked with mud, and a pair of work gloves hung from his pocket.

He was heading toward his old blue truck when he caught sight of the sheriff approaching. The sheriff slowed as he neared, bringing the car to a stop.

Ian hesitated, then changed course, rounding the front of the sheriff's vehicle and stepping up to the driver's side window.

"Sheriff," Ian said, a look of guarded concern on his face.

"Good day, Mr. Huggler," the sheriff greeted, catching the wariness in Ian's stance.

"Told ya I'd give Esther a couple days to settle back in 'fore I came up. Just need to ask her a few questions, and—" he gestured toward the boxes in the backseat "—brought her things. Figured she wouldn't wanna go back and get 'em herself. But you know how womenfolk are 'bout their stuff—lotta time gone into collectin' it all."

The sheriff gave a warm smile, surprising Ian with his candor and easing his natural defensiveness.

"I didn't tell her you were coming. Give me a few minutes to talk to her first. Everything that happened… well, you know—it was rough on her," Ian said.

"'Course, go on up. I'll wait here and finish my lunch," the sheriff offered easily. "She ain't got no reason to be scared of me. Just wanna ask a few questions 'bout Frank and Vic, that's all. Ain't fixin' to give her a hard time—girl's been through enough."

Perhaps he felt bad about dragging Esther down to Clive's, but Ian couldn't shake the feeling that there was more to it than that.

"All right, I'll head up there. She'll be at Clarissa's," Ian said, then added, "She lives there."

He wasn't sure if he should've said that last part, but he wanted the sheriff to know he wasn't just playing house with a girl the man likely suspected he had been fooling around with. Maybe it was an effort to salvage his reputation in the sheriff's eyes—or maybe something else entirely.

As Ian drove up the lane, he planned what he was going to say to Esther. He had played up her distress, though by all appearances, she'd recovered from the perils of the past week. She was back to her usual cheerful self—maybe masking it, maybe not—but there was a resilience about her that never failed to impress him. A tenacity that leaned forward, refusing to look back.

And every day, the love he offered to the girl from the hills grew, like seeds in the soil he had planted. He could finally admit to himself that he had hidden from it once, denying its very existence. But now, it felt as though he had thrown open the door, calling it in loudly—a beautiful thing.

As he pulled his truck up the lane, he spotted Esther returning from what he guessed was the chicken coop, a handled basket swinging in her grip. He jumped out quickly, not wanting to chase her inside—hoping for just a few minutes to prepare her.

"Esther!" he called out, his voice carrying across the yard as he strode toward her.

"Yer a little early for lunch, ain't ya?" she teased, a playful lilt in her voice. "Ya missin' me already?"

"Of course," he said smoothly, never one to pass up the chance to flirt. "But I need to talk to you—why don't you come over to the porch with me?"

She shifted the basket in her hands. "Clarissa's waitin' on these eggs. Mind if I drop 'em off first?"

She wasn't sure what he wanted, but he was acting too serious for her liking.

"Okay, but be quick about it, please. I've only got a few minutes." His tone was firm, and he was already heading toward the front.

"If ya say so," she muttered, making her way toward the kitchen.

Sometimes, Ian confused her—switching from playful to serious in the blink of an eye. She liked to push his buttons now and then, rile him up just to see what he'd do, but when he got serious, it always made her a little nervous. He was a large man, and while she trusted him—knew he'd never hurt her—there was a power behind his deep voice and his requests, and she knew it.

Esther set the eggs on the counter and made her way through the house, stepping out onto the front porch. Ian sat on the top step, and when she appeared, he patted the spot beside him, an unspoken invitation for her to sit.

"What's goin' on? Ya got me all worried, Ian," she said, her eyes narrowing as she studied him.

Ian leaned forward, resting his forearms on his knees, then reached over and gave her hand a light squeeze. "Aww, you don't need to worry. Just want to talk a bit."

"Really?" she replied, not quite trusting him as she sat down.

"Esther," he hesitated, "the sheriff is bringing up your things from Clive's today."

Her expression turned guarded as he went on.

"Looks like he packed it all up for you."

"Wait—what ya mean, it looks like?" she asked, her tone sharpening.

"He's down the road, waiting," Ian said.

In an instant, Esther bolted upright, alarmed. Ian stood too, reaching for her, trying to calm her.

"He's not here to take you away, lock you up, or anything like that," he said, wrapping his arms around her. "Do you really think I would even let him drive up the road if I thought he was coming here to take you? He's just bringing your clothes. That should make you happy—I know how you love pretty things."

Ian's words were meant to be calming, but Esther couldn't shake the uneasy thought of why the sheriff was really coming. She had taken Clive's money and hadn't said a word about it—or the photos—to Ian, wanting to pretend they didn't exist.

When Ian had asked why she'd gone to Clive's, she told him nothing. Yet now, she worried. Maybe the sheriff knew something. Maybe he even knew about the pictures.

The ones she hadn't burned yet.

"Darling, he does want to ask you about Frank and Vic." Ian paused, fearing he was running out of time as he caught the anxiety in her eyes. "Just tell him what you know. He's not going to lock you up. He promised me, and I believe him." Ian rubbed her arms, his level voice an attempt to steady her.

"I don't know anythin'. What 'em I supposed to say to him? My heart gets all crazy in my throat," she said, her voice wavering.

"Esther, I'll be there. You'll be fine," he replied, meeting her eyes with a steady look.

"No, Ian. I don't want ya there," she said, her tone suddenly resolute, catching him off guard.

A serious expression crossed his face. "Why? Why don't you want me there?" he demanded. What could she possibly say in front of the sheriff that she couldn't say in front of him?

But the dread of what the sheriff might ask twisted in Esther's gut, leaving her sick. If he knew about those damn photos, she didn't want to explain them to Ian—or worse, have him see them.

"No, Ian. I can do it by myself," she insisted.

Shaking his head, he said, "Absolutely not. The last time you were alone with the sheriff, you burned down a cabin."

"It's not ya choice," she said, trying to act confident, though her voice wavered.

"You want to bet?" he shot back, glancing over her shoulder at the police cruiser coming up the road.

Esther's heart pounded in her chest, her eyes threatening to well with tears. Ian made his way toward the car as she stood frozen on the porch—but she called after him.

"I'm serious, Ian," she pleaded as she sat back down on the step.

Not looking back, Ian snapped over his shoulder, "So am I."

And Esther knew there was no winning this argument. He was a stubborn man.

She bit her lip as she watched Ian greet the sheriff, the two of them standing beside his car for a few minutes—his posture relaxed, but it did nothing to calm the storm brewing in her.

She thought of getting up and just running through the house and out the back door, but she knew Ian would quickly chase after her—and she was certain he could outrun her. The sheriff, too, though he had a round belly, didn't appear that old, maybe in his early forties, and seemed athletic. Yes, the two of them could easily catch her, she surmised.

So, there she sat, wondering if Ian would still look at her the same after this, especially if he saw proof that darkness had truly touched her.

As Ian stood talking to the sheriff, he glanced over at Esther, catching her sharp look. He knew she was mad at him, but he'd deal with that later.

There was still a certain naivety about her, despite her experiences with town folk. Perhaps it was just part of her nature, but she panicked easily and fumbled her words. He was afraid she might do something reckless out of fear, not trusting what he'd told her about the sheriff.

"Well," Sheriff Ronell said before asking, "you wanna help me with these boxes?"

"Sure thing," Ian replied, taking the boxes the sheriff handed him and heading toward the front door, where Esther sat. Her arms were wrapped tightly around herself, her eyes casting daggers at him as he walked by.

"Really?" he muttered under his breath, noting her reaction with a small smile curling on his lips. "You're gonna find out quick—I like that expression."

"Shut up, Ian," she said, still fuming.

"Yep, that one," he replied, setting the boxes down on the porch, near the door. "Makes me just wanna kiss you more, your face all scrunched up."

Now he was just toying with her, which made her even more mad, but she quickly dropped her furrowed brow as the sheriff walked up.

Sheriff Ronell joined them on the shaded porch, setting down the boxes beside the others. He stood there, hands on his hips, as an awkward moment passed. Esther didn't rise to greet him, only turning her head slightly to look at him.

Ian, sensing the tension, spoke up, trying to make a friend instead of a foe out of Sheriff Ronell.

"Thank you kindly for bringing Esther's things up. That was very good of you." He smiled, glancing at Esther, silently urging her to express some gratitude as well. "Right, Esther?"

She begrudgingly stood, nodding as she adjusted her skirt. No matter how much Ian annoyed her, she still found herself drawn toward him, relieved he remained at her side.

The sheriff gave a long, loud sigh, his gaze drifting off for a moment as though wrestling with something difficult. This wasn't easy for him.

After confessing to Frank in the field, the acknowledgment of the secret had died with the man, but the burden itself still weighed heavily on his mind.

The young woman before him was his flesh and blood—his daughter—though she didn't know it.

But here he stood, trying to play the role of sheriff, duty-bound and official—though the lines blurred with every look into his daughter's face.

"Well," he said, pulling himself back, "I didn't figure you'd want to go back down there. Bad memories and all."

A sadness settled over his face and voice as he met Esther's eyes, the sincerity in his gaze almost startling her.

"Listen," he began, drawing a long breath. "I'm real sorry for takin' ya to your cousin's. I had no idea he was such a bad man, him bein' a preacher and all. I hope…" He paused, his face creasing with raw regret, "you can forgive me."

Esther didn't know what to do with his words. She glanced at Ian, seeking something in his expression, but Ian's face mirrored her bewilderment.

"I reckon I can," she said at last, her voice a little unsteady, "but I want you to know, I was never gonna throw myself into that fire. Just got a little too close to it, is all." She finally spoke that truth aloud, feeling both defiant and vulnerable.

The sheriff looked down, nodding solemnly. "Then I'm sorry for that too," he replied.

While she understood his words, knowing it was an apology, she couldn't fully trust his change of heart. He was humble now, lacking the hard edge of a lawman, with a softness in his eyes she hadn't seen before. But he still wore that shiny badge, and her caution remained, unwilling to let her guard drop completely. Wanting to get the conversation over with, Esther blurted out the reason she thought he was really there, her tone blunt.

"I don't really know nothin' 'bout Frank's or Vic's situation with Clive. Clive never did business in front of me much," she said, hoping her bluntness would end his questions.

The sheriff's posture shifted slightly, tilting his head, reading her carefully. He was good at his job, she could see that—his expression still kind, but she felt him see through her attempt to deflect.

"You reckon they had a fallin' out?" he asked.

Ian, sensing Esther's anxiety, placed a reassuring hand on the small of her back, a warm gesture that told her she wasn't alone, wanting her to pace herself.

Esther took a steadying breath, the warmth of Ian's palm somehow helping.

"Yeah, I guess they did," she whispered. "Clive cheated everyone, Sheriff. It was only a matter of time before he did it to your deputy."

The sheriff's expression tightened. "Did you know Frank was dirty, runnin' with Clive?" he pressed.

"Not 'til I saw 'em out at the lake, the day 'fore ya came for me," she replied. "It wasn't no accident ya found out about Gran's still."

"Yeah, I figured that much," he said, a weary tone creeping into his voice.

"Wait, what?" Ian's brow furrowed. "I'm confused. Out at the lake—Esther, the lake we were at?" His voice was sharp as he looked at her, piecing things together. "Was Clive out at the lake with Frank?"

Esther just nodded.

"Why didn't you say something? Why didn't you tell me?" Ian's frustration simmered beneath his words. "I would've done something."

"Like what, Ian?" she shot back. "There ain't nothin' ya could've done."

The sheriff, sensing the tension growing between them, redirected the conversation.

"Where ya suppose they were comin' from?" he asked, connecting the dots with practiced ease.

Esther's pulse quickened, realizing she'd already given away more than she'd meant to. She didn't know if she should lie to him, as she knew the answer. She was terrified to tell him the truth, knowing there was an unspoken code of conduct among the moonshiners—and one of them was simple: "You keep your damn mouth shut, and you won't die."

Esther turned to the sheriff, her fear fighting to take hold.

"Sir, I know ya don't know me and all, but I'm gonna beg ya not to ask me that," she said. "I don't wanna lie to ya, and I figure you'll know if I do, but..." She faltered, and Ian interjected, sensing her distress.

"Esther, maybe you shouldn't say that, or the sheriff's gonna think you know something," Ian said, his voice protective.

"But she does," Sheriff Ronell said, his tone kind but perceptive. "She's just worried if she says anythin', they'll come after her, right?"

Esther's voice dropped to a whisper. "They'll kill me if I tell ya."

The sheriff sighed, squinting as he looked down the road. "Aww, reckon ya might be right," he muttered.

Growing angry, Ian had heard enough. No way in hell was he letting her say another word.

"Go in the house, Esther," he commanded firmly. "This conversation is over." His usual warmth gave way to a hard resolve as he stepped closer to the sheriff.

"No need to worry, Mr. Huggler," the sheriff said. "I ain't gonna ask her any more questions. I ain't askin' her another thing about it, ever. You hear me, girl?" He met Esther's tearful gaze, his eyes softening.

"You ain't gotta worry. And anythin' 'bout your grannie's business is buried forever too," he added.

Ian's tense posture eased slightly, seeing that the sheriff genuinely intended to protect her, not wanting to put her in harm's way.

"I appreciate ya bein' honest with me," Sheriff Ronell said, a hint of regret in his voice. He wished he could extend the same honesty to her, but some truths were too tangled to unravel. "I advise ya to stay away from unsavory folks and best continue keepin' a low profile, 'cause Vic Porter is still out there somewhere. Whatever ya know about him, ya keep it to yourself. Don't talk to no one." He cast a serious look at Ian, emphasizing the importance.

"There's somethin' called the ATU—ya heard of it?" he asked Ian.

"Yes," Ian replied, his face drawn with concern.

"They're comin' to town in a couple weeks. They think they know where to look 'round here for moonshiners. And they don't care who they have to step on, or folks' reasons for makin' likker, and they'll bust in wherever they have to, guns drawn." The sheriff paused, seeing the flicker of fear in Esther's eyes.

"Don't worry, girl," he continued. "Like I said, they ain't gonna hear a word about you. Yer Gran was small potatoes. I'm just tellin' Mr. Huggler here so he'll make sure to keep ya away from anyone who could piece it together."

The sheriff turned to Ian, his face grave. "I reckon ya understand what I'm talkin' 'bout, right?"

"Yes," Ian said, working to process the warning in his mind.

"And another thing, Esther—you take Mr. Huggler up to where we tore up that still, and you scatter those pieces to the four winds. Don't leave a scrap of metal there, ya hear me?"

Esther nodded, still bewildered by the sheriff's unexpected compassion. It wasn't like him. Maybe he truly felt bad about taking her to Clive's, she thought.

Ian, too, had a perplexed look on his face, as though he was beginning to see the sheriff as more than just an authority figure. Today, he came across as a man genuinely trying to keep her safe, someone setting his ego and badge aside for her well-being.

Just then, Clarissa, who'd heard voices on the porch, came out, instantly lightening the tension in the air.

"Sheriff," she greeted him with surprise, "didn't know ya were here."

"Hello, Miss Clarissa," he replied.

Clarissa, realizing she'd walked into a serious moment, offered a smile. "Can I get ya some lemonade or sweet tea?" she asked.

"Actually, that would be real nice, thank ya," the sheriff said, nodding with appreciation.

"Well then, I'll be right back." She turned and disappeared inside, leaving them with a moment's privacy.

The sheriff looked back at Esther, his face softening once more. "I wanted to let ya know, when I was packin' your stuff up, I did it by myself. Ya understand? No one else was there."

He gave her a look that spoke volumes, though Ian didn't fully understand, his face showing a question he'd surely ask later.

"Also," the sheriff added, "I found some of Clive's mother's old jewelry. Knowin' she was your aunt, I figured it was family, so I threw it in there. Might not be worth much, but it's yours. Anything else belongin' to Clive will be seized by the ATU—his car, his house, even the old church," he finished.

"I don't want nothin' of his," Esther quickly replied.

"I figured as much, but just wanted ya to know," he said.

Just then, Clarissa came back, carrying a tray with neatly stacked glasses of lemonade. The sheriff graciously took a glass, as did Ian and Esther.

"Thank ya, ma'am," the sheriff said. "I'll have to drink and run, but not before I have a private word with Mr. Huggler. Ya mind walkin' me to my car?" he asked the tall German.

Ian nodded, and they walked to the sheriff's cruiser, leaving Esther and Clarissa on the porch.

Once out of earshot, the sheriff's face turned serious again.

"I've got a bad feelin' 'bout Vic Porter comin' 'round here. Whatever that girl knows, it's imperative she not say a word to anyone. I tried to wipe any sign of her from Clive's house. If anyone asks, she only visited him from time to time to go to church. She's been livin' here the whole time."

"You think the ATU will put it together? Her connection to Clive?" Ian asked, worry tightening his face.

"I'm leavin' it outta my report, and I'll do my best," the sheriff assured him.

"And another thing—on a completely different subject, and I think ya know what I'm talkin' 'bout. I meant what I told ya outside my station—ya mess around with that girl, ya better marry her." Sheriff Ronell's stern expression returned instantly.

Ian, knowing the sheriff's words were warranted, had no defense other than the truth, which wasn't much of one. He respected the man standing before him, no more than seven years his senior, yet a clear authority—and a man who obviously wanted to see Esther treated right.

"I'm going to marry her, don't worry. I'd do it tomorrow, but I think she needs a little time," Ian said, feeling vulnerable discussing this but knowing it was necessary. "Just know that I love her and will do right by her. You have my word," he added, hoping it would ease the lawman's concerns.

The sheriff's expression softened a bit. "Alrighty then. Next time I see her, I wanna hear folks callin' her Mrs. Huggler," he said with a faint smile.

Ian nodded in agreement as the sheriff quickly finished his glass of lemonade and handed it back.

"Y'all have a good day now," Sheriff Ronell said as he climbed into his car and drove off.

Ian stood there for a long moment, taking in the entire conversation and the layers of the sheriff's new, unexpected personality.

Chapter 7: Boxes

After Ian set the last of the boxes down on the floor in Esther's room, he shut the door behind him. And she knew why. He had questions—and he wanted answers.

Esther was grateful the sheriff hadn't pressed her further, hadn't asked for more than she'd given him. And he'd made no mention of what she kept hid away, things she'd rather forget—even if they weren't exactly well concealed, just shoved into a drawer within grasp.

Ian crossed his arms, not saying anything as he watched Esther shuffle through her things, pulling out a pair of red shoes and setting them on the floor.

"Think you can wait a bit to go through that?" he asked, slightly impatient.

She paused, setting down another pair of heels.

"I reckon," she said, "ya still grumpy at me?"

He scoffed. He hadn't been angry, only firm, which came from a good place, even if she disagreed with him.

"You've been fiery today," he said, a smile on his face, trying to lighten the mood a little. "Will you please get off the floor for a second?" he added, reaching down for her hand.

She reached her hand up, her wrist limp, as though she were being dragged into a conversation she didn't want to have. He pulled her to her feet, though she wasn't much help.

"My God, you're as dramatic as Rebecca," he said.

"'Cause I know you want to talk 'bout stuff I don't feel like talkin' 'bout," she said with a sigh.

She moved toward him in a playful sweep, wrapping her arms around his neck, hoping to distract him, looking up sweetly.

"Don't think ya kissed me all day," she played, trying to bait him.

For a moment, it worked—Ian had a hard time resisting her charm, her beautiful, playful, enticing eyes. They had only lain together those two times, and the last week hadn't been easy. Though Esther had clearly recovered—no more nightmares or delirium. Her appetite was back. The color and vigor had returned almost as they were last summer.

She hadn't even asked for liquor, though he wasn't sure if she ever went quietly searching for it, as he and Clarissa had made sure she wouldn't find any.

But when she stood there, pressing her body up to his, resisting became a struggle, and though he wanted to kiss her, the question in his mind lingered and needed to be resolved.

"Tell ya what, you have a real conversation with me, and tonight I'll tell Clarissa you need to come to my house in the evening—to do studies, learning to read," he said, thinking that might entice her.

"Ian," she said, her lips hovering near his.

"Hmm," he replied, thinking she might kiss him.

"That doesn't sound like much fun," she said, pulling away abruptly. "Not even romantic in the least bit," she added, moving back to look in her boxes.

Not liking that she teased him, he reached out and caught her wrist, tugging her against him.

"Esther, you need to learn to read, but I'll make it fun, don't worry."

"Yeah, I've seen the way you teach Benjamin and Rebecca. No thanks, Mr. Huggler."

Ian laughed—she had never called him that before, thinking he had actually never even heard her use his last name.

"You pronounced Huggler perfectly, like a real German," he smiled. "Not the way people in town do."

"I like that," he said as he pulled her body tight to his. He leaned to her ear, whispering warm and slow, "Now, I want to teach you how to spell it."

"Why do I gotta know how to spell it?" she asked in a hushed tone as well.

Still close to her ear, he said, "You might want to use it someday."

With that, Ian leaned down and kissed her neck softly, moving slowly to her face. He could feel her breath catch as he moved toward her mouth—the same mouth that had told him to shut up earlier, though his skin was thick, and it hadn't bothered him in the least bit.

And he hadn't kidded about how her scrunched-up face only looked cute to him. That was one of the motivations behind his kiss at the moment.

Esther knew exactly what Ian was up to, though the comment about his last name had caught her a little off guard. He had started saying subtle things to her over the past week, using terms that implied a future for them—like mentioning that his little house needed to be added onto, that it wasn't big enough anymore.

He didn't even try to hide the way he stared at her more, even kissing her on the lips in front of everyone at dinner the previous night—no inhibition in the action.

And when Abram had announced shortly after that he and Mitzy were having another baby, teasing Ian that it needed a playmate, Ian had just smiled at her, not saying anything, despite the look of panic on her face.

Now, here he was, planting kisses on her body and face, trying to trick her into a serious conversation and school lessons in his front room, when what she really wanted was to go into his bedroom and finish the thing they had started.

A bold thought crossed her mind, wanting to turn the game on him, like she couldn't stand the thought of him winning.

Just as his lips hovered over hers, she pushed him back playfully, just a foot or so, suppressing the smile that wanted to show as she put on a serious expression.

Noticing his look of surprise, she glanced down at the front of her dress, her hands moving to the buttons, caressing them. She could feel his breath catch as his eyes locked onto her hands.

Slowly, she unbuttoned the first button, then the second, looking up, giving nothing away.

Then the third and fourth, pausing as the dress opened slightly.

Ian was hooked, and she could see it—it almost wasn't fair, his previous look of determination shifting to something else.

She kept going until she reached her waist, letting it fall open on one side, baring her naked breast, as she hadn't bothered to put on a brassiere that day. Esther stood there, a slight smirk growing on her lips.

"God, Esther," Ian said as he grabbed her back, pulling her into his arms, his mouth dropping hard on hers, trying to capture her. His tongue, his body, every part of him had been caught in her trap.

"What are you trying to do to me?" he whispered in her ear, as he pulled back from the kiss. "If you don't button that dress up, I'm going to take you here, right now. And when Clarissa hears the floorboards rattling, you're going to have to explain it to her."

Somehow, Esther sensed he wasn't just teasing—there was seriousness behind his grip, his hands pulling at her hips like his body had a mind of its own.

"Really?" she asked softly.

Ian, seeing that she needed a little bit of proof, grabbed her hand and brazenly placed it on his crotch, making sure she felt every bit of hardness, holding her hand in place.

But instead of the shock, she smiled mischievously—not quite the reaction he thought she would have. She was playing games with him, and he was trying to let her know he could play them back, but it wasn't working.

With a look of determination, Esther reached for the buttons of his pants, pulling on them, opening two of them quickly.

"I ain't afraid of Clarissa. I'll just tell her I was movin' boxes around," she said with a smile as she unbuttoned another button.

"Esther, stop," Ian said, realizing their game was quickly getting out of hand.

While it sounded fun, Esther's bedroom door didn't even have a lock. All he needed was someone like Clarissa or Mitzy walking in, seeing Esther's hands in his pants.

"You win," he said, pulling at her hand, which was working its way down.

"Aww, Ian, big ol' brave Ian, 'fraid you gonna get caught with your britches down?"

"Um, yes," he said as he buttoned up his pants. "I'm not stupid enough to bed you in Clarissa's house."

"And you should be, too. Please do up your dress," he pleaded with a smile. "We should at least try to control ourselves—just a little, somehow."

Not wanting the responsible Ian to return just yet, Esther acted like she was about to button up her dress, but not before she grabbed both sides of the fabric, flashing both her firm breasts at the same time.

"Stop, please stop," he begged, laughing as he moved to cover her up, trying to get her to close her dress.

"I'm only a man, and I can only fight so hard. Where the hell did shy little Esther go?" he questioned.

"You're the one who came spyin' on me in my bath," she reminded him.

"I saw a whole lot more of you that night," he said, regret hitting him the instant the words left his mouth.

Esther paused, looking at the serious expression that suddenly came over Ian's face.

"What do ya mean?" she asked, waiting for him to answer, her eyes narrowing.

"Nothing—I was just playing around." He could only hope his slip of the tongue would pass unnoticed.

But she didn't let it go.

"No, Ian, what are ya talkin' about?" she pressed, studying his face, a shadow of worry crossing her own.

He had wanted to talk about serious topics, but not this one.

Clarissa had even suggested it was best to keep certain events of that night to himself, and somehow it had slipped out in the banter.

It felt like he was a hypocrite, not saying anything when he wanted her to tell him the hard truths she was keeping hidden.

So, he decided to bring it up, maybe giving it the tone of something casual, like it wasn't that important.

"Esther, do you really not remember that night?"

She looked away, then back at him, as if trying to piece together fragments and shadows behind the fog of nightmares and broken sleep. He could tell there were pieces—small, hazy flashes—buried in her mind.

"Did I do somethin', Ian? Somethin' bad?" Her eyes filled with worry. "Tell me what I did," she demanded, the torture of not knowing seeping into her.

"Let's sit down," he said gently, guiding her to the bed.

"Why ya always gotta make me sit down to tell me bad stuff?" she asked, but sat down nonetheless, her reluctance clear.

Ian managed a small smile, sitting beside her and taking her hand in his. He hated telling her things that didn't make her happy, and he would much rather be lying on this bed making love to her than reminding her of something they were quickly moving away from— a memory still raw in his mind, but not in hers.

"First," he began, a warm expression filling his face, "I want to tell you, I want you to really understand that I'm yours, and nothing you do can get rid of me. When I told you I loved you, Esther, I meant it. I don't treat those words lightly. Besides Addie, you're the only woman I've ever said it to."

Despite his loving sentiments, Esther's mind was whirling, the tension building—her need to understand which parts of those terrible dreams were real overwhelmed her.

"Please, Ian, just tell me what I did," she pleaded.

He could see the worry etched on her face and wanted to ease it.

"It wasn't anything bad, Esther. It just... frightened me. Really frightened me."

He took a breath, thinking it might be best to start with what she remembered, feeling for the edges of her memory.

"Do you remember coming to my house in the middle of the night?" he asked.

She shook her head, indicating she didn't, and he pressed on.

"What about talking about moonshining, your Gran?" he prompted.

"I dreamed about her," she murmured, trying to recall more.

He hesitated, then continued, "And the river. You said a lot about the river." He watched her face closely, seeing a flicker of recognition. He felt like he was brushing against something that resonated in her.

"Will ya just say what I did?" she begged, a look of panic rising in her eyes.

"Esther, I woke up with you gone from my arms, my bed. I was trying to help you weather the storm you were facing. At first, I thought you had just gone back to Clarissa's, but you discarded your clothes, took them off."

Ian took a deep, steadying breath. "All I could think about was what you'd said about the river. I got there as fast as I could, praying I wasn't too late." His voice broke slightly as he spoke, his fear from that night flashing in his eyes.

"I was in the river," she said, a quiet horror dawning in her voice. "I walked out in it..." The words were barely a whisper as the fragments in her mind began to form into something clearer.

It hadn't all been a dream—some of it had been real.

"Yes," he said. "I pulled you from the water—you almost got swept away."

Ian's fingers curled tighter around hers, his mind tracing the fragile thread of fate—had he strayed from it, he might have never reached her in time.

"Clarissa and I warmed you in the bath, and you came around, but Esther… there was a moment I wasn't sure you were even alive." He took another shaky breath, his voice rough with emotion.

"I've already carried one dead woman in my arms…" His voice cracked, raw in a way Esther had never heard before. Tears filled his eyes as he spoke, falling freely.

"I… I never thought I could possibly feel anything again," he continued. "But as I carried you up the hill, all I could think about was that if I had the opportunity, I would love you for the rest of my life. I would do it right, never letting anything bad happen to you."

All Esther could do was mirror a small portion of the emotion in Ian's eyes.

She wanted his love, longed to be consumed by it, but she couldn't let it reach her—a cold, icy river of fear stood in the way.

Oh, she'd bleed for him, die for him even, but to say the words—to open herself up—felt like more than she could surrender.

"Ian," she murmured, leaning in and pressing her lips softly to his.

"Esther, please—tell me. Say something. Anything to let me know I'm not just an old fool." The vulnerability in his blue eyes deepened as he went on.

"You see… I have this dream of a beautiful girl with wild, dark hair loving me. Someday marrying me, having children with me, walking by my side into old age. If that's something you can't give me, or… don't want to give me, then save me from myself. Because I can't—" His voice broke, the tears flowing again. "I'd run into any river for you—I'd do it a thousand times over—but please, just promise me you won't leave me. That you…"

Esther couldn't even breathe. Not only were Ian's words coming for her, but the memories had flooded back like an avalanche, as well as the faces—the people who had come to her from the beyond. Their words mixed with her tears, haunting her.

"Ian… I am tryin', please…," she begged. "I don't know how to take what ya tryin' to give me. I want to, God knows I do. I want to say those things back to ya. And maybe they are there inside me—I just don't know how to get to them," she cried back. "I don't want ya to give up on me. I ain't never had no one like ya in my life."

There was a sincerity in her eyes, warm and genuine.

That was enough for Ian, enough to give him the hope he needed to go forward, and he meant what he had said—he would go into the river for her, whatever that meant.

"I'll wait," he said.

And he would wait. He'd wait for her to tell him the things she couldn't say yet, to share what she hid so deeply.

Ian was resolved to prove to her that he wouldn't falter, that he could weather the storms she placed before him, intentional or not.

Chapter 8: School

Ian's promise of school lessons at his house had been no idle jest, and yet, despite her reluctance, Esther found herself seated at the long wooden table—an unwilling participant. The children, alight with enthusiasm over their newest classmate, remained oblivious to the quiet disinterest softening her expression.

Books lay open, small chalkboards placed within reach. Ian was instructing Rebecca, explaining how she always needed to capitalize the first letter of her sentences. He had her write about what games she had played that day, but even Rebecca was resistant.

"Pa, I didn't get to play what I wanted to. Esther was gonna help me learn to draw better, but you made her put her boxes away instead," she said.

A smile played on Esther's lips as Ian's daughter chided him. Distracted, her fingers found a piece of chalk nearby, and she began to draw on the small blackboard beside her.

Ian, seeing the smirk on Esther's face, retorted, "Well, Esther needs to not play around so much," letting the double meaning settle where it may.

"Esther, can we build a tree house tomorrow?" Benjamin chimed in, not wanting his father's words to ruin the plans he had been making.

"Benjamin, did you finish reading that chapter?" Ian tried to redirect, but the children were distracted by their favorite person sitting there.

Benjamin just shook his head, like he was joining Rebecca's rebellion.

"Do as your father says, Benji," Esther said. "If ya do, we'll pick out the best tree tomorrow."

A grateful Ian smiled at her, knowing the power she had over the children. It felt like his usual commanding presence didn't carry the same weight around her—like his children knew they could use Esther to plead their case for them, which she had on occasion.

There was a part of Esther that knew she shouldn't be belligerent about learning in front of his children, despite feeling awkward and embarrassed by her lack of education. His children were miles ahead of her, and here she sat, a grown woman attending school, though he hadn't instructed her in anything yet.

She quickly found herself getting drawn into the image she was creating on the chalkboard. It was a sketch of her favorite pair of shoes—the ones lost somewhere on Miller Highway. Oh, she was certain they had been ruined by the rain and mud, but she had loved them. Their pretty wedge heels, made with Italian leather, were one of the more expensive things Clive had allowed her to buy, not even flinching at the price, as he knew it would make her more submissive.

The uncomfortable conversation with the sheriff had actually been worth it in Esther's mind. She was happy to get her pretty things back, tired of having to borrow from a generous Mitzy—even using her lipstick.

Now, her treasured possessions had been returned, and without Clive's presence, they felt more enjoyable. Like she had won the Devil's game and got to keep the winnings, she thought to herself.

"Esther," Ian called, drawing her from her thoughts. "While that is a nicely drawn shoe—very accurate—can you please show me what letters you know?" he said, a formalness in his tone.

Instantly, Esther could see why Addie had switched Ian's name from Immanuel. Clearly, Immanuel was the man standing before her, instructing her in a sharp tone.

She erased the blackboard with her hand, haphazardly, glaring up at him slightly as he handed her a felt eraser.

"I don't know if I remember any of them," she said.

"Well, since you have a photographic memory, this should be easy for you," he said, opening up a book and setting it down in front of her. Ian then turned her easel over and pointed to the side with printed lines. "Use this side," he instructed. "Look at the letters, starting with A, and copy them—the big ones and the little ones next to them."

"Why they gotta have two of both? Seems like a waste of ink. Kinda greedy of them, like one isn't enough," Esther commented, drawing a laugh from the children.

"Please, Esther," Ian said. "Try to focus. There's a reason for it, just trust me."

"Fine," she said, taking it on more as an artistic challenge and looking at the shapes of the letters before her.

She could do this, she told herself, and she wanted to get it over with, as he didn't appear to be backing down.

Quickly and with ease, she started copying the shapes, moving along until she had completed the entire board.

"Here," she said, pushing the board toward Ian, who was reading a book at the table with them.

The children, wanting to see her accomplishment, came over.

Benjamin, who was the first to actually see her work, chimed in, "You write better than me."

Ian studied it, a smile creeping over his lips. "You have nice penmanship, Esther. Very nice. And the little spider you drew walking on top of the 'I'—a nice touch."

Esther smirked. She clearly knew the letter his name began with, and despite the defiance in her little embellishment, it actually pleased Ian.

He studied her work a little further, pausing for a moment. "But you forgot a letter, an important one. You left the 'E' out," he said, not wanting to discourage her hard work.

"Yeah, I know. I don't like that one," she said, taking the board from his hands and quickly erasing it.

Rebecca, disappointed, called out, "I didn't even get to see the spider, Esther."

"I'll draw you another one later," Esther said, trying to apologize.

"Esther, you know your name starts with an 'E,' right?" Ian questioned, knowing that was most likely the reason she didn't write it.

She just nodded, the discomfort plain on her face. Not wanting to diminish her success, he decided to drop it.

He turned the page of the book in front of her, pointing to the printed numbers.

"Now do the numbers," he insisted, not letting her lesson end just yet.

"Ian, I know my numbers."

"Then show me how far you can count, writing them down."

Esther grabbed the chalk and started to write. Ian watched as she worked her way through, counting up.

As Esther wrote, she thought of how Gran had carefully written the recipe for mash on a small card, always using numbers with a little picture of the ingredient beside them. It was something she had to follow with complete accuracy, as the ingredients were expensive and had to be adjusted based on what they had on hand. She knew basic math, and numbers had always worked differently in her brain. They followed their own logic—no funny rules, just common sense.

With no more room on the chalkboard, Esther turned to Ian, hoping this would satisfy him for the evening.

"Here," she said as she squinted at him.

Ian was just finishing up correcting a paper Benjamin had completed when he turned to her work.

"That was fast." He stopped, looking up at her, a smile twisting on his lips. "You clearly know your numbers... and your age as well... and mine too."

Benjamin, curious as always, came over to look.

"Why did Esther circle the 24 and the 36? She even put a little line with a 12 between them?" Benjamin asked.

"That's because she wants to remind me that I'm older than her and wiser than her," Ian said as he shot Esther a playful, wry smile.

"But there's no spider, Esther," Rebecca said sadly.

Esther pulled the board back to her, chalk in hand, as she asked, "You want it above the 7?"

"No, put it above the 11 for Benji," Rebecca said.

Esther glanced at Benjamin, who shrugged like he didn't mind. So, she quickly drew a little spider, even adding a web connecting it to the other numbers.

"Put a ladybug on mine," Rebecca added, not wanting to be left out. Esther quickly obliged, adding a little flower for the ladybug to climb on.

"Looks like lessons are done for the night—as well as art class," Ian said, shaking his head at the chalkboard. "You two get ready for bed."

"But Pa, you didn't read to us," Benjamin whined.

"Not tonight." Ian's voice was firm. "I have to finish up in the barn."

A wave of disappointment hit Esther, as she had wanted to spend more time at his house. It felt like she was being dismissed, sent home early—until Ian casually added, "Esther, you're helping me out there, aren't you?"

She looked to him, confused, trying to read his face as he stacked the books from the table onto the nearby shelf.

Then, with a gentle push, he guided his children toward the bathroom. He grabbed their toothbrushes from the cup and put them into their hands.

Within a few minutes, he was moving them to their bedroom, herding them like little sheep with fanned fingers.

But Rebecca broke free, running to her best friend, Esther, and wrapping her arms tightly around her waist, refusing to let go.

"Pa, I want Esther to live here with us." She looked up at her with a honeyed expression. "Don't ya want to just stay here? Ya can sleep in my bed with me."

Ian gently pulled her back from Esther. "I'm working on that, Rebecca."

"Yay!" She clapped her hands. "Ya can put another bed in our room!"

"She ain't gonna sleep in our room, Rebecca," Benjamin said, helping his father move her toward the door.

"Where's she gonna sleep, then?" the little girl asked.

Benjamin looked at his father awkwardly, like he didn't know how to explain what he understood. "Ya gonna tell her, Pa?"

Esther watched in delight as Ian struggled to find something to say—the right thing. She knew he didn't want to sound presumptive or overly self-assured after what he had confessed to her earlier in the day.

But with a certain confidence in his voice, he surprised her. "Esther's going to be in my room. Married people share the same bed."

It shocked her, leaving her unsure of how to respond.

She turned her head, like he had just proclaimed something she wasn't certain of.

She wanted to be with him, even to stay at his house, but the very word marriage loomed over her like the gentle closing of a cage door, the quiet certainty of clipped wings—unable to fly as she wished.

Ian had said he would be patient, and here he was saying such a thing in front of his children, raising their hopes.

Part of her wanted to just run out his front door, fly away, disappear into the sky before he could catch her.

But she knew he'd come after her, call her by name—and somehow, she'd stop, drawn back by the sound of his voice.

And then what?

She'd land, breathless, only to realize there was nowhere else she'd rather be.

Chapter 9: The View *

Frustration knotted within Esther as she lowered herself into the big armchair in the front room, landing with a thump.

Damn you, Ian, she thought. He kept saying things that sent little ripples of panic through her—things that sounded real and permanent, like telling the children she would be staying with them, sharing his room.

Esther's gaze drifted around the familiar space, taking in its cozy stillness. Her eyes landed on a well-worn book resting open on the side table, its pages dog-eared and margins filled with Ian's small, precise handwriting. Oddly, the sight of it unsettled her—evidence of a thoughtful man who made plans and left his mark on things. Often undeterred.

Annoyed as she was, she would still wait for him to finish tucking the children in, hoping to catch a quiet moment with him in the barn. She wrinkled her nose, unsure of his real motivation or whether he only wanted to continue the serious discussion from earlier, but her curiosity kept her rooted in place.

Within a few minutes, Ian reappeared, wearing his usual charming smile, his broad jawline catching the low light, only adding to his rugged masculinity.

He was so damn handsome, and she had to admit—the dimples on the sides of his mouth held a power all their own, effortlessly bending her to their will.

"Let's go," he said, reaching his hand down for her, his fingers solid.

She rose, her hand held firmly in his as he led her outside.

There was purpose in his quick steps, and Esther found herself working to match his long strides as the cool night air swept over them.

As they neared the barn, he suddenly changed direction. Bewildered, she glanced up at him. Clearly, he had no plans of going there—he was guiding her somewhere else.

"Where ya takin' me?" she questioned.

"You'll see," he replied in a light tone as he steered her toward his old Ford truck. It sat parked under the hazy glow of moonlight, its deep, familiar blue color blending into the darkness.

"Are we goin' somewhere?" she asked. "It's late, Ian. Dark outside."

"Yep," he said as he opened the passenger door for her. "Hop in, darlin'. We only have so much time before someone notices we've run off."

"Ya gonna drop me off in the hills—tired of me?" she teased as she cautiously climbed in.

"Maybe," he replied, shutting the door with a glint in his eyes.

Once inside the cab, Ian started the old truck, letting it rumble to life, the engine growling low and steady in the quiet night.

He glanced over at her, catching the puzzled expression on her face. He liked it—despite her reservations, she was sitting there, letting it unfold.

Leaning forward, he grabbed a bottle of cologne from the dash, dabbing it on his collar and the exposed skin of his chest.

Esther's eyes sparkled as understanding settled in—he was preparing for something else, something that sent butterflies fluttering in her stomach. She liked this version of Ian.

Noticing she was sitting too far from him on the seat, he patted the space beside him, his smile broadening.

"Come over here," he called. "This is your spot from now on."

Esther scooted over happily, leaning into his side. Saying nothing, she rested her head on his shoulder, feeling the solid presence of him against her.

With her settled close, Ian put the truck into gear, guiding it down the gravel road, past the dim glow of his house and out onto the small road that led away from the Reed Estate.

She had never really explored Clarissa's property, and she was excited to see where he was taking her, especially when he turned in the opposite direction she thought he would go. She leaned back as she eyed him suspiciously.

The road came to a small fork—one way was the familiar path she'd traveled her entire life, winding up into the Blue Hollows. But the other was a way she had never gone. Without hesitation, Ian turned onto the unknown path, his hand resting on her leg as he steered with ease, the moon casting a faint, gray light over the winding road ahead.

"I've never been up this way before," she said, as she looked out at the darkened trees slipping by.

"It's got a nice view," he said, stealing a look at her. "I don't know if I told you, but you look beautiful tonight. Very beautiful." His voice dropped—intimate, sincere.

"Thank ya," she replied, patting the front of her teal-blue dress, its fabric snug against her figure, highlighting her curves. "It's nice to have some of my dresses back."

"It fits your body perfectly," he murmured as the provocation in his tone sent a shiver of anticipation through her.

Yes, Esther thought to herself, this was the other Ian, the one who had snuck into the bathroom just to catch a peek.

"It's got a long zipper down the back," he added with a knowing smile as he looked for a spot to pull off the road.

A small clearing came into view, hidden from sight, like a secret waiting to be uncovered.

When the truck stopped, he put it in park, flicking off the lights and plunging them into darkness.

As their eyes adjusted, the waning light painted the landscape with a faint glow, and Esther could see it—a hymn of earth and stars stretched out below, silent and vast under the blanket of night.

"Aw, Ian, it's so pretty up here," she said. "I've never seen it like this before."

Turning to her slowly, he murmured, "You like it?" but without waiting for her answer, he cupped her face in his hands. "To be honest with you, Esther, I didn't take you up here for the view."

They were so close now, their nearness stirring the air between them, delicate as moth wings in the dark.

Esther felt her pulse quicken, her words barely a whisper as she asked, "Then what'd ya bring me up here fer?"

"What do you think?" he murmured, his voice a soft hush in her ear, sending a delicious thrill down her spine. "I wanted to go somewhere we wouldn't get caught."

Ian leaned further in, letting his lips rest on hers, tentative at first, then lingering.

The attraction between them was undeniable—pulling them closer, holding them there. His mouth moved with a firmness, her lips parting as he coaxed her, sharing both his warmth and his hunger.

She let her tongue brush his, a slow, exploring dance that felt new and ancient all at once.

He couldn't deny how good she was at this—responsive, passionate. She let him lead, but it felt natural, like her femininity answered his call without hesitation.

And she had a healthy appetite—he felt it in the way she kissed him back, like she couldn't get enough of the taste of him.

He pulled back for a moment, his need written in the stillness of his body, his gaze lingering on her face as if savoring every part of her.

"Esther," he said in a low and earnest voice.

"Yes?" Her voice was a dreamy echo of his.

"I want to make love to you," he said.

He could hardly wait a moment longer.

"In the truck?" she asked with wide eyes as she glanced around, wondering how it would work.

"Naw." A small grin tugged at his lips. "I threw some blankets in the back. Do you want to get out?"

"Ya really never planned on taking me to the barn, did ya?" She teased.

"Finished up my chores early. I had other plans for tonight," he said.

And he meant it—he'd been serious up in Esther's bedroom, wanting to take her there in that moment.

But caution had held him back, knowing they needed somewhere they couldn't be easily interrupted, somewhere far from prying eyes.

The sheriff's unexpected visit that day still lingered in his mind, a warning about not just "messing around" with her. But in Ian's heart, he knew he wasn't "messing around" at all. His intentions were clear-cut, and now he only had to convince her of the same.

Though he knew he could possibly use sex as a motivation for getting her to marry him, tonight he didn't have it in him to play that kind of game. He hoped that eventually, Esther would want to live with him, curl up beside him in his home every night—not just in the pickup bed.

"Give me just a minute," he said as he pulled away and hopped out of the cab.

Esther waited there, considering whether to take off her good stockings. She didn't want them to snag—they were hard to come by.

While Ian was setting up the back, she slipped off her shoes, unclipped her stockings, and carefully placed them in the dashboard tray for safekeeping.

When he returned, he opened her door, finding a barefoot Esther waiting for him.

"Aww, I missed that part," he said with disappointment as he reached for her hand.

"Sorry," she replied. "Ya can watch me put them back on when we're done, if ya'd like."

Ian nodded his head, like he intended to hold her to that promise.

"I'm gonna carry you to the back — it's kinda rocky here," he said. Before she could protest, he scooped her into his arms.

She let out a soft laugh, holding on to his neck as he carried her into the cool evening air. The scent of pine drifted down from the Blue Hollows, mingling with the earthy sweetness of damp earth underfoot, the sounds of night creatures humming around them like a quiet choir.

He set her down gently on the tailgate of the truck, steadying her as she shifted back onto the soft blankets he had spread out.

She glanced around, noting the careful way he'd prepared the bed, the blankets thick and inviting, layered like he'd gone to great lengths to make it comfortable.

"It's real soft," she murmured, her fingers grazing over the fabric as she crawled closer to him.

"Come here—baby." His voice was a low rumble as he adjusted his body into a comfortable position, leaning back against the rear of the cab.

He didn't want small talk—he'd waited all day for this, all day thinking about what she'd started showing him in her bedroom, unable to shake the thought from his mind.

He'd pieced together this plan for them, something spontaneous yet meaningful, romantic with the resources he had at hand.

She nestled up close to him, feeling the softness of the pillows behind his back.

"These from yer bed?" A small smile pulled at her lips. "I just put on fresh pillowcases today. Now they're gonna get all dirty," she lightly huffed.

"Esther..." Ian said in a husky and rough voice. "I want you to do what you were doing earlier." He leaned in, his mouth capturing hers in a kiss that was all-consuming.

He didn't hold back—a reward for his patience.

"What part of it?" she whispered against his lips, her fingertips grazing along the open neckline of his shirt, feeling the heat radiating off him.

He lifted her hand from where it rested, guiding it lower—much lower—until it settled on the metal buttons of his trousers.

"This part," he instructed.

Esther swallowed hard. It hit her all at once—a flutter of nerves, sharp and sudden. Like she was confident until Ian became serious, suddenly finding herself shy again.

Why did this always happen?

What was she supposed to do once she unbuttoned his pants?

What did you do with it once you uncovered it, having never actually touched the fullness of him before?

With Clive, she had always refused, turning her head away. It was one thing to have sex, another to touch a man.

Trying to act confident, she looked down, biting her lip as the intimacy of the moment wrapped around them, the distant call of a nightbird echoing in the trees.

She inhaled slowly, daring herself forward, fingers inching lower to the top button.

He leaned in, pressing a kiss to her neck, momentarily distracting her—the heat of his mouth enveloping her skin.

"Keep going," he whispered in her ear, his voice a simmering, dangerous heat against her skin—tender, yet edged with quiet insistence.

His tongue grazed her earlobe, sending a thrill through her that made her tingle.

The night seemed to close in around them, muted and still, save for the quiet rustling of their movements and his steady breathing.

She tried to focus on the task at hand as she unbuttoned the last couple of buttons.

There was a hesitation in her body as she considered how to proceed with the next part, thinking through the basic mechanics.

Even in the dark, she could feel the intensity in his gaze as he leaned in closer.

"Now," he murmured, his voice a quiet fire. "Put your hand in there."

He reached down with his hand, holding hers a moment longer than necessary, his thumb tracing small, calming circles over her knuckles before letting go, leaving her with the thrill of her own movement.

Ian spoke again, softer now, and in German. The words—"Ich brauche dich"—slipped from his tongue, half-swallowed and aching.

He confessed his need for her, a want that went beyond mere language.

And Esther could hear it—even if she didn't know what he was saying.

So, she gathered her courage and did as he instructed, her hand sliding gently behind his boxers, now loose at the waist, drawn forward by something stirring in her own body.

Despite having seen it before, touching him was something else entirely.

He was hard—firmer than she had expected—lightly pulsing beneath her fingers.

She hadn't yet decided whether to explore him fully, but she found the shape both attractive and strange in the same moment.

It was Ian, but a different part of him, a part he kept hidden only for moments like this, and now with her.

Not sure what else to do, she fumbled around, touching it lightly. She paused, then looked up at him—his chest rising and falling.

"Ian, I don't know what to do with it," she said, hoping he would give her more instructions, a clue as to what to do next.

"Aww, you're already doing it, just keep doing what you're doing," he said, as he kissed her again, his hands working to find the small zipper on the back of her dress.

But despite knowing the approximate location, he couldn't seem to find the little tab.

He pulled away from the kiss and, with a playful grunt, leaned her forward over his lap, pushing her hair lightly out of the way.

"I can't find it," he said, his big fingers brushing up and down her back.

"Guess ya can't take it off then," she teased as she sat up.

"Esther, you think I'd let a silly little zipper stop me? I'll turn on the truck lights and drag you in front of them before I give up."

She laughed, reaching up to easily find it and starting it for him. "Here," she said.

He found it, moving slowly so it wouldn't catch. Not sure if she was bare beneath, he held his breath—discovering quickly that she wasn't.

A delicate lace brassiere hugged her chest, shaping her breasts into a feminine, pointed silhouette—the style of the time.

"Where did this come from?" he said as he faltered on the tiny hooks of the next layer.

"I think some woman came up with this to keep a man from getting to her," he added, thinking back to when he had tried to take one off Adeline for the first time, catching her hair in it and pulling out a nice clump.

It had been a disaster for a twenty-three-year-old boy.

"Maybe you should just take it off," Ian said, not feeling confident about his rusty skills.

"But yer dressed head to toe," she pushed back, hoping it might give her a minute to build up her courage.

"You want to see how fast I can get this off?" He kicked off his boots, unbuttoned his shirt, and tossed it aside.

"Now you need to finish taking that dress off." His tone made it sound like they were taking turns.

She steadied herself as she stood in the truck bed, carefully pulling her dress over her head, standing above him now in her slip and bra.

He tugged at the bottom of her half-slip, pulling it over her hips, finding what he considered to be a very cute pair of panties and hosiery clips beneath.

Then, just as he thought she might take off something else, she knelt.

"Ya still got ya pants on, Ian."

With no further prodding, he stripped both his trousers and boxers off together, suddenly feeling the chill of the air.

"It's cold out here, colder than I thought it would be. As soon as you get that off, we should get under the covers," he said.

"Hold on… this thing's got some fight in it," she said, reaching around to the back of the brassiere. It was new, and the hooks were tight—refusing to be released. She struggled for a moment, tried again, then sighed from the effort. "It just ain't cooperatin'. Don't know if I can get it off."

"Turn your back to me," he said gently, not thinking about the fact that she was self-conscious about him seeing that part of her body.

"No, I can do it," she said as she kept trying, her stubbornness giving way to irritation. "Maybe I'll just have to leave it on."

Ian leaned in close, his fingers grazing her shoulders as he spoke.

"Esther, I've seen what you think you need to hide. There isn't a part of you I don't think is beautiful, do you hear me? Please, let me help you." His voice was steady as his hand lingered over her scars.

"I… I don't know. It's ugly, Ian, and I don't like it."

"Esther, your body is perfect because it carries you inside of it." His words were deeply sincere as he carefully turned her back toward him. She didn't fight him this time, allowing him to touch the place Gran had chosen as her spot to brutalize her.

The scars had lightened over the last year, as the constant barrage of abuse had kept them from healing properly. And in the darkness of the night, they were almost indistinguishable.

Slowly, Ian found each tiny hooked latch until the brassiere finally fell away. A sigh left Esther's mouth as it did.

There had been a shift in her mood.

She sat there, almost frozen, and Ian could feel something—a life force, an energy—drifting from her, as if pulling away from him, from the closeness they had been sharing.

It concerned him—he didn't want to upset her, and he felt her body shake. This wasn't what he had intended—he only wanted to make her feel good, to feel loved.

He tried to turn her to face him, but she wouldn't let him.

So, he pulled her into the protection of his chest, wrapping an arm around her.

"Are you okay?" he asked as he leaned over her shoulder. "I'm sorry if I made you unhappy."

How could Esther explain that it wasn't his fault—that it had never been his fault?

That she wanted to share her body with him, but didn't know how to get over the memory of the broken spirit tied to those scars?

How Clive had lusted after them, his hands clawing at her, almost always preferring to assault her from the back, his sick voice moaning in her ear.

Not sure what else to do, knowing maybe all she needed was to be held, Ian pulled a blanket up over them.

Resting his head against hers, he heard the faintest sound—a small cry. He reached up to touch her face, feeling the wetness of her tears.

"Please... don't be sad," he murmured. "I didn't mean to make you sad, my sweet Esther."

She said nothing, just let the tears fall, letting the warmth of his chest press against her back. He leaned his forehead to the back of her head, saying nothing, and for a split second, she almost caught herself wanting to confess a feeling—perhaps it was love, or something akin to it.

The words planted themselves on her tongue, deceptively so, which frightened her, as though they had a will of their own.

But then, they slipped back into the cave—the cave from her nightmares.

She didn't want Ian to carry the guilt for upsetting her. But the words she needed felt jagged in her throat—sharp-edged and hard to form.

Finally, almost like a flinch, she spoke. "He liked 'em, Clive I mean."

Ian stilled. There was a beat of silence before he spoke, as if he wasn't sure he wanted to know.

"Liked what?" he asked.

"My scars," she whispered.

She kept talking—not to explain, but to give way to her own voice.

"He told me they were a punishment fer denyin' him. That God would see me beat down 'til I gave myself to him. He wanted me to tell 'im that I loved him, but there wasn't a pair of pretty shoes that could buy that. There ain't nothin' in the world that can buy that."

Ian just listened, even though hearing it made his stomach churn, made him want to send Clive back to the hell he supposed he was already chained in.

But now, it was starting to make sense.

The girl from the hills—the one who had chased him.

She had begun to pull away the moment he turned and started loving her.

Oh, she was here in the truck with him—but not all of her, and he knew it.

She had asked him to love her in the barn last year, and now he had given in, heart and soul.

The words burst from him freely—escaped at last.

But hers? They were still bound, hidden away for safekeeping.

And that bastard Clive had tried to steal them from her—taking what was never his to claim.

No. Ian knew now, with absolute conviction, that Esther belonged with him.

She always had.

He had pieced it together slowly, asking himself when that feeling had first awakened in him—like a dormant seed breaking through the ground.

He was certain it had been the moment Sheriff Ronell's cruiser drove away with her the year before.

It had taken him longer than it should have to figure it out—unaware that thick roots had been growing with fury beneath the surface.

Now... he just had to wait for her to awaken the same way.

Esther continued, "I'm not sure, but I think Gran made some sorta deal with him, keepin' me fer him. But she knew if she ever actually handed me over, he'd never pay her another cent. So, this is where I was stuck fer years, Ian. Thinkin' somethin' was wrong with me."

"There's nothing wrong with you, Esther." Ian kissed her neck, pulling her closer.

"I'm a little crazy, Ian." She let out a controlled breath. "What kind of woman gets naked runnin' into a river?"

"That was just the alcohol, working its way out of you. My father said and did some pretty crazy things when he got off the bottle." Ian replied.

"I wasn't tryin' to kill myself, Ian... " Esther paused, sorting through her thoughts, deciding whether to tell him the whole truth—or just part of it. About what she had seen as she hovered between the earthly plane and what lay beyond.

"I heard someone cryin' in the river. I was searchin' for 'em," she confessed.

But Ian knew more of the story—he knew she was referring to Adeline, believing Esther's mind was confusing two stories—one true and one more of a myth.

Esther waited for Ian to say something, but he didn't. Finally, she turned to him. "Ya believe me, right?"

He hesitated. "I believe that's how you perceived it."

He knew the word might be above her vocabulary, hoping she would let it go.

But Esther caught his meaning, and it rubbed her the wrong way.

"So, ya think I be perceivin' some crazy things then?" she said.

"Esther, it was a rough night—please cut me a little slack, would you?"

And he was right.

Ian had brought her up here, trying to be romantic, spending time with her, and here she was, trying to start a fight again.

In that moment, Esther decided she was done purging for the night.

This was their time alone—she didn't want to waste it.

"Ian," she said.

"Yes?" There was hesitancy in his tone, unsure if she was still going to confront him.

"I'm not done yet." Her voice was steady, laced with determination.

"What else do you want to say?" he asked.

She tilted her chin up, smirking. "No, silly. I ain't done undressin' yet."

And with that, she rose, the quilt sliding from her shoulders like water.

Her bare breasts caught the moonlight, its glow tracing over her pale skin, making her appear almost ethereal against the dark sky.

Then, as if trying to call on the boldness from earlier in the day, she let the cool night air wash over her as she worked her panties and garter belt down.

Reaching up, her fingers found the pins in her hair, removing them one by one until long tendrils fell free—just the way Ian liked it.

A final shake sent the last of the pins tumbling, a quiet act of liberation.

She stood there, her silhouetted form complete, a strong breeze stirring her hair as she let him take in the sight of her—as much as he wanted.

And he wanted to take it all in—as his smile grew, so did the rest of him.

She wobbled slightly on the mushy surface, nearly losing her footing, but Ian steadied her, gripping her thigh firmly.

"Come back down here," he said, his voice low, roughened by longing, as he held out a hand to her.

She let herself fall back into his arms, his solid frame shielding her from the night's chill.

The scent of his cologne was intoxicating as he guided her down beside him, pulling the blanket over them once more.

Ian finally had her completely naked with him, and it felt nice—very nice.

He wanted to kiss her from head to toe, and he set about his task.

"Darling—tell me if you need me to stop—all right?" Ian's focus narrowed on her as he leaned in.

A flicker of confusion crossed her face, and he decided to hold back—save some of what he desired for another night.

He wanted to take his time, to show her how good this could be, to coax pleasure from her, to feel her melt under his touch and cry out for more.

He wanted to hear her gasp his name, lost in it until there was no doubt in her mind that she belonged to him in every way.

As he pressed his lips to her neck, he left behind a fevered whisper that traced the path of his mouth, his breath an exciting tickle against the cool of her skin.

He worked his way to her shoulder, the sensation drawing a giggle from her, but it only urged him on.

Lowering himself, his mouth traveled further, finding one of her breasts as his hand cupped it first.

For a moment, he hovered above, his presence teasing over her skin.

The heat of him was palpable before his lips finally met the delicate, pink-pigmented skin he'd been aching to taste.

Slowly, he let the tip of his tongue dart out, grazing her hardened nipple before tracing slow, deliberate circles around it.

Her body moved instinctively, as if trying to pull away from the intense sensation, her hands gripping his shoulders, soft sounds trembling as they escaped her parted lips.

Ian wanted more—more of the sounds she made, more of the way she arched into him, chasing the pleasure he gave her.

His hand trailed lower, seeking the heat between her thighs. His fingers slid through the silken dampness, parting her effortlessly as he searched for the delicate bud hidden there.

Shivers ran through her as his touch went deeper, focused and unhurried—tracing slow, knowing circles as he sought out her hidden jewel.

And when he found it, his smile deepened.

His fingertip glided over it, teasing, waiting for her body to show him just how much she needed.

A moan tumbled from her lips, and he knew—knew without question—he had her now. With ease—much easier than that damn zipper, he thought wryly as he established a rhythm, stroking her in a way that made her body respond like he'd found her secret.

An unknown force took hold of her, her movements growing more desperate, helping her build the waves she needed to finally meet the shore.

Lowering his head once more to her breast, he let his teeth nip at her nipple, lightly pulling it.

Esther's body tensed beneath him, her breath spilling out in urgent, unsteady cries. He sensed the shoreline was in sight—surprised by how quickly she was reaching it.

With urgency, he dropped his mouth fully onto her, sucking hard, determined to draw her in—riding tandem with his desire.

His finger worked faster, firmer, gliding effortlessly through the slick heat of her wanting body.

And it worked.

She crashed into the shore with a fury her body had never known—never shared with another soul—trembling as wave after wave took her under.

He didn't let up, guiding her through each crest, refusing to stop until she had nothing left to give.

Esther screamed as pleasure tore through her, her body releasing uncontrollably beneath him.

His name pushed from her lips—desperate, unrestrained. "Ian… Ian… oh my God, Ian!"

Her head kicked back as the last wave crashed over her, leaving her breathless—undone, her pulse pounding, chest rising and falling in shallow, uneven gasps.

Slowly, she opened her eyes, locking onto the solid, physical form of the man who had just unraveled her.

Her gaze was wild, untamed—the longing in them only more pronounced, deepened by the pleasure still humming through her veins.

Ian towered over her, his rugged face cast in shadow, the raw intensity in his eyes pulling her under all over again.

His own need was written all over him, his restraint stretched impossibly thin, barely holding.

"Ian," she whispered, her voice wrecked and sultry, each word deliberate, heavy with desire.

"I want ya inside me. Luv on me."

She was still shivering, still his to claim.

He needed no other motivation—her words called to him with the sweetest voice he had ever heard.

Lowering his body above hers, he found her like the perfect peach blossom—petals parted, perfumed and damp with morning dew, waiting for him.

She was ripe for him, taking him in slowly as he brought himself to her, savoring the moment as he entered.

All Ian could think was that she felt like paradise—her heat clutching at his stiff arousal, holding him securely, her body wrapped around him as if she'd been sculpted for him alone.

He braced himself, his body hovering over hers, drinking in the way her eyes met his in the moonlight—filled with a mix of anticipation and wonder, her chest rising in shallow, uneven rhythm.

He moved with purpose, his hands cradling the back of her head before lowering himself completely, his chest pressing against hers, feeling her hips rise to meet him in instinctive acceptance.

Rock-hard with desire, he moved within her, asking her body to give him everything it had.

"I love you," he whispered involuntarily against her ear, his lips grazing the delicate skin as he began to move, each thrust slow, reverent—a worship of the woman beneath him.

Unable to pace himself, he felt himself careening toward the edge faster than he had anticipated.

Wanting more momentum, he raised himself up, locking his arms as he drove into her with fervor—chasing his own release, seeing it clear in his body, not his mind.

He had told himself earlier he would pull out—he had meant to—but the way she clung to him, her legs locking tight around his hips, holding him in place, made it nearly impossible.

He knew it was reckless, but the moment overtook him, the wave already dragging him under.

"Sorry," he muttered, voice raw and strained, the words barely audible.

He thrust harder, ramming into her with a final, desperate drive before his release overtook him, spilling deep inside her.

A deep, guttural growl tore from his chest, and as he came, she only held him tighter, as if she had wanted this all along.

The world around them seemed to grow silent, their breaths mingling in the stillness, as Ian remained close, the weight of his body grounding her, holding her in a quiet rapture neither wanted to break.

He waited there for a moment longer, holding her beneath him, until she called his name, bringing him back to reality.

"Ian," she said breathlessly, "Ya kinda heavy."

He quickly moved off her and to the side. "I forget."

He leaned back on the pillow, his hand behind his head. "Darlin', that was something else. Felt like heaven itself."

She smiled in quiet agreement as she turned to face him, her eyes searching his before she asked, "Why'd ya tell me sorry?"

His face softened, a flicker of guilt passing beneath his smile as he brushed a stray lock of hair from her forehead.

"Because I told myself I wouldn't finish inside you... but I couldn't stop. I meant to pull out," he said.

"But why?" she asked naively. "That don't sound like fun."

"Esther, you know how babies are made," he chided playfully.

"But…" She paused, trying to figure it out, her brow furrowing. "I don't understand—you just stop, then it's over? Ya don't finish?"

He chuckled, then pulled her close, pressing a tender kiss to her temple as he wrapped her snugly in his arms. Her skin, soft and light as cotton, settled perfectly into the curve of his hold.

"No, it doesn't stop. It just… happens on your belly, or another place," he explained.

A strange truth registered in his mind—Clive had never been cautious with her. Ian wondered how Esther had avoided getting pregnant, but not wanting to ask, he forced himself not to dwell on it. He hated when those thoughts slipped in—unwelcome, intrusive— and tried to push them away as quickly as they came.

Esther's eyes went wide with confusion.

"What if it makes its way in, like through the belly button or somethin'?" she asked, genuinely wondering how it all actually worked.

A laugh escaped Ian despite himself, the innocence of her question catching him off guard.

"Why ya laughin' at me?" Her face grew warm.

"Sweetheart, babies don't really grow in your belly," he replied, still smiling.

"Naw, ya wrong, Ian! How does a belly get so big then?"

She sat up and crossed her arms, her defiant look only adding to the charm, despite her basic lack of knowledge regarding biology.

"It's a different spot, near your belly." He pointed at the place on her body, and she shook her head in disbelief.

"I'll show you a picture in a book," he said, his voice still gentle. "Soon you'll be reading those books, learning all sorts of stuff—not just where babies grow."

"If ya say so." She relaxed back into his arms, though there was a hint of reluctance in her voice.

"Esther, it's important to learn. You want our children to know how to read, don't you?"

There he went again, she thought, already planning a life with her without giving her the time he'd promised.

While she adored Ian's children, she wasn't even sure her body could bear another—her baby having died. She secretly worried she'd eaten too much wild carrot, a thing Gran once said could keep a seed from takin' root in a woman's body—one she'd relied on while at Clive's.

And the haunting warnings from Clarissa lingered in her mind, adding another layer of confusion—especially now that Clarissa had backtracked, admitting she may have misjudged Esther's symptoms. She'd told her the alcohol withdrawal was undoubtedly to blame for the lack of appetite and upset stomach, both of which had all but disappeared.

How could she even trust her own fragile body?

"Do you remember any of the letters you wrote earlier?" Ian's voice broke through her thoughts. It was gentle, though he wasn't about to miss an opportunity to help her advance.

"Really? Ya gonna ask me about letters while we're layin' here naked? Where am I gonna write 'em, huh?" She raised an eyebrow, a smirk creeping onto her face.

"Ya want me to scratch them into ya chest or somethin'?"

But Ian wasn't distracted from his agenda.

"That's a good idea—write them on my chest, but maybe don't scratch too hard," he teased, nudging her.

"No, Ian, ya just want to laugh at me more." She pulled her hand back.

"I promise I won't. Just try it. Every time you get one right, I'll kiss you. It'll be fun, come on." He pushed, hoping to make a game out of it.

Esther shifted her weight against him, looking up with a furrowed brow.

"Fine," she said with some reluctance, but wanting to kiss more. "What letter ya want me to make?"

Ian pulled the blanket down just enough to expose his chest. "Write an 'A.' We'll start at the beginning." His voice was a mix of patience and encouragement.

"Ya ain't gonna make me do all of them, are ya?" she asked.

"No, I'll switch it up." He eased her hand into position. "Just... please don't really scratch me," he added with a grin.

She tilted her head, shooting him a mock scowl, her eyes gleaming with mischief as she leaned closer, her finger hovering over his chest.

"Ya always callin' me a wild cat—maybe I'll prove ya right." She traced a perfect "A" on his chest with her fingertip.

Pleased, Ian grabbed her face, planting a big kiss on her mouth.

"Very good. Now, how about an 'R'?" His tone brimmed with approval.

"I don't know that one—I just memorize the shapes. If you told me what number it was, maybe I could figure it out." Her eyes narrowed in thought.

"You need to learn the names," he encouraged gently, stroking her cheek. "Here's a hint—it's the letter Rebecca's name starts with, and you have this letter at the end of your name."

Leaning up, Esther sighed, remembering how Rebecca always signed her name—like a person with a dress, standing sideways. She drew the shape on Ian's chest.

"Esther, you know more than you've been letting on." He smiled, kissing her again.

"Now draw an ',.'" he asked, knowing she had resisted it earlier.

"Ian, why ya tryin' to make me draw that letter so bad? I know how to write it."

"Just show me." His tone was gentle but persistent, knowing he might get a bit of sass back.

She scowled. "I'm done playin' ya stupid game."

Pulling out of his arms, she scooted away in the truck bed, creating distance between them.

"Come back here," he murmured, scooting up behind her and spooning her.

"I won't make you play it anymore tonight," he promised. "Don't be mad at me." His voice was tender as he wrapped her back up in his embrace.

"I thought maybe you'd just wanna hold me, not be Mr. Huggler."

Ian laughed quietly, pulling her even tighter against him, his chin resting atop her head.

"Okay, I get it," he said, closing his eyes and taking in the scent of her hair, letting himself settle into the warmth of the moment.

She felt so very nice in his arms. Just a few more minutes, he thought, and then they'd head back home.

They lay there quietly, wrapped in a thick blanket, Ian's arm draped protectively around her. The stillness of the night lulled them as the stars above twinkled faintly against the dark sky.

Chapter 10: Hair Pins

The morning sun rose, casting a flaxen glow over the rural landscape, painting the rolling hills in muted hues. Shadows stretched lazily across the ground, retreating as the light claimed its place.

Birdsong filled the tall trees, a symphony of trills and chirps that seemed to hum with life, welcoming the new day.

The scent of dew-kissed earth hung in the air, mingling with the faint sweetness of wildflowers. Everything felt untouched, as if the world was offering up its beauty for the very first time.

"Esther, wake up, wake up." Ian shook her bare shoulder lightly.

Slow to open her eyes, Esther looked up at his handsome face, gazing down at her.

"We fell asleep here. It must be after seven in the morning. The light is already in the sky." He sat up in the back of the truck bed, urgency in his tone. "I meant to just lie there for a few minutes and, well… how the hell are we going to explain this?"

Ian knew Clarissa was an early riser and had no idea how Esther would sneak in.

"Shit… my children." His voice edged in panic. "If they wake up without me there, they'll head over to Clarissa's. Get dressed, Esther, we've got to hurry back."

He scrambled to find his discarded clothes.

Esther, still tired, pulled herself up and wrapped the blanket around her torso. They had slept the night together, their bodies tightly intertwined—a sound, undisturbed sleep that surprised them both.

"I don't know why, but ever since you came back, I haven't been able to rise the way I usually do," Ian said, as he pulled up his boxers over his naked legs—not before Esther got an eyeful of his morning salute.

He caught the expression on her face, knowing she was about to say something smart, something that most certainly included the word "rise."

"Don't say it," he mused, grabbing for his pants.

"And please hurry." He shot her a look when he noticed she wasn't moving quickly. "It's going to take us a little bit to get back. I got your clothes, you can put them on in the cab," he said as he quickly gathered up her outfit.

"My hairpins are all scattered," she muttered, picking them up one by one.

"Esther, I'll buy you more of them." He swept up the blankets around her, flinging one into the air over the truck bed and out into the brush.

"Ian, they're expensive!" she panicked, scrambling to pick up the remaining ones, worried he'd throw more away. So caught up in saving them, she hadn't even realized she was crawling naked across the truck bed on her hands and knees.

And while Ian found it cute—no, very cute—he was in a hurry.

He slipped on his boots and leaped over the side, her clothes in his arms.

Reaching for her with his free hand, he said, "Let's go, darlin', I promise—I'll get you new ones."

"No, ya won't." She scooted to the side, eyeing him before reaching for his arm to steady herself. "And yer holdin' all my clothes."

"I know. Just hop on my back." He grinned, shifting his weight slightly as if ready to catch her.

"I'm as naked as a blue jay," she said, her arms instinctively folding over herself. "And I can walk."

"Esther, there are mean rocks and prickly weeds. Hop on my back." He turned his broad body to her, insistent.

She hesitated, biting her lip, her skin prickling against the cool morning air.

But when Ian gave her that look—the one that always softened her resolve—she dramatically let out a breath and climbed on, wrapping her arms snugly around his neck.

"God, Ian," she murmured, her breath tickling his ear.

She couldn't help but laugh as he carried her, drawing a chuckle from him as well.

"Ya carrin' me like a sack of 'tatoes," she mused as he opened the passenger door, turning backward and dropping her onto the seat.

He paused, taking in the view before him. She sat there naked, arms reaching for her belongings, legs slightly parted, her beautiful bare breasts practically calling him to touch them.

"You don't know how hard this is for me right now," he said, handing her the clothes and letting out a playful, over-the-top sigh as he forced himself to walk around the truck.

Inside, he started the engine. The truck rumbled cold in the morning air as he glanced over at Esther, who was rummaging through her things.

"I can't find my panties," she muttered. "I think they're inside the blankets."

He put the vehicle in gear and backed up slowly.

"Ian, did ya hear me?" she pressed.

"Can't you put your clothes on without them?" he asked, a smile playing at his lips. "I'll toss the blankets in the barn. You can come get them later."

Shooting him a sideways look of disapproval, Esther started working her half-slip up her legs. The truck rolled steadily down the hill.

But Ian reached over, his hand closing over hers, halting her attempt to get dressed.

"Don't be in such a rush." He winked. "It's a fifteen-minute drive. No need to hurry," he added, with his full grin.

"Well, hell—look what Satan done sent me," she drawled, grinning.

But his gaze had already wandered—drawn to the bare curve of her body.

"I just need to keep us on the road," he muttered, tipping his head slightly in her direction. "Scoot over here. I have something I want to give you."

Esther playfully took her time, deliberately keeping her distance.

With a low grunt, Ian reached for her, his hand gripping her thigh as he pulled her into him.

He didn't waste a second—wrapping his arm around her and kissing her like a man who knew what a proper good morning kiss ought to be.

With one eye on the road, he guided the truck down the winding hill, his free hand resting at the nape of her neck.

She pulled back, concern flickering across her face.

"Ain't this dangerous? Drivin' while neckin'?" she asked.

"This truck could drive itself. Now, if you sat on my lap, we might have a problem." He shot her a roguish look.

"Ian, how is it you're fully dressed, and I'm sittin' here without a stitch of clothin' on—buck nekkid? Is it really as late as you're sayin'?" She eyed him suspiciously.

"I wish I were that clever. But that doesn't mean I'm not reaping the benefits," he said.

Before she could respond, Ian suddenly shot his arm out in front of her.

"Hold on!" he yelled.

The brakes slammed hard. The jolt sent them both lurching forward just as a small herd of white-tailed deer darted across the road, barely missing the truck.

Esther caught herself against the dashboard, Ian's protective arm still braced in front of her.

Still catching his breath, he whipped his head toward her. "Are you hurt?"

"I'm fine," she said, still shocked but managing a small smile. "Maybe I should just get dressed."

"Damn deer, ruining my morning," he muttered, easing the truck forward again.

"Aww, hell." Ian groaned as a realization hit him. "I just remembered something. I promised I'd pick Abram up this morning—early. We've got to head down to Amos Crowder's place. His tractor broke down in the middle of a field, and we were going to help him."

The stress was clear on his face as he pressed harder on the gas pedal.

"You'd best get dressed." The serious Ian had returned.

Esther quickly put on her clothes, trying to make herself look presentable. With the few hairpins she had left, she tried to pin her hair up, but it wasn't working well.

"I really loved these pins." She looked down at one of them.

"I told you I'd buy you more." He glanced at her briefly.

"I ain't gonna let ya use your hard-earned money on 'em, Ian."

He scoffed. "They can't cost that much. What do they run, ten cents?"

"No, Ian." She hesitated, then added, "They got little rhinestones, and I ordered 'em special from the Spiegel catalog."

"How much do they cost, Esther?" His tone was skeptical, sure that she was over exaggerating.

"Three dollars," she said quietly, knowing he'd be shocked.

His head whipped toward her. "Good Lord, Esther, that's half a day's wage!"

"I know that," she said, bracing for a lecture.

But he didn't respond right away. Instead, he just shook his head, clearly bothered, as they drove in silence. The quiet stretched on, making her fidget uncomfortably.

"I ain't mad about it no more, Ian. Just forget about it." She tried to smooth things over.

Still, he didn't respond immediately. After what felt like an eternity, he sighed and turned to her.

"And Clive bought you these things? These expensive things?" His pride was clearly pricked.

"They're just stuff, Ian. I don't really care about 'em." Her voice softened, wanting him to let it go.

"Esther, I don't have that kind of money. Not to waste three hard-earned dollars on some stupid pins."

"Ya just gettin' mean now," she said, her arms crossing defensively as Ian turned onto the main road toward the Old Reed Estate. "I just ain't never had nice stuff 'fore. Sorry."

Ian glanced at her, noticing she'd turned her head toward the window.

It was hard for him.

He wanted to give Esther everything she wanted, but she had grown an appetite for finer things while living with Clive.

And the fact that she cared so much about items her cousin had bought—likely with illegal money—gnawed at him.

He didn't expect her to pack everything up and throw it in a fire, but he wouldn't have stopped her if she had.

As they neared the house, Ian slowed the truck, not wanting their wonderful night to end on a sour note.

He reached out to her, hoping she'd turn toward him.

"Esther, look, I'm sorry I called your pins stupid," he said.

She turned her head with a snap, the sting of his earlier silence still evident on her face.

Slowly, she began pulling the remaining pins from her hair, her dark waves falling.

"What are you doing?" he questioned.

"Ya really think I give a damn about these?" Her eyes were glossy with tears. "I'd rather be in rags here with y'all than sittin' at Clive's house, drownin' myself slowly in whiskey, pretty things all 'round me," she said, her voice breaking.

With that, she rolled down the truck window and hurled the pins out onto the side of the road.

"Don't!" Ian said as he reached out to grab her wrist, but it was too late. "I didn't tell you to get rid of them."

"But you don't like 'em, Ian. They're stupid."

"No, it's not that…" He struggled for the right words. "It's just that I'm a poor farmer, Esther. I can't justify spending three dollars on hairpins. I want to get you nice things, make you happy, but I can't pretend I can give you those things."

His expression was somber, raw, and honest.

"Well, I'm just a dumb hillbilly girl who can't read a lick, and don't know nothin' 'bout nothin'. Reckon ya got one up on me." Her gaze bore into him, defiant and still wounded.

"You're not stupid. Stop saying that." Ian reached out, beckoning her closer. "Please, move back over here," he asked in a softer tone.

Reluctantly, she returned to her spot.

He gently cupped her cheek with his rough, callused hand.

"Esther, I just don't want you to be disappointed in me someday. To look back and think maybe you should've found another man. A younger man, one with money who can buy you stuff from a pricey catalog," he said, like a man who badly wanted something, but refused to lie to get it.

She met his gaze—his handsome blue eyes steeped in quiet sincerity. And with a breath, all the what-ifs and maybes faded into irrelevance. He held her there, unwavering.

"Ian," she whispered, her voice a lull, laced with affection. "Can we just kiss and forget about this?"

With a relieved smile, he nodded and leaned in.

As their lips met, the worries of the world outside the truck seemed to fade, replaced by the warmth of two bodies in sync.

Everything he had felt the night before rushed back—the closeness, the sensations, the way she unraveled under his touch.

He had relinquished himself to her completely, offering every part of who he was—not just his body, but his thoughts, his spirit. He had made love to her.

"It was perfect, wasn't it?" he murmured against her lips as they briefly broke their hold.

She didn't answer, but pressed her forehead to his—that was all he needed.

Then—a sharp knock against the driver's side window. The sound cracked through the cab, jarring and abrupt.

They flinched, the spell between them breaking in an instant.

Ian turned to find Abram standing there, arms crossed, a knowing look on his face.

Ian quickly rolled down the window, shaking his head.

"Don't say it, Abram. Please don't say it."

"You told me six in the mornin'." Abram exhaled, clearly annoyed. "I crawled my tired ass out of a warm bed—with a nice woman beside me, mind you. I waited. Nothin'. Thought maybe your truck broke down or somethin', so I walked that same tired body over here, only to find your truck missin'." A flicker of amusement crept onto Abram's face as he glanced at Esther, who was doing her best to look anywhere but at him.

"I'm sorry, Abram." Ian fumbled for an excuse. "We took a drive, and it just... took longer than I thought."

"Hmm," Abram muttered. "I went over to yer house. Yer kids are up."

Ian rubbed the back of his neck. "Please tell me you didn't send them over to Clarissa's."

Abram let the suspense hang.

"Well... no, but I thought about it. I fed 'em. Told 'em you'd be back soon."

Ian exhaled in relief. "Thank you. I owe you. I really owe you."

Abram shrugged. "Can't say I didn't think about collectin' interest. Now, ya done, or do I gotta wait while you finish whatever it is y'all were doin'?"

Ian shot him a look. "Give me a minute." Ian's gaze flicked to Esther. "Then we'll head out."

Abram shook his head, waving him off as he stepped back a few feet.

Ian rolled the window up and turned to Esther. "You think you can sneak in the front door?"

"I'm gonna do my best," she said, hesitating as she glanced toward the house. "Ya think Abram's gonna say anythin'?"

"Nah. My kids, maybe. But not Abram." A faint smile touched Ian's lips. "Give me another kiss and run up the drive. I don't want to pull up there and alert Clarissa."

Esther leaned in, pressing a soft peck to his lips before slipping out of the truck, a shy smile lingering on her face.

"Ya have a good day," she whispered.

"I'll see you later, darlin'. Hopefully, this won't take all afternoon." His eyes lingered on her.

Just as she was about to shut the door, he called out.

"I love you." His voice was steady, certain.

Esther's heart tugged at his words, but she only returned his smile, looking briefly at Abram, who was making his way back toward the truck.

Not wanting to linger, she scurried past him up the driveway.

Abram climbed into the passenger seat, shutting the door with a sigh. In his hand was his lunch, wrapped neatly in a white cloth. He shook his head in disbelief.

"Lord, Lord, Lord. Ya sure do like trouble." He shot Ian a look. "Ya know Clarissa ain't gonna like this one bit, thinkin' yer just playin' with her niece."

"I'm not playing around with her, Abram," Ian said as he put the truck in gear and pressed the gas, sending them rolling forward down the road.

Abram didn't look convinced. Reaching for the shelf in the dash to stow his lunch, his hand paused. His brow furrowed as he pulled something out—a stocking.

Ian glanced over, immediately recognizing the evidence of his indiscretion.

"Well, now." Abram held it up with a smirk. "This here looks like you've been playin' with somethin', Ian."

"Shit," Ian muttered, snatching the stocking from Abram's hand.

"There's another one in here." Abram fished out the second stocking, dangling it teasingly.

Ian grabbed that one too, stuffing both into his pocket.

Abram shot him a sideways look, his grin downright satisfied. "When I said our baby needed a playmate, I wasn't meanin' the same age. Didn't reckon you'd get right to it."

"I'm a motivated man, Abram. What can I say?" Ian quipped, trying to maintain some composure.

Abram chuckled, but his expression turned more serious. "You oughta marry her first, don't ya think?"

"I intend to," Ian said, his tone firm. "She's just hesitant. Just needs a little convincing, is all."

Abram stretched his arms above his head, letting out a slow sigh. "Sounds like that Huggler charm ain't workin' like it should. That's what ya get for chasin' after a young girl. Yer an old man, Ian," he teased. "Could've had yourself an older woman with six kids already—one who just needed a man to chop firewood, if ya know what I mean."

"She's not that young, Abram," Ian shot back, "And she's just taking a little longer to come to terms with the fact that I'm the best-looking thing in the Blue Hollow Hills."

Abram chuckled again. "Well, at least you'll have time, time to try for an even dozen kids. She's young enough to keep poppin' out babies 'til you're gray as an old Bluetick Hound."

Ian threw him a look. "Shut up, Abram. You sound jealous. If you wanted a dozen kids, you should've gotten started sooner."

Abram shook his head. "Jealous? Ian, I got me a pregnant wife who throws things when she don't like my tone. Ya think I wanna multiply that by ten? And if ya get past four, I'm gonna just assume ya lost the bet."

"That's a shame, my friend," Ian said with a teasing grin. "I was gonna see if you wanted to start a contest. First to a dozen wins, but it sounds like you just don't have the stamina. Some of us are built for the long haul. Maybe you should've married yourself a German."

Abram scoffed. "Well, maybe I'll just have to take ya up on yer bet then. Ain't gonna have ya whoop me on this one."

"Deal. But I get first pick of your tools when Mitzy finally sticks you in the ground," Ian said as he shifted the truck into a higher gear.

Abram let out a deep laugh. "Ha! Joke's on you, I already told her. She just rolled her eyes and told me to go wash the dishes."

Ian just nodded, sure Abram had teased his wife about it before—just another running joke Esther's poor name had unfortunately gotten swept up in.

Their laughter faded into talk of the work ahead as the old Ford rattled down the dirt road, dust rising in its wake. The day stretched ahead, long and familiar, as it always did for men who worked the land.

Gingerly, Esther walked barefoot up the front steps of Clarissa's house, shoes dangling from her fingers.

The boards were cool against her soles, the early morning air thick with the scent of springtime.

She wrapped her hand around the doorknob, turning it with careful precision, willing it not to betray her.

But as the hinges let out a quiet creak, she sucked in a tight breath, muttering a curse as she slipped through the smallest gap she could manage.

The house was still, morning light filtering through the windows. She strained her ears for any sign of Clarissa.

Hearing nothing, she exhaled in relief. Just a few more steps to the stairs.

But as her foot reached the top step, a stern voice stopped her in her tracks.

"Told ya, I wasn't gonna cast a stone at ya, but that don't mean I ain't gonna tell ya—you're playin' with fire." Clarissa's tone was firm, laced with disappointment. "If ya ain't already pregnant, girl, ya gonna be. Best be ready to settle down."

Esther froze, turning slowly to face her aunt. Her heart sank at Clarissa's expression—a mix of displeasure and concern.

"I'm sorry, I just..." Esther faltered, grasping for an excuse.

"Ya think foolin' 'round is fun, and I get it. But let me tell ya somethin'. That man won't shack up with ya. He's got too much pride, too much honor. He's settin' his sights on marryin' ya. You keep that in mind. Just be prepared for that, girl," Clarissa said.

"I know that." Esther's voice dropped as she sank onto the top step, shoulders slumping under the weight of the conversation.

Clarissa's face softened slightly.

"Reckon ya hate me now." Esther's voice buckled under the weight of the words, a quiet tremor threading through each syllable.

Clarissa sighed, climbing the stairs to sit beside her. "Don't be silly. Yer my baby, my family, and always will be. But I love Ian too. He's the best man I know, and I just wanna make sure ya doin' right by him. I know ya care for him, but the way ya soundin' got me nervous—like ya don't know if ya can love him or not. It's got me worried."

"Aunt Clarissa, I... I ain't got a clue how to." Esther's voice broke.

Tears welled in her eyes and spilled over as she pounded her chest in frustration, harder each time.

"He says all these sweet things to me. He's so handsome, everythin' I could ever want. But for some reason, when he looks at me, talkin' about love, I can't feel it." The words choked in her throat.

Clarissa reached out, gently grabbing her hand to stop her. "Honey, please don't do that."

"What's wrong with me?" Esther cried. "I wanna feel it. And sometimes, I think I might start to, but then it just plumb up and disappears."

She paused, wiping her nose with her hand.

"When I thought he didn't have no feelin's fer me, I reckon I felt somethin' then—least, I think that's what it was. But every time he says he loves me, all I wanna do is run and crawl up under that ol' porch at Gran's."

Clarissa took a deep breath, wrapping an arm around her. "Ya wanna know what I think, honey?"

Esther nodded, her face wet with tears.

"I think ya need ya some time. Let Ian's words grow 'round ya, settle in soft-like. Don't go tryin' to force 'em. This business of gettin' hot for each other, it pushes things along—like that river out yonder. You might think ya strong enough to stand in the current, but it's gonna pull at ya."

She paused, letting her words sink in, then continued.

"And another thing. If ya decide ya don't want him, be easy on him. That man's got his heart set on ya now. He's big and strong, sure—but when a man loves ya, really loves ya, he ain't near as tough as he looks. Ya don't even know the power ya hold. Ya could break him like a dry twig if ya saw fit."

Esther sniffled, her voice barely a whisper.

"Aunt Clarissa, he'll hurt me 'fore I ever hurt him like that."

Clarissa tilted her head, studying her.

"Hmm. Girl, you sure don't hear yourself, do ya? That right there sounds a whole lot like love to me."

Chapter 11: A Woman's Work

L ate afternoon light filtered through the green curtains of the kitchen window, swaying slightly as if beckoning the springtime breeze in. The wind whistled through the crack in the sill, sweet and aimless, like it was singing a tune it was making up.

Esther held the oven door open, eyeing the baking loaves of bread nestled snug inside.

"Clarissa, I don't know if they're done or not." Esther bit her lip. "I'm scared to pull 'em out and they ain't cooked through—like last time."

The older woman, tying her apron back on, came over to inspect. She reached into the stove and tapped on the crust with her fingernails, her movements practiced and confident.

"They need a few more minutes, honey. Crust ain't springin' back yet, and look at that color—it don't look near tasty enough." She carefully shut the door. "You'll get this. Ya missed out on cookin' time with me when ya was young, but we'll make up for it."

Esther smiled as she moved to the sink, washing the last of the mixing bowls, her hands lingering on the edge as though stalling, trying to be patient.

Just then, Rebecca and Benjamin bolted through the back door, their energy filling the kitchen.

"Esther, ya said we could pick out the tree today," Benjamin said, sounding frustrated.

Clarissa quickly cut him off. "Esther's got woman's work to tend to. Y'all run on now, go play outside." She handed each of them a cookie with a stern but affectionate nod.

Benjamin, not easily deterred, faced his aunt. "You and Pa are makin' Esther not fun anymore. She ain't played with us much since she's got back."

Esther's hands paused mid-scrub, a sad expression crossing her face. She missed those carefree times but knew she needed to start growing up and take on the harder tasks expected of her now.

"I promise ya, Benji, I'm gonna build it with ya. Why don't ya scout out a few good trees—ones that ain't too hard to climb." Esther dried the last dish and set it on the rack with a quiet clink.

"Can we draw later, Esther?" Rebecca chimed in, her bottom lip pushed out in a dramatic pout.

"Yeah, but y'all best clean up everything in the front room first. It'll make your Pa happy and maybe give us time tonight." She turned to put a large flour canister on a tall open shelf.

Rebecca wrinkled her nose. "Benji's right. You ain't fun no more."

With a light chuckle, Clarissa ushered the children back out the door, giving them a light pat on their bums. "Do as she said, young'uns."

Once they were gone, she turned to Esther, a proud little smile tugging at her lips.

"Ya turnin' into a real mama," Clarissa said as she grabbed a broom from the corner and began sweeping under the table, pulling out the chairs.

Just as she did, a spent Ian walked through the door, letting it clank as it bounced shut.

Esther was in the middle of putting the last of the baking canisters on the top shelf, stretching on her tiptoes, reaching as far as she could—but still coming up short.

"Well, hello, my beautiful ladies," Ian said as he stepped up behind her, purposeful, taking the container from her hands and setting it in its place.

She looked up to see his face streaked with sun and dust, along with the smudges and sweat darkening his shirt. A pungent musk clung to him, bolder than she liked but not completely off-putting.

Ian gave Clarissa a brief glance, then turned back to Esther. He kissed her forehead, his hands resting at her waist, the intimacy of the moment telling its own story.

"Lord, Ian, ya need ya a good soak," Esther playfully said as she pushed him away.

"I do, but I'm starving. I had to steal Abram's lunch, and it wasn't much." His stomach gave a loud grumble. "See?" He rubbed it sheepishly.

"Now, why'd ya go and do a fool thing like that?" Clarissa mumbled as she set a skillet on the stove with a practiced clatter.

Ian shot a questioning look at Esther behind the older woman's back as she went to the fridge. His eyebrows arched as he mouthed, "Did she catch you?"

Esther shook her head, but her response wasn't convincing. His lips tightened into a thin line—worried.

"Sit yer weary bones down," Clarissa instructed, pulling a large pork chop from the fridge and dropping it onto the cutting board with a soft thud.

Clarissa spun around just in time to catch the look of two folks trying hard not to look caught. Her eyes lingered on Esther for a moment longer, a knowing glint in them. She pointed to the pan heating up.

"This is yer job now, girl. I got other work callin' me. Fresh cornbread's under the towel." A tentative smile found its way onto Clarissa's face, lifting her cheeks. "Don't know what I should do with ya both," she muttered as she left.

Ian waited, his fingers drumming idly on the table as he shifted his attention to Esther.

"What did she say to you?" His voice was low.

Esther busied herself with a rag, wiping a spill from the counter.

"Ain't nothin' for ya to worry 'bout." Her tone was breezy, but her movements betrayed her unease.

Ian frowned, then sank into the chair with a long breath, his long legs pushed out in front of him.

"Good Lord, you're right, I do need a bath. How can you even stand being near me?" He grinned as he lifted his arm and gave a dramatic sniff.

Without meeting his eyes, Esther took the pitcher of iced tea from the icebox and poured a glass, setting it down beside him.

She moved back to the stove, dropping a teaspoon of lard into the pan. The sizzle of the pork chop filled the room as she added salt and pepper.

"You're really making me food?" Ian teased, leaning forward. "You look so cute, come here."

He reached out, but she darted past him.

"Ian, I'm cookin'. Don't go messin' with me," she said, fighting a smile.

"When you're done, come sit on my lap so I can kiss you." There was no mistaking the pull in his voice—he'd missed her all day.

She turned just enough to glare at him, amused. "Yer filthy."

Not missing the opportunity to be suggestive, he said, "Sweetheart, you don't know how filthy I really am." Then, with a mischievous smile, he leaned over, tugging lightly on the hem of her dress.

"Stop," she whispered, batting his hand away. Her eyes darted toward the hallway. "Yer gonna get me scolded again."

Ian's grin faltered, replaced by a more concerned expression. He bent toward her, just slightly. "Clarissa said something?" His brow furrowed. "She doesn't know what we're really up to, right? You didn't say anything—right, Esther?"

Esther turned, holding a plate in her hands like a shield. "Ya want butter and honey on your cornbread?" Her tone was carefully neutral.

"Just butter, not too much," he said, worry lingering under the surface. "You didn't answer me. You kept it between us, right?"

She set the plate down and busied herself slicing the cornbread, her hands steady despite the tension in her shoulders.

"Eat your food and quit worryin'. I ain't said nothin', Ian."

Her voice was stiff, with a slightly strained pitch.

Ian leaned back, studying her.

As she passed by, he caught her hand and tugged her into his lap, the suddenness of it catching her off guard. With a small scream, she landed square on his legs.

"I just know how women are," he said, his tone light but his grip firm. "They talk about stuff—stuff that oughta stay private."

She eased her arms around his neck, her head tipping to the side like she was setting him up.

"Ya think ya know women so well, do ya?"

He shook his head—her softness had already undone him, and he didn't care. He kissed her slowly, taking her in, maybe trying to soothe whatever had begun to unravel inside him.

"Esther," he murmured, his lips brushing her ear. "I've got something in my pocket for you."

She pulled back, eyeing him.

"Stop, Ian." A laugh bubbled up in her throat as she swatted his chest. "I ain't reachin' in there."

"No, really," he chuckled, reaching into the pocket of his trousers and pulling out a handful of small hairpins, her hairpins. He set them down lightly on the table before her.

Her breath caught as she stared down at them, her hand hovering midair.

"Ian... ya ain't have to do that," she said, her voice thick with emotion—pure appreciation.

"They make you happy, and I'd do anything to see you happy. And I don't think they're stupid—they look real nice in your hair," he said, sincerity lacing his tone.

Her hand trembled as she picked up one of the pins, running her thumb along its smooth surface. A soft, almost teary smile spread across her face.

"Thank ya," she whispered.

He leaned back slightly with a satisfied grin, but before he could reply—

A bitter scent filled the air, sharp and unmistakable.

Burnt bread.

Esther's eyes widened. "Oh no!" She spun, bolting to the oven.

She yanked the oven door open, but before she could grab the pan, the heat lashed at her fingers. "Damnit!" She jerked her hand back with a yelp, waving it frantically in the air.

Ian was beside her in an instant, grabbing a hot pad to pull the loaves out.

"They're not that bad," he said, setting the loaves on the counter. "I've seen Clarissa's look worse."

"No, Ian, they were almost perfect, and I've ruined 'em," she groaned, sticking her finger in her mouth to cool the sting.

He guided her to the sink, turned on the faucet, and let the cool water run over her hand.

"They look fine," he said gently. "I'd take a slice."

"But ya ain't picky 'bout food," she muttered.

"Thanks," he replied dryly, lifting her finger to blow on it. "You want to know what else is in my pocket?" His grin returned, distracting her.

Esther arched an eyebrow. "Ya already done tried that bait."

He leaned closer, his voice dropping to a whisper.

"Your panties and stockings are in my pocket, sweetheart. Have been all day."

Esther's breath hitched. "Ya been workin' all day with 'em in there?"

"Yep," he said, his grin widening as he watched her cheeks flush.

Not sure how to react, clearly flustered, she let a small smile slip through. "Ian, yer food's gettin' cold."

He lingered, savoring the effect he had on her, before finally sitting down.

"This looks good," he said, digging into the food with gusto. "Not burnt at all."

Esther sat beside him, her gaze drifting to the window.

The late afternoon light had softened, casting the Blue Hollow Hills in a hazy glow.

Ian noticed her expression, his fork already loaded with food. "Darlin'," he said as he took a bite, then continued, "I was thinking we should go up there tomorrow. We need to do what the sheriff told us—get rid of that old still. Make it look like it was never there."

A sigh pulled deep from her chest, slow and thoughtful. "I know," she said.

"I'll take a shovel. How big is it?" he asked.

Esther's fingers drifted over the table, tracing the worn dark grain beneath them.

"That soil up there's mighty rocky. Kettle's pretty big. Ya might beat it down, but it'd take all day to bury it." Her hand stilled, her thumb pressing against the wood, something unreadable settling behind her eyes.

"Naw," she said quietly. "I know somewhere we can put it. Ain't nobody ever gonna find it."

The chill in her voice sent a shiver through him.

He studied her, watching something shift in her. He wanted to ask, to push, but decided to let it be what it was.

"Tomorrow, then," he said, setting down his fork and reaching for her hand.

"Tomorrow," she repeated, her eyes returning to the place she had called home for most of her life—though it had never really been that.

Chapter 12: Never Home

Early morning crept in on the backs of low-hanging clouds drifting down from the Blue Hollow Hills. Mist wove through the orchard as dew clung to the leaves, unwilling to release the last hold of night.

Esther stood perched beside the blue Ford truck near the old barn, the engine idling as it warmed. A sweater pulled tight around her shoulders, she watched as Ian loaded an assortment of tools, setting them over the tailgate into the bed.

He hefted a shovel with ease, the metal scraping against the back before landing with a heavy clank. Wiping his hands on his pants, he glanced around for anything he might've forgotten.

"I checked the river this morning. It's come down some, but I'm not sure we can get across. We'll most likely have to do it on foot—it's still too high for the truck," he said, half to himself.

"Ian, there's tools up there already. Probably everythin' ya be needin'. Why ya bringin' all this?" Esther eyed it all, shaking her head.

"I don't want to have to return to the house if they're all rusty or won't work. I'd rather be prepared than waste my time," he said, short on patience.

She decided to pick her battles, letting him have this one. Still, she didn't want to forget something important.

"We need us a lantern. Can I grab the one from the barn?"

Ian nodded, a perplexed look crossing his face as he leaned against the truck, watching her retreat. Esther's steps were slow, almost hesitant, her body drawn in as if bracing against something more than the morning chill.

She'd been quieter ever since he brought up going to the Blue Hollows the night before. Not a word at the table during their evening studies. No questions. No playful comments or drawings.

No, she'd been serious. And when he walked her back to the front porch afterward, he'd tried to get frisky, asking if she wanted to practice undoing the buttons of his trousers again. She gave him only a small, distracted smile, dismissing him with a quiet, 'I'm tired,' before heading inside.

It hadn't really troubled him, though. Her silence was most likely an inevitable dread taking root, fed by the certainty of where they were going and what needed to be done.

He'd tried to ease it, make her smile, tell her it was going to be all right, but until it was out of the way—done—it was bound to poison her joy.

As they drove up the narrow dirt road toward the familiar hills, Esther pointed out a spot she thought he could park.

"This here's your last good place to pull off," she said.

When they stepped out of the truck, she grabbed the lantern before he could reach for it, then motioned for him to follow.

They followed the fast-moving river for what felt like ten minutes before she turned to him, breaking the silence.

"This is where we can cross." Her gaze drifted toward a cluster of large boulders jutting from the water.

"It's a little precarious, Esther." He eyed the path they'd have to take across. He wasn't worried about himself spanning the distance, but wasn't sure she could.

"I don't know what that word means, Ian, but I've crossed here 'fore. I can do it."

"Let me go first and reach for you, fair enough? And hand me that lantern," he insisted.

She slipped off her shoes, leaving them by the side of the river.

"Don't you need those?" he asked.

"Ian, my feet know this hill. I know where to step, and I'll only slip on the rocks in these shoes."

He figured she was right and didn't push the issue.

The river's current still ran swift, rushing past the large gray speckled rocks, its fury not yet spent. He couldn't help but wonder if there were places where the water spread wider and ran shallower. But Esther had picked this spot—said it was their only option.

If Ian thought he could put this off any longer, he would have—but he wanted it done. No proof left that Esther or her family had ever been tangled up in this illegal business.

The fresh air filled his lungs as he stepped easily onto the first boulder, steadying himself before reaching back for her to join him.

To his surprise, Esther darted forward, ignoring his outstretched hand.

She leapt confidently onto the next rock, her bare feet gripping the slick surface with ease. Before Ian could say a word, she was ahead of him, almost running across the rocks. His chest tightened.

"Slow down! Wait for me." His voice was sharper than he meant it to be.

She didn't stop—not until she'd made it all the way across, unassisted. Not even fazed, she waited for him on the other side as he carefully crossed.

"Damn it, Esther, don't do that."

"Ian, do you know how many rocks I've jumped? Ya ain't got to worry 'bout that," she said, turning to walk in the direction she already knew they needed to go.

She'd spent her life in these hills—if anyone knew the terrain, it was her.

Still, Ian huffed, not hiding his disapproval. He didn't trust that river and its power.

It was a strange thing—walking in a place Esther had known all her life, while he was still a stranger to it. He'd seen these hills from a distance, sure—but never stepped foot in the Blue Hollows.

As she walked ahead, he found himself watching her—each step weaving through the land with effortless familiarity. She knew where every tree stood, as if expecting them, as if born of the forest itself.

"There's another river up this way. It feeds into the big one," she said, pointing to the smaller stream.

Ian hadn't even known that, despite pulling water from the big river to feed the orchard during the summer months for years.

It felt right that Esther wore her hair down, wild and unruly like the first time he had seen her. It swayed as she moved, dark and untamed, spilling down her back.

The girl from the hills. The one he'd fallen for.

As they worked their way up a small, overgrown trail, Ian thought of Esther's grandmother. He had only ever once seen her face up close—and only for a brief moment. He remembered the cruelty etched into her features, made all the more stark by the way she hadn't even bothered to justify beating her granddaughter.

The next memory he had was of pulling her lifeless body far from the falls, after she had been dragged quite a distance.

She had been wedged between two rocks, and Ian had to wade out into the rushing river, throwing her limp torso over his shoulder to bring her to shore.

Esther's Pawdad had been easier to find, his body almost sailing into a soft bank, caught up in the brush.

Abram had helped him carry the old man's body up through the undergrowth to a spot where they could bring the truck down closer. The work had been slow—grueling in every way—and neither of them had said much. There was something about lifting a man who once stood so tall that made the silence feel necessary.

Except for the very few things Esther had said about her grandparents, Ian hadn't known them. They had avoided the Old Reed Estate, only seen in hurried passing—not even turning their faces to meet the eyes of the people there, including himself.

A sober reality hit him—he'd actually spent more time with those people dead than alive. People who had been Esther's whole life for years.

"We're almost there," she murmured as she passed the large flat rock she had always considered her favorite spot in the hills, placed perfectly beside the water.

She hesitated for a moment, reaching down to touch its dark granite, as if it had been her only friend.

Ian slowed his pace, letting her take her time. There was something sorrowful in the way she paused, her fingers tracing its edge.

It made his chest ache, picturing her here—alone, unheard—no one to share in her laughter, no one whose face lit up at the sight of her.

For all its beauty, this place had been steeped in cruelty, the rough hillside shaped by hardship—a world that had given her little and taken far more.

He wanted to speak, to offer her even the smallest assurance that as long as he walked this earth, this would never be her life again.

But what words could unmake years of loneliness and savagery?

Esther pushed forward, lingering for a moment on the place where she'd once scooped endless buckets of water, only to haul them up the steep incline to the old moonshine still. The tally reaching the thousands—it had been her chore, even when she was just a small child.

Her fingers tightened, as if the heaviness of it still lingered in her grasp, bracing against the tide of memories—a life she had worked at erasing from her very mind.

She released a breath she was holding, trying to let go of the angst this place stirred in her. With a glance over her shoulder, she checked if Ian was still behind her—almost forgetting that he was.

But there he stood—steadfast, just off to her side, quiet, as if he hadn't wanted to disturb her.

The long walk had given Esther time to steel herself. To prepare for the ghosts that still lingered.

Had they driven up the hill, the trip would've been faster—perhaps too quick for the time she needed.

"How are you holding up?" Ian's voice was soft, his brow knitting as he tried to read her expression.

She nodded, but it was brief, absent—more habit than meaning.

The tension in her shoulders was visceral, her grip on the lantern tight—she hated this place. He knew that much.

He wondered if, through fresh eyes such as his—eyes that hadn't endured or seen what she had—she might have felt differently about the breathtaking Blue Hollows.

Tall, statuesque pines climbed skyward, their needles whispering in the breeze like a gentle melody. Below, the meadows wore their spring blankets as a lush green carpet covered the earth—wildflowers scattered like brushstrokes on a canvas.

The dirt, soft beneath their feet, stood in stark contrast to the jagged rocks that littered the path.

And his beautiful Esther—he couldn't deny—looked like she belonged here, a spirit, a creature of the woods.

It had never been the place.

It couldn't be.

It had been the people who called it home. And not just any people—Esther's grandparents.

With a weary breath, Esther climbed the last stretch of the hill, drawing closer to where the tattered distillery lay in wait, like a shadow of its former self.

The climb left her more winded than she expected, and she paused, surprised by the burn in her lungs and legs. She shifted her weight, aware now of the tenderness in her feet.

Maybe her time at Clive's had softened her. Shoes from the world beyond these hills had spoiled them.

"This is it, Ian." She pointed at the wreckage ahead.

Her voice was subdued as she swept her eyes over what remained of her grandmother's legacy.

The sheriff and his deputy had done a number on it—pipes lay scattered and bent, wooden pieces splintered, but the destruction hadn't been completed.

The scene felt like an act of unfinished violence, halted last summer by the chaos of Esther's disappearance and the smoke rising from her grandparents' cabin.

Ian crouched low, his sharp eyes taking in the details.

The big still pot, blackened and battered, caught his attention first. It was larger than he'd imagined, twisted and punctured in several places—likely beaten with hammers. He ran his fingers over the worn tarp that had once covered it, brittle at the edges. The copper piping had greened over with time, almost disappearing into the dirt, like the woods were trying to claim it back.

"This'll take some work," he murmured.

A few feet back, Esther stood looking down at the scattered pieces, a tired vacancy in her eyes.

"Where did your grandfather keep his tools?" Ian cut in, interrupting whatever she might've been thinking—or not.

"Up further. Follow me," she said matter-of-factly, as she started up the hill again, the path narrowing.

The remains of the cabin came into view first, its charred timbers sprawled like forgotten corpses, overtaken by greenery. Sunlight filtered through the trees, dappled patches illuminating the destruction as if nature itself sought to reclaim what was left.

Esther's steps faltered as they passed the ruins—evidence of what her own hands had done the year before.

Unable to walk on, they stopped for a breath. The faint smell of soot lingered, mingling with the fresh, earthy scent of spring growth.

Ian rested his hand on the small of her back, offering her silence wrapped in care. He watched Esther's face, the way she studied the spot, as if sifting through them for something only she could see.

Her mouth was taut, her arms cinched tightly around herself. It was a reckoning—confronting a life burned to ashes.

Beyond the cabin, tucked into the tree line, stood Pawdad's shed. The structure leaned precariously to one side, its roof sagging under the weight of years and weather, yet it had survived the fire.

Ian approached the rickety door first, pushing it open. The rusty hinges groaned in protest, the sound cutting through the stillness. Inside, the air was thick and musty, the scent of oil and wood lingering.

The shed's interior was cluttered with tools—rusted hammers, saws, and jars of nails scattered haphazardly on shelves. A thick layer of dust coated everything, softening the sharp edges of tools that had long since been forgotten.

"Pawdad wasn't much for organization, was he?" Ian's lips twitched with a faint smile.

"He knew where everythin' was," Esther said with a small shrug, then picked up a rusted hammer from the workbench and held it out. "Will this work?"

Ian eyed it skeptically. "It'll do." His gaze shifted, spotting what he was really looking for. He reached into a cobweb-filled corner and pulled out a long wooden shovel, turning it in his hands. The handle was rough, splintered from years of use.

"Did he have any gloves?"

But she didn't answer right away, her expression distant, resting on where the cabin once stood.

"Esther?"

"I reckon they were in the house," she said.

"Never mind," he said, shaking his head and shifting his attention to the tools. "This'll do."

Back at the clearing, where the remnants of the old still lay scattered, Ian set to work. He crouched by the mess, his hands firm on the twisted metal as he pried loose pieces that had fused with the forest floor.

"Hold this steady for me." His tone had that certain edge—what Esther called the working Ian voice. Not harsh, but direct. Not mixing words.

She knelt, gripping one end of the warped tubing. Her fingers felt clammy despite the cool morning air, but she held firm, concentrating as he worked to pry loose a stubborn joint.

The rhythmic clang of metal echoed through the clearing, each strike rattling the quiet air.

Ian grunted as he leaned his weight into the pry bar, the metal groaning in protest before giving way with a sharp clang.

The large moonshine kettle was the most challenging. Its size and weight made it nearly immovable without significant effort. He pressed his shoulder against the battered side, leveraging it enough to shift it, revealing the scorched earth beneath.

"We'll bury what we can near here, but not on the site." He motioned to the smaller, rusted pieces scattered nearby.

Esther nodded, her gaze flicking to the pot before shifting away. "I'll get some rocks."

She returned with an armful of stones and set them down beside Ian, who was digging shallow pits beneath the dense brambles a short distance away.

They buried the smaller components first, freshly tilled earth quickly disguised beneath leaves and twigs. Ian piled the rocks over one of the spots, adding a larger one himself to make it look undisturbed, as if it had always been there.

"This feels a little strange, Ian."

"Yeah? What do you mean?" He glanced up, meeting her eyes.

"My whole life, we'd bury and unbury this damn thing. Always bringin' it back to life, resurrectin' it. Now it's gonna be laid to rest for good—same as my grandparents."

He paused, his hands resting on his knees. Her words hung in the air, heavy with meaning.

"In a few years," he said, "the earth will eat it all up. Break it down like it was never even here. Just like a body, I suppose."

He nudged her shoulder, smirking. "Not that I'd know—grave robbing's not really my trade. But if it were, I'd be wealthy enough to keep you in hairpins and out of reasons to be cross with me," he added.

Ian chuckled at his own joke, despite the seriousness on her face. "Oh, come on, Esther. That was a little bit funny. It's worth a laugh."

She gave him a brief courtesy grin, making him shake his head.

"You usually think I'm funny. And honestly? Most days, I'd agree," he said.

She exhaled, resting her chin on her knee. "Ain't it nice when a fella can entertain himself? Ya mighty clever, Ian."

He scoffed, shaking his head. "Now that's downright mean, Esther. Here I am, up here breaking the law with you, and you can't even give me a proper smile?"

He reached over, playfully grabbing her bare foot, dusted with dirt and scratched from rough ground, as he finally coaxed a sincere expression from her.

"Darlin', where was it you were thinking about putting the big pot? I don't think any of Pawdad's tools are strong enough to bend it—it's gonna have to go in whole."

"I know." She nodded as she brushed back a piece of hair from her face.

Chapter 13: Laying It to Rest

When it came time to move the copper kettle, Esther led Ian further up the ridge. She knew exactly where to take it— a natural hollow she'd discovered as a child, hidden behind a thicket of wild blackberry bushes.

The climb was steep, the earth loose and uneven beneath them, sharp rocks jutting from the hillside like hidden teeth.

Ian carried the heavy, awkward pot over his shoulder, the rim pressing painfully into his back. A makeshift harness of rope and an old tarp strained against his chest. Though his breathing remained steady, a few beads of sweat formed on his forehead under the warming afternoon sun.

Esther noticed the subtle shifts in his posture, the way he kept adjusting the pot's weight as it bumped against him. Each step seemed to throw him off balance, and he moved with careful deliberation, trying to make the pot feel less like a burden, though the uneven terrain only made it harder.

The rope dug into his skin, tightening with each step, and in a passing glance, he looked over at her, his face revealing the discomfort he was trying to hide.

"You sure this spot's good?" he asked, his voice breaking the quiet.

"It's safe," she replied firmly. "No one'll think to search there."

The hollow was just as she remembered—a small, rocky cave tucked into the hillside, its entrance almost entirely obscured by thick, tangled thorny bushes.

She pushed the dense branches aside, wincing as they snagged her sleeves, the sharp thorns biting into the fabric and pricking her skin.

She hissed in discomfort but kept moving, her hands firm as she cleared the brambles, knowing exactly how far she had to push them before she could enter.

Ian set the copper pot down with a grunt, brushing his hands against his pants as he met her eyes.

"Should've brought my canteen. Didn't know it would be such a hike," he muttered, wiping the sweat from his brow.

Esther glanced at him, offering a small, understanding smile.

"I'll take ya to the spring on the way back down. We got our drinkin' water from there."

Pulling a match from a small compartment of the lantern, Esther struck it quickly. The flame flickered briefly before it steadied. She lit the lantern in her hand, then lifted it high as she crouched slightly, holding it toward the low entrance. The warm light spilled over the threshold, casting soft shadows on the stone.

"Ian, I can just put it in without ya," she said, her voice soft, secretly hoping he wouldn't insist on going in.

"No, I want to see what it looks like in there."

There had been a hesitancy in Esther's voice, and he wanted to make sure it was indeed a good spot.

"Ya gonna have to crawl in." She glanced toward the entrance. "Ya think it'll fit through that narrow openin'?"

"It'll make it through. How far does that cave go?"

"It's real deep. Never actually reached the end of it," she said. "There's a part that drops off—only dropped rocks down there, goes real far."

"But Ian, I can take it in. I know the way."

"Esther, you just told me about a place where I'd never be able to reach you if you slipped, pushing a big pot. Hell no, absolutely no. I'm coming with you. If the pot can fit through, so can I. I can crawl, if need be."

Ian stood there, hands on his hips, shaking his head, as if he couldn't believe she'd actually asked to take it in on her own.

And Esther knew he was right—she could never maneuver the large pot through the narrow turns. With a resigned sigh, she signaled him to follow her.

This rock fortress had been where she hid—her refuge. Only one other person had ever been here. It was the place she had run to once the porch had become too narrow to fit under. The place she came when her back had bled, her knuckles raw, her belly empty, her soul broken.

The flickering light of the lantern cast shadows on the dark cave walls—jagged and jutting out—the ceiling taller than Ian had expected.

He had crawled in, but now he could stand up. A couple of spare inches hovered above his head, surprising him. He leaned back down, dragging the pot through the entrance. It slid easily as he set it down beside him. The stone around them was cool, with a musty, damp smell in the air, but the earth beneath them was soft, like dust.

Esther picked up the lantern and held it toward the passage ahead.

"Darling, did you come here as a kid?"

"Yeah," she said, giving no further explanation. "Follow me."

Ian lifted the pot into his arms, the black soot staining his already dirty shirt. He let Esther lead as she maneuvered them through a narrow section, which opened into what felt like a good-sized room. The dim light from the lantern painted the rock with soft, flickering shadows.

It was then that Ian realized the walls were covered, not with prehistoric drawings, but those of a lonely girl living on a hill.

Large, sweeping images of the things important to someone who knew nothing else—mostly animals, wild beasts, and unknown faces, perhaps the products of a wishful mind or the result of long hours spent dreaming alone.

Birds flew across the ceiling, their wings outstretched as if ready to take flight. He wondered how she had reached so high, her hands leaving marks in the charcoal, smudged on rock as though they, too, had once been alive. Smaller handprints smeared the walls—a testament to her younger years, the touch of someone who had lived in this quiet, isolated world.

The drawings felt like fragments of an untold life, etched into the stone and left to linger in silence. She had let him see her hymn book, drawings done in pencil, but he never could have imagined this—a mural of young life, vibrant yet trapped in the stillness of the cave.

A knot tightened in Ian's chest. There was something raw and painful in looking at it. He hated the thought of his beautiful Esther being here, alone.

Then he saw it.

A small shrine in the shadowed corner—like a rock altar, built tenderly and with care, stones stacked with purpose as if to honor something precious.

The faint glow from the lantern moved in waves over it, casting soft, undulating shadows.

Small, carefully placed offerings lay before it—pieces of worn cloth, clearly fashioned into simple baby clothes, a small carved wooden bird, and dried flowers, as though someone had tended to it with reverence.

Ian stopped, unable to take another step. His body seized, as if the air itself had rushed through him like a spirit, pulling the breath from his lungs and leaving him gasping.

This was a sacred place, he thought. The silence here whispered of something intimate, precious, reaching far beyond the cave's stone walls.

Esther was already trying to move on down another narrow tunnel, the lantern held ahead of her, hoping he would pass by it. But she knew with certainty—he had seen it. He couldn't pull his eyes away.

The truth of what lay before him was undeniable.

"Esther, please, come back here," he called, his voice firm but gentle as he set the large pot to the side.

He wasn't going anywhere until she returned, his stance unwavering as he watched her, waiting for her to heed his words.

With a deep breath, Esther turned back, the lantern held out in front of her, its light cutting through the darkness and illuminating the stone wall.

This corner of the cave was not covered with animals or trees, but with the drawn images of a baby.

Her baby.

Not dead, but alive in the wall art—one wrapped tightly in a blanket, another of a small child with chubby cheeks and wide eyes, and a boy's face, beaming with a wide smile, as if frozen in a moment of joy.

The drawings gave the cave a pulse, conjuring a world that had never been.

A dream she had held in her heart, one that never came true. A path she was never destined to walk.

"Ian, please," she said, not wanting to acknowledge it. It cut through her like shards of glass—ruthless, without an ounce of mercy.

But all Ian could do was look at her face, wiped of all emotion, almost icy, chilled from what lay around her.

"Esther, is this where your baby is buried?" he asked, crouching down and clearing some debris off what was clearly a small limestone headstone, carved and shaped tenderly with what appeared to be primitive tools.

He reached out, tracing his finger over a small bird's nest, an egg nestled inside, its outline carefully etched with something sharp.

Just above it—no name.

Just an E.

Alone.

With nothing else.

"Oh, Esther," he whispered, his heart breaking with understanding.

There was a profound loneliness about it, as if it needed more—needed more details, more of a truth to validate a life that had been so important to a young girl living in the hills. A way to give it meaning beyond the cold, hard stone.

Important to her—her small baby.

Esther didn't want to give him an explanation, but he was staring at the very thing she had been trying to hide from him.

Knowing this, she felt compelled to tell him at least what the "E" stood for. But as she opened her mouth, a flood of tears worked their way out, as if they had been building up with every silent moment, every stone-like expression. The tears came like a storm—uninvited, unstoppable.

"His... his name was Ezekiel, like my grandfather."

Ian leaned up, gazing at her with tenderness in his eyes.

He knew what a spot like this meant to a person, thinking she had never shared it with another living soul. His heart ached for her, for what she had carried all these years, hidden in the silence of the hills.

Esther's resistance to the letter "E" had nothing to do with her own name.

It was the only letter she knew of a name she couldn't write, a life she couldn't speak about, a secret she had lived with until she shared it in the barn with him.

"Esther, do you want me to write the rest of his name on there?" he asked.

Instantly, a river of tears rushed from her eyes. Almost panicked, she nodded firmly, her body shaking.

Dropping to the ground, she frantically searched for a rock—anything he could use, desperate.

"Don't worry, my love. I have something that'll work." Ian smiled softly, his voice warm and full of reassurance as he pulled a pocket knife from his pocket.

His steady eyes met hers in the darkness, offering her his peace in that fragile moment.

He sat down firmly, his movements slow and intentional, calling for her to bring the light closer. She found a spot near him, her tears still falling, unrestrained, as he reached for the precious flat stone, setting it carefully in his lap.

"Did he have a middle name?"

"No," she choked out, her voice barely above a whisper.

"Did you give him the last name Primm?"

She nodded, her breath hitching as her eyes met his.

Ian felt a strange relief wash over Esther's body as he began to carve, as if, with each stroke, he was releasing a sorrow she had carried for years.

It was like righting a wrong, honoring a life that had been passed over, unimportant—his place in the world now, at last, properly recognized.

Ian paused between carving the names, leaning over and kissing her forehead with tenderness, his lips lingering for a brief moment as if to offer some quiet comfort.

He continued, digging into the soft gray stone, the strength of his hands pressing firmly as the letters took shape.

"Do you know when he was born?" he asked.

"I'm not sure. I tried to figure it out," she said. "I think around the beginning of April."

"That's okay. Lots of headstones only have the month, or sometimes just the year," he said as his hands worked the stone. "1933, right?"

"No, Ian, it was 1932."

A slight gasp slipped from Ian's mouth as he quickly did the math in his mind. Esther's baby had been born only six months after Benjamin. Both Esther and Adeline had been pregnant at the same time.

His mind suddenly filled with the dream of what young Ezekiel would have looked like now—a boy similar to Benjamin, but with a freckled face like his mother, dark hair, and definitely a spirited personality. Loud and playful, with a fine sense of humor, no doubt.

He could imagine how Benjamin would have loved having him as a friend—the adventures they would have shared, the trouble they would have gotten into.

The sadness of it never being a possibility pushed his own tears to the surface as he scribed on, writing more than he had planned—words that sat in his own heart.

Esther didn't question what he was doing or what he was saying. She just leaned against him, resting her head on his moving shoulder, trusting him.

When Ian was done, he paused, holding it back to inspect, bringing it closer once again to fix a few minor imperfections. He blew away the dust, a small smile tugging at his lips.

He hoped Esther would be pleased that he had done it justice.

Her eyes studied it, clearly moved as she spoke softly.

"It looks real nice, Ian."

He carefully lifted the stone, placed it back in position, and straightened the rocks around it to help it stand upright.

"Here you go, little Ezekiel." His voice was soft, speaking to her baby as one might. "You're a beautiful little boy... so perfect."

Compelled to speak more, he continued, his words gentle and full of warmth. "And, little Ezekiel... if you are ever lonely or scared, go find a nice lady named Adeline. She has a big smile like yours."

"She'll be sure to take good care of you, hold you, rock you until your mama comes for you someday." Ian's voice cracked as he faced Esther.

"And Addie... she'll be happy to do it... as your mama is doing the same thing for her... here."

Drawing in a reverent breath, he finished, "Sleep now, little one... sleep until we meet you again in heaven."

Ian's words, a gift to Esther's pain, so powerful they released a frozen dam inside her, shaking away years of sediment and stone.

In what could only be described as a deep, gut-wrenching cry, it rose from her—rising up from a haunted and buried chasm inside her soul.

The sound reverberated off the rock walls, echoing down the long, blackened passages. It moved out of the cave, filling the quiet of the Blue Hollows.

Ian swept her into his arms almost immediately, his own tears mingling with hers as he gripped her tight in his embrace.

He wanted her to truly feel him there with her, to know she wasn't alone anymore.

There were many things Ian wanted to teach Esther, beyond writing, and about the world.

One was how to grieve.

A thing done better in the arms of another human being, not alone in a cave, hidden in the mountains.

Clarissa had given this to him, letting his dam break over and over as it flooded his world. And after some time, a long time, it slowed.

Finally, it no longer released with such fury, not tearing away the hillside inside him. Now, most of the time, it was a small stream, coming down at unexpected moments.

And Esther, his beautiful Esther, had rebuilt him again, though he didn't know if she knew that.

She made him want to feel alive, to not just carry on with life, but to be inside of it.

And now, he wanted to give that to her as well.

Help her dream a bigger, greater dream than just escaping the hell she had been in.

Without rush, with no pressure to cease, he held her until the last of her cries had escaped, as she wiped the snot from her nose, awkwardly trying to rub it on the inside of her dress, not knowing what to do with it.

"Here," Ian said, handing her a hanky.

"Thank ya," she said, blowing her nose, almost filling it up.

She scrambled to find a pocket to put it in, realizing her dress didn't have any. "Should've worn my slacks. Ain't got any pockets to put this in."

"I've never seen you wear pants," he said playfully. "But I'm sure you'd look real nice in them."

"First time ya met me, I was wearin' overalls," she said, thinking back.

"That doesn't count, and those most certainly are not the same thing. You can't see a girl's bottom side in those," he said, standing up, dusting the dirt off his pants.

She just shook her head, thinking he was only being honest.

"Darling, are you ready to finish this quest?"

"What's a quest, Ian?"

"You've never heard of a quest before?" he asked, reaching down to help her up. "That's why reading is so worthwhile."

"How is it, Ian, ya always bring everythin' back to readin'? I swear. I could be nekkid, or sittin' in the belly of the earth, and ya'd find a way to slip it in."

He laughed, thinking of the double meaning as he picked up the big copper pot, directing her to continue leading while she lifted the lantern.

"I'm never going to give up," he said stubbornly.

"That's what I'm worried about," Esther said, walking ahead of him, leading him forward in an ancient tunnel.

They walked for a few minutes, the walls tight on both sides, having to climb over a couple of large boulders, scooting themselves along in a narrow gap. There was water seeping down the rocks, a slick spot in the dirt.

Esther pointed it out, making sure Ian saw it.

"We're almost there," she said.

"Esther, how come you weren't terrified of this spot? It's kind of spooky, especially for a young person."

"Oh, I was scared of this part, certain it was the door to hell, like in the Bible."

Ian just laughed, though the thought bothered him, as he knew it wasn't a joke—she had actually believed it.

"Slow down, it's over here," she said, pointing, visible fear on her face.

"Esther, you know this isn't really the way to hell, right?" he questioned, but she didn't appear convinced.

As he neared the hole, he peered over. The large pit was almost vertical, and far more vast than Esther had explained.

"Don't get too close," she said, grabbing the back of his shirt, as if she could actually stop him from falling.

For a second, Ian thought about teasing her about tripping—but decided against it. She might not take it well.

He liked that she was holding on to him tightly. It made him feel like she cared—like when she'd made him food the night before.

"Well, I'm going to toss it. You have any last words?" he asked, grinning just a little.

"Like what?" she asked.

"Don't worry, I know what I'm going to say," he mused.

With a surge of force, Ian hoisted the old, tarnished moonshine kettle above his head, holding it like a trophy before hurling it into the dark void.

The clang of metal against rock echoed sharply, each thump and rattle marking its descent as it tumbled into the unseen depths, swallowed by the abyss.

"I send you down to hell," he yelled with mock fervor as it fell. "Back to your masters, Gran and Clive. May you stay there with them forever, tormenting them as they tormented this poor girl. Tending the fires of an empty pot until the end of time."

Ian finished, trying not to let the laugh in his voice escape, doing it all to amuse her.

Worried she hadn't taken it the right way, he turned to her—and caught the soft curl of her lips.

"Wasn't ya just telling me I was dramatic a couple of days ago? Ain't no doubt ya Rebecca's pa," she said, pulling him to move away from the edge.

"I wanna leave," she added, her tone insistent.

"Lead the way," he agreed.

They moved easily, entering the last chamber. Esther paused, letting her eyes linger on the headstone again, now complete— finished as it should have been. She gave Ian another grateful smile.

"Let's go home, my love," Ian said, taking her hand, his rough fingers holding hers tenderly.

Ian, not wanting anyone ever to discover the cave, moved the spiky blackberry bushes back into place, working to conceal it. As they stood back, they agreed that anyone passing by would never know what lay beyond it.

They worked their way down the hill faster than they had gone up. Esther led from memory, and Ian followed, stopping briefly to drink from the spring.

There was a new lightness in her step, as if she had been unshackled from the chains that had bound her to that cave. Ian had only been joking, but he found himself wondering if, in that moment when he tossed that old kettle, his words had meant more— something symbolic, something meaningful.

As they neared the Primms' cabin, Esther quickened her pace, eager to pass it by. Her grip on Ian's hand tightened—almost enough to pull him off balance as she led him down the hill.

"Shouldn't we put the tools away?" A responsible Ian reminded her. It almost pained him to leave them lying on the bare forest floor, though there wasn't much use left in them.

"Let 'em rust," she said, dragging him along.

"Really?" he asked, looking back as though he had disrespected her Pawdad by leaving them there.

"Ian, let them rest with him, too."

"Very well. Then that's where they belong," he said, lifting her hand gently, pressing a lingering kiss to her knuckles.

Once they had crossed back over the river, shoes back on her feet, Ian led Esther back to the truck, opening the door for her.

As he did, a strong breeze blew past them, rattling the hinges, accompanied by the strong scent of pine. It was as though the hills were bidding them farewell.

"Esther, we're not far from the turnoff," he teased, giving her knee a quick squeeze.

She just rolled her eyes as he shut her door.

"Is that a no?" he questioned as he climbed into the cab, an actual look of disappointment on his face.

"You forget what ya said only a few minutes ago? 'Bout havin' work to do?" she reminded him.

Ian started the truck, his brows drawing together as he glanced her way. "The kids are right. You're not fun anymore."

"Are ya really tryin' to put a baby in me or what?" she said, half playful, half serious.

"Would you be mad if I did?" he teased, voice low as he pulled her closer on the truck bench.

Before she could answer, he kissed her—fierce and tender all at once.

He pulled away, breath heavy, and reached over to gently tug her ear toward him, his fingers grazing the side of her neck.

He whispered slowly, as if confessing a truth.

"I'd do it if you wanted me to."

His breath lingered warm on her skin, sending a shiver down her spine and drawing a small gasp from her lips.

Esther raised her eyes, thinking for a second he was still teasing—but when she met his gaze, she saw something in his eyes—something real, something far beyond the playful banter.

He was serious.

A tightness settled in her chest.

What had gotten into him?

Clarissa had been wrong, she thought. Ian would shack up with her if he thought he didn't have another choice.

"God, Ian, ya so damn handsome. An' ya have already made some mighty pretty ones so far, but… ya really think that's somethin' ya should do?"

He smiled, but it didn't feel sincere. He leaned back, the responsible Ian trying to claw his way back in as he turned to stare out the side window.

He didn't look at her right away.

"You're right," he said finally, brushing it off. Then he gripped the gearshift as the engine roared to life.

"I'm sorry," she said, afraid she'd pushed him away.

"Oh, I'm not giving up, Esther. I'm a patient man," he said, glancing at her with a half-smile. "Someday you're going to give me a lot of children. I'm not worried about it."

Tilting her head, she asked, "Children?"

With a growing grin, he said, "Abram and I are racing to a dozen, and he's catching up."

Chapter 14: Fishing

Weeks had passed at the Old Reed Estate, where spring moved through the land like a slow, sweeping hand, coaxing pink petals from their stems and scattering them gently across the front porch and orchard paths.

It was late April now, and in quiet moments, Esther often wandered the trees, comforted by the feeling of being lost among them. Their vibrant blossoms had faded, replaced by a lush canopy of green leaves and clusters of tight fruit buds.

She paused near the portable metal fencing, resting lightly against it as she watched the sheep grazing beneath the shade, nibbling quietly at grass and weeds.

The sheep did more than feed—they worked, clearing away the tangle of undergrowth, moving in a rhythm as old as the land itself.

As if sensing the attention, two fuzzy lambs trotted up to the fence, their small noses twitching as they investigated her presence. Esther smiled, leaning over to pet them, but they darted back to their mother before she could touch them.

Distracted, she hadn't even noticed Ian approaching until his hands suddenly gripped her sides.

"Sweet Jesus! Almost jumped in with the sheep, Ian."

"Sorry, darlin'. Just wanted to tell you we were going." He squeezed her tightly from behind, his large arms wrapped around her. "Are you sure I can't convince you to come?" he asked.

She turned to face him. "Naw, but it'll be fun for ya boys. Saw Clarissa making y'all a nice big lunch."

"Will you walk me up?" Ian asked, reaching for her hand with a smile as they made their way toward Clarissa's driveway.

Time was slowly creating an ease between them now, washing away their earlier worry. Ian had grown more patient, careful to give Esther the time she'd asked for.

Following Abram's sage advice, he made sure to send her home early each evening—careful not to let her "play wife" at his place. It wasn't easy. He often caught himself yearning to revisit the passionate places they'd already ventured.

He wasn't denying that he wanted to push the boundaries, exploring the edge of the cliff with her. And despite his impulsive offer to make a baby with Esther, he'd quickly retracted it, recognizing its recklessness.

Ian had resolved to be more careful now, and they had settled into something comfortable—despite the occasional pout from Esther when she tried to convince him to invite her into his bed.

He'd even gone so far as to lock his door, knowing full well that if she showed up, he wouldn't be able to turn her down.

Temptation walking barefoot through his house.

The time she wanted came at a cost—one that cut both ways. The punishment was hurting him, too. But he was playing the long game, holding just enough back.

There wasn't a morning when he didn't anticipate seeing her face in Clarissa's kitchen, just as eagerly as the children did.

And at the end of every long day, he found himself heading straight for her, often before he'd even washed away the sweat and dirt of his work. Esther felt like a reward, her smile and bright gaze welcoming him as though it had been forever since she'd last laid eyes on him.

Being with her was bliss—even when she frustrated him, which was often enough. Yet he was beginning to accept that as simply part of who they were together.

The passiveness she'd once shown was fading, giving way to a stubborn confidence. Now, as Esther became surer of herself, she didn't hesitate to speak her mind—especially when she believed he was wrong.

If he was honest, though, few things frustrated him more than trying to pin down a straight answer from her when she wasn't inclined to give one.

And there was that thing sitting unaddressed in the back of his mind—something Esther refused to even talk about, leaving him increasingly unsettled with each passing day.

Ian was a studied man, one who took notes—tracking the weather, the seasons, every blessed tiny detail of the orchard. He even recorded important dates and events in his private journal—things that needed to be remembered.

And he had noted something—paying more attention to it than she would have liked.

He'd asked Esther about her womanly time—her monthly—but she'd dismissed him outright. It didn't feel like shyness. She was short with him, shutting him down with a sharp glance, refusing to give even the smallest bit of information.

He wasn't ignorant—he had studied biology in school back in New York and knew how it all worked. And after years of struggling to conceive Rebecca with Addie, he understood it far too well.

Not wanting her to be cross with him, he had left it alone. But over the last week, she had been acting differently—telling him she was tired out of nowhere.

Earlier that day, he had found her curled up on the small porch swing, fast asleep. Napping wasn't something she usually did, always saying it was "the Devil's business."

She had also complained about feeling off, her body aching—especially her breasts when he tried to playfully grab at them when no one was watching, actually swatting hard at him.

At first, he wondered if it was just a reason to make him keep his hands to himself—a quiet retaliation for sending her back to Clarissa's each night. But then he caught her holding them protectively in the kitchen after he hugged her.

He'd counted back, tracing the days like chalk marks on a wall. Every sign pointed to what he suspected—an early pregnancy.

A baby conceived in the dark corner of a barn—a night Ian could only recall in fragments, but one he was certain had left a good part of himself behind.

Yes, he thought to himself, he would have another talk with her tonight, making her sit down and really tell him.

Because if she was, her waiting time was over. Plain and simple. They would need to get married—and quickly—to salvage her reputation. Despite the people of Larkin being rural folk, they weren't ignorant of such things and would do the math.

"What are ya thinkin' 'bout, Ian?" Esther said, drawing him from his thoughts as they neared his parked truck.

"We'll talk about it later." He smiled. "I don't want to leave you. Come with us," he begged, tilting his head sideways, as if his charm might do the job.

"I can't. I got plans of my own," she said, her voice secretive as she wrapped her arms around his neck.

He pulled her body tight against his. "Like what?"

"You'll see when ya get back," she teased, pushing her lips out for him to kiss.

But he bypassed her lips, easing close to her ear to whisper, his voice low and hurried as Abram approached from the house.

"Does it involve getting naked with me?"

Esther loved playing the part, pretending to be shocked as she slapped his arm, knowing he only taunted her with such statements. Ian knew full well she wouldn't have time to fire back—not with Abram so close, their lunches tucked under his arm.

"I'm not gonna kiss ya goodbye now," she said, trying to pull away. But as soon as she did, he whipped her back, dipping her low.

He planted a big, wet kiss on her mouth, holding her there despite her giggles and pleas for him to let her go.

"That's gross," Benjamin said as he rounded the house, a fishing pole in one hand and a dangling can of worms in the other. "She can't even breathe," he added, looking to Abram, expecting him to agree.

But Abram just laughed as he opened the truck door, ushering the boy inside and placing the pole in the back.

"I'll save ya, Benji. Hide ya eyes the best ya can," he said with a smirk.

Ian didn't let up. He held Esther there longer, wanting to make his point.

"Ian, she gonna be here when ya return. And ya son is right—she's gonna pass out from no air," Abram said, shaking his head as he settled into the passenger seat.

Still dipping her back, Ian finally pulled up from the kiss, her laughter escaping as she tried to stand. But he easily held her in place, her back resting in his muscular arms.

"Let me up," she begged, breathless.

"Promise. Promise you won't ever take your kisses from me," he insisted.

"I promise, I promise. Now, lemme up," she said as he finally pulled her upright. She wobbled a little, and he reached out, steadying her until she found her footing.

"You made me all dizzy." She smiled, pressing a hand to her stomach as if steadying herself. "Benji's right—you sucked the air right outta me."

Ian's playful grin faded somewhat. "You okay? Need me to walk you back to the house?"

"Yer just bein' silly. I'm fine, Ian. Ya boys need to get on now," she said, recovering and waving him off.

With that, Esther stepped back toward the house, blowing a quick kiss as they pulled away.

The truck rolled down the driveway to the main road—Ian honking once and throwing a final wave out the window.

As the vehicle disappeared from view, Esther turned toward the front porch, walking slowly, her hand still firm against her body.

Then it hit her—hard.

She wasn't going to make it inside.

Her gut churned with a force she couldn't fight.

Desperate, she found the only spot she could, dropping to her knees beside Aunt Clarissa's pretty pink azalea bushes, and heaving, emptying the contents of her stomach with force.

Slowly, she leaned up, wiping her mouth with the back of her hand before taking a long, steadying breath.

"Oh, Lord," she whispered to herself.

This wasn't the first time. And Esther knew it had nothing to do with hard drink. Her mind had been clear for weeks now.

After one desperate search for Clarissa's liquor—only to find it gone, sure that Ian had removed it—she'd given up, letting the burden go. The relief that came from no longer chasing after it had been a tender mercy.

But this? This was different. Her body felt changed. She could barely lie on her sides, her breasts so tender that it hurt to have anything near them, not even able to wear a brassiere.

Luckily, no one had noticed yesterday morning when the smell of sausage frying in the kitchen hit her like a punch. She had hardly managed to excuse herself, muttering something about fetching eggs before stumbling outside. She didn't even make it past the old tree before the meal came back up, leaving her breathless and shaken.

Now, with her gut settling again, she leaned back against the porch railing, staring at the horizon.

Well, she thought to herself, Ian might have just gotten his wish.

He'd been more patient—if that's what you could call it—but she knew deep down he wanted this, wanted a family with her. And Lord help her, it terrified her.

Sober and with a clear mind, Esther knew she had missed her time by a couple of weeks, hoping her math was correct.

But somewhere in her mind, a dark thought lingered—was there a chance, however slim, that it could be Clive's? The very idea sent a shiver through her.

Using reason, she reminded herself of Clive's impotence—it had been a growing problem for him. She'd taken to plastering him with alcohol every time he tried to get at her, purposely making it worse.

The last time, clumsy and intoxicated beyond reasoning, he hadn't even been firm enough to get inside her before passing out, pinning her face down beneath his bulk.

Esther closed her eyes against the memory, her breath catching. Clive had been a big man, a solid weight around his middle. She had struggled to wiggle free, her breath pushed from her lungs, legs pinned wide under his limp body.

She'd called his name with what little air she could gather, hoping to wake him. But it wasn't until she started to see stars that he rolled off, grumbling in a drunken haze.

If he hadn't moved, she was certain she would have died that night, smothered beneath him.

Her breaths came slower now, measured, as she attempted to peel herself free from the haunting vision still clinging to her thoughts.

She had pieced together the timeframe of that night.

A brand-new magazine had arrived from Paulson's Mercantile that day. She recalled glimpsing it among the belongings the sheriff brought her weeks ago, hidden neatly at the bottom of a box.

Acting casual, she'd asked Benjamin what month began with the letter F.

Esther was almost sure she'd had her monthly after that—she remembered using it as an excuse to get up in the night and move to Clive's couch.

It gave her some peace, even if the whispers of doubt stirred in her head.

Still, a quiet panic drifted up from where her fears lived.

She needed more time.

If she told Ian, she knew exactly what he'd do—he'd put her in his truck and drive her straight to Jasper to marry her that very day.

Maybe it wasn't what she feared—or worse, what some hidden part of her secretly wanted.

But the old whispers rose again, cruel and insistent, reminding her that something was broken deep inside—that her body didn't know how to hold life the way it was supposed to.

She didn't even know how far along she'd been all those years ago, only that she'd failed.

She remembered holding Ezekiel in her arms—tiny and perfect—with his full head of hair, delicate fingernails, and soft eyelashes brushing gently against her memory.

Ian hadn't let up teasing her about having a large family, either. He could be so pushy and frustrating—even if that was just his way of trying to let the idea grow on her.

And what was this thing he needed to talk to her about tonight?

He'd had the gumption to ask her outright, just last week, when she'd last bled, leaving her mortified.

Couldn't he be like other men—just walking around clueless until his woman told him?

Esther shook her head as she stepped inside the house.

The lingering scent of ham frying in the skillet met her, curling into her nose and hanging there—rich, heavy—sending her stomach twisting wildly again.

Chapter 15: Esther's Surprise

Esther slid the chicken into the oven, her eyes drifting toward the clock as she silently repeated Clarissa's careful instructions. She scanned the kitchen quickly, checking off each task in her mind—potatoes peeled, greens seasoned, biscuits neatly arranged and ready to bake. Her gaze finally settled on the counter, where bowls and utensils waited in tidy stacks, every detail of the evening meal thoughtfully prepared.

She stepped back, smoothing her apron down with both hands as her gaze roved over the kitchen.

Everything was ready—a meal she had made entirely by herself, unassisted. The thought sent a quiet surge of pride through her. It was a surprise for everyone, but mostly Ian. He always said he loved it when she cooked, and she had dabbled here and there with a side dish or two, but she had never served such a feast. She wanted to show him that, despite not learning to read as quickly as he had wished, she had polished her culinary skills.

She looked at the clock once more, remembering what time Ian had said they'd be back, and calculated quickly. It needed to be just right—hot and ready by the time they returned and cleaned up. Satisfied, she folded her apron neatly and set it in a spot where she could easily retrieve it later.

Now, she had time to wait—to sit on the front porch as she'd promised Rebecca, drawing paper dolls together, coloring them, cutting them out, dressing them in elegant city clothes. That was Esther's favorite part.

Earlier, she had told Clarissa to take it easy, but Clarissa had only waved her off, insisting on scrubbing the upstairs bathroom. Stubbornness ran thick in this household, but today, it didn't bother Esther. She had done her part. Now, the work was behind her.

The porch welcomed her as she stepped outside, the late afternoon sun pooling on the wooden boards, painting them gold. Shadows stretched long and thin, curling around the porch's edges, and the ferns swayed gently in their hanging baskets. There was a softness to the scene, almost romantic.

Down by the fence line, Mitzy sat cross-legged in the grass under the shade of a wide white oak, her dress pooling around her. Jeremiah darted back and forth nearby as he stumbled after a butterfly that stayed just out of reach. His giggles cut through the stillness, the sound pure and joyful.

Esther smiled but quickly noticed that someone was missing.

"Rebecca?" she called, stepping forward. Her voice carried over the porch rail, but there was no answer.

Mitzy glanced up, brushing dirt from her hands as she stood.

"She went down the road, lookin' for those white flowers she likes to make crowns with," Mitzy said, her eyes flicking toward Jeremiah as he suddenly lunged for something on the ground. "What ya got there? Spit that out!" Her voice sharpened as she rushed forward, prying at his small, eager hands before he could shove whatever it was into his mouth.

Esther sighed, her gaze drifting toward the dirt road. She knew exactly where Rebecca had gone. They'd passed that spot a couple of days ago—a patch where water settled deep in the furrows of the field Ian had planted. Wild daisies and clover grew thick there, the kind of place a little girl with a big imagination couldn't resist.

"I'm gonna get her," Esther said, her voice resolute as she stepped off the porch. The gravel crunched under her feet as she made her way toward the main road. The driveway gave way to hard-packed dirt, its surface grooved by years of truck tires, wagon wheels, and heavy boots. A white-painted fence ran alongside it, stretching past Ian's house before turning to wire and disappearing into the fields.

Around the bend, she caught sight of Rebecca. The girl's small silhouette danced against the backdrop of the tall grass, her arms full of flowers. Esther's lips twitched in amusement.

"Rebecca!" she called again, louder this time. The young girl didn't turn, making Esther suspect she was ignoring her on purpose.

"I know ya can hear me," Esther said as she drew closer, her voice carrying a hint of exasperation. Finally, Rebecca turned, her face lighting up with a wide, innocent grin.

"Esther, look how many of them I found!" she exclaimed, holding up her bundle of flowers proudly before bending to gather more.

Esther put her hands on her hips, trying to appear stern, though a smile tugged at the corners of her mouth.

"Rebecca, why ya got to make me come down here to get ya? We ain't gonna have time to draw ya dolls if we don't head back."

The little girl pouted, clutching her flowers tightly.

"But Esther, I wanna make crowns for the little dolls."

She leaned over, meeting Rebecca's gaze head-on. "We can draw 'em crowns," she said gently, her tone coaxing. It worked. Rebecca hesitated, then nodded, turning reluctantly to walk back with her.

The two of them made their way up the road, Rebecca's small hand clutching hers, the other clutching her fresh flowers precariously.

Esther kept glancing over her shoulder, her gaze flicking toward the valley, as if expecting the boys to return any moment.

But something in the air felt off—an undercurrent of sound just beneath the usual hush of the countryside, a faint hum threading through the silence.

Then she heard it—a low rumble in the distance, faint at first but growing steadily louder. Not Ian's truck. This was heavier, deeper, a sound that sent a prickle down her spine. Her body tensed instinctively, fingers tightening around Rebecca's small hand.

A familiar dread crawled over her skin, one she hadn't felt since tearing through the fields outside Clive's home, fleeing for her life as Deputy Frank chased her.

Just then, a gust of wind barreled past them, stirring the trees, sending a strange chill through her.

The sound deepened into a guttural growl that made the ground hum beneath their feet.

Rebecca tugged at her hand. "What's that, Esther?"

She didn't answer. Her eyes were fixed on the bend in the road, where the noise was coming from.

Her stomach twisted as the rumble deepened, closing in fast.

A truck, this time of year? Coming up this way? It didn't make sense. Something was wrong—a feeling she couldn't shake.

Esther tightened her grip on Rebecca's hand and picked up the pace, dragging her along.

"Rebecca," she whispered cautiously. "Stay by me."

The sound swelled, and then the truck appeared.

Its hulking frame ground up the road, a cloud of dust rising around its wheels, shrouding it in a hazy, ominous veil.

Esther's breath hitched as she recognized the type—one used for hauling peach crates during harvest. It didn't belong here, not now.

Then she saw them—men packed into the back of the truck, their silhouettes jagged against the late-day sun.

Their voices carried on the wind, sharp and unruly—hooting, hollering, breaking the stillness like a crack of thunder.

Adrenaline surged through Esther, her grip fiercely locked on Rebecca's hand.

"Rebecca, RUN!" she screamed, nearly yanking the little girl up the road.

Her mind raced, raced with dark stories of men who hunted those who didn't stay within the lines drawn for them.

She knew those kinds of men existed—had heard their ugly voices outside Clive's church, speaking words so vile she'd never want Clarissa or Ian's children to hear.

Rebecca stumbled, her legs too small to match Esther's frantic pace.

"I can't run this hard!" Rebecca gasped, her voice breaking with fear.

Esther risked a glance over her shoulder. The truck's massive frame loomed closer, barreling up the road, dust curling from its tires.

The men in the back shouted and laughed, their voices carrying over the wind like something wicked.

Then one of them stood, swaying with the truck's movement, his arm lifted, pointing straight at them.

Panic clawed at her chest. The house was still too far, the distance stretching endlessly before her. She grasped for options—anything that could buy them a moment more.

The fence appeared like an answer as it ran alongside the road. If she could reach it, maybe she could throw Rebecca over—give her a chance to hide. But could she lift her high enough in her panic?

Would the men follow?

No time to think. Esther made her choice.

She scooped Rebecca into her arms just as the truck roared past, its tires kicking up a spray of dirt that pelted her legs. It sped recklessly along the road, close enough that she could feel the air shift with its passing.

Terror ripped through her as her foot caught on uneven ground. They stumbled—then fell, hitting the earth hard, tumbling into a shallow ditch with Rebecca still clutched against her chest.

Dust and grit filled their mouths. Esther spat, scrambling to her knees. Rebecca whimpered against her, small hands gripping her tightly, but Esther didn't hesitate.

"Hold on to me, Rebecca," Esther said, hauling the little girl back into her arms. Rebecca was crying now, her sobs broken and breathless, but Esther ran.

The house. The big house. It was safer than Ian's. It had to be.

Ahead of them, up the road, the vehicle skidded to a halt, its brakes screaming like a wounded animal.

She gritted her teeth. Her legs burned. Her arms buckled beneath Rebecca's weight.

But the house was close now—its solid shape rising like a beacon.

Ahead, Mitzy stood frozen on the porch, clutching Jeremiah tightly against her chest. Her wide eyes darted between the truck and Esther's frantic sprint.

For a moment, she hesitated—then sprang into action, caught between her own fear and the desperate need to get Esther and Rebecca inside.

"Get in the house! Get in the house!" Mitzy screamed.

Following her own command, she whirled, yanking the door open, her panicked cry ringing through the house. "Clarissa!"

Behind them, the truck slowed, its tires crunching against the road as it turned. Coming back.

Esther's heart pounded. The porch steps blurred beneath her as she stumbled forward, shoving Rebecca ahead of her.

"Go! Go!" She all but pushed the little girl through the door, the slam of wood echoing behind them as she twisted the lock, her hands fumbling at the latch.

Rebecca stood in the entryway, her small body trembling, tears streaming down her face.

"Hide, Rebecca! Hide in a cupboard!" Esther barked as she rushed past Mitzy, who stood shaking, her baby wailing in her arms.

Esther ran to the back door, latching it tight. Then she hurried through the house, checking the windows, fingers skimming over the locks, testing each one. Ian had made sure they were all working last year when the men from the prison had started working the fields.

A thud of hurried footsteps sounded from the stairs. Clarissa nearly missed the last step as she stumbled down, breathless.

"Who are they?" she asked fearfully, having seen the men from her window.

"I don't know," Esther said, whipping around. Her pulse roared in her ears, but her mind stayed sharp, already working, already thinking ahead.

There was Rebecca—still standing in place, unmoving, her small body tight with fear.

"Go get in the linen closet! Hide in the bottom!" Esther said, her tone razor sharp and firm as she faced Mitzy. "Take your baby up there, too. Put him in with her!"

Rebecca's silent tears kept falling, harder now.

Esther dropped to a knee, gripping the little girl's shoulders, forcing her to meet her eyes.

"We're just playin' a silly game, ya hear me? Ya gotta hide. Keep Jeremiah happy until we come get ya, okay?" Esther's tone softened, trying to sound steady—like holding out a hand to someone teetering on the edge of a ledge.

The little girl's big brown eyes locked on hers as she gave a tiny nod, afraid but willing.

Mitzy hurried them toward the stairs, and Esther moved to the window, peeking out as the truck rumbled into the yard.

Its horn blared—a guttural, animalistic sound that made everyone flinch.

The men hollered, their voices deep and mocking, saying lewd things meant to ignite fear in women—crude enough to curdle blood.

"Aunt Clarissa!" Esther yelled.

Before she could say another word, Clarissa was beside her, shoving something into her hands—a large revolver, its weight solid and cold.

"Ya'd know how to use this better than me, girl."

Esther didn't reach for it. She swallowed hard, forcing her voice to be calm.

"Aunt Clarissa, those men are armed. Every one of 'em got a rifle in their hands. This little gun ain't gonna do nothin'."

Clarissa's breath hitched. Her eyes flickered with something beyond fear. Something old.

"They're comin' for us again," she whispered, her voice laced with a terror Esther had never heard before. A history Clarissa hadn't often spoken of, but that never left her.

The commotion outside escalated, the truck's engine roaring as the men revved it harder, their impatience vibrating through the humid, heavy air.

Esther moved back to the window just as Mitzy came flying down the stairs.

"I don't know 'bout y'all, but I'm gettin' a kitchen knife," she declared, fierce and unshaken. "I'll cut 'em before they touch my baby."

Esther barely heard a word. Her eyes stayed pinned to the men in the truck.

"How come they ain't gettin' out?" she murmured.

But just as the words left her lips, the truck's driver's side door groaned open.

An imposing man stepped out—broad, unhurried, moving like he had all the time in the world.

His worn overalls hung loose on his oversized frame, stained from years of labor, his long black beard swaying with each step.

Then his voice boomed, slicing through the thick, uneasy air.

"Primm! Primm! Ya come out here, Primm!"

Esther's stomach lurched.

They weren't here for Clarissa. Or Mitzy. Or the children.

They were here for her.

The realization hit like a hammer to the chest.

These weren't just drunks looking to stir trouble.

These were moonshiners—bootleggers.

And they had come for Esther Primm.

"What are they yellin'?" Clarissa asked, her knuckles tight around the pistol's handle as she braced herself.

Esther could feel the pieces sliding into place. One by one. With a sickening kind of clarity.

The Alcohol and Tobacco Unit was moving into town. The sheriff had warned her. And now, fear had spread like wildfire among the bootleggers, sending them scrambling to tie up loose ends.

She was a loose end.

Not because of her grandmother. No, that wasn't it. It was Clive. It had always been Clive.

And these men believed she held his secrets.

Outside, the truck inched forward, its horn blaring, rattling the windows. One of the men yelled something vile—about dragging the women out by their hair, one by one.

Esther turned slowly, her gaze pausing on Clarissa. When she spoke, her voice was eerily calm.

"They're not here for ya," Esther said.

Despite how her heart hammered—causing a tight, stabbing pain in her chest—she forced her face into something unreadable, something that spoke of determination. She had no choice.

"They're callin' for me," she said

A sad understanding passed between the three women.

"They're men from the hills," Esther murmured. "Moonshiners."

They sat in the quiet reality of it for a tense moment—a beat of silence thick enough to choke on.

"I need to go out there," Esther said, her voice shaking, though a grim finality settled into her expression.

There was no way—no way—she would ever put these people, the ones she loved more than life, in danger.

She thought of the small children hiding upstairs—Mitzy's sweet baby and Rebecca, a little girl she couldn't love more if they shared the same blood.

She had to do this.

"No!" Clarissa said firmly. "Let 'em try to get in here 'fore you go out there. We'll fight 'em together."

"I can't," Esther said. "There's young'uns in here, and those men could tear through these walls with those guns. They don't even need to walk through the door."

"Please don't, Esther," Clarissa pleaded, gripping the girl's face with both hands, the revolver still clutched between them. "Yer my baby," she wept. "I don't wanna lose ya."

"She's right, Miss Clarissa," Mitzy's voice wavered, but her words were steady. "Dear God, ya gotta let her do it. If she goes, maybe we got a chance. If we sit here, they're only gonna get mean and do what she said."

Clarissa's hands trembled as she tried to force the gun into Esther's. "Take this gun, then."

But Esther just shook her head.

"I can't outshoot those men, Aunt Clarissa." She turned to Mitzy, nodding toward the weapon.

"Give her the gun. A gun'll do more than a knife."

Mitzy hesitated only a second before reaching over and taking the revolver from Clarissa's unsteady hands.

Esther turned back to Clarissa, cupping her weathered face, holding it gently with all the care inside her.

Clarissa was the only mother she had ever known. The woman who had loved her from the beginning. Her kin, her rock, her lighthouse in a world that had never been kind.

"Aunt Clarissa, ya ain't my aunt. Yer so much more. Yer my mama, you hear that?" Esther's voice broke, but she pressed on, her tears slipping down her cheeks. "I love ya. Thank ya for doin' all you've done for me, prayin' for me when I probably didn't deserve it."

Clarissa let out a quiet, broken sob, and Esther pressed her forehead to the older woman's for one fleeting moment before stepping back.

"Tell them young'uns I love 'em too," she said, trembling.

Just as Esther finished speaking, a deafening crack split the stillness.

A bullet tore through the paned window of the front room, shattering the glass and splintering the wood. Shards rained onto the floor, the shot barely missing Mitzy.

The women screamed.

Instinct took over. Clarissa and Mitzy ducked low, scrambling toward the center of the house, seeking safety in its walls.

But Esther stood unmoved by the front door, her hand tightening around the knob, submitting herself to fate.

Slowly, she turned it.

Opening the door inch by inch, a silent surrender, letting the men know she was coming out.

She cast one last glance over her shoulder, her voice barely a whisper—soft, fragile, like it had been forcefully pulled from her.

"Tell Ian... that I... love him. And that I'm sorry I'm so onery sometimes."

Clarissa's breath hitched, her face twisting with emotion.

"I will," she rasped, her voice thick. "He loves ya too, girl, I'm certain of it." She swallowed. "But ya already know that."

And Esther did. She had seen it in every action he had taken, every sacrifice he had made. She couldn't tell him herself—but Clarissa could send the words for her.

The evening air was thick with tension, heavy with the acrid scent of diesel and gunpowder.

Esther took carefully measured steps as she walked out onto the porch.

She descended the steps, her pulse drumming against her ribs, her mind fighting her, telling her to turn and run.

But she held her head high, shoulders squared. She knew how to pretend she was alright when she wasn't.

If this was the firing squad, then so be it.

A defiant fire burned in her eyes.

She had been loved. Had endured worse than this.

But the dark voices stirred—the ones that had once whispered to her, urging her to toss herself into that cavernous hell after holding her dead baby.

They mocked her, calling her a coward.

Esther fought them, reminding them she'd stood at the gates of fire undefeated, and more than once.

At Clive's. At the very edge of ruin.

The men watching her held no power over her.

And Esther was relieved Ian wasn't here to witness what she had to do. He would have stopped her, never letting her set even a foot onto that grass.

No, he wouldn't have let her walk straight toward a pack of angry men who had just fired into a home without a second thought, not caring if they hit a living body.

Ian would have put himself in front of her, taken any bullet meant for her.

Yes, it was a good thing he wasn't there.

That's what she told herself as she moved toward the truck.

They couldn't see it, but she wasn't alone. She had angels walking beside her—the kind you don't see, but know are there when others love you.

Swallowing her fear, she called out, her voice steady despite the way her bones rattled with warning.

"What ya want with me?"

The grizzled man stepped closer, the last light of day slanting across his face. His teeth were yellowed, his dark beard unkempt, and his eyes—sharp with malice—pinned her in place.

"Primm," he growled, his voice rough as gravel. "Ya know who we are, right?"

Esther held his gaze. "I reckon."

There was something eerily familiar about him, something her mind couldn't quite place.

The man tipped his head at the truck, gesturing lazily. "Ya see that fella up there?"

She followed his motion. A husky figure perched on the truck bed, his rifle raised with lazy confidence, aimed dead at her.

"Yes," she said.

A slow, creeping sickness of knowing slid into place.

Boones.

The man speaking was Big Hands Boone.

Big Hands nodded toward the man on the truck again. "This here's my son, Zeb. He can hit a rabbit clean from two hundred yards—don't waste bullets."

His tone was almost conversational, but each word cut sharp, his boots crunching closer on the gravel.

Esther's gaze flicked back to the truck bed.

Zeb stood like a shadow of his father. Not quite as massive, but broad, thick-chested—commanding attention without needing to try.

His beard, jet black and heavy, was a younger mirror of the one on Big Hands—though Big Hands was streaked with gray. The resemblance was unmistakable.

Zeb's demeanor was hardened. Something eerie, calculating. He rested the rifle against his shoulder naturally, as if it had grown there.

It was then that his dark eyes found hers.

He looked at her just a second too long.

Like he knew her.

Her breath caught.

She looked away quickly, but the icy chill remained.

That brief moment—that lingering stare—it had stirred something dark, like it'd slipped out from one of the places she kept sealed off, even from her own memory.

"Girl, we're givin' ya one chance," Big Hands drawled. "'Cause ya were Pearl Primm's kin. But if we hear 'bout ya sayin' a peep to anyone, that man up there's gonna come and clear out every blessed person livin' here. Ya understand?"

Esther met his gaze, her chin lifting just enough to let him know she wasn't afraid—at least, not enough to cower.

"I already done know that," she shot back, her tone edged with defiance. "Think I wanna get locked up myself? Reckon y'all should keep my damn name outta yer mouths too, right?"

The words came out sharp, raw, like she had pulled them straight from Gran's throat. This was their language, and she spoke it fluently.

She took a step closer.

"I ain't never said a thang, and I'll see ya all in hell 'fore I do. Now get off my land and be done with this nonsense."

The weight of her voice settled in the thick evening air, convincing enough to make the man hesitate.

He stepped back, a slow grin curling up one side of his mouth. Then came the laugh—a long, rattling thing, drawn-out like he had just heard the best damn joke of his life.

"Ya is Pearl Primm's girl, fer sure," he mused, shaking his head as he started toward the truck. But then he turned back, his grin fading, voice dropping to a mutter.

"'Cept ya is a…"

Words spat like filth off his poisoned tongue—meant to cast shame on her for who she loved, for who she called family.

With that, their truck rumbled to life, shifting into reverse, tires kicking up loose gravel as it peeled backward.

It clipped the corner of the painted fence, sending splintered wood scattering across the road before rolling over it without a care.

They were finally leaving—gone.

Their laughter, a pack of jackals, trailed off as the truck barreled down the road. The driver leaned on the horn one last time, a final warning that rang out.

Esther stood frozen in place, her legs threatening to buckle underneath her.

When the truck finally disappeared, when the sound of its engine faded into nothing, she let out the breath she'd been holding in for support.

And collapsed.

The gravel bit into her knees, but she didn't feel it.

Her chest heaved. Silent sobs wracked her body.

She had pulled the darkness of her Gran over her like a shield, let it shape her words, her stance, her fire. She had become something terrifying to protect the people she loved.

But it had hollowed her out.

The front door creaked open behind her.

Mitzy and Clarissa rushed out, their feet crunching over the rocks.

They had been watching from the window, waiting.

They had seen Esther standing before those men like she could take them all on, her voice steady, her chin high, her presence unshakable.

Their Esther. Willow-thin Esther.

She had shown a toughness most wouldn't have mustered.

But now, sitting there alone in the rocks, they could see the truth.

It had been an act.

A performance.

And it had taken everything out of her.

Clarissa's chest ached as she dropped beside her, wrapping her arms around Esther and rocking her gently, trying to fill the space that the terror had stolen.

The girl had done it—done what she had to.

Chapter 16: On the Table

The old Ford truck hummed low as it crawled up the dirt road. Inside, the air smelled of fresh fish and the lingering warmth of the day. Ian's hand gripped the wheel loosely, his eyes relaxed, scanning the darkening road ahead.

Across from him, Abram leaned his arm out the open window, a faint smile tugging at his lips as he glanced at Benjamin, who sat squished in the middle, chattering excitedly.

"Ya think she'll scold ya for bein' late?" Abram teased.

Ian grinned as he said, "She'll have every right to. I gave her a time, and I've gone and stretched it."

"Think she'll yell, Pa?" Benjamin asked as he leaned forward.

Ian chuckled, shaking his head. "Esther doesn't yell, son. She gives you that look—you know, the kind that makes you want to fix whatever you've done."

Abram laughed as they neared the estate. Ahead, Clarissa's house came into view.

But the humor drained from Abram's face as the truck's headlights swept across the fence line.

He straightened, his brow furrowing. "Ian. Look."

Ian slowed the truck, his gaze snapping to where Abram pointed. A fence post near the driveway was splintered, lying awkwardly on the dirt. Fresh wood gleamed under the headlights.

"That's new," Ian said, irritated.

Benjamin, still oblivious to the shift in the truck's cab, leaned forward. "What's wrong?"

"Some fool ran over one of our posts," Ian muttered, sarcasm barely masking his agitation. "Such a nice, neighborly thing to do." Another damn thing to fix.

As they approached the house, the soft glow of the lights greeted them, though the warm, inviting sight didn't quite match the dull annoyance Ian couldn't shake.

He parked near the porch, stepping out as Abram followed, his eyes scanning the yard as he stretched with a yawn.

Ian moved to the back of the truck and pulled the string of fish free, handing it to Benjamin, who was now hovering close.

"Take these inside, son," Ian said in his usual firm tone. "Clarissa can cook them up tomorrow."

Benjamin grinned, hurrying toward the porch, the fish swinging in his hands. But just as Ian turned to follow, his steps faltered.

The glint of shattered glass caught his eye, scattered across the wooden boards of the porch.

He froze.

"Abram," Ian called over his shoulder, his voice turning hard as he strode forward.

Abram joined him quickly, his gaze falling to the shards before trailing upward—to the dark front window, where a gaping hole yawned in the glass.

"What the hell?" Abram muttered.

Ian's attention darted to Benjamin, who had already reached the door, his small hand grasping the knob. He jiggled it and frowned.

"It's locked," the boy said, confused. "It's never locked."

"Step back, Benjamin," Ian ordered, his boots crunching over broken glass as he moved to the door.

Benjamin obeyed without question as Ian pounded against the wood, yelling, "Clarissa! Esther! Open up!"

The silence held too long, and it was too still.

Each second tightened the coil in his chest.

He knocked again, harder, not letting up.

Then—finally—the sound of hurried footsteps echoed inside. The door creaked open.

Clarissa stood in the dim light, the lines of her face deeper than Ian had seen in a long time.

"What's happened?" he asked as he pushed forward.

Hesitant, she didn't reply right away. She just leaned back, holding the door open. Her silence spoke almost as loudly as her words.

Ian entered first, with Abram close behind.

As they moved through the hallway, the warmth of the dining room light spilled out to greet them.

The scene, though it looked idyllic, carried the wrong kind of stillness.

Ian stopped in his tracks.

Esther sat at the head of the table, Rebecca cradled in her lap, the little girl clinging to her as though she had cried herself to sleep.

Beside her, Mitzy held her baby close, her back stiff, as if bracing, like she hadn't let herself breathe since it happened. Her eyes found Abram, lingering there—not accusing, not forgiving—just searching, like she was still trying to believe he was real.

The table was set like a grand meal had been planned—fine linens neatly draped, untouched plates waiting.

But the faces around the table told a different story.

Something had gone terribly wrong here.

And to make matters worse, at the center of the table sat Clarissa's revolver, shattering any remaining illusion of peace.

Ian's eyes locked onto the weapon, then snapped back to Esther.

His boots hit heavy against the floor as he crossed the room in quick, determined strides.

"Esther," he said. "Why's there a gun on the table?"

Not saying a word, she kept her hand on Rebecca's head, her fingers moving slowly through the little girl's hair. When she looked up at him, her face was pale but composed, though he could see the strain in her eyes—the weight of whatever had unfolded.

"Visitors," Clarissa said from behind him, her voice flat. "Men from the hills."

Ian turned sharply. "What men?"

"A group of not-so-friendly moonshiners," she replied, gripping the back of a chair for support.

"Moonshiners?" he repeated, almost in disbelief.

"They came in a big truck. Shot at the house," the old woman continued.

Rage and worry surged behind Ian's eyes as he scanned the faces in the room, the people who meant everything to him.

Clarissa's words were enough. But the revolver lying within arm's reach drove it home with a punch.

Abram rushed forward, fury woven into every word, barely holding it together. "Of all the damn people to come up here, why moonshiners?"

"How many?" Ian asked as he tried to put it together.

Clarissa's lips pressed into a thin, rigid line as she said, "Quite a few. Over a dozen, I reckon." Her eyes met his, weary but steady, confirming what he already feared.

"My God," Ian muttered under his breath.

Abram's stony gaze landed on Esther, then shifted to Mitzy. His wife—his wife—sat there, shaken, clutching their baby to her chest.

And the longer he stared, the more his frustration boiled over.

"I'm just gonna say it," Abram snapped, his voice honed to a point. "This is 'cause of you, Esther. You've been bringin' trouble to this place since the day ya showed up! Yer like a damn curse."

The words were cold and accusing.

Esther turned her head to him, trying to hold back what already showed on her face. "Abram—I…"

Before she could finish, Mitzy cracked through the tension like a whip. "How dare ya!"

She shot to her feet. Jeremiah, startled awake in her arms, began wailing.

"How dare ya say that! Ya weren't here, Abram. Didn't hear what those men were yellin'. Sayin' what they'd do to us." Mitzy's voice trembled, but she didn't stop. "Didn't hear them gunshots."

Abram took a step back, giving her space, but she only moved closer. Mitzy wasn't finished.

"Ya weren't here to see these babies hidin' in the closet, their mamas thinkin' they were gonna die!" Her words came faster now, laced with emotion. "And Esther? She didn't hide. Wasn't off fishin'. She went out there—to them—a whole truck full of men with guns pointed at this house—at her head. She did it to save ya son. She's got more courage than y'all ever have."

Abram flinched, his fists unclenching at his sides.

Ian, however, was focused on Esther—on what Mitzy had just said.

"You went out there? Why? You shouldn't have done that, Esther," he said, his voice strained with every word, his shoulders tight and drawn like a bow.

Exhausted and unable to even muster a stronger defense, Esther mumbled, "I ain't have no choice, Ian." The strain was clear, but so was the conviction. "The young'uns were inside. What else was I supposed to do?"

He paused for a moment, taking in what she said, then shifted—his expression darkening again—as he ran a hand through his hair, exhaling sharply before turning on Abram.

"And you—" Ian's voice came like a threat given shape as he pointed at him. "Don't you goddamn dare say anything like that ever again. That's your last warning."

His eyes burned with something visceral, something aggressive.

"She's going to be my wife. And I won't tolerate it," he added.

Abram glared back at him, his own jaw set hard as he held his tongue.

They had butted heads before, but this time, he knew he had gone too far. The fire burning in his friend's eyes wasn't something to mess with, and he was certain in that moment Ian would raise both fists to him if he ever said another derogatory thing aimed at Esther.

The silence hung between them, heavy and strained, until a small voice broke through.

"Papa?"

Rebecca.

Tear-streaked and quivering, she climbed down from Esther's lap and made her way to her father, her small hands reaching for him.

Her scared eyes locked onto his, searching for reassurance.

Ian's hardened expression softened in an instant.

He scooped her up, holding her close as she clung to him.

"Pa, I hurt my knees runnin'… I dropped my flowers, too." The words came out shaky, like she'd been crying, as she buried her face against his shoulder.

His grip cradled her, his large hand rubbing slow, soothing circles on her back.

He pressed a kiss to her hair, murmuring against her temple, "You're okay, sweet girl. You can pick more tomorrow."

But over Rebecca's head, his gaze found Esther's.

The intensity in his eyes didn't waver.

"Who were they, Esther?" His voice was low, controlled, but edged with firmness. "Do you know who those men are?"

Esther rose slowly, bracing herself on the edge of the table. Her hands splayed across the wood for support.

She hesitated—just for a breath—before nodding.

"I have an idea." Her voice grew quieter now, though she tried to sound confident. "But I ain't gonna tell ya, Ian."

He was clearly not pleased.

"Not going to tell me?" His pitch rose before he caught himself, reining it in. "Esther, they came to my house. They put my family in danger. If you know who they are—"

"I told them I'd keep my mouth shut,." she said as her gaze met his straight on. "If I say anythin' and ya go stirrin' up more trouble, what ya think's gonna happen then? They'll come right back."

Abram, still standing with his arms crossed, let out a derisive snort. "We can't let them bastards think they can just ride in, wave their guns around, scare our women, and get away with it. Hell no. We don't go beggin' for trouble—but we sure as hell ain't gon' let it slide neither. There's ways to make 'em think twice. Quiet ways, if it's gotta be. But I ain't sittin' on my hands while they think we're easy pickin's. I'll make it so that big truck never runs again."

"They ain't comin' back, Abram," Esther said firmly. Her voice didn't waver.

"And how do ya know that?" Abram asked.

"Because they know I'm one of 'em," she said as her words landed awkwardly in the room. "And I ain't given them a reason to doubt that." A strange certainty settled over her face, like she believed everything she had just professed.

But the strain in Ian's expression was unresolved as he shifted Rebecca in his arms, adjusting her weight against him. Her small hands were still clutching his shirt.

And the heavy set of his brow spoke it plainly before he even had to open his mouth.

"This isn't over," Ian said. "But I don't want to talk in front of the children."

Across the room, Benjamin stood frozen, wide-eyed, his small body stiff. The string of fish hung limp in his hand, the catch itself now lumped on the floor beside him, forgotten.

Clarissa, noticing the boy's state, leaned down behind him, her touch gentle as she rested a hand on his shoulder, her voice slipping into something softer, almost cheerful.

"Well now, what'd ya bring me here?" She bent to pick up the fish, brushing off a bit of dust. "Looks like we're gonna have us a fish fry 'morrow night," she said lightly, nudging Benjamin toward the kitchen, steering him away from the tension lingering thick in the air.

Esther, wanting nothing more than to slip away from the conversation, turned to go as well. Without looking back, she muttered just loud enough for everyone to hear, "No use wastin' good food. Supper'll be on in half an hour."

Ian watched her walk out, his mind churning, trying to grapple with everything that had just happened.

Then a small voice pulled him back.

"Pa," Rebecca whispered, looking up into her father's eyes. "Were they gonna kill Esther?"

His gut twisted, but he forced a reassuring smile. "Of course not."

But Mitzy gave him a look—one that stripped away the lie as soon as it left his mouth.

In a low whisper, she leaned in. "Ya should've seen her, Ian. She marched out there like she was gonna take 'em on one by one. She'd never let anyone hurt that little girl of yers."

Ian swallowed, nodding once, slowly.

He already knew it.

There was something in Esther, something fierce and protective when it came to his children—a fortitude she could summon for them, even when she couldn't seem to summon it for herself.

And despite every instinct inside of him screaming against what she'd done, how could he blame her?

She had done what he would've done himself.

When Esther had promised to take care of his children, she'd meant it.

Chapter 17: Cistern

The morning light filtered softly through the dense branches of a sycamore tree, its wide canopy dappling the ground with shifting patterns of sunlight.

Ian knelt beside the old cistern, his shoulders tense with focus as he worked to repair its weathered stone rim. A small bucket of mortar sat within reach. The trowel scraped against the rock with a steady rhythm, the sound carrying faintly through the hush of early May.

A few feet away, Esther stood with her arms tucked around herself, taking in the deliberate way his hands moved—careful, efficient, strong. There was a quiet satisfaction in it, a kind of ease that made it impossible to look away.

"Always wondered what this was," she said after a while, breaking the silence.

He didn't look up, his attention fixed on filling a crack in the stone. "Is that so?" he replied, his voice even. "It's tucked back here for a reason. Only really used during dry spells, long before wells ran deep enough to matter."

She stepped closer, the damp grass soft under her shoes. The sight of the cistern fascinated her—the moss creeping along its base, the way it seemed to blend into the landscape, as if it had grown out of the ground itself.

"How long's it been here?" she asked.

Ian sat back on his heels, wiping the back of his hand across his forehead. "Longer than me or you," he said. "Maybe as old as the estate itself. Built to last, but not without a little care now and then."

She crouched beside him, fingertips brushing the rough edge of the stone. "Why'd ya bring me out here?" A slow smile touched her lips. "Don't reckon ya thinkin' this is a good spot to get nekkid."

He chuckled, the sound low and warm. "Not a bad idea. But no, that's not why I brought you out here. We need to have a little talk."

The humor in her expression faded. She reached for the trowel he'd set aside, turning it over in her hands.

"Why don't you just show me how to do this instead?" she said, trying to distract him before he started lecturing her about not taking study time seriously.

He lifted an eyebrow, studying her with that quiet patience of his, then took the trowel from her hands and set it aside. Without a word, he stood, drawing her up with him, his grip firm but unhurried. His hands closed around hers, warm against the lingering chill of the morning.

Ian's gaze held hers—fixed, intent—as he drew in a breath, bracing himself for what he was about to say.

"I'm going to ask you something serious." His voice was calm and measured. "And I don't want you to get mad at me or tell me it's not my business."

Esther's lips parted, the beginnings of protest rising in her throat, but Ian gave a small shake of his head, as if already expecting resistance—already knowing this wasn't going to be easy.

This was worse than she thought. And he wasn't being Mr. Huggler—he was being the serious Ian—the one she didn't know how to talk to, the one who flustered her.

"Esther, I am a patient man. Or at least I tell myself that I am," he said, pausing as her gaze drifted, waiting until her eyes came back to him, making sure she was really listening.

"But I want to be an honorable man, too. And I'm asking for the truth. Please give it to me."

Her heart started pounding faster as she anticipated his impending question.

It had been a week since the moonshiners had come onto the property, and she refused to give Ian so much as a shred of information about them. He'd been so cross about it one evening, he didn't even say goodnight—just walked out of Clarissa's door, muttering a few choice swear words about how impossible she was being, then slammed it behind him. But she had held firm.

Both he and Abram had kept close to home since then, never straying far, never out of earshot.

It meant they hadn't gotten everything done as they'd planned, putting off important projects, but the quiet had begun to settle back over the Old Reed Estate—despite the lingering threat still hanging over them.

And now here he was, pressing her again. She feared he'd try to make her give up their names, but she didn't even know them all— just two. A man and his grown son. A surname that sent a chill up her spine. Faces she recognized—kin to Clive through his father's side, of no relation to her.

"Esther, please look at me," Ian urged, his voice softer now.

"I am, Ian," she shot back, a thread of impatience creeping into her tone. "Ya always get me so nervous when ya start talkin' like this."

He smiled a little, giving her hands a squeeze.

"I like that you get nervous. Means I excite you."

She rolled her eyes, tipping her head up at him, lashes fluttering in mock innocence.

"That sounds like a better idea. Why don't ya just take me for a drive or somethin' instead?" she asked.

He shifted his feet, as if steadying himself. He couldn't keep dancing around it. He just needed to say it.

"Esther, when did you last have a monthly?"

She jerked back slightly.

"God, Ian. Is this what ya brought me out here fer?"

"Esther, I've seen you run out the back door more than once this week, emptying your food under the big oak. You think I don't notice those things, but I do."

He paused, watching her face, trying to read what she wasn't saying.

"I saw you in the chicken coop," he continued. "You were rubbing your belly softly, as if you believed no one was watching."

Her lips parted, but nothing came out.

"Ian, that don't mean nothin'," she finally managed, though she knew he wasn't buying it.

"All right then," he said, pressing on, his voice calm but unwavering. "Just answer a simple yes or no question."

She shook her head, like she wanted no part of whatever deal he was trying to make.

He braced himself, knowing that chasing the truth with her was like chasing a rabbit—quick, elusive, always darting away at the last second. His grip on her hands tightened just slightly as he said, "Esther... have you bled since we made love in the barn? Or the truck?"

Her stomach twisted as his words struck with precision.

Damn you, Ian, she thought.

She should've stayed at the house. Should've never followed him out here to the old cistern.

She didn't answer. She couldn't.

And Ian saw it—saw her.

She wanted to close her eyes, to block him out, to keep him from reading her the way he always did. But it was too late.

Her silence was an answer.

And worse—he saw something else too.

A somberness. A knowing.

"You are—" he took a deep breath, the reality of it hitting.

He had wondered if she would just deny it, like she had before, but here she stood, saying nothing, though her eyes were telling him a different story.

He let go of her hands, lifting his to her face, his thumb brushing gently across her cheek. He wanted to push just a bit further—to hear it again in her silence.

"Esther, are we having a baby?" he asked, already knowing the answer. His gaze locked on hers.

Something flickered across her face—fear, maybe—as her eyes filled, lashes heavy with unshed tears. She squeezed them shut, as if that might hold everything in, keep the truth from spilling out.

Ian had seen enough.

He knew.

And she didn't want to say it out loud.

She had already let herself want this, want his baby, but she knew what it meant, and that frightened her.

"God, Esther... you are," Ian murmured, his arms pulling her in, holding her close.

But she was stiff against him.

He eased back just enough to see her face, his hands resting firm at her waist, a nervous smile tugging at his lips.

He couldn't hide it. He was happy. More than happy. He loved her, and the thought of her carrying his child—an extension of them, of this life they were building—only deepened everything he already felt.

Ian had to admit, when Adeline first told him she was pregnant all those years ago, he hadn't responded the way she'd wanted. He'd been uncertain, more afraid of failing as a provider than the idea of fatherhood itself.

But now?

Now, he had been a father for eleven years. He was seasoned. And it no longer scared him.

Then a truth hit him—like the bricks he was trying to mortar—they needed to tie the knot, and soon.

Ian knew the blood test for syphilis took a couple of weeks to come back, and he'd have to take her to Jasper for that part of it. By his calculations, Esther was seven weeks along. By the time they could make it legal, she'd be nearly nine.

"Esther, you know this means we need to get married as soon as we can," he said, his voice practical, straightforward.

He forgot, for a moment, what marriage meant to her—how it wasn't just a promise but a cage. She feared it, thinking it would hand him control over her life, something too close to ownership. He had tried to reassure her that that wasn't the case, that she'd still be free to make her own choices.

But she hadn't believed him.

"Ian…" Her voice wavered as tears filled her eyes.

"Yes, my love?" he asked, watching her struggle, wanting nothing more than to ease it.

She swallowed hard. "I don't know if I can do that." Her voice cracked on the words.

"Esther, you're going to be just fine," he said. "You're so damn brave. My God, you stood up to a group of men in the drive, guns pointed at you. Clarissa said you made her feel strong. And you know what a tough broad she is." He smiled, hoping she'd see herself the way he did.

Then, after a pause, his voice softened. "And she told me something else. Something I'm still waiting to hear from you… along with a long list of other things," he added, his tone teasing.

He searched her face, tilting her chin up so she couldn't look away. "Clarissa told me that if something happened, she was to tell me that you loved me. That you wanted me to know that."

A quiet moment stretched between them. Then Ian leaned in, his mouth brushing against hers, slow and tender. He could feel the hesitancy in her, but ignored it, focusing on the warmth of her lips against his.

Why did he always do this to her? Use his kisses to smooth over the hard things he would say. Act like everything was all right, like she could just say those words back to him like any regular woman, despite never knowing if she could.

Esther was getting used to his constant declarations of love, the way they slipped so easily from his mouth, a daily thing now, especially before saying goodnight.

But why had Clarissa told him?

Now, whenever he said I love you, he would know, know she had said it, thinking her silence was now implying it. And maybe it was. She wasn't sure anymore.

At the moment, when she thought she might be saying goodbye to the people she loved, she hadn't wanted Ian to be haunted by the thought that she had never confessed that.

"Esther," Ian murmured as he pulled back, his hands firm on her hips. "We've got to take a drive tomorrow."

"Fer what?" she asked.

"A silly little test we have to take, it's not a big deal. We can make a day of it, though. I need to pick up a few tools in Jasper, so we'll kill two birds with one stone." His voice was too optimistic, like he'd been planning this forever.

She narrowed her eyes. "Ya wanna know what?"

"What, darling?" he asked, flashing a grin—way too big a grin. Like he'd just won a game, she wasn't aware they were playing.

"Well, those words Clarissa told ya—they were for ya if I died, and I ain't dead. So, they don't count," Esther said, grasping for a way to turn the tables, to win something back.

She wasn't about to let him have the complete satisfaction of knowing he'd all but gotten her to confess she was pregnant, and that she was going along with his silly test—if only because she didn't want to miss out on a trip to Jasper.

And then, of course, there was the matter of a confession of love—something he'd been waiting on. Perhaps, more than anything, it was the one thing he wanted most.

Ian just laughed, the sound rich and warm, before leaning down, his breath stirring the fine hairs near her ear. His voice dropped, slow and confident.

"There's something I'm going to do to your body one of these days that'll have you screaming you love me from the top of your lungs. Might even feel like you died and came back to life." He lifted his eyebrows, as if he had just spoken a simple truth.

Esther gasped, eyes snapping to his, heat rising up her neck. What was he talking about? Hadn't he already done that? What else could he mean? Was he just playing with her—teasing her naughty-like?

"I'm not sure what ya mean," she said, working to sound unimpressed, but he was already turning back to his work.

"Not so fun when a person doesn't give you a straight answer, huh?" he tossed over his shoulder as he picked up his tools.

His mood was light, whistling some tune as he set the last brick into place. When she scowled at him, he only winked.

No, he had won this round.

And he knew it.

And he knew she knew it, too.

He was overjoyed—truly happy—and despite how much she liked seeing him that way, she couldn't shake the unease curling in her stomach.

A heavy thump echoed inside her.

He expected her to marry him.

To be Esther Huggler.

Someone he could boss around forever.

She was scared.

She didn't know the husband Ian. And what if she didn't like him?

Chapter 18: The Drive

E sther gazed out the window of the old truck as she and Ian drove, the long, straight rural highway stretching ahead of them. The landscape shifted as they made their way to Jasper—vast planted fields giving way to rolling green hills, the sky stretching open above it all.

"Ian?" she asked.

His hand rested firmly on the top of the steering wheel, his eyes steady on the road ahead. "Hmm?" he murmured, turning to her with a smile.

For a moment, she just looked at him.

A freshly trimmed beard, pressed formal clothes—no boots this time, but polished dress shoes instead. His wavy, dark blond hair was combed back, drawing attention to the strong cut of his brow, the natural crease in the middle that never quite left him, happy or sad. It only made him look more rugged, more like himself.

"Is this where Clive and I crashed?" she asked.

Ian glanced at her before turning back to the road. "We passed it a few minutes ago."

She frowned slightly, glancing out at the passing fields. "You don't think my good shoes are still out there, do you?" A wistful question slipping out—soft, unguarded.

"Aww, I doubt they'd be worth finding now." He paused, then added, "But if you want, we can look on the way back. Do you remember where you dropped them?"

Esther just shook her head—she didn't have a clue. It only stung knowing those pretty Italian leather shoes were likely stiff from rain and heat, left behind like a good friend she hadn't meant to abandon.

"Ya probably right," she murmured, leaning her head against his shoulder with a sigh.

Ian loved when she did that—cozied up to him, fitting herself there like she belonged. Her hair smelled so damn good, too. A soft, pretty scent that he now tied to the thought of her.

Despite her hesitation about today, she had dressed up to the nines, stepping out in a red dress he had never seen before. The neckline plunged lower than what she usually wore—just a bit too revealing—her bosom now filling out, making her curves more pronounced, giving her cleavage.

He was sure other men would notice, just like he had, but he tried not to let it bother him.

She looked beautiful.

Waiting in the driveway, he had told her that the second she stepped out the door—and he waited a good long while, even sending Rebecca in to fetch her. But the moment his eyes landed on her, the delay had been worth it.

Esther's voice suddenly pulled him out of his thoughts. He blinked, realizing she'd been chatting away, and he hadn't a clue what she'd said. Shaking off his distraction, he listened as she kept talking.

"Tell me about New York," she said. "What kind of things do folks do there?"

He exhaled, leaning back slightly against the seat. "Well, there are more people than you've ever seen in one place," he said, thinking even his words weren't adequate to describe it.

"Is it much bigger than Jasper?" she asked, trying to recall the pictures the children had shown her, but struggling to grasp the scale.

He chuckled, shaking his head. "Yes," he said, glancing at her. "You might not even be able to imagine it. Buildings taller than any tree you've ever seen. People pushing past each other on the sidewalks, always in a hurry."

Her eyes widened. "I want to see it someday. I want to see all the shops, the pretty clothes."

Ian smiled, studying her. "Yes, you would love that part, I'm certain." He leaned back, a flicker of amusement crossing his face. "You'd fit right in, dressed like this. Though…" he added, nodding toward the front of her dress, "you might get more attention than you want."

Esther looked down playfully, seeing the pushed-up tops of her breasts.

"It's like they done grew bigger overnight," she said. "Don't know what to do with 'em now."

"Oh, I have a few ideas," Ian said as he kept his eyes on the road, though the grin stretching across his face gave him away.

"Ya got a dirty mind, Ian. Ya know that? If people heard us, they'd think we were layin' with each other every blessed night."

"Doesn't matter. We've done it just enough, Esther. That's how we got into this situation in the first place," he said, matter-of-factly.

"Only a couple of times, and it's been a while," she complained, shifting slightly as she tried to tuck her bosom in a little more—not that it did any good.

"You said you wanted to wait, so I waited," he said.

"Practically pushin' me out ya door every night," she shot back, a thread of resentment laced in her voice.

Ian just smiled to himself. She wanted him. Wanted more of what he could give her. And he had been holding it just out of reach.

Though he'd thought it damn near impossible, he had managed to keep it in his pants—mostly. Never actually crossing the line since that night he'd taken her for a drive up near the hills.

At times, it had been torture. Especially when she had grabbed at him, told him she wanted him that way, tried to provoke him into forgetting himself. Oh, he'd let his hands wander over every inch of her body, kissed her until she was breathless, but no—he hadn't taken her.

Because if he did, there'd be no more waiting.

Sex made him feel possessive of her, like he needed her beside him in everything he did—especially sleeping in his bed. And that wasn't going to happen until they stood before a judge, until she took his name.

No, he wouldn't shack up with her, despite her pretty much offering to.

And Clarissa sure as hell wouldn't let him.

Ian eased the truck to a halt at a four-way crossing, the old vehicle creaking beneath them as it settled for a moment. Then, with a smooth shift of the clutch, he moved forward again.

"Well, sweetheart, you're gonna be living at my house permanently—and soon," he said, knowing full well it would rattle her a little. And it did.

Esther sat up straighter, her lips pressing into a firm line as she shifted her dress.

"Sometimes ya just mean to me," she muttered, inching a little farther away from him on the bench seat.

Ian turned to her, amused. "Can you please explain to me how that is mean? I swear, Esther, a fella wants to marry a girl, and you think that's mean? You are definitely a different gal than most, that's for sure."

"Ya know what I mean," she huffed as she crossed her arms. "Ya got me trapped, now ya just gloatin' 'bout it."

Ian reached for her, fingers curling around her wrist as he tried to pull her back closer.

"I'm not gloating, I'm happy. And, Esther, you're the one that started kissing on me in the barn, knowing I had been drinking. Maybe I'm the trapped one. Ever thought about it that way?"

"Naw," she admitted, flustered, scrambling for a quick comeback. But her mind went blank.

Ian turned serious, his voice steady as he shared something she needed to hear—something painful, but true.

"A child born out of wedlock isn't a child people treat kindly. You wouldn't want our baby to carry that shame their entire life, would you?"

He had said something real, something that cut to the heart of it—a reality of the society they lived in.

"I was," she whispered, turning to him, a sadness settling in her eyes.

"I know," he said gently, his voice carrying both empathy and conviction. "That's why we need to do this, and now. I can't allow a child of mine to go through what you went through. Do you understand?"

She didn't answer, but she didn't need to. The words had settled inside her, cutting through the fear and shifting her focus to something else—protection. Protection for an innocent baby, their baby, though she still refused to say the words out loud.

Esther bit her bottom lip, then slowly shifted back toward him on the seat. Ian took the invitation for what it was and slid his arm behind her, resting it along the top of the bench.

After a moment, he spoke again, his tone lighter.

"Did I tell you my brother, Freddie, is coming for a visit?" He glanced at her, his mouth pulling into a small grin. "I don't think we can wait for him to get here before we get married, but you'll get to meet him. He's a real city man. It'll give you an idea about those folks."

"What's he like?" she asked.

"The exact opposite of me. A couple of inches shorter, dark hair. Doesn't sound German at all—sounds British, like he's from England."

"I don't think I'd really know the difference," Esther admitted. "You are the only person I know that ain't from around here."

"Maybe, but trust me—it's different," he continued. "We left Germany when I was twelve, but my younger brother was only seven. Like Rebecca's age."

"Was it hard, just up and startin' over somewhere like that?"

Ian paused, his fingers flexing slightly on the wheel. "It was different," he said, considering his words. "My father had taught us some English, but the children in school weren't too happy about a dopey German boy being in their class."

He chuckled lightly as he continued, "I got into a lot of trouble, thinking I had to protect the reputation of my home country. Nothing like fighting off a group of boys on your own. Good thing I was a big kid. But it wasn't so easy for Freddie. Let's just say those boys quickly learned he had a big brother who didn't mind being sent to detention."

"I would've liked to have seen ya then," Esther said, reaching up to touch his brow playfully. "Did ya have the same serious face back then?"

Ian smirked. "I have a few photos. I'll show you when we get home—let you decide for yourself."

He glanced over at her, something soft passing through his expression.

"I can almost guess what you looked like when you were young—your face is still so youthful," he added. "As a matter of fact, Abram has told me on more than one occasion that I look like I could be your father."

Ian laughed, though a part of him wondered if people would really think that.

Esther only smiled back, thinking that she could tell him she didn't have any photos of herself—young or now—but that wasn't entirely true.

Clive's power—the photos he had used to control and manipulate—rested in the leather pouch she kept hidden. It was something she had avoided, too terrified to sift through the stack, knowing there were probably more of her in there. Ones she hadn't seen. Photos taken in a drunken haze or worse—in moments she couldn't remember at all.

She cursed herself for not burning them the moment she got home that day. But she hadn't been in her right mind. And as time passed—the sheriff visiting, the weight of it all settling on her—she started to question whether holding on to such a powerful tool might actually be in her best interest.

Those photos could protect her if the ATU came after her. Men of power were in those images, caught in ways that could ruin them completely. It was something Frank would have killed to keep hidden—proof of just how much control they held.

And yet, it was just as hard to keep them as it was to let them go.

"Esther. Esther," Ian's voice came louder now, snapping her out of her thoughts. "Are you listening to me?"

She turned to him with an apologetic smile. "Sorry. What were ya sayin'?"

Ian's eyes flicked to her, studying her face like he was trying to read what had just been running through her mind.

"I was just saying, Freddie is gonna talk your ear off. He's one of those people who doesn't know how to stop once he gets going."

She nodded absently, barely registering Ian's words.

He frowned. "You feeling all right? I mean, I know you're nervous and all, but the blood test is only a little prick."

Her head snapped toward him, panic rising in her voice. "What are you talkin' 'bout, Ian?" She sat up straighter. "They gonna poke me with somethin'? Ya ain't tell me that part."

"Esther, how do you suppose they get your blood?"

"God, Ian, I don't know, pop ya in the mouth or somethin'," she muttered, almost dead serious.

Ian's laughter came quick, rolling out of him before he could stop it. "You think—" he had to pause, catching his breath as he continued to laugh, "you actually thought they would hit you? In the face? Honey, you can't actually believe that. Please tell me you haven't been sitting here in this truck, thinking I was takin' you somewhere to get roughed up for a vial of blood."

He was still laughing, shaking his head in disbelief.

But Esther didn't find it funny.

He was laughing at her. At what she didn't know.

And it hurt.

"I ain't never been to no doctor 'fore, Ian," she said, her voice edged with defensiveness.

Ian's laughter faded as he turned to look at her fully, realization settling in. She wasn't joking. She was telling the truth.

And suddenly, it didn't seem so funny anymore.

Ian knew he was in trouble.

He had mocked her, assumed she would know something that had never been part of her world. He reached for her, trying to pull her closer despite the resistance in her body, his other hand gripping the wheel as he worked to pass a slow-moving tractor.

"I'm so sorry. That was stupid of me to laugh at you. Please don't be mad at me. I wanted today to be nice," he said, his voice softer now, almost pleading.

But she didn't say anything.

And he was right—he'd never let anyone rough her up or hurt her—but moments like this made her wonder what he really saw in her. He was smart, had seen the world, and she... she had only known an isolated and simple life.

Ian exhaled, desperate to ease the tension. "If you want to slug me in the arm, if it'd make you feel better, go ahead. I deserve it," he offered with a small smile, hoping to calm the storm in her.

She didn't budge.

He needed something stronger. Something she wouldn't ignore.

"What if I let you stay as long as you want at my house tonight?" he said, throwing down the card he'd been holding. "Doing whatever you want. I'll read to you, listen to music, kiss you—whatever."

That got her attention.

Esther turned to him, eyes narrowing. "I can stay as long as I want?"

He nodded earnestly.

She tilted her head. "Sleep in ya bed, the whole night?"

Ian flicked a glance at her, a slow smile creeping onto his lips. "Yes. But you're the one that has to explain it to Clarissa. That's the deal. Take it or leave it."

But Esther wasn't done negotiating.

"What about that thing ya were talkin' about yesterday? That thing ya said ya'd do to me, the one ya said ya never did."

Her tone was serious, her eyes locking onto his with a directness that nearly made him drive off the road. He swerved back onto the highway, gripping the wheel tighter.

"God, Esther, you're gonna make me kill us," he said with a nervous laugh. Then, after a beat, he added, "But yes. I will do that. Happily, I might add."

"Is it really gonna make me say all kinda nonsense?"

"I'll do my very best," Ian said, watching the wheels turn in her mind, the curiosity flickering in her expression as she tried to piece together what it could be.

Anticipation danced across her face, and he had to bite back a smile.

It was cute—how she really had no clue what he was talking about.

And the thought of sharing that with her for the first time—of being the one to show her—well, it excited him. A lot.

One night wasn't playing house, right? He tried to justify it to himself. The resolve in him had been held together by a tiny fraying thread.

He wanted to be close to her. To feel her lying underneath him. To love on her as long as he walked in this world.

And today was a start toward the real thing.

A strange relief settled inside him, knowing they were moving forward—together. Toward a life that wasn't just his anymore. A life with her.

And the sweet life growing inside the woman who would be his wife.

His Esther.

Chapter 19: Cola

The truck rumbled along the dirt road as Jasper came into view, its modest skyline marked by brick buildings, a water tower, and the occasional steeple reaching toward the heavens.

Compared to sleepy Larkin, Jasper felt alive, a small city with just enough bustle to give it a sense of purpose. Esther leaned her head out the window, taking in the shop signs and the steady flow of townsfolk as Ian slowed the truck to navigate the main street.

"Looks busier than Larkin," she remarked.

Ian grinned, his hands steady on the wheel. "A little. Not so big you'll get lost, though."

She glanced at him, the red fabric of her dress fluttering against her knees as the breeze caught it. His gaze lingered, remembering the last time he'd seen her in Jasper—stepping out of Clive's car at the movie theater. So much had changed since then.

Now, that pretty girl was sitting beside him. A dream come true.

Ian wore an easy expression as he turned the truck toward a quaint diner, nestled quietly along the hum of a busy street.

Its striped green-and-white awning fluttered in the wind, the sound of a distant train whistle mingling with the chatter of passersby.

The truck rumbled low as he guided it to a stop out front.

"I've got some errands to run," he said. "You'll be more comfortable here while I take care of them."

Esther eyed him, her curiosity piqued. "Errands? What kind?"

He hesitated, then gave her a quick smile. "Just need to pick up a few tools. Won't take long. Place is a dump, though—don't want that pretty dress of yours getting dirty."

Esther tilted her head, unconvinced. "Ian, I don't mind going with ya."

"Nope," he said, hopping out of the truck before she could argue. With that, he came around to her side, opened the door, and offered his hand, the sun catching on the faint freckles along his forearm.

"I'm going to leave you here. Now go on inside. Get yourself a soda, maybe a slice of pie."

She hesitated as her feet touched the pavement. "Ian—I don't want pie."

"I promise I won't be too long," he said, pulling a few bills from his pocket and pressing them into her hand. His tone softened as he added, "I'm not abandoning you here, darling."

Her fingers curled around the money. "Ya promise?" she asked, her voice edged with unease.

"I promise," he said, smiling as he leaned in to give her a quick peck. "I'll be back in half an hour."

"Ya better," she muttered, glancing around. She'd never been out on an outing like this by herself, and the idea of it made her stomach tighten.

Ian chuckled, rounding the truck with a playful smirk. "If I don't come for you, someone will snatch you up. Don't worry."

Esther wrinkled her nose at him. "Really, Ian. Reckon ya think you're mighty funny."

With a Cheshire grin, he climbed back into the truck.

Reluctantly, she stepped away, watching as he backed up his vehicle slowly.

Gathering her courage, she made her way toward the diner.

The bell jingled as she pushed open the door, glancing over her shoulder just in time to see Ian lift a hand in farewell before driving off.

Inside, the diner was warm and lively, thick with the scent of fresh coffee and fried chicken. A long counter stretched along one side, lined with stools, while booths hugged the windows and walls.

Esther smoothed her dress and took a steadying breath, acutely aware of the glances that followed her as she walked to the counter.

"Afternoon, miss," said the man behind the bar, his apron stained from a morning spent serving breakfast. He was older, with a friendly face and a twinkle in his eye. "What can I get for ya?"

"A Double Cola, please," Esther said, her voice soft as she slid onto a stool.

She and Clive had once driven to a diner out in the middle of nowhere—a smaller, untidier place than this. He had ordered for her, but for once, she had actually liked what he picked. A Double Cola had been one of those things.

"Well now, aren't ya just the prettiest thing to come through that door today?" the counterman said with a wink, setting a glass on the counter and scooping ice into it. He took it to the spout and returned with a fizzy drink, sliding it toward her with a grin. The final touch, a paper straw.

Esther wondered if this was what it felt like in the city—places like this, people gathered, talking, laughing.

"That one's on me," the older man said, wiping his hands on his apron.

"Oh, I couldn't," Esther said, reaching for her money.

"Sure you can—" he started to say.

"I've got it," came a voice from behind her—smooth, deep, and unfamiliar.

It carried an easy assurance that made her turn.

A tall man stood there, his brown suit tailored just right, his dark hair slicked back.

His smile widened as he stepped closer, handing a coin to the man.

"A beautiful girl in a pretty red dress shouldn't pay for her own drink."

Esther's cheeks warmed as recognition flickered through her.

The man from the movie theater.

The one she had smiled at in the dark, hoping to make Ian jealous. The one who had smiled back.

And now here he was again, looking at her the same way—except this time, in the bright light of day.

"Aww, I don't know… I don't know ya," she said, hesitant but polite.

The man leaned in, like he was sharing a secret.

"But you do," he said confidently. "You're friends with Margie Mae, aren't ya?"

Esther frowned slightly, confused.

His smile only deepened. "She's my aunt."

"Yer aunt?" Her brows lifted in surprise.

"Yep. Name's Hank Calhoun," he said, offering a hand.

Esther faltered for only a moment before taking it, her grip light.

But his thumb pressed against the top of her hand, holding on just a second longer than necessary. It sent an uncomfortable flicker through her, and she shyly smiled as she pulled away, setting her hand on her glass.

"It's good to meet ya, Esther," Hank went on, his tone smooth. "I went down to Larkin a few weeks back hopin' to run into ya, but no such luck. Margie said she ain't seen ya in a while. Said ya were livin' up on some estate. Almost drove up there, but figured that might be a little too forward."

"Wait, how do ya be knowin' my name?" Esther asked, confused.

Hank chuckled. "I saw you outside the theater with Aunt Margie. Looked like some men were about to brawl over ya, though I don't blame them."

His grin widened. "Figured then wasn't the best time to say hello. But today must be my lucky day. I saw ya outside comin' in, and, well—I couldn't help but chase ya in here."

Esther was at a loss for words.

He was laying it on thick, and while she wasn't sure what to make of it, she couldn't deny she'd never had someone approach her quite like this before.

And the fact that he had even thought about coming up to the Old Reed Estate? That was something else entirely.

"Ya may not know this, but the whole town stopped to stare at ya out there," Hank said, his voice dropping low, flirty. "Though you're even prettier up close."

Esther let out a nervous laugh, glancing down at her drink. "Thank ya, but I don't think that's true."

"Oh, it's true. I saw you years ago, ya know. Back when ya were just a girl in Larkin. I smiled at you, but your grandmother—well, she didn't seem too pleased."

Esther blinked, surprised by the memory.

"Gran wasn't one fer pleasantries," she said, almost under her breath.

And now Esther knew exactly who he was.

She hadn't forgotten that day—how his face had lingered in her mind all these years.

He had grown, changed, but there was something about him that now felt profoundly familiar.

"Well, I'm glad to see ya now," he said. "Makes up for lost time."

Esther opened her mouth, thinking she ought to say something—anything—before this went on any further.

But before she could, the diner door jingled.

Her breath caught, like she was doing something she shouldn't.

She turned instinctively, her heart giving her a quick jolt as she spotted Ian's unmistakable form.

His eyes found her immediately, narrowing as they flicked to Hank.

He strode in with his regular confidence, his movements calm—too calm—as he approached the counter.

Esther smiled at him, though a flutter of nerves curled in her stomach. "Ian, this is—"

But Ian didn't let her finish.

Without a word, he sized up Hank, a cool smile on his lips as he reached for her soda—plucking it clean from her hands.

Ian slowly lifted the drink to his lips, moving the straw aside with his finger and drinking straight from the rim—taking a long and deliberate sip.

His gaze never wavered from Hank, who straightened under the silent challenge.

The moment was drawn out and awkward.

"Well…" Hank finally said, his smile faltering just enough to be noticed. "I'll be seein' ya around, Esther. Tell Margie Mae hello if you see her."

Hank tipped an imaginary hat, pivoted on his heel, and walked out—shooting Esther one last lingering smile over his shoulder. Making sure Ian saw it.

With a light clink, Ian set the empty glass back on the counter and leaned against it, arms crossing over his chest.

"That was rude," Esther whispered, turning to him, her brow furrowed.

Ian's lips twitched into a smirk. "No, darlin'. That wasn't rude. That was somethin' else."

He offered his hand. "Come on. We've got an appointment to keep," he added.

She glared at him but didn't press further.

They stepped outside, bright sunlight spilling across the pavement like nothing had happened.

Ian opened the truck door for her, but she stopped before climbing in.

"Ya really were rude, ya know? Hank is Margie Mae's nephew," she said again, her voice firmer this time.

Ian's grin only widened as he leaned in slightly.

"Hank, is it?" His expression didn't shift as he let the silence stretch before speaking again. "Well, Esther… Hank and I don't like each other."

She frowned, confused. "Ya already know him?"

Ian held her gaze, the smile still playing on his lips.

"We do now," he said, giving her no further explanation.

And with that, he shut the door, leaving her to stew as he walked around the truck and climbed in.

The engine roared to life, the wheels kicking up dust as they pulled onto the road.

Esther crossed her arms, eyeing him. But Ian's grin lingered, unshaken.

He wasn't about to let anyone—especially Hank or whoever— think they could take what he'd already laid claim to.

Not when he had just been off picking out a wedding ring for that girl.

Chapter 20: Doctor

Ian eased the truck to a stop outside the small doctor's office, the engine's low rumble fading as he turned the key.

He glanced at Esther, who sat stiffly, hands clasped tight in her lap, clearly nervous. She hadn't said much since they'd left the diner. He'd tried to coax a smile from her, keep things light—but she wasn't having it.

With a quiet sigh, Ian stepped out of the vehicle. He tugged his shirt into place, tucking it beneath his belt—a slight pause, betraying a nervous edge he tried to hide. Circling around, he opened her door.

"Come on, darling." He held out a hand, his smile warm, easy.

Esther didn't take it right away, her eyes flicking to the clinic's front window, a shadow of hesitation passing over her face.

"Do we really gotta do this, Ian?" she asked, her voice tight. "Can't we just get married somewhere that don't make ya do somethin' like this?"

He leaned in slightly, his outstretched hand still waiting.

"It's just a formality. A little paperwork, a tiny bit of blood, and we're done. Then we can go celebrate." He smirked. "Or find you a soda that doesn't involve that Hank fella."

She rolled her eyes, but the corner of her mouth twitched. He caught it.

"Promise it'll be over before you know it," he added.

She exhaled, long and reluctant, before slipping her hand into his. He helped her down, and she lingered for a moment, as if gathering herself, before walking with him toward the office.

But a few steps from the door, she slowed, pulling back on his hand.

He stopped, taking her in with a patient glance.

"Esther, if I drag you in kicking and screaming, they're gonna think I'm forcing you to marry me."

"Aren't ya?" she said with a sour expression, but no longer resisting.

The clinic door creaked as Ian pushed it open. The air inside carried the faint bite of antiseptic, the wooden floorboards groaning under their feet. Behind a desk, a middle-aged woman glanced up, her smile warm and welcoming.

"Well, y'all must be gettin' married," the woman said, her eyes crinkling at the corners. "Congratulations on the engagement! Gonna be a June wedding?"

"Thank you, ma'am, but no, we're getting married as soon as the tests come back. Two weeks, right?" Ian asked, his voice polite as ever. He brushed a light hand against Esther's back, a steadying gesture more than anything. She nodded shyly.

The woman slid two stacks of papers across the counter. "Give or take. Just need y'all to fill these out and bring 'em back when you're done."

Ian took the papers and guided Esther toward a small bench by the wall. He sat, flipping through the forms while she lingered beside him, her fingers fidgeting with the folds of her dress.

"I'll take care of this," he said, sensing her unease.

The pencil scratched softly against the page as he filled out his own forms. The quiet of the office settled around them, broken only by the occasional rustle of paper. When he reached her section, he hesitated, then leaned in close.

"When's your birthday?" he asked gently, hoping she wouldn't make a thing of the fact that he didn't know.

Esther hesitated. "I reckon it's in March," she admitted, her voice hushed.

A quiet pang of guilt hit him. His jaw tightened as her words sank in. He'd known her for over a year and had never thought to ask.

"March what?" he pressed.

She shook her head. "Ain't sure. Just March. Clarissa might know."

He nodded slowly, something unreadable clouding his expression. "Alright. Let's say the first," he murmured, jotting it down. "We'll figure it out later."

Once the paperwork was done, he carried it back to the desk. The woman took the forms with a bright smile.

"Thank you kindly. Miss Primm, we'll get started with you first," the woman said, glancing directly at Esther, whose eyes went wide as they darted to Ian.

"Can he come with me?" she begged.

The woman chuckled, shaking her head. "Oh, no, hon. That wouldn't be proper. It'll only take a few minutes."

Ian rested a hand on Esther's arm, a quiet reassurance in his touch.

"You'll be fine. I'll be right here waiting," he said.

She swallowed hard but nodded, following the assistant down the narrow hallway. At the last second, she glanced over her shoulder, looking like a lamb sent to slaughter.

A smile threatened at the corner of Ian's mouth—he knew he shouldn't smile, not when she looked that pitiful—but the image caught him off guard.

He cleared his throat and sat back on the bench, stretching his legs out. His fingers drummed against the armrest as his gaze wandered around the waiting room.

A few minutes passed. Then, from somewhere in the back, a sudden clatter broke the quiet.

Ian's head snapped up, his body tensing. He was on his feet before he'd fully registered the sound, eyes directed toward the open doorway.

The assistant rushed past, her face flushed.

"Everything's fine," she assured him with a quick smile before disappearing through the door.

He remained standing, his gaze fixed in that direction.

When Esther finally emerged, her cheeks were flushed, her eyes dark with anger. She didn't say a word—just stormed past him toward the door.

"Esther—" Ian started, stepping after her.

"I'll be in the truck," she snapped at last, letting the clinic door slam shut behind her.

He exhaled, rubbing a hand over the back of his neck.

The assistant reappeared a moment later, motioning him forward. "Mr. Huggler? The doctor's ready for you."

The exam room was small, sterile, and scrubbed down to a harsh shine. A single table stood in the center, and beside it, a tray of medical tools lay scattered across the floor.

The doctor—a stout man with a kind face—was crouched down, gathering them with a chuckle.

Ian sat down on the edge of the examining table, brow creased. "What happened?" he asked.

The doctor straightened, shaking his head with a grin.

"Your bride-to-be didn't take too kindly to having her blood drawn. Kicked me square in the shins and sent my tray flyin'."

"She's a spirited girl. Sorry about that," Ian said as he gave a wry smile, wondering if he should have prepared them for that.

The doctor chuckled. "You'll have your hands full when she has a baby someday, I'll tell you that much."

Ian's smile faltered, though he forced a polite nod. He hadn't mentioned it on the forms, knowing Esther would've panicked if the doctor started asking too many questions—fuel to an already burning fire.

The blood draw was quick, and within minutes, Ian was back at the truck.

Esther sat stiffly in the passenger seat, arms folded tight, her expression downright stormy.

He slid in beside her, the seat creaking under his weight. "You okay?"

She turned to him, eyes flashing.

"It wasn't just a prick, Ian. That needle hurt. And then that doctor... he tried to touch me. Right—right on the knockers."

Ian blinked, then immediately knew what she meant. The doctor had checked his heart with a stethoscope before taking his blood.

Biting back a laugh, he rubbed a hand over his jaw.

"He was just listening to your heart, Esther. That's what doctors do."

"Are ya sure?" She narrowed her eyes. "Sure felt like he enjoyed touchin' 'em."

Ian reached out, brushing his fingers over the top of her hand. "I promise, Esther. It wasn't anything improper."

But she didn't look convinced.

Sighing, he turned the key, the truck jolting to life beneath them. He backed out, easing onto the road as the countryside stretched ahead.

As he pulled onto the rural highway, he shot her a playful expression, hoping to lighten the mood.

"You're moody today, you know that?" he said.

The glare she gave him could have soured fresh milk.

"That ain't helpin', Ian."

He chuckled softly, shifting gears. "You think old Hank would like that look?" He kept his tone light, but the name still lodged like a small irritating thorn.

Esther's patience snapped. "Hank, Hank, Hank—you think yer so funny, speakin' his name over and over," she said.

Ian just laughed, which only drove her further, pushing her to say something vindictive—something she knew would grate his ego.

"Well, ya think he was just foolin' around, but he went lookin' for me in Larkin. Almost drove out to the house." She flicked her gaze toward Ian, gauging his reaction. "Told me I was pretty more than once, too. Said he liked this dress."

The shift was instant.

The air inside the truck thickened, and the teasing burned away in a heartbeat. Ian's face went rigid, the lines of his jaw sharp, his mouth pressing into a tight line.

What had been play—maybe even a test, seeing if she'd brush off the encounter, if she'd mock Hank right along with him—had turned into something else entirely.

"Well, of course, he liked your dress," he said, Ian's voice cold, dismissive.

Esther's head snapped toward him. "What ya sayin'?"

Her voice had sharpened now—they were fighting.

Ian jerked his head, his eyes cutting toward her, heavy with meaning.

"I don't know, Esther. What do you think?" His gaze dipped, just briefly, to the neckline of her dress, eyeing her cleavage.

Her temper flared.

"If ya didn't like me wearin' it, should've told me to go back in the house," she shot back, sharp as a blade.

Ian let out a dry, sarcastic laugh.

"Like I could tell you anything. You always do what you want anyway."

She wasn't about to let that slide.

"I thought ya told me I could. That no one owned me. Now ya here, tryin' to do it," she said.

"My God, Esther." His grip tightened on the wheel. "You need to get those crazy ideas out of your head—the ones that tell you I want to own you. I want to share my damn life with you." He exhaled sharply, then turned toward her.

"Tell me the truth—are you just mad at me because I never asked when your birthday was?" he questioned.

Esther scoffed. "Ian, I told you—I don't know when my birthday is. Why would I expect ya to know it, if I ain't got a clue myself?"

"Then why did you say Clarissa might know?"

"'Cause she done helped birth me," she said.

Despite still feeling defensive, still angry, Ian couldn't shake the confusion creeping in.

"Esther, what the hell are you talking about?"

"I was born at the estate, Ian," she said as a matter of fact, though edged with a challenge.

He frowned. "Are you sure?"

"I was born in the room I'm sleepin' in now," she insisted, voice adamant. "Clarissa was my mama—the first year of my life, 'fore Gran came and got me."

Ian stiffened, the words making no sense—certain that had never been the case.

"I think you're wrong, Esther." He tilted his head, convinced she had tangled up someone else's story with her own.

"Ya don't know everythin' like ya think ya do," she shot back, doubling down, her voice rising.

"Esther, I think I would know," he said with certainty. "I was married to Adeline. And the only baby Clarissa ever had was named Rebecca—and she died."

He took the next bend in the road a little too hard, maybe going faster than he should.

"Well, that baby didn't die. And I'm Rebecca, Ian," she said, watching him, waiting for him to put it together.

He laughed—a short, sharp sound, more annoyance than amusement. This conversation was ridiculous. It was stirring up something raw, something he didn't want to touch. Adeline had struggled with that loss for years, and now Esther sat here, claiming something impossible.

"My God, Esther, you are white—if you haven't noticed." He scrubbed a hand over his face, wondering where exactly the day had started to go wrong. It had begun with promise. He'd been excited to take her to Jasper.

And it didn't help that some stupid bloke had come along, trying to snag *that girl*—like she was sitting out on a shelf, waiting to be snatched up. The thought made his jaw clench.

Oh, it really made him fume, thinking about how Hank had actually come to Larkin looking for Esther.

He knew with absolute certainty that if the man had weaseled his way up Clarissa's drive, he'd have sent him packing in the other direction—before the bastard even had a chance to get a sweet nothing past his lips—tail between his legs.

Ian prided himself on being calm under pressure, always keeping his composure, never wanting Esther to think him weak—unsure. Because he wasn't a weak man.

"Why ya gotta say such stupid stuff, Ian? Like I'm so ignorant I don't know what color my skin is." Esther huffed, shoving the money he'd given her for the diner back into his lap. "Ya really get me so hot sometimes."

He glanced down, seeing the exact bills he'd handed her earlier. Then she added, smirking, "Hank bought me my cola."

His head snapped up.

"You let him buy you something?" Ian barked, his voice uncontrolled. "I gave you money—why the hell would you let him pay?"

"'Cause he offered," she said meekly, actually realizing that it hadn't really been proper, and he was right.

Ian scoffed, shaking his head. "So, are you just gonna take whatever he offers you?" Ian's voice filled the truck, loud, echoing off the windshield. "And trust me, that fella wants to offer you a whole lot of things"

His fingers curled around the wheel. The words were out before he could stop them.

"Maybe you'd rather marry him instead of me? Let him raise my baby as his?"

He turned to her, a flash of anger burning in his eyes.

"And for all things holy, can you at least get that stupid, delusional idea out of your stubborn head?" he snapped, continuing, his frustration boiling over. "The one that makes you think you were somehow Adeline's sister. I know you want some connection to her, but she's gone, Esther. Do you even hear how insane the things you say sound? Like I would ever marry my dead wife's sister."

His voice eased as he pressed the truth into her, blunt and final.

"My God, we named our baby after Rebecca because she died, Esther. So, you can't be her."

But Esther clapped her hands over her ears before he could finish.

"I'm not talkin' to ya anymore." Her voice was tight, raw. "Ya just barkin' like a big ol' dog on a rope—annoyin', thinkin' ya scary when ya ain't."

She scooted as far from him as possible, adding, "And I ain't listenin' to a single damn word ya say."

And so, she sat, hands pressed tight against the sides of her head, face turned away, unmoving—rejecting him completely. She stayed like that for a long while, arms stiff, shutting him out without a word.

Ian clenched his jaw, not loosening his tight grip on the wheel, staring out at the road ahead. The fight inside him hadn't burned out—there were still things he wanted to say, things she needed to hear, but she'd shut him down.

He'd been too loud, louder than he should've been, and pushing her now would only make it worse.

So, he let her be, sitting in a long-drawn-out silence.

Until suddenly, without a word, he veered off the side of the road, yanking the old Ford to a stop with a sharp jolt. The tires kicked up dust, the abrupt halt jarring them both forward.

Miller Highway stretched ahead, long and narrow, disappearing into the horizon like an unreachable destination. There was an irony in that moment, as if the distance spanning between them in the cab felt even more vast.

For a split second, Esther wondered if he was going to throw her out of the vehicle, having had enough of her moldy expressions.

But he didn't.

He sat there a moment longer, hands resting on the wheel, eyes fixed on the same vacant space. He sighed, never lifting his brow.

Then, with quiet purpose, he opened the door. Stepped out. Shut it behind him.

Esther sat rigid, her heart hammering.

For a breath, she braced for him to appear at her door, to force some kind of resolution between them. Wondering what she would do with herself if he actually left her standing on the side of the road.

But he didn't.

He never came.

A flicker of panic crawled up her spine.

Shifting in her seat, she strained to see where he'd gone, twisting to peer out the back window. Nothing.

Then, finally, she spotted him—his tall frame in the distance, walking away, disappearing down the stretch of road.

No, Esther told herself, he wasn't dumping her on the highway—not over what she'd said about Hank. And yet, she knew her words had wounded him, just as she'd meant them to.

But Lord, he made her so mad.

Ian wouldn't listen, wouldn't believe her, acting like she hadn't heard Clarissa right, like she didn't know the truth of her own birth. Like those childhood memories of Adeline—playing in the hills, laughter carried on the wind—weren't real.

As if it hadn't been hard enough for her to accept them into her own reality. The line between dreams and truth fragile.

So, she sat and waited, the bench beneath her growing warm as the afternoon sun heated the cab. Her gaze drifted to the fields—lush and full of life now, so different from that dark, rain-soaked night when she'd run from Clive.

There was nothing she could do but wait for Ian to return—however he came back to her.

She considered climbing out and walking off in the opposite direction—God knows where—just to prove he couldn't yell at her, couldn't make her sit there like a fool.

But almost as if on cue with the thought, the driver's side door swung open.

Ian stood there, still irritated, broad shoulders squared, the heat of the day clinging to him. A bead of sweat traced its way down his forehead, his expression set in stone.

Without a word, he tossed two leather-wedged heels into the cab, landing near her feet.

Esther blinked.

Ian had found her shoes. The dark brown leather still gleamed despite the weather they'd endured, dirt clinging to them but nothing a good polish couldn't fix.

Joy flickered inside her, warm and immediate. She wanted to smile, to thank him. But the look on his face held her back, his frustration still painted across his features, like even going to find them had been a chore he resented.

So, she said nothing.

She just turned her head toward the window, unimpressed.

Without a word, Ian started the truck, easing it back onto the road.

They drove in silence, mile after mile stretching between them. Neither willing to let go. Neither willing to bend. And though they weren't fighting, the quiet sat thick between them, almost worse than the shouting.

It felt dreadful—the kind of silence that begged for words, for something to break it. For healing that neither of them appeared ready to offer.

Esther wanted Ian to apologize. Not just for snapping at her, but for making her feel like she was... what was that word he used? Delusional? She wasn't sure of its exact meaning, but she'd understood the message well enough.

And for Ian—she had insulted him. Worse, she had insulted Adeline. The memory of his dead wife and the intimate things she had confided in him were sacred. Esther had twisted them into something that felt like a mockery—something Addie had spent years trying to reconcile.

He found himself wondering what the hell he had been thinking—why he'd chosen the most difficult girl in the world to love.

Addie, though complicated, had been easier to reason with. There hadn't been a language barrier the way there was with Esther—he was constantly needing to explain himself. Ian was always trying to bridge the distance, always rewording, always clarifying.

Briefly, he glanced at Esther, the steady vibration of the truck rocking them as they climbed the hill toward the Old Reed Estate.

And there she sat—silent, distant, and so damn beautiful it wasn't fair. The sunlight was hitting her just right, softening her features, catching on the curve of her cheek, the shape of her lips—the ones he liked to kiss.

Her heavy-lidded blue eyes stayed forward, sharp with feeling and far-off thoughts, locked on a place he'd never been invited—like she was waiting for the wheels to stop so she could vanish from his sight, and still, he couldn't stop glancing over at her.

She hadn't even thanked him for finding her shoes.

And it hadn't been easy.

The first shoe had been simple enough, inches from the road. But the other... he'd had to work his way down into a ditch, the tall grass disguising it.

Discouraged, he glanced down at his slacks—his good slacks, the ones he only wore on special occasions—now streaked with green stains. His polished shoes—muddied.

Couldn't she see his effort?

That he did it for her, the same way he did everything else?

Maybe he'd moved too fast. Perhaps she needed more time—more of the world before settling into this life with him. After all, she had never really seen what other men were like. Clive didn't count.

No, Ian hadn't given her that chance. And now, he was starting to think it was coming back to bite him.

Because Hank—that bastard—was most certainly in pursuit of her.

From the looks of it, he had money. That much had been obvious from the tailored suit. He was attractive, as far as Ian could tell. Confident. And worst of all, he had that air of entitlement, the kind Ian knew women liked.

And Esther?

Well, maybe she liked it, too.

And the way she had looked at Hank while talking to him—that sweet, easy smile she gave him. The way she held his gaze. She had liked his attention.

And why shouldn't she?

She was stunning. She had found her confidence.

A voice in Ian's head reminded him that it was his fault—that he hadn't shown restraint, that he had no honor, not after what he'd done to her, binding her to him for a lifetime with the gift his body had given her.

But it was too late for that now. The deed had been done.

There was no undoing it.

So, all that was left was to move forward.

As they pulled into Clarissa's driveway, he shifted the truck into park.

Before he could say anything, Esther was already reaching for the door, making it clear she didn't want him to come around and open it for her, which didn't surprise him one bit.

She moved quickly, grabbing the shoes he had found for her, dangling them by their dirty straps as she turned away.

But before she could shut the door, Ian finally spoke.

"I'll never let another man raise my child."

His voice was firm, the depth of his resolve clear. He meant every word. Esther could do whatever she pleased, but she wouldn't shut him out of his child's life.

She stopped, glaring at him. His tone was cold, unyielding—that Ian, the dark, direct one, left her feeling cornered.

"Don't ya think I know that?" she said, matching his tone with her own.

Then she slammed the passenger door hard enough to rattle the entire truck, leaving him there alone as she hurried up the front porch steps and into the house.

Silence settled around him, almost deafening. He gripped the wheel again, his mind sifting through the wreckage of the day, trying to pinpoint the exact moment everything had gone wrong.

Inside, Esther moved swiftly toward the staircase, her breath coming in uneven gasps now that she was free from his gaze. The tears she'd been swallowing down with all her might rose to the surface with the same intensity, blurring her vision.

Clarissa, hearing the front door, met her halfway. One look at Esther's glossy eyes told her the whole story. It wasn't the expression she had hoped for—not after knowing what Ian had planned that day.

It had clearly not gone well.

"Honey, what's wrong?" she asked, reaching for her.

But Esther rushed past without stopping, feet racing up the stairs.

A moment later, the slam of her door echoed through the house, evidence of the storm that had followed her inside.

Clarissa stood in the hall for a moment, wiping her hands on her apron, turning the problem over in her mind.

Was there a gentle way to bring two people back together—two people who so clearly loved each other?

She had promised herself she wouldn't meddle. But this time, she made an exception.

Determined, she stepped onto the front porch, her eyes immediately catching sight of Ian, still sitting in his truck.

She made her way across the yard slowly, considering her words. By the time she rounded the truck to the driver's side, she found him already out of the cab, leaning against the seat, feet planted in the gravel. The door stood open beside him, but he made no move to leave. Arms crossed, shoulders tense, there was something lost in his expression.

He saw her approach and let out a sharp breath, shaking his head, like there was no point in small talk—like they might as well cut straight to it.

"God, Clarissa, she drives me crazy," he said, exasperated.

Clarissa smiled, stepping closer, resting a hand on the warm metal of the truck as she stood beside him in the shade.

"Trouble's part of the package, messy business love," she murmured, her voice calm, knowing.

Ian huffed a tired laugh, raking a hand through his hair, gripping it like he might pull it out.

"I tried. I really tried. I wanted today to be special, but everything just spiraled out of control." His voice wavered slightly, like he didn't even know where to begin.

Clarissa reached out, smoothing a hand over his arm, a quiet gesture of reassurance. He turned to her, his eyes glistening, unburdening himself to the one person he trusted most.

"I don't think she wants to marry me," Ian said, his voice catching, the truth of the words thick in his throat. Saying it out loud made it feel real—too real. "Not really."

"What would give ya that idea, honey?" she asked, her voice gentle.

"Everything," he exhaled. "She pushes back on everything. I find myself trying to manipulate her, bargain with her—using whatever I can just to get her to go along with it." His shoulders sagged as the words left him.

The older woman smiled, like she knew a secret he hadn't figured out yet.

"Honey, you've forgotten this part of it—this is how it is, bein' with a woman. We ain't easy. Sorry, my dear."

A small smile ghosted across his lips, but it didn't last.

"She says the craziest things," he went on. "Most of the time, I try to let it go, knowing she doesn't mean anything by it, but sometimes it feels like she's doing it on purpose—trying to work it under my skin." Ian shook his head, exasperated.

"You wouldn't believe what she told me today," he added.

Clarissa tilted her head, choosing her words carefully. "Maybe ya should just tell me what ya talkin' 'bout—since ya both seem a little prickled."

Ian took a long, deliberate breath, weighing his next words. He had a choice—gloss over it like he usually did when things got too sensitive, or lay it all out and hope Clarissa had some kind of answer.

He needed help—her wisdom.

"She thinks she was your baby," he said finally, watching Clarissa's expression. "The one that died."

His gut tensed immediately, afraid he'd offended her the same way Esther had offended him. "Please don't judge her," he added quickly. "I know she comes up with some crazy ideas."

Clarissa didn't react right away. She just stood there, time pooling in the space between them.

And then, slowly, something settled in her face.

Not shock. Not offense.

Resignation.

She had known this moment would come. Had been holding back, maybe out of fear, maybe out of knowing it wouldn't be an easy thing for Ian to hear.

But the time had come.

And there was no turning back now.

Adeline's memory had been preserved in a perfect state, untouched by flaws, despite the reality of who she had been.

And Clarissa hadn't wanted to change that—not when Ian needed something to cling to in his grief. But that truth no longer served a purpose.

So, despite Adeline's request, Clarissa would tell him what she had kept buried.

She took a steady breath.

"But Ian, she is. My baby never died, and I didn't give birth to Rebecca. Annie Primm did—Esther's mother."

The words hit him like a punch to the gut.

His eyes snapped to hers, searching her face, as if he could find a different truth there.

"What are you talking about, Clarissa?" His voice was tight, the ground beneath him shifting.

She held his gaze. "Adeline shared with me that she only told you a half-truth—a lie about her sister, though I don't know exactly why. But I have a few ideas." Clarissa hesitated, watching his face, knowing this would cut deep.

"And Ian, I don't think those secrets are doin' you any good anymore."

His body tensed. His pulse pounded in his ears.

No.

Adeline wouldn't have lied to him—not her.

He struggled against the truth as it ripped through him, trying to absorb what Clarissa was saying, trying to hold onto the reality he had always known.

"But... but... we named our daughter after her," Ian muttered, grasping at something he knew.

"After Esther, yes." Clarissa's voice softened, full of sorrow. "She was that baby, ripped from my arms and taken to the hills when she was just over a year old. Honey, why do you think I always call her my baby? Why I cried so hard when they took her away again? She had been mine."

Clarissa reached out, trying to rub his arm, but he remained rigid beneath her touch.

His breath came unevenly as his mind tried to process what she was saying. It was too much—too much history, too much betrayal, too much to untangle all at once.

And suddenly, his hurt turned sharp.

"Clarissa," he said, his voice edged with something bitter, "you let me fall in love with her—knowing this? Knowing all of this?"

The frustration that had been swirling inside him now had a direction. And it turned on her.

"And ya been happier than you've been in years, honey," she said, stepping closer, cupping his face in her hands. "There's been a light in your eyes since the day she came home. Why would I take that from ya?"

The words sank into him, deep and undeniable.

And with that, the fight in him wavered. The full force of it all cracked something open inside him, and before he could stop it, the tears came.

He set his jaw hard, trying to steady his breath. "But how do I..." He faltered, searching for words he couldn't quite find.

"Accept it?" Clarissa finished for him, her voice smooth, steady. "I reckon ya just do. Ya keep on lovin' the woman yer wife loved as a sister before ya. Findin' in it the same sunshine. Ain't nothin' wrong in doin' that."

He swallowed hard.

"I… I don't think I can stop loving Esther," Ian admitted, knowing the truth in his own words. "I just can't. She's grown into me, rooted herself."

"Then, given this truth, ya move forward, honey. Acceptin' it for what it is."

Her words rang true, clear in his ears.

And Ian knew he would try. He didn't have a choice, not really.

Certain he'd sit with it, turn it over in his mind, maybe even go up to Addie's grave and have a stern talk with her.

But now, there was something more pressing—something bigger knocking at his door.

He had hurt Esther.

He'd called her delusional when, in reality, she had been the one who had known the truth all along.

Now, knowing that—knowing he'd been wrong—guilt dragged him under like an undertow, pulling him out to sea.

"Ya got bigger problems, Ian." Clarissa sighed, her tone knowing, like she was reading his thoughts word for word—which she probably was. "How ya gonna make up with that cryin' girl up there?"

His stomach tightened. "She was crying?"

Clarissa nodded. "Yes, honey. And ya gotta make peace and wed her 'fore she starts showin'," she added, a glint in her eye, like she had just called him out—laying down the truth they'd been trying to hide.

Within an instant, Ian's chest tightened.

Had Clarissa just said their secret out loud?

Panic flashed through him, but before he could say a word, she kept going.

"Ya think you were the only one who noticed her runnin' for the door every time I cooked in a skillet? And I live with her, Ian. I hear her retchin' her gut up a couple times a day," she said in a sobering tone, like it was the most obvious thing in the world.

"Aw, Clarissa…" Ian shook his head, trying to find the words—an apology, an explanation, something. But nothing seemed appropriate.

"How ya ever thought ya were bein' sneaky is beyond me," Clarissa said, shaking her head. "Stayin' out all night in a love nest, grabbin' at each other when ya thought no one was lookin'—boy, ya was only foolin' yerself."

He exhaled slowly, guilt weighing heavy on him.

"I'm so, so sorry, Clarissa. Please forgive me. Know—know I'm ashamed of myself." His voice was raw, unsteady. "I know I've probably lost your trust, that I didn't act like a gentleman."

She let out a small laugh. "My goodness, Ian. Ya act like ya think I'm a saint. Like I ain't never laid with a man outside of holy matrimony."

Her frankness startled him.

She smiled, softer now, her dark, round eyes holding him like a mother's.

"I'm always gonna think you're the best man I know," she said. "You've done more good in your lifetime to outweigh any wrongs ya might do. And my girl—well, she needs someone like ya to help her through this world. She's gotta have a solid man like ya. She won't survive without ya. Too much bad's happened to her, and you—you'll make sure nothin' like that happens again."

Her voice cracked, emotion catching in her throat. "She's safe with you."

He swallowed hard, his throat tight. "I can never live without her. She's ruined me forever," he admitted. "Even if she can live without me."

Clarissa cocked her head, watching him closely.

"I told ya, honey. When it mattered, she said those words fer ya."

Clarissa went on,

"They were more real in that moment than at any other time. She wanted ya to know she loved ya, even though she was scared of sayin' it—maybe just as much as those men waitin' out there fer her."

She reached out, squeezing his arm, her voice steady.

"But Ian, they were her words, and she meant them, more than she'll let herself admit. And it'll get easier with time."

Ian inhaled, the relief spreading through him slowly.

Clarissa watched as it settled into his face, the sharp edges of his worry softening, just a little.

There was a renewed resolve in his countenance.

He trusted Clarissa more than anyone else on earth, and she had told him to keep going.

To push forward.

She had offered him grace, not condemnation. Hadn't made him feel like a failure for disappointing her—or himself.

And yet, her own admission had surprised him, shaken him even. Who had she been talking about?

She had been married to Obadiah for years. Ian suddenly found himself curious, wondering just how many secrets women really kept safely tucked away.

Clarissa gave him a squeeze on his arm, breaking through his thoughts.

"Now, ya need to go and make up with yer girl, Ian. We've got a weddin' to plan."

Her voice carried an optimism he hadn't felt in hours.

Without thinking, Ian reached for her, sweeping her up into a bear-sized hug, lifting her clean off her feet.

Clarissa let out a startled laugh, swatting at him.

"I just love you," he said, his voice full, the weight in his chest lighter.

Chapter 21: Sorry

Ian stood outside Esther's bedroom door, hands at his sides, waiting—praying she would answer. He hadn't been sure how to approach her, but he knew she needed to hear an apology.

"Esther, please open your door."

He knocked again, resting his forehead against it. His voice dropped to a whisper, raw with desperation, hoping she could hear what words alone couldn't fix.

"Sweetheart, please. I'm sorry. Please—please just open it," he pleaded. "I know I was wrong."

But Esther didn't answer.

He could have pushed the door open, but barging in would only make things worse. So, he stood there, waiting, thinking she might change her mind. She didn't.

"We never ate lunch. You want me to bring you something?" he asked as his own stomach grumbled at the thought. "Abram needs my help, but I don't want to leave until I talk to you." He tapped his fingers against the wood, a final, reluctant plea. "Can we talk later? I promise I won't yell."

He took a step back, then another, trying to pull himself away. But it didn't work.

If she could just see his face—see that he meant every word—maybe then she'd listen.

Against his better judgment, his fingers curled around the doorknob. Slowly, he turned it, easing the door open wide enough to peek in.

"Esther?" he whispered, remembering Clarissa had said she'd been crying.

But when he opened the door, the room lay bare. No sobbing girl. Nothing.

His gaze swept the space, landing on the floor. Her pretty red dress lay where she'd tossed it off in haste, and the shoes from the highway sat discarded beside it, forgotten just as carelessly.

No—Esther had changed and slipped out the back door while he had been talking to Clarissa.

Ian hesitated, uncertain whether to go looking for her or let her work through her anger alone. Back when he and Addie had fought, he'd learned to give her space, let her cool down. It had usually worked. But Esther was an entirely different creature, and the thought made him nervous.

The river glistened in the sunlight, much lower now, the spring runoff having long since passed. Esther had felt drawn to it, the need to find privacy, a place of solace. Perhaps she hoped that the familiarity of nature around her might mend what felt torn inside. So, she had made her way down to the rocky bank.

She tried to listen to the trees, to hear their voices carried in the breeze that rustled through their branches.

But her mind was still tangled in Ian's words—his tone, sharp and angry, like she had broken something of value.

Esther knew her part in it, too. She had flaunted Hank in front of Ian, worse than at the theater. She had thrown it in his face on purpose, wanting to salt his wound, making it sting.

Now, standing alone by the river, she realized—she'd gone too far. And Ian had been right, too, about her being moody. She felt herself sliding back and forth, like a ship at sea—half the time wanting to just purge her guts, early pregnancy doing its best to make her feel crazy.

She would never admit it, but Hank's attention had been exciting—something new. Different from Ian, though handsome in his own way. Definitely not as strong, she reasoned, like weighing two options.

Ian had broad muscles, the kind that felt solid and safe when he wrapped her up in them.

Hank had a polished, easy smile, the kind that could probably charm the socks off most girls.

But it just didn't compare to Ian's either. His smile did something to her, melting her from the inside out.

She could still see it—the way Ian had grinned that first time they'd picnicked in Clarissa's backyard with the children, all sunlight and laughter, like he belonged there.

She wished she could go back to those days. Back when all she wanted was for him to look at her, to let his gaze linger as she walked by.

It had been a dream, the wanting of him—distant and sweet.

But now that she had him, she wasn't sure what to do with him—she hadn't thought that far ahead.

She liked the idea of having a man, but marriage had never felt like a real, attainable goal. Gran had soured it in her mind, and Clive's power over her had tainted it forever.

She wondered if a guy like Hank would just want to marry her, too, like that was all a fella knew to do with a girl.

As Esther continued walking along the river's edge, she came upon a large, sun-warmed rock perched near the water.

It called to her, so she went to it, slipping off her shoes and dipping her toes into the coolness. The whooshing of the current was soft, almost like music in her ears, lulling her, calming her.

She sat there, bathing in the hush, as a beam of light pierced through the trees, landing on her. It settled almost perfectly over her lower belly, a quiet reminder of something else—something important.

A little egg, growing in its nest. A real person. A baby.

Ian had given this to her, just as he had given her so many other things.

As a matter of fact, he always made sure she had what she needed. Even stopping on the highway to hunt down a pair of shoes he knew she liked, staining his pants in the process.

He never overlooked the little things, the kind things. Like carving Ezekiel's headstone with his name, a beautiful gentleness in the act. Though she wasn't certain what all he had written, he had done it to give her peace, and she knew that.

No, Ian, despite his rough edge, built into a powerful body. He'd always shown her the utmost care. Always protective of her, never letting anyone hurt her.

My God, he'd searched for her in the rain, never giving up, then brought her home.

He had stood up to Clive, making him pay for what he had done to her, willing to take the entirety of the punishment, no matter the cost, when he thought there was one.

And she knew he would be this selfless for a child of his, as she had already seen him doing this for Benjamin and Rebecca.

Most days, after hours of hard labor, spent and tired, he still came home and gave them what was left of himself.

He'd smile, make them pull out their books, listen as they rattled off the mischief of the day, then tuck them in with a tenderness that never wavered.

There wasn't a doubt in her mind that he would love their child the same way, giving it what she had never known. A father's love. A father's protection.

Emotion welled up inside Esther as she thought about the tall blond man.

His face every morning when he greeted her in the kitchen. The way he'd wink at her or steal a quick kiss when he thought no one was looking.

The way he had looked deep into her eyes when he made love to her.

And he loved her. She knew this much.

The girl from the hills.

He told her every day, but the real proof was in the way he treated her.

It was something she could trust.

That thought was powerful—almost magical.

A strange, unexpected feeling stirred in her core—right where her heart lay.

It felt like heavy rocks crumbling away, a bright light breaking deep into the place where the haunted hurts lived.

They held a scared girl captive, whispering in her ear not to trust love, not to believe.

But now, that ray of light burned through, warming what had long been frozen.

She whispered, her voice soft—but sure.

The words she felt. The ones she had been too afraid to say.

"I love you, Ian Huggler."

The moment the words left her lips, something in her unlocked.

She closed her eyes, feeling it rise, spreading through her like a caged animal set free.

The feeling almost felt good. She wanted to say it again.

"I love you."

She smiled, feeling almost silly, leaning back, letting the weight of those words settle.

Letting the sound of them hum in the surrounding air.

She knew it'd still be hard to say to him out loud, but now she knew the truth of it inside herself.

A secret she hoped someday she could share with him.

But she knew something else, and, for certain, the ornery words they had shared with each other now threatened the new feelings she was experiencing.

How could Ian not help but think that she somehow wanted something more from Hank, as she had made it sound that way.

She had let him buy her a drink, knowing full well that her man had already seen to that. And she had been mean. She saw it in Ian's face, just for a fleeting second before he masked it.

And though the way Hank looked at her had made her feel desired, Ian made her feel that every day. He wanted more than what she offered on the surface, past the painted lips and pretty dress.

A determination took root inside her—nervous but certain. She pulled herself off the rock with urgency, found her shoes, and slipped them on.

She moved swiftly.

On a mission now. To fix what she had done wrong—to make sure that the German man knew she wasn't going anywhere with Hank or anyone else.

She ran, pushing past the dense overgrowth along the narrow path, charging toward the upper orchard. The estate was vast—too vast—and if she didn't find him now, she might have to wait until evening to speak to him.

But she didn't want to wait.

She needed this fixed, needed Ian to know.

As she reached the orchard, the trees stretched above her, their canopies thick with summer leaves. She wove between them, her breath quick, her mind set on the house at the top of the hill.

Her feet moved fast, light, like they were being carried by something more than just her own will—like they were caught in the current of what lay inside her.

I love him. I love him.

She whispered it in her mind, over and over. If marriage mattered to him, she would give him that.

She would want the thing he wanted. Because she trusted that the married Ian was the same man who had shown her, time and time again, who he truly was.

When Esther reached the top, breathless, she scanned the horizon.

Disappointment gripped her chest when she didn't see Ian's beautiful old truck anywhere.

She took a deep breath.

Think.

Resolve swelled in her again as she tried to recall what Ian had told her earlier. There was always something waiting for him.

The sheep.

He had said that he and Abram needed to move the fencing and take the flock to a different part of the orchard. She assumed he had meant the lower orchard, where the trees were older, larger, denser.

She took off down the hill, nearly stumbling in her rush, scanning between the long rows.

Her pulse quickened, her eyes searching—

Then, a flash of blue.

The Ford truck.

And there—just beyond it—Ian.

He and Abram were loading the large portable fence panels used to corral the sheep, their movements steady. The animals were already gathered into a smaller pen.

Abram stood in the truck bed, hauling up the long sections of fencing while Ian passed them up from the ground.

For a moment, she just stood there, watching him.

Her Ian.

Sweat-dampened and working hard, sleeves rolled up, muscles flexing with every lift. The very sight of him sent something warm surging through her, a mix of longing and relief.

She hadn't realized how badly she had needed to see him.

Without another thought, she picked up her pace, heading straight for him.

He didn't hear her, but he felt her—like a shift in the air. That unmistakable feeling of being watched. Ian lifted his head, his eyes landing on Esther, who was making her way toward him from a good distance away.

His gaze locked onto hers, a weariness in his eyes, as if bracing for whatever she had come to say. Her expression gave nothing away.

The May sun framed her, casting a golden glow over her narrow frame as she wove through the lush greenery of the peach trees, reminding him of the times he used to steal glances of her, long before he could admit how she'd undone him.

It would be easier, he thought, if she weren't such a pretty girl. But there she was—searching for him, wanting to talk.

And no matter how much work still needed doing, this—this thing with her—was at the forefront of his mind.

With a quiet exhale, he set down the heavy panel in his grasp.

"I'll be back," Ian said.

From the truck bed, Abram looked up, following his gaze.

"She's only gonna yell at ya more," he muttered, figuring Ian had told him just enough to feel better—without letting on how bad it really was, knowin' he'd stepped in it good.

Ian didn't argue.

He unscrewed the cap of his canteen, took a quick sip, then set it on the tailgate. His jaw worked for a second, like he was sorting through the right words—or maybe bracing for whatever came next.

"I'm sure I deserve it," he said, voice level.

Then he started toward her.

His broad shoulders never slumped, carrying that quiet confidence, even if he really didn't feel it in the moment.

But as he drew closer, and Esther's features sharpened in the light, he caught something in her eyes—something softer than he had expected.

And just like that, the knot of tension inside him eased.

She was happy to see him, and he was happy to see her, too.

His smile joined hers, wanting her to know that all was well inside him—despite the hard truths he'd learned that day. Things that weren't her fault any more than his, strange as they were.

Her eyes lit up, an effervescent smile carried high on her cheeks as he approached, her eyes gazing up at his.

This was her man walking towards her. She could feel it now.

"You came down here," he said, breaking the silence as he neared.

"Reckon I had to," she admitted nervously.

"Why's that, darling?" His voice remained steady and warm as he stepped even closer, his tall frame towering over her, his strong presence drawing her in.

So, she moved closer to him, nearly touching him, their nearness humming.

Her eyes never left his, holding him there, letting him see the warmth she sometimes tried to hide—especially in such intimate moments like this.

It made Ian catch his breath—not a boldness of desire, but something deeper. An openness. A trust he had been craving from her.

"Ian," she said softly. "Ya still wanna marry me?"

"Of course," he answered, without hesitation, without a second thought.

"I love you, Esther."

This time, she didn't push the words away. Didn't ignore them as she had before. She stood there, absorbing them, letting them settle over her like warm rain.

She drew in a deep breath, steady and sure.

"Well, Ian Huggler, I wanna marry ya real bad too."

Tears welled in her eyes as the words poured out of her, delivered straight to him—swift, certain.

And they made their mark.

He felt them hit, sinking into his chest, warm and strong.

His eyes lit with joy, a brightness as fierce as the beam of sunlight that had found her earlier.

This was it.

His breath hitched, knowing with absolute certainty—it was her.

It was always going to be her.

He reached for her, cupping her face in his strong hands, his gaze steady, searching hers.

He had called her to that unnamed place once before—the night he had first realized he loved her.

That place where two people go when they choose each other, despite the risks. Despite the fear. A place where past pain might still linger, but it wouldn't hold them back.

Where they would stand side by side—risking together—knowing that life could hurt, but love was worth it.

"I'm going to do my best never to make you regret your decision," he vowed. "I promise you that."

A shift came over him—serious, sincere, with regret painting every word.

"I can't promise I won't act a fool now and then... that I won't listen when you're telling me the truth." He looked hard into her eyes, making sure she could see his apology was genuine. "And I'm sorry. So utterly sorry I raised my voice at you. I was just so jealous—"

"Shh..." Esther pressed a finger to his lips, cutting him off, sparing him from carrying the full weight of that guilt or humiliation.

A teasing glint flickered in her eyes.

"Aw, Ian, I ain't got a care for that silly boy... what was his name? Hank?"

"He's too skinny fer my likin'," she added, her tone soft as butter. "Don't look like he's ever chopped wood a day in his life."

"That right?" Ian smiled, well aware she was just trying to indulge his ego—which he liked. "You like your wood chopped, do you?" he teased.

Esther playfully squeezed his large bicep. "I sure do like yer arms a lot, not gonna lie."

His voice dipped suggestively as he lowered his head closer to hers. "I think you like other parts of me, too."

A warmth spread across her face. "Yeah... that's true," she admitted, her voice dropping as natural shyness crept in.

His eyes darkened with mischief, a slow grin stretching across his lips. "I owe you something—a promise I made for coming with me today."

She smiled in response—almost too quick—knowing exactly what he was referring to. Well, not exactly.

"I don't know what ya talkin' 'bout, but it got me feelin' kinda tickled inside," she said.

That little admission sent a thrill through him. Acting on instinct, he swept her into his arms, holding her tight against him. The thought of loving on her, of making her feel good—well, he loved that idea.

He pulled back just enough to tilt his head down, his mouth hovering over hers. Then, with some of that stored-up energy he'd been holding onto, he kissed her—slow, deep—just a taste of what was to come.

Esther's knees went weak as Ian pressed in close, his mouth moving over hers, his warm tongue urgent—irresistible.

They had shared many kinds of kisses, but this—this was different. She could feel not just his desire but the depth of his love, raw and unguarded.

They kissed hard, lost in each other, wrapped in the shelter of the trees, their world narrowing to just the two of them.

Until a loud voice shattered it.

"Ian, while I'm enjoyin' seein' y'all standin' over there lovin' on each other like I'm not here, the problem is... I am."

Abram's tone was lighthearted, but the interruption was enough to make Ian grunt out of frustration. Slowly, he turned his head, still holding Esther firmly in his arms.

"You can't be serious," Ian muttered. "Do you know how many times I've watched you and Mitzy do this? Where do you think I learned how to do it right?"

Abram leaned against the truck cab, grinning. "Well, you almost got it, but still gotta few things to learn."

Ian grinned as he murmured near Esther's ear, "I'm sure I do."

She buried her face in his chest, his warmth rising to meet her.

Abram sighed dramatically. "But not jokin', Ian—can we finish this chore up? I'm just standin' here, waitin', feelin' like a sad galoot. Please, Miss Esther, can I borrow him back?"

Esther hesitated, making Abram wait before saying, "Long as ya know where to return him."

"Will do. Thank ya. And I see yer logic—don't want him wanderin' 'round the trees, lookin' like a lost pup," Abram shot back.

"Could ya put out a few breadcrumbs fer him to follow? Like in that story, Hansel and Gretel?" she quipped, not missing a beat.

"Now that there's a mighty bright idea. Got some old cornbread in my lunch Ian ain't managed to eat yet," Abram said, letting out a loud laugh.

Ian just stood there, taking it like a good sport. He figured he'd rather have them teaming up on him than standing on opposite sides. And he could tell Abram was trying to make amends for his words after the moonshiners had come. He appreciated it.

Esther glanced up at Ian. "I can leave," she offered, letting him know it was all right for him to get back to work.

He narrowed his eyes at her playfully. "Why do you have to say it like that? It makes me nervous."

"Alright, I'm gonna try to say it nicer. I'll be waitin' fer ya at the house, patient-like, Immanuel Huggler," she said, trying to sound more convincing.

He chuckled. "Not sure if the 'Immanuel' part is better, but I'll take it." He gave her one more proper kiss before releasing her.

But just as she turned to leave, he reached back, giving her a playful swat on the backside. She spun around, eyes wide in mock shock.

"Yeah, I saw that too," Abram called from the truck.

"Well, I reckon I learned that from you, too," Ian shot back.

With that, he turned toward the waiting task, a wide, unapologetic grin still plastered across his face.

Chapter 22: Shaping a Life

The kitchen was alive with the scurry of small hands, the air thick with the scent of sugar and flour. Esther stood at the wooden counter, rolling out the pale dough that would soon crown her peach pie. Across from her, a blue bowl cradled the fruit, the peaches steeped in their own sweetness, waiting for their turn.

Rebecca sat perched on a stool, her little face scrunched tighter than a possum caught in a trap. Sticky dough clung to her fingers as she wrestled with the stubborn edges of her small pie crust.

"Why's it always gotta fall apart?" she huffed, her voice sharp with frustration. She couldn't help but glare at her lopsided project, like it was working against her on purpose.

Esther glanced over. "I like how it looks," she said.

Benjamin snorted from his side of the table. "Mine don't fall apart, Rebecca. Look, it's perfect."

Rebecca shot him a withering glare. "I ain't askin' ya, Benji."

"Enough, ya two," Esther cut in, her voice soft but firm. She brushed a loose strand of hair back, leaving a streak of flour on her cheek. "Pie's for eatin', not fussin' over."

The door creaked open, a cool draft curling in, laced with the damp smell of dirt and the orchard. Ian stepped inside, his broad frame filling the doorway, wind-ruffled hair catching in the low light. His face was tanned from the day's work, the shadow of a smile playing at his lips as he took in the scene.

"Well now, what's all this?" His voice rolled through the kitchen, warm and rich, settling in like it belonged there.

Rebecca abandoned her crust and leapt off the stool, barreling toward her father with flour-dusted hands. "We're makin' pies, Pa! Real pies!" she said.

He crouched to catch her, lifting her with ease despite the smudges she left on his already dirt-streaked shirt. "Is that so?" His grin deepened as he turned to Esther. "And here I was thinking I'd just walked into heaven."

Esther answered with a smile, though she kept her hands busy, smoothing the rim of her pie with deliberate care. "Well, it ain't gonna be heaven if ya don't get cleaned up quick. Clarissa's got supper on in ten minutes."

As if on cue, Clarissa's voice rang in from the hall. "Ian, you best not be trackin' orchard dirt into my kitchen. Go wash up 'fore we sit down."

Ian straightened, setting Rebecca down. "Yes, ma'am," he called back, throwing his daughter a playful wink as his gaze settled on Esther.

"Who are you making that for?" he asked, nodding toward the counter. "That one just for me?"

Esther raised an eyebrow but couldn't hide her pleasure that he had noticed. "That depends. Ya like peach pie?"

"Love it," he said. "Especially if you're the one making it."

Benjamin groaned, letting out an exaggerated gag as Rebecca giggled beside him. "Gross, Pa. Now you sound all sappy like Abram," he muttered.

"Go on, Ian. Wash up 'fore Aunt Clarissa comes to chase ya out again," Esther said, pretending to look worried.

Ian chuckled but didn't move. He rubbed a hand over his jaw and glanced toward the back door.

"Hey, did anyone by chance go into the barn today?" His voice stayed casual, but Esther caught the slight edge beneath it.

She flicked him a glance, still rolling the dough. "Not today. Why?"

Ian exhaled through his nose.

"The barn door was wide open. Chicken coop too." He hesitated before adding, "Found a dead hen. The neck was snapped, no blood."

Esther's hands stilled. "That don't sound right."

"Abram walked the grounds—said he didn't see anyone. But he found some strange boot tracks near the barn," Ian continued. "Didn't match his. Didn't match mine either."

Esther dusted off her hands, her brow pulling together. "Ya think someone's sneakin' around?"

"Possibly. Could have been someone passing through, looking for easy pickings. But times are hard." Ian's gaze lingered on her. "Desperate people do things they wouldn't normally do. I'm just wondering why they wouldn't take the chicken if they bothered killing it."

She studied him, picking up the weight in his words.

"Maybe they saw one of y'all comin' or somethin' and run off."

He nodded, then looked toward the children, lowering his voice but keeping it light.

"Listen to me, both of you," he said. "If you see anyone near the house who don't belong, you call for me or Abram. Don't go wandering off on your own."

Benjamin squinted up at him. "Is it bad folks?"

Ian shook his head. "I'm not saying that. I just want you to be careful. No harm in being a little cautious."

Rebecca, oblivious to the weight of the conversation, sighed as she inspected her ruined crust.

"Maybe a ghost done it. Maybe the panther," she muttered.

Benjamin rolled his eyes. "Rebecca, why would a ghost kill a chicken?"

"Just keep an eye out," Ian said. "I don't want you worrying over it, but if you see anything, I want to know. Ghosts, panthers… or ghosts chasing panthers. Whatever order they come in."

Rebecca perked up, pushing out her chest. "I'd fight that panther… if it was smaller than me. Don't know about a ghost, though. How ya fight a ghost?"

"I reckon ya just pray," Esther said with a serious tone.

Rebecca squinted at her. "Does Jesus fight the ghost?"

Benjamin shook his head. "Jesus don't fight ghosts, Bitsy. He just tells 'em to git, and they do."

Rebecca frowned. "How?"

"Like Aunt Clarissa," Benjamin said as he lifted his brows, dead serious. "Ain't nobody talkin' back when she's starin' ya down."

From the other room, Clarissa's voice called out. "Ya best believe it, boy. And if y'all don't finish cleanin' up, yer gonna see just how scary I can be."

Ian grinned, shaking his head in animated agreement. He kissed the top of Rebecca's head, then glanced down at the little pie she was making. "Looks tasty, but you should listen to your aunt, or she'll come in here spooking you."

Clarissa's voice shot back without missing a beat. "I heard that, Ian. Ya still standin' there in ya muddy boots?"

He glanced down at his boots, eyes widening like he'd been caught. "And just like that, I'm going to leave. See—scary."

Rebecca giggled, and Benjamin sighed, like he didn't think his father was all that funny.

Just then, Clarissa strode into the kitchen, wiping her hands on her apron, one brow arched.

Ian clutched his chest, feigning mortal injury. "Alas, banished for my muddy boots and undeniable good looks!"

He turned toward Esther, catching the twitch of a smile she tried to hide.

Clarissa planted a hand on her hip, eyeing him. "Boy, ya might be a handsome devil, but I'm still gonna cast ya out! Shoo, now—go on."

Ian raised his hands like he was dodging trouble and hustled toward the kitchen door, making a grand show of escape before the older woman could get to him. His boots thudded on the wooden porch as the door swung shut behind him.

From the other side, his muffled voice called, "I'm gone, I'm gone! Please don't put a curse on me, Clarissa!"

Clarissa let out a good-natured laugh, shaking her head as she readjusted her long gray braid over her shoulder.

"That man's yer problem now, girl," she said with a smile at Esther. "All puffed up and pleased, like a schoolboy just picked for the first dance. Reckon you said somethin' he needed hearin'."

Esther just nodded in silent agreement.

Rebecca, always delighted by a bit of drama, beamed after her father's exit.

But her grin faded as she turned back to her dough, poking at it with a sigh. She flopped back onto her stool with flair. "My pie looks like a critter got to it," she lamented, drawing a rare laugh from her older brother.

"It'll cook up fine. Let's get 'em in," Esther said as she slid her pie into the oven. And yes, Clarissa was right. Ian was her problem now—the idea still new, still settling, growing inside her.

These had to be the moments that mattered—the laughter, the rhythm of shaping dough, the warmth of belonging stitched into ordinary things.

Loving Ian's children had always been effortless, but the quiet certainty that she would stay—that she was theirs now—felt like something new. A precious gift. As if she'd been walking toward this life all along, even before she knew the path existed.

A future full of moments like this was waiting for her.

Dinner had come and gone, and the kitchen hummed with the clink of dishes and Rebecca's endless chatter.

"I've dried twice already, Benji!" she huffed, hands on her hips.

"You ain't done nothin' but talk," he shot back, tossing a dish towel over his shoulder.

Esther worked at the sink, her sleeves rolled up, washing the last of the bowls, her movements slower than usual. Ian leaned against the counter nearby, arms crossed, his eyes thoughtful as he watched the familiar rhythm of the kitchen.

"You're looking a little worn out, sweetheart," Ian murmured, his voice low enough that only she could hear.

He stepped in closer, his breath warm against her ear as he added, "Maybe you oughta come over later. I'll take care of you... love on you a little."

"Ya tryin' to keep that promise?" she whispered, her smile faint.

Before he could answer, her hand flew to her mouth. She excused herself, hurrying from the kitchen.

Ian's gaze lingered on the hallway she'd disappeared down. He hated seeing her like this—and couldn't pretend he wasn't to blame.

Without another word, he returned to the dishes, grabbing a towel and joining Benjamin at the drying station.

"Guess I'm helping you tonight, Benji," he said, ruffling the boy's hair.

Benjamin grumbled, ducking away.

From her perch on the stool, Rebecca swung her legs, stacking clean plates into a neat pile. "Where'd Esther go?"

"She's not feeling so well," Ian said, though his eyes drifted back to the hallway, the thought of checking on her still tugging at him.

When Esther returned a few minutes later, she looked pale but determined. She waved off his concerned glance, brushing her hair back as she propped herself against the counter. "Ain't nothin'. Just caught me sideways, that's all. It'll pass."

Ian reached for her hand, his touch gentle, his eyes attentive. "You sure? You look like you need to sit down."

"I'm fine," she insisted, though her voice lacked its usual strength. "Been so dang tired, feels like someone tied sandbags on my feet."

He frowned but didn't argue, though he was insistent, taking her by the hand. He guided her to the cozy sitting room at the front of the house. A glass lamp cast a dim, honeyed light, inviting them in.

Esther didn't put up much of a fight, sinking down on the cushion without a word.

"Just rest a little," Ian said, his voice soft but firm. "I'll finish up in the kitchen, and you can save your energy for later." There was a slow smile on his mouth, teasing.

With a nod, she let out a quiet breath, lying down. Her eyelids were already heavy.

"I reckon I could," she whispered, her words hard to make out. "Guess a body that don't rest ends up devil-bit 'fore dawn."

"Not sure exactly what that means, but you can explain it later, darlin'," he mused, leaning over to kiss her forehead before returning to the children in the kitchen.

After he had dried the last pan and hung it up, Clarissa poked her head around the corner, already dressed for bed in her robe. The children had already been sent home.

"Thought ya might wanna know, that girl's sound asleep on my sofa," she said, her voice laced with tenderness. "Plum tuckered out."

He gave a half smile. Clarissa didn't need to ask—she already knew. As he turned away, a flicker of disappointment crossed his face. He'd been looking forward to being alone with Esther.

Drying his hands, he spotted Clarissa still standing there.

"Glad to see ya two getting' along. Does my heart good," she said. "Looks like she done come around, like I told ya."

"Clarissa, did you sprinkle some of your magic on it? I wouldn't be surprised if you had," he said, part amused, but mostly serious.

"Oh, this ain't my doin', honey. I ain't never told ya, but I dreamed 'bout ya both that first night she came here. Saw ya holding her hand tightly. Like God or maybe that ol' river out there knew where she belonged, brought her home," she said, her voice almost reverent. "Not to me, but to you."

"Well, I'm not about to argue with good fortune," Ian said, smiling, even if he wasn't sure he believed it.

And Clarissa wasn't going to push it. She'd just leave it with him—a seed planted in his mind for another time. With a good night, she headed toward the stairs.

Ian made his way to the sitting room. Standing in the arched doorway, he rested his arm on it. Esther was curled up on the sofa, her breathing steady.

He couldn't help but take her in, the warm glow of lamplight tracing the delicate lines of her face. Her long lashes fanned against her cheeks, her pretty hands tucked close to her body as she slept. Peaceful.

He was tempted just to pick her up and carry her to his bed—so she could sleep there from now on, curled up against him like she belonged.

But he knew it wouldn't look right. Clarissa would most certainly object, despite knowing full well what had already passed between them.

It was one thing to turn a blind eye—another entirely to flaunt it in plain sight. A bold statement, dismissing the decorum of a genteel society.

With a sigh, he pulled the knitted blanket from the back of the couch and draped it over Esther, his hand lingering for a moment. Then he crouched beside her, close enough to feel the slow warmth of her breath against his skin.

A smile touched his lips.

She had said she wanted to marry him, and he had seen the sincerity in her eyes.

It made him so damn happy.

There was a sunshine in her, something that seeped into his chest, warming him from the inside out.

And though he knew he should be ashamed for putting her in the family way out of wedlock, he wasn't—not really. The act, yes. But not the result.

Esther was carrying his child, and the thought filled him with a raw joy.

"I can't wait to see you holding a little baby in your arms," he whispered, not to wake her.

But here, in the silence, he confessed himself further. His fingers brushed lightly through her hair, his face drawn with regret.

"I still feel bad for raising my voice today," he murmured. "I hate when you're mad at me. I should've trusted you knew the truth."

"It stings, knowing Addie told me something that wasn't true. And I don't know why."

"But she knew you," he continued, softer still. "She loved you— cried over you so many times. Telling me you had died, maybe because it felt like you had."

Esther stirred, shifting slightly—her head turning just enough to suggest she heard him.

When she settled again, he went on.

"You had Addie's love long before I did. And if it doesn't feel strange to you... I'll do my best to let it be what it is."

Esther would be his wife, choosing each other in the simple promise exchanged between them under a canopy of green.

A certainty—a belonging—to one another in this life.

There had been nights before Esther when the grief drowned him, when morning felt like an ugly reminder of what he'd lost. He had thought that part of his life was over—loving a woman—the door shut and locked behind him.

But Esther had changed everything. She had torn through the sorrow, not by replacing what was gone, but by being something wholly her own—something fierce and consuming, something alive.

This girl, this woman, raised in the hills above the estate, carved from hardship and resilience, bound to him by a fate so strange it almost felt deliberate—as if some unseen hand had meant for them to find each other all along, just like Clarissa believed, far-fetched as it sounded.

"Goodnight, my love," he whispered as he kissed her softly on her lips.

With a slow breath, he reached for the nearby lamp, dimming its glow. Then, casting one last look at her peaceful face, he turned and left her to her sleep.

Chapter 23: Two for One

The peace of the morning was shattered with the sharp bleating of sheep, their cries loud and insistent as they barreled through the garden rows, trampling tender sprouts under their careless hooves.

Ian's voice cut through the chaos, sharp with frustration.

"Damn it, get back here!" He lunged forward, arms wide, trying to steer the unruly creatures away from the wreckage. A few more choice curses slipped out under his breath, his boots kicking up dirt as he moved.

Esther sprang forward to help, but her presence only added to the confusion, as a woolly body slammed into her side, knocking her off balance. She staggered, hands hitting the earth before she could completely fall.

"Esther, please get out of here!" Ian barked, his voice rough with exasperation—and something bordering on worry. Then, turning toward Rebecca, he jabbed a finger toward the old canning table beneath the covered outdoor area. "Rebecca! Get on that table, now!"

Rebecca hesitated, her brown eyes flicking between Ian and the chaos before she climbed up, crossing her little arms as she watched it unfold.

Benjamin stood beside Ian, gripping a long stick, his lean body taut with determination. He swiped at the air, herding with all the grit of his father, his face a mirror of Ian's focus.

"This isn't how I wanted to spend my day," Ian muttered, shaking his head. "Of course, Abram's in town, and these damn sheep are actin' worse than wild dogs."

Mitzy approached from the edge of the garden, her apron fluttering in the breeze as she lifted Jeremiah onto the table beside Rebecca. "I can help," she offered.

Ian barely spared her a glance, waving her off. "Abram wouldn't like it if I let his pregnant wife chase after his pet sheep," he said gruffly.

Mitzy arched a brow, planting her hands on her hips. "And why can't Esther help? She's standin' right here."

Ian's jaw tightened as his eyes flicked to Esther, lingering a beat too long. He didn't answer, but the look in them was enough. Protective, edged with something else—something she recognized. A slow, knowing smile curled her lips as the realization settled.

It took some wrangling, but eventually Ian and Benjamin managed to herd the sheep down toward the lower orchard, guiding them along the dirt road by the barn as Ian's truck rumbled up with Abram behind the wheel.

Abram jumped out, taking in the scene with a smirk. "Takin' 'em for a stroll?" he called out.

Ian shot him a look. "Will you just help, Bo Peep?"

Abram chuckled but fell in step beside him, the two of them disappearing toward the orchard to get the sheep back where they belonged—relieving Benjamin of his duty.

Back at the garden, Mitzy lingered, Jeremiah balanced on her hip, her gaze was sharp as she turned to Esther.

"So, ya havin' a baby, huh?" Her tone was light, but curiosity ran beneath it.

Esther froze. Her eyes flicked toward Benjamin, who had returned and was helping Rebecca climb down from the table.

"Shh," she hushed, afraid the children might have overheard.

But Mitzy wasn't one to let up. A teasing tone colored her words as she whispered, "That why y'all are marryin' so quick? Ian stick a lil' Huggler in ya?"

"Mitzy, please," Esther begged softly.

But Mitzy just shook her head with a big smile. "It's none of my business," she said casually. "I'm gonna go fetch Clarissa some eggs." She began to walk away, then called back, "Sounds like we'll both be good and fat in a couple of months."

Esther stood there a moment, watching Benjamin and Rebecca chase after Mitzy, excited to see the new chicks in the coop.

As she headed toward the big house, Mitzy's words clung to her. It felt like everyone already knew. The secret was unraveling faster than Esther could pull it back together. And if Mitzy suspected, would she mention it to Abram?

And then there was Aunt Clarissa—well, she had brought it up that morning, making it clear she was well aware of her condition. She had said it was better for her and Ian to marry sooner rather than later, encouraging her to start thinking about what she would wear to the wedding—it would be important and might require some planning.

Clarissa's words had been sobering, and though they stirred a flicker of panic inside her, the idea of dressing up pretty for a special day sounded enticing.

An elegant baby blue tailored suit dress—something Esther had ordered during her time with Clive—hung in her closet. It featured delicately shaped lapels, a pencil skirt, and a matching button hat adorned with a stylish half-veil. The only problem was that it hadn't fit her frame as she wanted and needed extensive alterations to suit her narrow hips.

Margie Mae had encouraged her to keep it, promising they would work on it together at her house. Skilled in the art of tailoring, Margie Mae had made the offer without hesitation, and the thought of spending time with her, learning such a skill, was something Esther liked.

Esther slowed as she neared the house, still caught in the daydream of soft blue fabric and careful stitches, when a sudden shriek shattered her reverie.

"Esther! Esther!"

The children's screams cut through the air.

Esther spun around just as their cries came again.

"A bear! A bear's chasin' Mitzy! Into the coop!" Benjamin belted as he and Rebecca came tearing toward her, their voices shrill with panic, their small legs flying over the dirt.

Benjamin held tight to his baby sister's hand, tugging her along, his grip fierce with determination.

"Go to the house!" Esther yelled, panic clawing its way up her throat. "Find Aunt Clarissa and stay there!"

Esther turned without a second thought and rushed toward Ian's house, her feet hitting the ground hard.

This was up to her—the men were too far away.

What choice did she have?

She knew Ian kept an old shotgun on the mantle. Her chest tightened at the memory of Pawdad's lessons, praying the gun was still in working order.

She'd never bothered to ask Ian about it.

She flung the door open, rushing inside. Her hands trembled as she reached for the weapon, its weight familiar yet foreign in her grip. This wasn't Pawdad's gun. She had never fired this one before.

A small box of shotgun shells sat near it. She pulled only three— no use in taking all of them.

Two slugs went into her mouth, gripped between her teeth, held firm the way her Pawdad had taught her. The cool brass pressed against her lips.

Pawdad's rough, unmistakable voice echoed in her mind, so clear it was almost as if he were standing beside her.

"Always bring three shells—one fer the bear, one if ya miss, and one in case he's got himself a friend."

Esther felt time was slipping away as she ran back outside, leaving the door swinging open behind her.

Her breath came in sharp gasps as she tore across the yard, praying she'd make it in time.

She shoved the first slug into the chamber, feeling it slide into place as she kept her pace. Her mind worked to steel itself. It had been a long time since she'd last fired a gun.

For the first time, she wished her old, wiry-bearded grandfather were here. He would have been calm, reminding her not to let her nerves shake the weapon. He would have chastised her, saying the gun could feel her fear.

Mitzy's screams tore through the air, sharper now.

Inside the wire coop, the black bear was already closing in, its massive paw raking at the wooden hutch where Mitzy had climbed in with her toddler for safety. She was pressed back as far as she could go, shielding Jeremiah with her body as its claws splintered the wood.

The creature moved with single-minded determination, each swipe drawing a blood-curdling shriek from Mitzy and her crying child.

The chickens were no better—frantic clucks and flapping wings filled the air, feathers floating like bits of chaos. Some had already burst through the broken door, fleeing in a frenzy.

Determined to brace herself, Esther planted her feet in a firm position and raised the shotgun to her shoulder.

A sharp gasp escaped her before she forced it down. She took aim, aligning her body, working to ignore the mayhem before her.

Her eye locked on the bear, its dark, hulking form looming over the coop.

The gun's sight lined up perfectly.

A sharp crack split the air, the shotgun's roar deafening.

The kick slammed into her shoulder, but she didn't flinch, absorbing the brunt of it.

Mid-swipe, the bear collapsed, its body crashing onto the slanted ramp leading to the hutch. A harsh snort escaped its throat, followed by a few shallow gasps—and then, silence.

Esther lowered the gun slowly, her ears ringing. She stared at the still body, waiting for it to move, just in case. But it didn't.

"Mitzy!" Esther called, her voice trembling. "It's dead! It's dead!"

A shaken Mitzy peeked her head out, her face still wild, her eyes darting, though relief had begun to settle in. Little Jeremiah clung tightly to her, his small arms wrapped around her neck.

Before Esther could catch her breath, a strange sound caught her ear—sharp and distant, like someone whistling.

Then came another—a rattling, low and hollow, echoing from the large storage shed out back—the one used for garden tools, plows, and sacks of seed.

Her heart pounded as she turned toward it.

She moved cautiously, leaving Mitzy behind. The noise came again, sharp and irregular, metal and wood clattering as something shifted inside.

What's that? Her mind flicked to the possibility of a smaller animal, maybe a fox, drawn by the loose chickens still flapping about.

But as she stepped closer, a rancid, greasy smell hit her—thick and unmistakable. It clung to the air, heavy, sour. Bacon grease? No—deer.

She rounded the corner, and there it was.

A deer carcass.

Stripped and split, ribs exposed, limbs twisted unnaturally—left out in the open like bait.

Esther's stomach turned.

What kind of wild animal had dragged it there?

And why here? Why like this?

Her eyes lifted to the barn. The door was ajar.

Wide enough for something large to slip through.

That door was never left open.

She hesitated as she leaned her head inside, peering into the dim interior.

Her blood ran cold.

Another bear.

It stood among scattered tools and torn seed bags, its massive shape shadowed but unmistakable. Worse, it had already seen her. Its deep-set gaze locked onto hers, and for a moment, neither moved.

She hardly had time to grasp its immense size before it started moving toward her.

The gunshot hadn't scared it. It had only made it angrier.

She moved slowly, willing herself not to betray the fear clawing inside her. But it was hard to mask, especially as the bear snorted, the sound breaking the quiet like a warning.

This one was bigger than the first. Esther's pulse hammered as realization set in—it wasn't going to back down.

She needed distance, enough space to line up a clean shot.

She bolted.

The bear lunged after her, its dark eyes locking onto her, a low, guttural growl rumbling deep in its chest.

Reaching the clearing near the barn, Esther spun, quickly shoving a shell into the shotgun.

Her fingers fumbled against the smooth metal as the bear picked up speed, its massive body closing in, the ground trembling beneath its weight.

She fired—too soon.

The slug hit dirt, kicking up a cloud of dust. The bear didn't stop.

Terror gripped her, twisting her insides.

Her hands shook as she scrambled to load the last shell, panic surging as the bear bore down on her. Its shadow stretched over her, dark and massive.

She forced herself to focus, Pawdad's voice replaying. "Yer the master of the gun. Force it to hit what ya see."

With a final, desperate breath, she fired.

Down in the lower orchard, Ian and Abram had nearly finished pushing the sheep when the sharp crack of a shotgun sliced through the silence.

Ian froze, his head snapping toward the sound. Without a word, both men abandoned the sheep and sprinted up the hill, fire moving through their blood.

At first, Ian's mind leapt to the moonshiners—maybe they'd come back. But the upper orchard and the house were still.

Abram shouted as they ran, "The sound came from over here, near the coop!"

Ian didn't hesitate, his legs burning as dread twisted inside him.

When they crested the hill, moving past the barn, they saw it.

Behind the chicken wire, a black bear lay sprawled in the dirt, dead. Near the hen house stood a trembling Mitzy, Jeremiah clutched in her arms. Blood seeped from a deep claw mark on her forearm, her breath ragged.

But she was alive. Shaken. But alive.

Abram rushed to her, gripping her as if he couldn't believe she was standing there. Relief flooded his face as he murmured reassurances, guiding her out of the coop.

"Thank God yer alright," he breathed. "Good Lord, woman... that thing damn near got ya," he said, his arm steadying her, his eyes darting anxiously to the bleeding wound.

Then, the second shot rang out.

Ian was already halfway to the house, searching for Esther—sure she'd been the one to fire the gun.

He stopped, dead—spun instinctively toward the sound.

He had hoped she was inside.

But the gunfire had come from the opposite direction.

Behind the old shed.

He took off, his strides eating up the ground.

Then, a third shot punched through the air.

All he could do now was pray. Pray that the shot had hit its mark. Pray that Esther was unharmed.

He rounded the shed, his boots skidding across the dirt. Then he saw it—an enormous dark form, collapsed on the ground like a toppled giant.

His gaze tore through the scene, searching, panic clawing at him. *Where the hell was Esther?*

His eyes briefly landed on the dead deer in the dirt, then flicked to the shotgun lying beside the black beast. His stomach dropped.

He saw her.

She was underneath it.

"Esther!" Ian's voice wrenched from his throat as he lunged toward her.

Her pale face was visible beneath the enormous animal, her lips parted as she struggled for air. She was moving, but faintly, her strength fading under the crushing weight.

Ian dropped to his knees and shoved against the bear with every ounce of strength he had. But the thing was massive—clearly a male, and unusually large. The dead weight barely shifted.

"Damn it!" Ian growled, his voice raw with desperation. He threw a frantic glance over his shoulder. "Abram!" he bellowed, but he didn't wait. Planting his feet, he braced his legs for leverage and pushed again, his boots grinding into the dirt. The bear shifted—barely.

Not enough.

"C'mon, move!" he roared, his hands sinking into the coarse fur as he strained against the animal's bulk. Every muscle burned, every fiber of his being demanding that he free her, but the weight refused to yield.

Abram appeared moments later, his face tight with determination as he took in the situation. He had heard the second shot.

Without hesitation, he moved beside Ian, their combined strength straining against the bear's body, working to dislodge it.

Abram took hold of the bear from the opposite side.

Together, they heaved, their combined strength forcing the massive carcass to shift—then roll.

Just enough to drag Esther free.

Ian scooped her into his arms, his heart pounding as he tried to rouse her. Her face was white, her lips tinged purple, her eyes unfocused and glassy.

He gave her a small but urgent shake, his voice cracking. "Take a breath! Take a breath, Esther!"

For a terrifying second, nothing. Then—

A gasp.

Sharp and painful, it tore into her lungs like a knife, forcing air where there had been none. It was agonizing, like being ripped from the beast itself.

Another breath followed, harder, just as painful. A weak moan broke from her lips as her body fought for air. Her lungs spasmed violently, a choked cry escaping her throat.

Ian's eyes never left her, his own chest rising and falling with hers, willing her back.

Then—relief. Her breaths were coming steadier. Her eyes, though wet with tears, were finding focus.

"You're okay," he said, his voice steady. "You're all right. Just keep breathing, nice and easy. You got the wind knocked out of you and hard."

Esther's tears spilled over as she tried to sob, but the effort sent fresh pain lancing through her chest. Ian gently coached her, his breaths slow and deep, guiding her into a rhythm. She followed his lead, each breath easing the spasms bit by bit.

Abram's voice broke through the moment, thick with concern. "She gon' be all right, ain't she?"

"She is. I've had this happen to me plenty of times—well, maybe not from a bear," Ian said with a small smile, his eyes never leaving her face.

"Does anything else hurt besides your lungs?" he asked.

She weakly shook her head, her trembling fingers gripping his arm for reassurance.

"The feeling will pass," he promised her. "Just breathe, darlin'."

And it did, though slowly, as he sat cradling her in his lap, his solid presence comforting.

Ian glanced up at Abram, who stood staring at the bear, his mouth open.

"My God, Ian, look at the size of this fella," Abram murmured, awe creeping into his voice. "Must be six hundred pounds—biggest one I've ever seen in my life."

Ian nodded, his focus still on Esther.

"You couldn't just wait for me?" Ian teased, the corner of his mouth twitching with a smile. "Now Benjamin's never gonna believe I know how to shoot that gun."

Esther tried to smile, but the movement made her wince. The pain still lingered, but a spark had returned to her eyes—a sign that her strength was coming back.

She swallowed, her voice barely above a whisper. "Gonna... hang his hide... on Clarissa's wall."

Ian laughed, relief washing over him.

"I'm going to carry you to the house, you hear me?" he said, shifting to stand. "I don't want you walking until Clarissa checks to make sure you didn't split a rib."

He set her gently on the ground for a moment before rising, then bent down and lifted her with ease.

"I'm fine," she muttered. "Just got a... lil' hug from this furry fella." But the words had barely left her lips before a cough wracked her chest. She winced, a low moan slipping out.

"I'm sure you are," he said lightly, shifting her weight in his arms as if to start toward the house.

Abram reached down, scooping up the shotgun from where it lay.

Glancing down at her, Ian teased, "Pretend I'm carrying you over the threshold after we get married."

She just shook her head, unable to muster a witty response. Instead, she let herself lean into him, drawing what comfort she could from the warmth of his body.

But Ian didn't take a step.

Something on the ground caught his eye.

His gaze drifted—past the blood-darkened earth, past the body of the bear—landing on the deer carcass just beyond the shed again.

"Abram," he said, voice low. "That deer... you see how it's laying?"

Abram glanced over, frowning. He walked toward it, crouching beside the stiff body.

"Yeah," he muttered. "It ain't been dragged. Too clean. Looks like it was put here, deliberate-like," Abram said.

Ian adjusted Esther in his arms, uneasy. His eyes swept the ground around the carcass, brow furrowing.

"Someone's messing with us," Ian said, quiet but certain. "Might've even brought the bears in. Left this out like bait."

Abram didn't answer right away. He stood, wiping his palms against his trousers, his expression tight.

Then he gave a single nod. "Yeah... yeah, I was thinkin' the same," he said, pointing at what looked like boot prints near it.

Ian didn't say a word, but he returned the nod—he'd seen it too.

He continued on toward the house, his jaw set firm, the tension still clinging to his shoulders.

Once in the kitchen, Clarissa quickly removed her dirty apron, gesturing toward the table. "Set her down on there," she instructed.

Ian gently lowered Esther onto the wooden surface, his hands resting briefly on her back before he stepped away.

"Anythin' pokin' at ya? Sharp real-like?" Clarissa asked, pressing along Esther's ribs with firm, practiced hands, inspecting each one with care. Her touch lingered briefly on Esther's lower belly. "Any cramps, pains down here?"

"No," Esther murmured, her voice worn. "Think the ground hit me harder than the bear."

Benjamin and Rebecca sat nearby, wide-eyed.

"Pa, did Esther kill the bear?" Benjamin asked, his voice laced with both amazement and worry.

Ian turned to him, his face shifting into an exaggerated look of surprise, his playful expression meant to ease the boy's nerves.

"What do you mean?" Ian said, eyes wide. "She didn't just kill one—she killed two bears."

Benjamin's jaw dropped. "Really?"

Ian nodded, his grin widening. "Two bears, Benji. Big ones."

Rebecca gasped, her little hands covering her mouth.

Esther managed a weak smile, still cradling her ribs.

"Reckon I didn't have a choice. Didn't wanna be lunch fer that ol' furry booger."

Despite Ian's easygoing words to the children, he cast a look at Clarissa—one that said everything. Beneath the teasing, he knew how close it had been.

Clarissa met his gaze, her expression shifting as the weight of it hit her, too.

Rebecca, who had been silent, moved closer to Esther and gently placed a hand on her arm, her eyes searching her best friend's face. Her tender voice trembled with worry as she asked, "But... but what about your baby? Did it get hurt?"

The little girl's question hung in the air, drawing a collective gasp from nearly everyone in the room.

"Rebecca, what are you talking about?" Ian's voice shot out, sharp with surprise.

"We heard Mitzy talkin' about it," Benjamin chimed in like it wasn't a big deal, his casual tone only adding to the tension.

Mitzy's face flushed as she quickly spoke up. "I'm so sorry! I thought they couldn't hear me."

Her apology was earnest, but her shoulders sagged under Ian's pointed glare. He mouthed, *Thank you*, the sarcasm unmistakable.

Esther's stomach twisted.

Now, everyone at the Old Reed Estate knew.

Across the room, Abram, who had been silent until now, shifted awkwardly before quietly slipping away, eager to remove himself from a conversation he had no business being part of.

"But, Pa, is the baby in her belly okay?" Rebecca pressed, her big eyes brimming with genuine worry.

Ian let out a slow breath, realizing there was no dodging it now. The children would find out soon enough, and he didn't have the heart—or the energy—to come up with a creative way to sidestep the truth.

"Yes," he said.

Esther's eyes flashed with frustration.

She hadn't even said the word baby out loud yet, and now everyone else was saying it for her. She shifted, uneasy, moving to get down from the table. Ian was at her side immediately, his hands steadying her as she eased to the floor.

"Do you feel good enough to stand?" he asked, his hand holding her elbow.

She nodded. "Think I wanna lie down fer a bit. Do ya think I can help ya with chores later, Aunt Clarissa?"

"Honey, of course," Clarissa said.

"Let me help you," Ian said, insisting despite Esther's half-hearted attempt to wave him off.

As they moved toward the hallway stairs, Benjamin—who had stayed behind talking to Clarissa—blurted out, "How'd Esther get a baby inside her?"

Clarissa's eyes widened. She stammered before exhaling. "Oh my. That's somethin' to ask ya pa, not your old aunt."

Ian froze mid-step, his patience fraying. "Benjamin, can you please just leave it—for God's sake?" he muttered, not turning around, hoping to avoid an even more awkward explanation.

More than anything, he prayed the children hadn't quite pieced together that he was the baby's father. That was a conversation he wasn't ready to have—not before he'd even married Esther.

As Ian and Esther reached the top of the stairs, she suddenly stopped and leaned toward his ear. "Ian, I didn't want anyone to know."

"I know. I'm sorry, darling," he said in a low voice.

Chapter 24: Abram

A week had passed since Esther shot the bears. The bruises had faded to faint smudges, and she moved with her usual ease now, though Esther couldn't shake the feeling that she was becoming a bit of a local legend.

Neighbors Roy Lee and his wife, Lucy, had come up to the estate with their children to see the big ol' beast for themselves. Like Abram, they agreed—it was the biggest bear they'd done seen. Roy Lee, grateful it hadn't made its way down to his small farm, admitted he wasn't sure he'd have had the nerve to shoot something that size barreling straight at him.

Esther brushed off the attention, as it made her feel uncomfortable. But Ian refused to let up, always finding some playful—or wildly inappropriate—way to remind her.

Telling her things like, "My hell, Esther. You drop a six-hundred-pound beast like it's nothing—what's a man like me supposed to do except let you have your way with me?"

And he hadn't stopped there, either—every day since, he'd found some way to slip in another comment, always grinning, always waiting for her reaction.

"Ya best watch yerself, Mr. Huggler. That ol' bear didn't stand a chance… Ya reckon ya could?" she huffed.

The laugh he let out was low, dark, and amused—like the idea didn't bother him one bit. Like he was asking if she promised to do that very thing.

As she walked down the narrow dirt road, Esther chuckled to herself, replaying the conversation in her mind.

Today, she was making her way toward the sprawling field where Ian was at work. In the distance, she spotted his familiar form clearing a clogged ditch with a shovel, his body moving with ease, making the hefty chore look effortless.

He looked up, his expression brightening at the sight of her. Stopping, he rested an arm on the shovel and let out a playful whistle.

"You're wearing slacks," he said, noting the cute, tailored pants—something she hadn't worn in front of him before.

"Ya like?" Esther asked, spinning to show them off. "Figured I should wear 'em while I still can."

"I like them," he said, grinning. "Spin one more time for me—but slower, so I can get a better look at them." His tone turned mischievous.

She did as he asked, turning again—slow as molasses—but shot him a suspicious look.

"Ya tryin' to get a look at my hiney?" she asked, almost sounding like she'd be disappointed if he wasn't.

"Of course," Ian said without hesitation. "And if I didn't have dirt all over my hands, I'd come over there and grab you."

Esther shook her head, smiling. "I swear, I've gone and done hitched my wagon to a wild horse."

"Yes, darling, but I'm the kind of trouble you can't seem to resist," he said, smiling but serious.

She just rolled her eyes, as if conceding defeat.

But Ian's gaze lingered on her. Even as her eyes looked away, he remained transfixed on his pretty bride-to-be.

"Well…," Esther said, "Abram's gonna drive me over to Margie Mae's place."

She caught the way Ian's face fell, disappointment pulling at his features almost instantly.

"I don't understand why it's going to take so long just to fix up a dress," he said, not wanting her to leave.

"'Cause it does, Ian. It's lined inside, and all of that has to be unpicked and sewn up right. I'll be back the day after 'morrow, I promise. Margie Mae said she and Ralph will bring me back up here when we're done. Plus, a girl's gotta get it all done right for her weddin' day. You don't want some homely bride headin' to the courthouse with ya," she said with a smile, determined.

He grinned wide, his voice almost serious as he said, "I wouldn't care if you wore a flour sack, Esther. You'd look beautiful in anything."

She smiled. Ian always said things like that to her, and it felt good, especially since she'd gone most of her life without hearing praise or flattery.

"And, sweetheart, I'm planning on taking off all your clothes when we get home from the courthouse anyway," he added, purely for shock value.

Esther gasped.

He smirked. "I got an idea—why don't you stay, forget Margie's, and I keep my promise to you? Show you that thing I haven't had the chance to do."

She laughed, curiosity tugging at her.

But her desire to look the part on her wedding day—that was a powerful motivation, too.

"Guess I'm gonna have to wait, then," she said, her tone full of sass.

"No? Damn it, Esther," Ian said, smiling, though the disappointment was clear in his voice. He beckoned her with his finger. "At least come over here and give me a nice kiss before you go. I won't touch you with my dirty hands."

"Ya promise? Don't want to be walkin' 'round with a big paw print on my backside."

Ian cocked his head, eyeing her like he couldn't believe she didn't trust him.

"Come here," he demanded, raising his hand like he had no intention of letting it touch her.

Esther made her way down to him slowly, her eyes narrowing. "I'm serious, Ian. I'm ready to go, and I don't wanna have to find somethin' else to wear."

He just smiled, saying nothing.

As she stepped closer, his gaze locked onto hers, holding her there, sending a warm, curling feeling through her. She leaned up and kissed him softly on the lips.

"I'm going to miss you," he murmured, almost brooding.

"I'm comin' back, Ian. I promise," she reassured him, struck by the thought that for such a big, confident man, he could say the most tender things.

She kissed him once more, resting her hand against his chest. "Can't wait fer ya to see what I'm wearin' on our weddin' day."

The excitement on Esther's face made him happy, knowing she was just as eager for their fast-approaching nuptials.

The distant rumble of an approaching car cut through the quiet, growing louder as it neared. It was Abram, driving Obadiah's old Ford Fordor Sedan. Though aged, Abram had kept it in fine working condition and used it whenever Ian's truck wasn't available.

The car rolled to a stop beside them, dust settling around the tires.

"We best get goin'," Abram drawled, a big old grin spreading across his face as he leaned his arm out the window. "Clarissa has put your stuff in the back."

"I appreciate you taking her," Ian said, wishing he had planned to take Esther to Margie Mae's himself.

Abram waved him off. "Well, I got a whole lotta errands to run for Miss Clarissa—she's wantin' to put on a nice spread fer y'all when ya get hitched. I'll be gone a good portion of the day, scavagin' the countryside."

"I'm a-comin'," Esther said, turning to go.

But not before Ian made a playful swipe at her, reaching for her with his mud-covered hands.

"No!" she shrieked, jumping back. "Ain't ya got a lick of shame? Nothin' but a devil wrapped up in a man." She laughed, breathless. He grinned back at her, unrepentant.

With one last glance at Ian, Esther climbed into the car beside Abram, and they were off, leaving Ian to return to his work.

The drive to Margie's was uneventful, but excitement stirred inside Esther—the thrill of going somewhere new, of having an outing on her own.

She and Margie Mae shared a kinship, bonded by their love of fashion and all things beautiful. Margie Mae's guidance had shaped her in more ways than one. She had given Esther tips, taught her how to style her hair, and even spent time practicing the art of walking with her.

Margie Mae's gregarious personality was infectious, and she had enjoyed her time with Esther just as much. She and Ralph had only two boys, both married now and living in different towns, leaving her longing for company. When Margie heard that Esther wanted to fix up her suit dress, she couldn't have been more excited if it were for her own wedding.

As they rode down Miller Highway, Abram glanced over at Esther, a smile on his face. He looked at the pretty girl who had captured his best friend's heart. And Ian—well, Ian was happier than he'd ever seen him. The man even had a new pace in his step, hardly minded the hard work these days, and didn't grumble the way he used to when frustration got the best of him.

But something had been weighing on Abram, something long overdue that needed to be said. It wasn't easy for him to be humble, to let his feelings show. But Ian's girl deserved to hear the words he'd been turning over in his head, saving them for the last stretch of the drive.

Clearing his throat, he broke the silence. "I wanna tell ya somethin', if ya don't mind."

Esther turned to him, her face open, listening, though she didn't say anything. So, he continued.

"You may not know this, 'cause I don't show it much, but Mitzy—well, that woman's got me all wound up around her, like ya done to Ian. I've loved her since the day I saw her, though she had another fella courtin' her."

Esther smiled, leaning back.

Abram let out a breath, shaking his head. "That girl drove me crazy, thinkin' I wasn't ever gonna be enough fer someone like her. Made me prove I was serious, too. Weren't takin' no nonsense from me neither."

"What happened to the other fella?" Esther asked.

Abram laughed. "Oh, I got my ways, got my ways," he said, chuckling louder. "When a man really has his mind set on a girl, he ain't gonna let another one swoop her away. But that's a story Mitzy's gonna have to tell ya." He grinned, leaving the mystery unanswered.

His smile faded, though, as he shifted in his seat. "But the reason I'm talkin' about Mitzy, well..." His voice hitched, struggling. "My whole life was in that chicken coop. Everythin' I have."

Tears filled the man's chiseled face, his strong eyes betraying a tenderness Esther had never seen in him before. A rawness that felt almost out of place on a man like Abram.

"When ya heard there was a bear, ya didn't even think about yerself." He turned to her, wanting her to hear the sincerity in his voice. "Ya had as much to lose as Mitzy, and you did all ya could to see her safe. Esther, ya saved my family. Ya risked yer life for the thing I could never live without." His words filled the cab of the vehicle.

Esther swallowed, her heart squeezing at the weight of it all. "I love Mitzy and Jeremiah," she said softly, meaning it.

"I know. But ya did somethin' I can never pay back, and I ain't never gonna forget it." His grip tightened on the wheel. "I haven't always treated ya right, said harsh words at ya. Blamed ya for things that weren't yer fault. And I see I was wrong."

He paused, knowing the next words wouldn't come easy. Apologies didn't slip from his tongue often, but Esther's sweet nature made it easier—he knew she wouldn't rub his nose in it.

"I'm sorry. Will ya forgive me?" he asked, glancing at her.

A warm smile spread across her face.

"Aww, Abram, ya gettin' all mushy on me?" she teased, trying to lighten the heavy mood. "Ya forget—you helped drag the bear off me. Reckon we're squared up."

He smiled back, knowing she had heard him and answered in the way that felt natural to them both.

"And he was a big ol' bastard," he laughed. He leaned back, his grip easing on the wheel. "Got two pelts waitin' to be tanned. Ian's determined to make 'em pay for comin' onto the Old Reed Estate. Gonna turn 'em into a reminder for any others that get that idea in their head."

"I know—I'm worried he's gonna put one of 'em down in his front room, makin' me walk on it," she said.

"Oh, that's what I'm figurin' to do with the one that chased Mitzy and Jeremiah. A nice big ol' bear skin rug to warm her cold toes."

"Sweet Jesus, Mitzy ain't gonna like that." She knew Mitzy, just like her, wouldn't want some big, furry beast stretched out on the floor.

Abram smirked. "Ya sure?" His voice was playful. "Remember, I got my ways. I'm thinkin' I can convince her."

Esther just kept shaking her head, a laugh slipping from her.

"Yer hurtin' my confidence," Abram teased. "Got me wonderin' if I still got influence."

"Oh no, you should try. Try if ya think ya can," she grinned, egging him on.

"Well, that's exactly what I'm gonna do," he said. "Got to show Ian how it's done. How a man stands up in his own home." Abram chuckled back. "But I got to tell ya, when it comes to you, I worry the man ain't got the hard resolve." Abram glanced at her, more thoughtful now. "That's 'cause he'd do anythin' to see you happy. That big German man's got it soft fer ya."

Abram turned slightly, catching the way Esther soaked in his words. And though she already knew this much about Ian, hearing it from someone else—someone who was as much a brother to Ian as a man could be—made it feel different.

As they neared Margie Mae's home, the pretty little house came into view, nestled down a tree-lined lane. It wasn't as grand as the Old Reed Estate, but it had its own charm—a two-story home with a wraparound veranda and flowers blooming in every direction, just as one would expect from someone like Margie.

When Abram pulled up, Esther straightened, preparing to step out just as Margie Mae came rushing onto the porch, waving in a big, excited Southern greeting.

"Let me get ya door," Abram said, quickly hopping out and making his way around the vehicle. He opened it like a perfect gentleman, grinning like he'd just brought Margie Mae a present.

"Thank you, Abram," Esther said, pausing for a moment, wanting to thank him for more than just the car ride. "Sure glad Mitzy got ya fer her man," she added with a genuine smile. "Though ya really gonna have a problem tryin' to get her to let ya bring that pelt inside."

Abram smirked. "Oh, she's gonna be stretched out on it by the time you get home."

He laughed, but the moment the words escaped his mouth, he knew he'd gone too far—forgetting for a second that he wasn't talking to another man.

But Esther wasn't the type to be offended—she just grinned, used to hearing Abram and Ian speak without a filter.

As he handed over the belongings Clarissa had packed for her, Margie Mae was already making her way down the steps, her eyes lighting up when she saw the dress.

"I forgot how pretty the color was." Margie Mae reached out to touch the fabric. Her voice oozed with delight. "This is gonna be fun, and I had some ideas 'bout addin' a little more to it. Come see what I was plannin'." She linked her arm with Esther's, already leading her toward the house.

"You ladies have a pleasant afternoon," Abram called as he tipped his hat and climbed back into the car.

Margie Mae responded without turning her head, her attention fixed on the dress in her hands.

"We'll bring her back up the day after 'morrow,'" she said, leading Esther inside. "That is, if I don't just decide to keep her for myself." Her voice held a teasing lilt, but there was no mistaking the fondness in it.

Chapter 25: The Dress

Margie Mae had a room all her own, a space devoted to sewing and the quiet hum of creation. It was how she filled the empty nest, stitching away the silence left behind. Her youngest son's old bedroom had been transformed, the walls now covered in Margie Mae's eager sketches—dresses that had once lived only in her mind, now waiting to be brought to life.

The two women fell easily into their familiar rhythm of conversation—movie stars, the latest fashions, the towering stacks of magazines Margie Mae had scattered around like old friends.

"This room is just perfect, Marg," Esther said, sinking into a wide, overstuffed chair, her gaze drifting over the fabric-strewn tables and drawings lining the walls. She sighed, stretching her legs out. "I'm gonna move in here—claim it as my own."

Margie Mae chuckled. "I'd let ya, if ya wanted."

Esther grinned. "Don't think Ian'd allow it. Man's got it in his head to marry me."

Margie Mae tilted her head, her voice teasing but edged with something weightier. "Well, I can see why ya'd want to marry that man. He's easy on the eyes. But does he treat ya right?"

"Oh, he's real good to me, Margie Mae. Probably too good," Esther said as she hesitated, a small smile tugging at her lips. "I'm kinda mean to him sometimes."

She thought back to the time he'd scolded her for letting the kids slide down Aunt Clarissa's wooden stairs on pillows, warning her they'd break an arm. So, to prove a point, she had grabbed a pillow herself and sailed down ahead of them, just to watch his expression twist in that way that both irritated and amused her.

Ian had been furious. Playful as he could be, he didn't abide reckless risks. Later, when they were alone, he'd asked—quietly, still bothered—if she even realized she could've hurt their unborn child. She hadn't. At least, not in the moment. It had been a thoughtless act, meant only to ruffle his feathers.

She had waved him off, calling him a rather large stick in the mud, saying that if a bear hadn't gotten the baby, a little bump down the stairs probably wouldn't have mattered. But deep down, she had wondered if maybe he was right.

Margie Mae's voice pulled her back.

"Well, long as he's good to ya. And he can give ya the things ya need—maybe even a few of the things ya like." A knowing smirk crossed her lips as she smoothed Esther's blue outfit over the long sewing table. "'Cause, girl, we both know ya like the nice things."

Esther didn't respond, but she knew what Margie Mae was really implying. Ian might struggle to give her the finer things—the kind of life Clive, for all his darkness, had lavished on her, but at a price.

The type of money that could wrap around a person like silk, even when the hands holding it were rough and cruel. A luxury she'd likely never know again.

If Ian had hemmed and hawed over the cost of three-dollar hairpins, well, he'd have fainted at the price of her favorite shoes— the ones he'd rescued from the highway.

No, Ian was frugal—she knew that well enough. But there were more important things than money.

The day slipped into evening as Margie Mae and Esther worked, their hands busy but their conversation even busier, drifting from fashion to local gossip. Margie Mae spoke of the red-haired girl Esther had once seen at the mercantile—the one who had batted her lashes at Ian.

Caroline Suggs. A woman her age, already notorious for scandal. She'd strung along two boys at once, promising marriage to both. Each had bought her a ring, each had proposed in the same week—only for Caroline to refuse them both, claiming she had her eye on someone else entirely.

Esther couldn't quite decide what to make of her. It was foolish, what Caroline had done, but there was a power in it, too—something bold, something Esther secretly admired. Not that she'd want Caroline anywhere near Ian again. No, that woman had better keep her distance.

But the confidence? The way Caroline had made men stumble over themselves? That, Esther had tried to emulate.

The conversation shifted then, turning sharp in a way that made Esther uneasy. Margie Mae brought up Clive. Said she'd heard rumors about him running illegal liquor and asked if Esther had known what had been in the back of the car that night at the movies.

Esther answered truthfully enough. She hadn't had a clue. But she left out the rest—the parts that still sat like a stone in her gut.

Margie Mae, however, wasn't ready to let it lie.

"I wanna be real honest with ya," she said, voice dipping lower, as if she wasn't sure she should say it at all. "And ya may not have noticed, but your cousin Clive—I think he had his sights set on ya."

Esther stiffened. She knew. Of course, she knew. But she wasn't about to admit it, not here, not now. Instead, she gave a small, uncertain shrug.

"I don't know," she said meekly, feigning ignorance as best she could.

"Oh, honey, it made me so uncomfortable. I was gonna say somethin' to ya, thinkin' maybe you hadn't caught on. But he was just outta line. Like you'd ever pick someone like him, when you could have near any bachelor in the county," Margie Mae said with conviction.

Esther laughed, unconvinced. "I don't think that's quite true, Margie."

Margie Mae paused, straightened, and set her hands on her hips. Her expression turned firm, full of certainty that only came from knowing the truth.

"Esther, you really don't see it, do you? You have a power over men, and ya don't even realize it. If I'd had a face like yours, I sure wouldn't have settled for Ralph," she said, her tone as serious as ever.

"Margie!" Esther exclaimed, surprised. She hoped her friend was joking, but the look on Margie Mae's face said otherwise.

"Don't get me wrong, I love Ralph—he's a big sap, treats me right, gave me a nice house and all—but I never had what you have. That thing that makes men wanna fight over ya." She let the thought settle between them before adding, "Just don't waste it. Get all you can with it."

A smile brightened Margie Mae's round face as she continued.

"And if Mr. Huggler is that, well, good on ya. Just remember, despite his incredible good looks, life's got more comin' at ya than love-makin'. That tall man's not got much to offer—small house on land he don't own, two youngins needin' raisin', and a complicated life, bein' German and all."

Her voice softened with warning. "Things won't always be so merry when you're tryin' to feed ya babies. And he's the type of man that'll give you plenty of 'em. Trust me, you'll want him to."

Esther didn't bristle. She knew Margie Mae meant well, speaking from a place of love, offering the kind of advice a girl like her needed. But there was something Margie didn't know— something she couldn't know.

She was right about Ian. He was good at making babies. And one of them was already growing inside the belly Margie Mae had just measured with her tape.

Sensing the conversation had turned too serious, Margie Mae shook it off, settling into a familiar rhythm. "Now, Cary Grant," she said with a sigh.

The two women quickly fell into playful agreement that if Cary Grant were an option, they'd pick him over Ralph or Ian any day. Their laughter filled the room, spilling out into the dimming evening as the last of the daylight stretched thin across the walls.

That night, tucked beneath the covers in Margie Mae's guest room, Esther thought about Ian—where he was, what he was doing, whether he was thinking about her too. She thought about his children, how they hadn't been too happy about her leaving. Rebecca had clung to her, wide-eyed and stubborn, declaring that she was her best friend and didn't need any others. The memory brought a soft smile to her face.

By morning, the women were back at work, determined to make up for lost time. They focused on bringing Esther's vision to life, though it was clear Margie Mae was living vicariously through her, every stitch and seam threaded with excitement.

They'd wasted enough time the day before, so there wasn't a moment to spare. Margie Mae guided Esther through the basics—how to lock a stitch, how to hide it, how to roll a knot off the tip of her finger after wrapping the thread just right.

Esther took to it quickly. Margie Mae's instructions were simple, and Esther had an eye for precision. She could see a straight line as easily as she could draw one. When she sketched her ideas onto paper, Margie Mae went quiet, her expression unreadable. Then, with a slow exhale, she shook her head in disbelief.

"Lord have mercy," she muttered, handing Esther one of her own rough sketches. "Fix this one up for me."

Esther did, making minor adjustments, sharpening details, refining the flow. Margie Mae watched in amazement, half laughing, half in awe.

Before long, the room was filled with their laughter, their chatter turning playful. They joked about launching a clothing line called Hillbilly Chic, convinced Hollywood would snatch it up. Margie Mae teased that Esther ought to model for it, which only made them laugh harder.

By mid-morning, Margie Mae declared it was time for lunch and tea, insisting they take a break on the front porch. Esther quickly noticed that Margie Mae had gone all out—setting out a proper spread, every plate and dish neatly arranged. She was a wonderful cook, too.

Esther, however, barely touched her food.

Margie Mae didn't press the matter, assuming it was the sort of thing women did before their wedding, trying to stay slim for the dress.

Outside, on the broad wooden porch, Esther helped set out tea, small cookies, and a bowl of nuts, the scent of warm wood and sunlight wrapping around them.

"Hope ya don't mind," Margie Mae said, setting a pretty napkin onto the table, "but Lavina Ronell and her daughter are stoppin' by for a bit. Have you met them before?"

"I haven't. Ronell?" Esther asked, trying to clarify.

Margie Mae nodded. "Sheriff's wife. They don't live too far from here. I'm takin' in some of their daughter Fannie's dresses—she's as thin as you."

As if on cue, the sound of tires crunching over the drive caught their attention. A car pulled in, dust settling around it.

From the driver's seat stepped a blonde woman in her early forties, her hair neatly swept up, her presence calm and composed.

From the passenger side emerged a young girl, maybe fourteen, with dark waves cascading down her back, much like Esther's.

Margie Mae and Esther stepped forward to greet them, first turning their attention to Lavina, as her daughter lingered behind.

"Well, hel-lo, you two," Margie Mae said warmly, reaching out to welcome the visitors.

But Lavina barely heard her. Her eyes locked onto Esther, widening as if she had seen a ghost. A small, sharp breath hitched in her throat. She tried to speak but faltered.

"Thank ya for invitin' us, Margie," she managed, though her gaze never left Esther, holding there long enough to stir unease.

Margie Mae, oblivious to the shift in the air, pressed on cheerfully.

"This here is Esther Primm—soon to be Huggler, I might add."

Lavina reached out, taking Esther's hand with a softness that felt almost hesitant.

"Primm, is it?" she murmured, the name rolling over her tongue like something half-remembered.

Before Esther could answer, the sound of footsteps drew her attention. Fannie Louise had finally made her way up the porch, coming to stand beside her mother.

Esther's breath caught.

She understood now why Lavina had looked at her that way.

The girl was her mirror. Dark hair, light freckles—features so eerily similar they may as well have been cut from the same cloth.

Even Fannie Louise seemed to notice, hesitating as her gaze flicked to her mother, her expression puzzled.

Margie Mae, noticing the resemblance, let out a breathless laugh.

"Oh my goodness, you two are like twins!"

"Are ya kin? Distant cousins?" she teased, trying to break the tension.

"Not that I know of," Esther said, hoping to steer the moment away from whatever it was threatening to become.

They settled onto the porch, the afternoon slipping by in simple conversation. From time to time, Esther caught Lavina looking at her—studying her with a quiet, searching expression.

Margie Mae kept the chatter moving, filling the space with the usual talk of town life. But beneath it, something unspoken hovered between Esther and Lavina, a thread stretched taut, neither of them quite willing to pull at it.

After what could only be called a pleasant afternoon, Lavina and Fannie Louise prepared to leave. But before stepping off the porch, Lavina turned back to Esther, reaching for her hands with a soft, deliberate touch.

"It was good to meet ya," she said gently. "Yer a lovely girl. I wish you well, and congratulations on ya upcomin' nuptials."

There was warmth in her voice, but something else, too—something Esther couldn't quite name.

"Thank ya, ma'am," Esther replied, her tone sweet.

She exchanged one last glance with Fannie Louise, who had remained unusually quiet throughout the visit.

Once the sheriff's wife and daughter had gone, Margie Mae let out a breath and shook her head.

"I swear, Esther, you and that girl could be sisters. I just don't see how you ain't."

The words settled deep, stirring something restless inside Esther.

That old, nameless voice—the one that had haunted her since childhood—rose again, whispering like the wind through bare trees.

The same voice that had sent her searching men's faces in town, hoping to see her own eyes staring back.

She had always wondered. Who her father was.

If he was still alive. If he had ever lived in Larkin at all.

Until today, she hadn't found a soul who resembled her—not one. She'd long since convinced herself that he'd been a stranger passing through, a man her mother, Annie, had only known for a moment.

But Fannie Louise—she was different. She was the mirror Esther had been looking for.

And Lavina—Lavina had paused at the name Primm. She had studied Esther too long, her gaze lingering not just in recognition, but in search of something as if she were piecing together a puzzle in her mind.

The thought wouldn't leave Esther, even as she and Margie Mae returned to their work.

She stood before Margie Mae, the wedding skirt turned inside out as pins slid into the fabric. Margie Mae worked quickly, her hands practiced, but Esther wasn't present.

Sheriff Marty Ronell's face had settled in her thoughts.

Their last encounter at her home. The way he had apologized. That strange, strained tone in his voice. The kindness—unexpected, unfamiliar.

And his vow.

That if he had known the truth about Clive, he never would have taken her there.

The needle slipped through the fabric. But Esther was elsewhere, unraveling something bigger than seams.

And then there was the way he'd practically told her and Ian to lie about her time at Clive's. How he'd said he'd do what he could to keep her name out of any reports, making it clear—without saying it outright—that he intended to do the same himself.

No, Esther thought. That was strange.

Her mind drifted into dangerous territory—one of those places where wild notions take root. The kind you only dare say out loud in your own head.

Could Sheriff Marty Ronell be my father?

The idea was ridiculous. Absurd.

Esther let out a sudden laugh, shaking her head at herself. She must've lost her mind.

Margie Mae, pinning a seam, glanced up at her with a curious smirk. "What ya laughin' at?"

"Nothin'. Just somethin' stupid," Esther said, her eyes dropping back to the skirt.

Margie Mae narrowed her gaze. "Well, somethin's caught yer tickle."

Esther forced a small smile. "Just thinkin' about my weddin'," she lied.

Margie Mae beamed at that, pleased with the thought. She stepped back, resting her hands on her hips, admiring the shape of the skirt.

It seemed like the right moment—maybe even a perfect moment—to bring up something important. Something Clarissa might not have mentioned yet. The thing a mother figure ought to say, with such a special day so near.

Clearing her throat, Margie Mae motioned for Esther to sit.

"Honey, ya know how it works, right? Between a man and a woman? Ya know what to expect that night?" Her voice was gentle, careful. She assumed Esther was still untouched, too naïve to have crossed that threshold.

Like a cottontail caught in an open field, Esther froze, wide-eyed, unsure how to respond. She nodded quickly, hoping that would end the conversation.

Margie Mae wasn't convinced. She took Esther's hand in hers, giving it a small squeeze.

"I just want ya to be prepared," she continued. "Knowin' he's gonna wanna do some things to ya that might feel... uncomfortable. Not just kisses, ya understand."

A warm smile softened Margie Mae's face, but Esther felt trapped, her mind scrambling for a way out. She nodded again, more forcefully this time, praying it would be enough.

Margie Mae carried on, unaware of the tension stiffening Esther's shoulders.

"Don't be surprised when a man gets a strange kind of hunger—a hunger fer you. And, well, ya might even find yourself buildin' yer own kind of appetite," she said, pausing, as if expecting Esther to absorb her meaning.

In truth, Esther wasn't absorbing anything. She was trying to find an escape.

"But ya know how men gobble too fast at the dinner table?" Margie Mae went on. "They do that in the bedroom too. Leave ya sittin' alone at the table when they're done, ya get my drift?"

Esther nodded so fast she nearly gave herself away.

Margie Mae sighed, shaking her head.

"Well, honey, ya need to remind 'em to come back and help—maybe clear the dishes. Ya gotta be firm about that."

She said it like a woman passing down wisdom, hoping Esther would piece it together once she was married.

But Esther already knew exactly what she meant. And Ian had made sure she was taken care of the last time they'd been together— every part of her.

"Thank you, Margie Mae," Esther said, eager to return to the task at hand.

Margie Mae studied her for a moment, then let the subject drop.

"We've got a few more hours, then I need to stop and fix Ralph some dinner, or that fella's gonna be cross. Gets real grumpy when his belly's empty—turns into a downright grouch," she added.

Esther nodded in agreement. "I think Ian gets that way, too. Like food can turn a sour mood sweet."

Margie Mae chuckled, then hesitated.

"One other thing, Esther," she said hesitantly. "And I hope ya don't get mad at me for this one. But I did somethin' I'm kind of regrettin'… and I can't change it now."

Esther frowned. "Not sure what ya mean, Margie?"

She couldn't imagine Margie Mae doing anything wrong. Whatever it was, she was surely overreacting.

Margie Mae stilled, setting her work aside. She met Esther's gaze, a flicker of hesitation crossing her face before she decided to come clean.

"I invited my nephew, Hank Calhoun, to dinner tonight," she confessed.

Esther's stomach dropped.

"Margie…" she said slowly, already reading the intent in the older woman's eyes.

"Listen, Esther," Margie Mae rushed on, as if trying to soften the blow. "I just wanted ya to see there were options. And, well… that boy's got it bad for you. Drove all the way to Larkin last month, askin' me how to get to the Old Reed Estate—which I refused. Knew it wasn't a good idea, him just showin' up unannounced. Didn't reckon you'd get engaged and married so fast."

Esther sighed, not knowing how to feel. She didn't want to be mad at Margie Mae, who was always so generous, so full of love. And deep down, she knew her intentions were good.

Still.

She wasn't sure how Ian would take this—so maybe she'd just leave this part out when recounting her time at Margie Mae's house.

Deciding to make the best of it, she resolved she could endure one meal with Hank Calhoun.

Dinner arrived faster than she was ready for. In the guest bedroom, she smoothed her dress, then reached for her red lipstick. A strange flutter stirred in her chest as she ran the color over her lips, sharp and bold against her skin. She scolded herself for it.

If Ian ever entertained such a thought—entertained another woman—she'd be furious.

From the window, she caught the glow of headlights sweeping across Margie's driveway. Ralph had already returned, so the sound of the door could only mean one thing.

Hank was here.

"God, please help me," Esther muttered, her heart pounding as she made her way downstairs.

Pausing on the steps, she wavered. The urge to turn and flee clawed at her, but she pushed forward, each step carrying her toward the trouble she knew awaited her.

In the dining room, Hank Calhoun stood off to the side, talking with Ralph.

Tall. Clean-cut. Dressed sharper than usual, like he'd made an effort.

The moment his head turned and his gaze found hers, Esther felt her pulse quicken.

She ducked her head, stepping lightly, as if she could slip past unnoticed. She wanted the safety of the kitchen. She wanted Margie.

But it was too late.

Hank was already making a beeline for her, his stride sure, his smile practiced. Before she could step away, he had her hand in his, shaking it firmly.

"It's so good to see ya. You look real beautiful tonight," he said smoothly, his wide grin searching her face.

Before Esther could respond, Ralph piped up.

"Oh, you've met Esther before?"

"Yes, I've had the pleasure a few times," Hank said, still gripping her hand like he had every right to touch her. She was about to yank it back when he finally released it—just as Margie Mae came rushing in.

Despite everything Margie had said earlier, Esther didn't miss the way she was sizing them up, as if trying to picture them as a couple. It made Esther's skin prickle.

She just needed to get through the evening.

So, she took a steady breath, reminding herself that Clarissa had taught her how to carry herself at a formal table. If nothing else, she could rely on that.

"Margie Mae, can I help ya, please?" she asked, hoping for an excuse to slip away, even for just a moment.

But Margie Mae was no help.

"No, honey, it's all ready. Hank, will ya pull out a chair for Esther, please?" she said, gesturing toward a seat at the long dining table.

The chairs had been arranged close together at one end, meant to create a sense of warmth and intimacy. But she knew what that meant. Hank was going to be right next to her.

Her mind jumped to Ian, likely sitting at Clarissa's table at that very moment, having his supper. The thought made Esther's pulse stutter.

He wouldn't like this. Not one bit.

Lord help me, she thought, forcing herself to breathe as Hank settled in beside her. The heat of his body radiated too close.

And, as if things couldn't get worse, he was wearing cologne— a nice one.

The scent wrapped around her, making his presence feel even closer. She worried it might linger on her clothes afterward, like some sort of evidence.

Hank Calhoun was an opportunist, and he knew this was his one shot.

Margie Mae had made sure of that, letting slip that Esther was getting married soon. And Hank? He wasn't about to waste his chance. His aunt had planted a seed—suggesting that if Esther realized she had other options, she just might reconsider.

Ralph, seated at the other side of the table, tried to keep the conversation going.

"Hank, how's that job at the bank? I hear you're movin' up the ladder real quick."

Hank smiled, smooth as ever.

"Yes, I just bought myself a nice little house. There's a garden spot you can see from the back porch—perfect for children to run around."

Then, leaning in close, his breath warm against her ear, he murmured, "Just needs a female's touch."

Esther forced a polite smile, but inside, her thoughts spun like a windstorm.

No.

Ian would not like this.

She could almost see it—his jaw tightening, his knuckles turning white, fighting the urge to wring Hank's neck.

As the meal stretched on, a deep unease settled in her stomach, and not just from the company. Her morning sickness, stubborn and lingering, now crept into the evening. She took slow, steady breaths, hoping the pallor of her face wouldn't give her away.

Hank, however, didn't let up. He was more charming than she remembered. More attractive too—something playful in the way he moved, like he knew exactly what he was doing.

When she reached for her spoon, he did the same, his hand brushing against hers, lingering just a second too long.

Esther pulled away, but before she could dwell on it, Margie Mae appeared with small bowls of ice cream, setting one in front of her.

The coolness was a relief, settling her stomach enough that she could at least rejoin the conversation, pretending, for now, that everything was fine.

After dinner, she stood to help clean up, as was the custom at Clarissa's, but Ralph and Margie Mae waved her off.

"Go on outside," Ralph said, wiping his hands on a napkin. "It's cooler out there. The house has gotten too warm."

Esther hesitated. She could excuse herself, retreat to the guest room. Say she wasn't feeling well.

But Ralph had already mentioned playing a game of Rummy later—a game she'd never played but had heard about plenty. If she disappeared now, it would seem rude.

Hank, wasting no time, rested a hand on the small of her back and guided her toward the veranda.

His touch felt different than Ian's.

Though this wasn't her fault, guilt stirred inside her, bubbling up like something she couldn't quite push down. Sitting on a porch with this man—being here—felt wrong, like some small betrayal.

When Hank motioned toward the swing, Esther declined politely.

"I prefer to stand. Been sittin' a lot today."

Light raindrops began to fall, soft and scattered, speckling the wooden steps as she stared into the darkness, unsure of what to say.

Hank stood too close, the nearness unsettling. He lifted an arm, resting it against a tall pillar, his body at ease as he watched the storm roll in.

"Looks like the heavens are gonna pour down for us," he murmured, his voice low, thoughtful. Then he turned to her, his expression shifting.

More serious now.

"Esther, I know you're gettin' married," he said, his eyes soft but heavy with something else.

She looked up at him, her mind knotting with unease.

If he knew she was getting married, why had he flirted so boldly at dinner?

"But I'm not a man to give up so easily," he continued, his jaw tightening with quiet determination.

"A girl can always change her mind." A slow grin curved his lips, almost teasing. "Given the right reasons."

She gave a hesitant smile, hoping to let him down gently.

"I've given him my word, Hank. That has to mean somethin'."

She wanted to believe that would be enough, that he'd hear it and step back. There was something almost endearing about the way he wore his heart on his sleeve.

But her words didn't have the effect she'd hoped.

Hank inched closer, boxing her in against the railing. "But Esther," he said, his voice dipping lower, steady and sure, "ya didn't say it's because you don't like me. And I can appreciate you wantin' to keep your word with that fella, but I want you to know somethin'— somethin' I told my friend all those years ago when I saw you in Larkin with your grandmother."

Despite his closeness, she stayed still, curiosity flickering beneath her expression. That memory of Larkin—she held it tenderly in her heart.

"I can see you wanna hear it," he went on, watching her closely, "so I'm gonna tell ya."

He leaned in just slightly, his voice smooth.

"I told my friend that you were the girl I was gonna marry. That I'd marry you, or no one else."

His eyes bore into hers, searching, willing her to get caught in them.

Esther resisted.

Her mind scrambled for the right words, for something to defuse the moment without making it worse.

"I would've loved to hear that back then," she muttered, being honest. "But that was then, and I reckon a lot has changed since."

"No," Hank said firmly. "Not really."

His gaze didn't waver.

"I'd marry you today if I thought it was the only way to get ya."

Esther gave a startled laugh, the absurdity of it catching her off guard. He had to be teasing, playing some kind of game.

But the look on Hank's face said otherwise.

He was serious.

My God, she thought. What is wrong with these eager men?

Her suspicions had been right—Hank wanted to pull her into matrimony even faster than Ian.

He stepped in closer, his voice dipping into something smoother, something coaxing.

"Esther, shouldn't ya at least try kissin' me first before you turn me down?"

His hand slid to her waist.

Esther couldn't deny the flutter it caused—the way her pulse skipped, then slammed hard in her chest. But it wasn't just the newness of the moment, or the way it caught her off guard.

It was the sharp warning beneath it.

Because she knew, without a doubt, that if Ian ever did this with another woman, she could never forgive him.

The trust would be shattered forever.

With that thought, she shoved Hank away, her brows furrowed as she wrestled with the intoxication of his closeness.

"I'm gonna marry Ian Huggler next week," she said, her voice firm.

She wanted Hank to hear it, to let it settle, to crush any hope still lingering in his mind.

But he wasn't ready to accept it.

He leaned in again, but Esther planted a hand against his chest, keeping him at arm's length.

"Do ya love him?" Hank asked, his voice low, searching. He pinned her with his gaze, looking for something—some crack, some hesitation.

"That's... that's none of yer business, Hank," Esther shot back.

She realized too late that it wasn't the best answer, but flustered as she was, it was the only one she had.

Hank smirked. He wasn't done.

"What if I drove up to see you before ya get married," he pressed, testing her resolve, "so we could talk a little more."

Esther didn't need to think twice. The image of Ian's reaction was already clear in her imagination.

"Don't do that! Please! I'd hate to see ya with a busted lip—or worse," she said quickly. "Ian don't like ya, and he says you don't like him either. Yer just lookin' fer trouble, and Ian—well, he's a big man."

Hank laughed, shrugging off the warning like it didn't matter, like Ian didn't intimidate him in the slightest.

"Well, he's right—I don't like him," Hank admitted, his voice dripping with confidence. "But the reason is simple. He's got somethin' I want, and he knows I'm comin' for it." Hank paused, eyes narrowing. "He knows I could take it... but I'm runnin' out of time."

Esther's stomach tightened.

"Hank, ya need to let me go—whatever idea ya got in yer head. I'm gonna make that man my husband," she said, her voice sharp with finality.

Just then, the front door rattled.

Hank stepped back as Ralph pushed onto the porch, a deck of cards in his hand.

Esther seized the moment.

She slipped past Hank, muttering, "Excuse me," before rushing back inside.

She wanted to leave. To run home. To put all this behind her. But the rain was coming down harder now, trapping her in place.

Inside, she made her way to the bathroom, her hands trembling slightly as she gripped the edges of the sink and stared into the mirror.

Her reflection met her gaze—flushed cheeks, wide eyes, frustration, and disbelief written all over her face.

"How did such a crazy thing just happen?" she whispered.

She looked deeper into her own eyes, past the confusion, into something solid.

Then, softly, just for herself, she whispered, "Ain't nothin' gonna stop me from marryin' ya, Ian Huggler. Not that fella out there. No one."

Her hand drifted to her belly, a quiet reminder she wasn't alone on this journey. Their baby was with her.

The thought steadied her, strengthened her.

She drew in a breath, shoulders squaring as the certainty settled deep. Then, without hesitation, she left the bathroom and stepped back onto the porch, rejoining Margie Mae, Ralph, and Hank.

Chapter 26: Finding the Way Back

The road winding up to the Old Reed Estate felt long and drawn out, twisting its way deeper into the foothills. The sun hung low in the sky, casting golden light across the valley as Ralph drove cautiously, unfamiliar with the rugged terrain.

In the back seat, Esther sat quietly while Margie Mae chatted in the front, still glowing over their accomplishment—a perfectly tailored, ready-to-wear outfit for Esther's wedding day. It had taken longer than expected, leaving Esther with a lingering guilt for not returning earlier as she'd promised Ian.

The car swayed along the winding road, and her stomach lurched. She swallowed hard, pressing a hand to her belly. Hoping the nausea would pass, she cracked the window, letting the warm breeze wash over her face.

Mercifully, the sickness subsided just as they neared Clarissa's house. Excitement bubbled in her chest as they drove up the driveway—she was home. Ian and the children were just beyond that front door, and two days away had felt far too long.

Margie Mae, who had never been up to the estate, let out a breath of surprise as the orchard stretched out before them, rows of trees sloping into the land beyond. Then her gaze lifted to the house itself, her brows raising.

"My goodness," she murmured. "This place is much grander than I thought it would be."

Ralph gave a low whistle. "Mighty impressive."

Few folks ventured up this way, despite knowing the estate's location and history. The Reed family had once owned a good portion of the valley where Larkin now stood.

Clarissa's history, however, was more tangled. Town gossip had long claimed she was Jeppson Reed's daughter—a rumor so persistent it had settled into near fact, despite no one actually asking her about it. While that connection lent her an air of legitimacy, whispers of her illegitimate birth and her mother's race still lingered in certain circles.

Margie Mae had always tried to keep an open mind—more so than Ralph, perhaps, who remained set in his ways despite being married to such a strong-willed wife. That open mind, rare for the time, had forged a quiet kinship between her and Esther—one that didn't need to be spoken aloud, just quietly understood.

The three of them climbed out of the car, Esther carefully cradling her outfit, now wrapped in paper after she and Margie Mae had pressed it to perfection. As her eyes scanned the property, she searched for Ian's old Ford—only to feel a small pang of disappointment when it wasn't parked near the barn.

Brushing the thought aside, she led Margie Mae and Ralph up the wooden steps. The house stood before her, warm and familiar. Home.

Ralph reached for the door and pushed it open as Esther stepped inside, calling out, "Aunt Clarissa?"

Clarissa appeared almost instantly, her smile warm. "Welcome, welcome, y'all. Come sit down, and let me get you some refreshments."

"Well, thank ya, Miss Clarissa," Margie Mae said, settling onto the sofa, her gaze sweeping across the room. Ralph hesitated before finally joining her, quieter than usual.

"I'm just gonna run this to my room," Esther said, lifting the wrapped package slightly. "Won't be but a minute."

She disappeared down the hallway, leaving Margie Mae and Ralph alone in the front room.

Ralph exhaled, looking around. "It's much nicer than I thought."

"I always wondered what it looked like," Margie Mae admitted, eyes lingering on the high ceilings, the carefully arranged furniture. "Such a fine old house—reckon it's twice the size of ours."

She admired the long drapes, their fabric old but well cared for, the colors rich without any fading.

"Honey," Ralph said, shaking his head, "it's much bigger than that."

Just then, a dull thump came from the front door, followed by the sound of it opening and closing.

They both turned as heavy footsteps crossed the hardwood planks of the hallway.

Ian walked in with broad strides, almost moving past the sitting room without noticing them. Then he stopped short, turning back around, his tall frame filling the entryway.

Margie Mae gasped softly, startled by the sheer presence of the man before her. For a moment, she sat there, taking him in. She had nearly forgotten just how ruggedly handsome he was. In that moment, she understood exactly why her young friend was so eager to marry the man.

A broad grin spread across Ian's face.

"Well, hello there. Appreciate you bringing Esther home," he said warmly.

Ralph stood, crossing the room to shake Ian's hand. "How ya doin' this fine evenin'?"

"Better now," Ian replied, playful and easy. "Now that you've brought my girl home. Where's she at?" He glanced toward the hallway.

"Said she'd be down in a bit," Margie Mae chimed in from the couch.

Ian turned toward her, remembering his manners.

"Well, aren't you looking nice today, Margie Mae," he said, flashing an even bigger grin. "New dress?"

Margie Mae beamed. "Well, actually, it's almost new—only wore it a couple times," she admitted, clearly enjoying the attention.

Ian laid on the charm, even catching Ralph rolling his eyes.

"The color yellow suits you," he said sincerely. "Matches your personality and hair—bright and sunny."

Margie Mae practically glowed.

"I swear, Ian, yer such a flirt. No wonder that girl wants to be Mrs. Huggler," she teased as he winked—almost enough to make her heart flutter.

And she wasn't exaggerating—she'd never seen Ian's full charisma at work before, and she was pretty sure Esther liked it more than she let on.

Sensing his wife's obvious schoolgirl attraction to the tall man, Ralph cleared his throat and changed the subject.

"How far up the hill does the Old Reed Estate go? Way up into the hills?" he asked, steering the conversation toward something that interested him, trying to get a better sense of the vast land still tied to the property.

Ian considered it. "Well, quite a ways, to the big river, but beyond that is Primm land. Belongs to Esther, I suppose."

He rubbed the back of his neck, the weight of it settling in. He hadn't really thought about the legal side of it—how the land would have to be claimed, how one day it would be theirs—just another complicated thing to figure out.

"Nice land up there?" Ralph asked.

Before Ian could answer, Clarissa entered the room, carrying glasses of iced tea and a plate of her famous molasses cookies.

The sight of the treats brought a twinkle to Margie Mae's eyes. "Thank you, Miss Clarissa. Ya gonna join us?" she asked, hoping to bond a little with the older woman.

"I'd love to, darlin', but I've got a pot I'm tendin' on the stove," Clarissa said. "Please, stay as long as ya like. Yer welcome to join us for supper if you'd like."

Before Margie Mae could answer, Ralph cut in.

"Oh, no, we couldn't. Don't wanna drive down that hill in the dark," he said, earning a sharp, disappointed look from his wife.

Margie Mae sighed, but masked her displeasure. "Maybe next time. Sure hate to miss out."

Clarissa, catching the disappointment, offered a smile. "Well, ya both are invited to join us on Friday afternoon when the bride and groom return from gettin' hitched. We're havin' just a little get-together, and I'm sure Esther would love it if you came—she speaks very highly of ya both." She glanced at Ian for support.

"Please come," Ian added, directing his words at Margie Mae, knowing she'd see to it that they showed up.

Before Ralph could protest, Margie Mae answered with certainty. "We'll be here."

A creak on the stairs caught Ian's ear, and he turned toward the hall, his face lighting up with expectation. He hoped it was Esther. He had missed her terribly. Though he had kept himself busy, he didn't like knowing she wasn't safely asleep in her room at Clarissa's.

"Esther," he called, his deep voice warm, steady, carrying down the hallway.

She turned the corner, her heart skipping at the sight of him. His happiness radiated as she ran toward him, launching herself into his outstretched arms.

He caught her easily, wrapping her up and lifting her off the ground, spinning her as she laughed loudly, her arms locking around his neck.

"Do you know how much I missed you?" he murmured, excitement spilling over before he kissed her, full and unreserved, right there in front of everyone.

Clarissa, passing by on her way to the kitchen, chuckled at the display.

"Okay, okay—let me down," Esther insisted playfully, aware of their audience.

"No," Ian teased, though he set her down gently, his arms still firm around her waist.

Margie Mae grinned. "Well, aren't ya two the cutest things ever. I think he might like you just an itty bit, girl."

Ian leaned down, meeting Esther's eyes. "A little bit, maybe," he teased.

Esther looked up at him lovingly, brushing her fingers along his cheek. Now and then, Ian showed his boyish side, and this was one of those times.

As much as she wanted to stay wrapped up in him, they had company, and Esther knew she ought to act proper. Slowly, she worked her way out of his embrace, tugging him along with her into the sitting room.

Ralph, still curious about the land, asked, "What's the acreage of the orchard? Looks like a lot of trees."

Ian's tone shifted, slipping into something more businesslike.

"Almost eight acres, but we're planning on adding to that."

"Good Lord, that's a lot of peaches," Ralph said. He couldn't help but wonder if Clarissa had more money than he'd assumed, not realizing the realities of a working orchard.

"And you pick all of those?" Margie Mae asked, her voice laced with disbelief.

Ian chuckled. "No, no. We bring in commercial pickers." He glanced at Esther warmly. "Though this pretty lady here can pick her fair share."

"I wouldn't mind seein' a little of it," Ralph admitted, curiosity winning over.

Ian hesitated for only a second before nodding, though truth be told, he'd rather steal a few minutes alone with Esther.

"Well, come on, I'll take you out there. You girls want to come? Fair warning—I just flooded part of it, and you might get a little muddy."

That was enough to discourage Margie Mae, who shook her head.

"Maybe we'll just visit with Clarissa in the kitchen," she said, glancing at Esther for agreement.

Ian led Ralph toward the door, his arm sweeping in invitation. The moment they stepped outside, Ralph launched into more questions—about the volume of fruit, the number of trees, the operation of it all.

As Ian was about to shut the door behind him, he leaned back inside, catching Esther's gaze. His lips parted in a quiet whisper. "I love you."

She smiled, watching him disappear.

Margie Mae sighed as she followed Esther into the kitchen, carrying her glass of tea and a cookie. "He really is cuter than I remembered," she mused.

Clarissa welcomed the company as the women settled into small talk, but Esther found herself distracted. Her eyes kept drifting to the window, watching for the men to return.

She knew Ian loved talking about trees with anyone willing to listen. She only hoped he wasn't talking Ralph's ear off—though it was good for them to bond. And maybe, if all went well, Ralph would bring Margie Mae around more often.

After a good half hour, Esther saw the men making their way back up the gravel drive. Ralph appeared winded but satisfied, having enjoyed the tour. Ian's expression, however, was unreadable, and she thought he looked tired.

"Wanna go join 'em?" Esther asked Margie Mae, motioning toward the men outside.

Margie Mae nodded, bidding Clarissa farewell before following Esther down the back steps.

As the men approached, Ralph called out, still catching his breath.

"We best get goin', Margie Mae. Sun'll be settin' soon."

Esther smiled as Ian neared, looking forward to having a moment alone with him. The children were likely still at Mitzy's, which meant they had his house to themselves.

But when she tried to catch his eye, he turned his head away.

It was almost like he was avoiding her.

Her steps slowed, an uneasy feeling creeping in.

By the time Margie Mae and Ralph reached their car, Esther could see it plainly—the coldness in Ian's expression.

What's wrong with him?

The thought stuck as she hugged Margie Mae goodbye. "Thank ya for helpin' me. I had a wonderful time visitin' ya," Esther said.

"Next time I see ya, girl, ya gonna be a married woman," Margie Mae said with a wink.

Ian gave a polite nod, though his eyes told a different story.

Esther eyed him carefully, her stomach twisting. Something had changed.

Ralph offered his own goodbye, thanking Ian for the tour before opening Margie Mae's door and shutting it with purpose. His steps quickened as he glanced at the dimming horizon.

Esther and Ian stood side by side, watching as the car backed down the drive.

She turned to him, still searching his face. Maybe he was just hungry.

"Ya need somethin' to eat?" Esther asked, nudging closer, trying to pull a smile from him.

"I'm not hungry," he said curtly.

Then, without warning, he turned and headed back the way he had come, his steps quick and deliberate.

Her stomach dropped.

He was mad.

Mad at her.

She hurried after him, reaching for his arm to stop him, to pull him back. But he resisted, his muscles taut beneath her grip.

"Ian, where ya goin'?" she called after him.

He didn't answer.

Her mind scrambled for answers. What could have caused this?

And then, just as she caught up to him, he stopped abruptly.

He turned, his icy stare slicing through her like a knife.

"So, you had dinner with good ol' Hank last night," he said, his voice sharp. "How was that?"

Esther sucked in a breath, her heart thudding.

She hadn't planned on telling him, never to mention it ever.

"Is that why you wanted to stay there two days, Esther?" Ian's voice rose, rough-edged, disbelief laced with anger. "My God, we're days away from getting married!"

"Ian…" she began, trying to reach him, but he was fuming.

"Will you please look at me?" she begged.

He turned, but when he spoke, his voice carried an edge of accusation.

"Esther, I know you find him attractive. I saw it in your smile at the diner. Are you going to tell me otherwise?"

She hesitated. She couldn't deny the truth outright—it might give her away. Instead, she steadied herself and said, "Ian, I didn't know he was going to be there. I swear on the life of our unborn child."

The moment the words left her lips, silence fell between them.

For Ian, hearing her say it out loud—our child—momentarily relaxed the anger that had overtaken him.

For Esther, it made everything feel more fragile. She scrambled for more words, knowing full well how delicate the situation had become. She could only imagine how furious she'd be if their roles were reversed.

There was no choice but to tell the truth—or at least the part that mattered most.

"I ain't gonna start off by lyin' to ya, Ian. I respect ya too much for that. But just know, I didn't know anythin' 'bout this 'fore goin' over there."

Ian's gaze bore into hers, unflinching.

"You can't tell me he isn't trying to pursue you, Esther, because I can see it in your face. And you like it," he stated flatly.

She didn't answer right away.

And Ian sighed deeply, as if trying to accept something he couldn't—and never would.

She lifted her chin. "Not gonna lie to you about that either. Yer right. He likes me an awful lot, Ian."

She saw the way his jaw tensed, his entire demeanor tightening once more.

"I told him I was gonna marry ya. Nothin' he could do about it," she added, hoping it would ease the storm inside him.

He exhaled sharply, shaking his head.

"Esther, you tell me something… and I'll accept it, even if you lie to me, because I want to marry you and can't stop myself. But…"

He hesitated, the words catching in his throat. He didn't want to ask. Didn't want to know. But he had to.

"Did… you let him kiss you?" he asked bluntly, his eyes locked onto hers—firm, unyielding—waiting for the answer that could break him.

"No! I didn't, Ian. I promise ya, I'd never do that to ya, ever," she said, her voice rising, insulted. "Ya think I have no self-control, no decency? Like I can't control myself?"

"Did he try to?" Ian pressed, his voice edged with frustration. He could sense there was more.

She took a deep breath, wrestling with the temptation to lie and be done with it. But Ian deserved the truth, so she spoke, her voice as composed as she could muster.

"He tried, Ian. Said he wanted to marry me. Said if he couldn't, he didn't want nobody else. Told me he was fixin' to come up here, talk me outta marryin' ya. But I told him you'd beat him senseless if he did."

"You weren't lying," Ian muttered, his hands on his hips, his anger simmering beneath his features.

"Hank's a bold fella, persistent, too. But Ian, I've made up my mind. I'm gonna be Esther Huggler on Friday, and I ain't got no other plans but that."

Ian stood there, his eyes scanning her face, trying to trust her words. She looked sincere, but his anger hadn't fully abated.

When Ralph had casually mentioned during their walk that, at dinner the night before, Margie Mae's nephew, Hank, had said he was buying a house, it hit Ian hard, filling him with jealousy.

He had missed Esther desperately, and the wait to make her his wife was becoming unbearable. And knowing now that Hank lurked in the shadows, waiting for his chance to make a move, only made his suspicion burn hot.

Esther stepped closer to him. "Yer gonna have to trust me like I be trustin' ya. Hank can offer me whatever he wants, but it ain't gonna work. If I could've found a way to get ya to come fer me last night, I would've. But we don't have a phone here, and I ain't never even used one 'fore," she said with a small smile, hoping to lift his mood.

But Ian's expression remained firm, his face unmoved.

"Esther, why can't you just tell me that you love me?" Ian asked, frustrated. "You realize it'd make me feel better, but you just won't say it. We're going to the courthouse in three days, and you've never said the words to me. Don't you think you should?"

"Please, Ian," she begged, despite knowing how desperate he was to hear them, words she could whisper to herself but couldn't bring to her lips when it mattered most.

"No, Esther. I want you to say it. I don't want to get married until you can," he said, his tone cutting. "I'll call off our wedding until you do," he threatened.

Esther's heart pounded, his ultimatum forcing her to confront the weight of her silence. It didn't matter that she knew he was right. He was pushing her beyond what she could do. It felt like standing at the edge of a cliff, with Ian demanding she leap and learn to fly.

Even though it wasn't the same, it felt like it—that familiar sick pressure Clive had put on her, his voice still haunting her to this day.

Tears welled in her eyes as she tried to force the words to her tongue. She opened her mouth, willing herself to push them out. *Just say them. Tell him ya love him. Do it*, she urged herself.

But the words refused to reveal themselves. Even as tears spilled over, she pushed harder, almost holding her breath under his gaze.

Ian's eyes softened, but his voice still carried a plea.

"Please, just say it… just tell me so I know I'm not a fool. Esther, they're only three simple words."

The more he begged, the farther the words fled. She could only shake her head, her voice emerging as a trembling whisper.

"I… can't…"

Then she crumbled.

"Clive… he broke 'em."

Ian's breath hitched.

"But I'm not your cousin. I would never hurt you like that," he said, his voice gentle now, aching.

"Like what, Ian?" Her voice wavered, something deep inside her cracking wide open. "Ya think it's so easy, but ya don't know what it was like. How my…" She faltered, then let the words pour out in a trembling rush. "Like how my face was shoved into a mattress? His disgusting body layin' on me—pushin' his way inside me? Ya wanna know what he'd say to me the whole time?"

She choked as she answered her own question.

"He'd say, 'Esther, tell me ya love me. Tell me ya love me,' over and over. He'd keep sayin' it, tryin' to pull it out of me the entire time."

Ian's face twisted as he saw how far he'd pushed her. His jealousy, his fear—they had taken him someplace he never meant to go. Now, the vivid image of Clive raping the woman he was going to marry was seared in his mind, and he couldn't bear it.

"I see it, Esther. I get it. Please stop. Please stop telling me," Ian said as he reached for her, desperate to fix the chasm he'd created.

But it wasn't so easy for her to stop. The dam had broken, and there was no holding it back.

"I was so happy comin' home to see ya," she cried. "I just wanted to see ya, have your arms around me. And now yer tellin' me you don't wanna marry me 'cause I can't say somethin'? Well, Ian Huggler, there's a lotta things I can't say right, and ya done known that about me from the start, I reckon," she said, as she turned away from him.

The long, darkening road down the hill to the orchard stretched before her, beckoning her away from the turmoil behind. She began walking toward it, leaving Ian standing there alone.

An evening breeze swept through the orchard, cooling the May air as it blew past her. Esther didn't look back. She just kept walking forward.

She wasn't trying to make him chase her.

She was just tired.

Tired of trying to fix herself.

Tired of trying to justify why she was the way she was.

The voices returned—those old, cruel companions whispering for her to stop trying. They told her that the scared young girl in the cornfield still lived inside her, that she always would.

Clive had stolen her voice then, and now his words echoed in her mind, ghostly whispers curling around her like a shadow she could never outrun.

She tried to remember what she had done after—after he had pinned her to the ground, ripping away her virginity.

She remembered the taste of dirt on her tongue, the grit clinging to her teeth as her face pressed into the soil.

How he had stood above her, fixing his pants like nothing had happened, his breath heavy.

How he had even offered her a hand.

Told her to get up.

And then, he had left her there.

Her body bleeding. Her spirit fractured.

No one had ever explained to her what a man's body could do.

But she had learned quickly.

It wasn't just the physical pain that hurt—it was the memory of having smiled at him earlier that day.

Clive had said something funny, and she had laughed.

Had that been enough to encourage him?

She remembered the way he had tried to hold her gaze, how she had refused to meet his eyes.

Gran had left her at the church that afternoon, running an errand into town. A cluster of parishioners stood near the entrance, chatting, but Esther had been too shy to join them, finding refuge in the back.

Clive had seized the opportunity.

Approaching her with his characteristic slickness, he insisted she accompany him, claiming he had something to show her inside his house.

She knew better but was too timid to say no outright. And Gran had warned her never to go inside his home.

So, she had pretended to follow him, then darted away, slipping into the safety of the tall corn, thinking she could lose him there.

She had been wrong.

He had followed, almost as if it were a game.

A game between a grown man and a terrified girl.

A game between a hunter and his prey.

Esther stopped walking. Her mind snapped back to the present, the nightmarish thoughts retreating as she realized she had made her way down the entire hill.

Around her, the golden hues of dusk had deepened into twilight as the sounds of night had begun—night birds calling in the distance, the rustling of unseen creatures stirring in the shadows.

She stood still, unsure where to go next. To her left, the fields stretched wide beneath the deepening twilight.

Behind her, someone approached—quiet, deliberate footsteps drawing nearer.

Her tears had dried, but the sting of Ian's rejection still clung to her, raw, causing a dull ache in the middle of her chest.

"Esther," Ian's voice broke the hush of the evening. "Where are you going?" His tone was soft, careful.

"I don't rightly know," she mumbled in a steady but distant voice. "Don't really ever know where I am at… most times… maybe 'cept when ya standin' next to me."

"It's the same for me, too," he admitted.

Silence settled between them. Neither moved, both watching the last traces of light slip from the sky.

"I'm not going to make you say it, Esther," he finally said. "While I want them—hell, I'm starving for those words to slip from your lips—I'm going to believe they're there somewhere. I'll try to wait for you to give them to me.

He took a deep breath, his thoughts settling as the edges of his anger faded.

Esther could hear it now, what was truly behind his bruised words.

"Ian, I know why ya so cross." Her eyes met his, steady and certain. "Ya think I'm gonna go far away, disappear on ya. Like I ain't got no say in it."

He didn't answer, but his expression shifted.

"But I have a choice," she went on. "Ya told me that yerself." She paused for a breath. "And I choose you."

He exhaled, the tension easing from his shoulders. He heard her—really heard her. And she was telling him, plain and clear, that she wouldn't leave.

Not for another man.

Not for some far-off horizon.

Not lost to the unknown abyss.

A small grin tugged at his lips.

"Did you really tell Hank I'd beat him up?" he asked, slightly amused.

Esther managed a faint smile.

"You know I'm not really a violent man, right?" he added, thinking back to how Clive had pushed him to an extreme he usually avoided. Ian prided himself on using words until there was no other choice.

She gave a small, knowing smile.

"Hmm. I've seen ya get pretty angry 'fore, Ian."

He chuckled softly, stepping closer.

"Trust me, Esther, I've had to hold my tongue more times than I wanted to—avoiding fights even when I'd have been in the right."

His face grew more serious as he continued.

"You don't know the vile things people said to Adeline and me when we moved here. We thought we had it bad in New York, but here—" he exhaled. "There were times I had to fight with every bit of myself not to turn into something uglier than the words they used. I held back for her peace, tried to grow a thick skin like she had."

Esther stepped closer, lifting her hand and tapping a finger against his thick brow.

"Don't know about skin, but ya got a thick skull."

His lips twitched with amusement.

"Of that, I'm certain. It's a German trait."

Raising his hand, he cupped her cheek, his palm warm against her skin.

"Why do you have to be so darn pretty?" he asked. "Makes being mad at you damn near impossible."

"Ya think our baby's gonna look like me, or you?" she asked, her thoughts drifting toward the little life growing inside her.

Hearing her say that—talk as if she was looking toward their future—it settled something deep inside him. His grin widened as he spoke.

"You'd better hope it doesn't have my big head."

"I want 'im to have yer nice smile, maybe a dimple or two," she said, gazing up at him.

And just like that, the tension between them melted away. They were back—back to the warmth and the softness that always seemed to pull them home.

He wrapped his arms around her waist, drawing her into a firm embrace. The warmth of his body pressed against hers.

"Mitzy's probably brought the kids back already," he murmured, a touch of regret in his voice. "Guess we missed our chance for some time, just us two."

She nestled in his arms, tilted her chin up toward him, her voice full of quiet certainty. "But Ian," she said, "ain't we got a whole life waitin' on us?"

Chapter 27: Roses and Smiles

Preparations for Ian and Esther's wedding luncheon were well underway, with less than two days to go. It was just a small gathering of local friends and neighbors—forty people at most—but you'd have thought Clarissa was feeding a thousand the way she planned, her spread reflecting the grandeur of her taste.

There hadn't been a proper celebration at the Old Reed Estate in years, not since Obadiah's seventieth birthday—the year before he passed. When Ian and Adeline had wed, they had married quietly in New York, without so much as a toast. So, in Clarissa's eyes, this was her moment to host the kind of gathering she had never gotten to before—and for two people she couldn't love more if she tried.

"Esther, did Ian ever find those old lanterns like I asked? I don't want it getting' dark while folks are still eating," Clarissa said, sliding a pan of dainty butter cookies into the oven.

"Abram said he thought they were up in the attic of his house… or maybe he said the barn, I ain't actually sure," Esther admitted as she wiped the table down with a wet cloth. "But he and Ian headed that way."

Clarissa huffed, shaking her head. "Why'd it take both of 'em? They needa hold each other's hands?"

Despite the joke, her anxiety lingered. Food was a sacred thing to her—people leaving her table hungry was an offense Clarissa couldn't abide.

"I swear, Mama Clarissa, yer more worried than I am," Esther said, pausing as she smiled at the woman who had given her so much. "Don't ya need a rest? Ya been goin' all day."

Clarissa returned the warm expression, but she wasn't about to stop. She leaned over, pulling a heavy metal baking dish from a deep cupboard.

"Now don't ya go sweet talkin' me with that 'Mama' stuff," she warned, though the warmth in her voice betrayed her. "Even though ya know I love hearin' it." She set the dish down with a sharp clink. "When those boys get back, I'm gonna give them a few choice words and kick 'em right in their hind ends. I've got plenty more for them to do."

Esther just laughed, knowing full well Clarissa might actually swat at them if they took too long.

"Honey, did ya get the linens on the line? I swear, it best not rain on Friday. We should be ready to move everythin' inside, if need be," the older woman fretted, glancing out the window.

"I already took 'em in," Esther reassured her. "Ironed two so far."

The patter of hurried steps down the front hall broke the busy rhythm of the kitchen.

Rebecca burst into the room, her eyes filled with urgency. "There's someone here," she announced.

Esther barely had time to process the information before Clarissa waved a hand. "That'll be some of the neighbors bringin' extra chairs. Esther, tell them to leave 'em on the porch."

But Rebecca shook her head. "I don't think he's a neighbor."

Esther's brow furrowed as she pulled off her apron. "Hmm," she muttered, heading toward the front door with Rebecca.

Before they could even get halfway down the hallway, Benjamin appeared. "The fella out there told me to come get you," he said.

"Me?" Esther asked, stepping outside and pushing past a large hanging fern that blocked part of her view of the driveway.

And then she saw him.

Leaning against a sleek, newer model car, a bouquet of red flowers in his hand, he was dressed as sharp as ever.

Hank Calhoun had kept his promise.

Esther's stomach dropped.

"Good hell, are ya kiddin' me?" she muttered, her pulse jumping to her throat.

She turned sharply to Rebecca and Benjamin. "You two stay here. And I mean it," she warned, her voice firm.

Taking a breath, she stepped off the porch.

Hank was already watching her, smiling too big, like he didn't care one bit that she was obviously annoyed.

"Now, I know ya told me not to come up here," he started, voice smooth as ever, "but you ain't gonna stop me. I'm not that easy to get rid of." His grin widened. "And I don't have much time, since yer dead set on gettin' married come Friday."

He lifted the flowers toward her. "These're for you—might make ya not so mad at me."

Esther folded her arms. "Ya need to leave, Hank. Now." She pointed toward his car. "Get in and go. Please. I'm beggin' ya."

Hank barely blinked. "I made up my mind. And ya need to hear me out." His gaze didn't waver as he added, "You want me to leave? Then take a walk with me first."

He held out the flowers again.

Esther glanced over her shoulder and noticed the children watching them. She turned back to Hank, her voice firm.

"They're nice and all, but I ain't gonna take those from ya. Put 'em back in your car."

Turning to the children, she instructed, "I want ya to go inside." But they didn't move from their spot, curiosity evident in their eyes.

"I mean it, I'll be in a bit," she added, but they didn't budge.

Hank seized the moment, raising the flowers again. "Oh, it's going to take longer than a bit, maybe half an hour. Don't ya remember ya promised me a walk?"

Frustration crept into Esther's voice. "Hank, I'm tryin' real hard to be nice and all, not be rude 'cause ya Margie Mae's kin, but for the love of God, please go. And I ain't promised ya nothin'.'"

He stepped closer.

"You really think I'm that easy to shoo off, lovie?" he said, winking.

"Please stop," she pleaded as he advanced, extending the flowers toward her again.

"At least just take these. Would be a shame to waste them—cost a pretty penny," he coaxed, inching nearer.

Desperation colored her voice. "If I do, will ya leave? 'Cause the man I'm gonna marry is gonna be drivin' up that driveway any minute, and I don't want you two to run into each other."

Hank's confidence didn't waver. "Good, I would like to have a talk with him, too."

"Well, ya might not get the chance to talk. Remember I told ya, he didn't like ya much," she warned.

Acting on impulse—and more out of desperation than anything else—Esther decided she needed to stop being so nice, to be more direct.

Without thinking too much, she snatched the flowers from Hank's hand and turned toward his car. She reached for the passenger door, only to find it locked. Her face flushed with frustration.

"You wanna go for a drive?" Hank asked, figuring that'd be a better idea anyway.

"No," she replied, rounding the car and heading toward the driver's side. But before she could open the door, Hank grabbed her wrist.

"Now, don't you think about throwin' them flowers in there," he warned, his grin never wavering.

"I'm tryin' to send ya home," she said, tugging against his grip, "and I don't want 'em."

But Hank was stronger than she expected, and he held on tight.

"Tell me you love this Ian fella," Hank said, his tone suddenly serious. "And I'll let ya go."

Esther let out a sharp laugh. "Ha! I ain't never gonna tell no man I love 'em."

"Esther," Hank said, still holding her arm, "you're gonna tell me you love me."

She pulled harder, her frustration growing.

"Hank, I swear to God, let me go! If I can't tell the fella I'm gonna marry that, I sure as hell ain't gonna tell you." She shot back, panic rising in her chest.

She stretched her arm, reaching for the door handle, pulling at it with everything she had.

"Esther, just get in the car with me. Stop being so damn stubborn. I'm just asking for a few minutes of yer time," Hank coaxed, thinking she was on the verge of giving in.

But she wasn't.

She tried again to throw the flowers inside, but Hank yanked her away, dragging her farther from the car. It was like a tug-of-war— Esther straining to break free, but he just laughed, his grip refusing to loosen.

"I sure do like that spit and fire of yers, Esther," Hank said, his voice amused as he tugged her away from the door again.

Her heart raced. Was he really going to force her to get in the car? Was he going to make her walk with him if she didn't want to?

Then, just as her frustration reached its peak, a low rumble rolled up the drive.

She didn't have to look. She knew the sound of that truck by heart—the soft growl of its engine, the way it eased over gravel like it had every right to be there.

And sure enough, Ian's blue truck pulled in, its bumper nearly brushing Hank's car.

Esther didn't even have time to acknowledge him. Her focus was on breaking free from Hank's grip—worried about the appearance of it.

The flowers had long lost their shape, now wilted and hanging loosely in her hand, the petals scraping the ground with each twist of her wrist.

Ian was out of the truck in a heartbeat, not even bothering to shut the door. Abram followed closely behind, his eyes flicking nervously between Ian and Hank, unsure of what might happen next.

"Going somewhere, Esther?" Ian's voice was low, his gaze fixed firmly on Hank.

"Yes, she is," Hank answered, his grip tight on Esther's wrist. "She's goin' for a walk with me." He held her firmly in place, his exasperation clear.

"No, I'm not, Hank. Lemme go," Esther managed, looking up at Ian, a slight relief registering as their eyes met.

"Don't beat him up, Ian. He's Margie's nephew," she pleaded, struggling again against Hank's hold.

In a burst of frustration, she threw the flowers directly in Hank's face.

Ian's expression remained serious, but his calm now felt unnerving. There was something different about him—this must be the fighting Ian Esther hadn't seen before.

"She asked you to let her go," Ian said, his voice steady, hands on his hips, knuckles flexing in quiet readiness. "Might be in your best interest if you do."

"I'm not hurting her," Hank said with a grin, glancing at Esther as though he was the one in control.

"And ya know she isn't in love with you, right?" Hank added, his smile widening as though he were delivering devastating news. "I asked her, and she can't even say it."

But Ian only laughed—a deep, hearty sound, rich with amusement—that made Hank pause.

Uncrossing his arms, Ian leaned back slightly, resting a hand on his stomach, as if Hank's words were a joke.

"Just let her go, boy. You're embarrassing yourself." Ian's tone was mocking, the words tossed out like an insult as he added, "Why would she mess with the likes of you?"

Bewildered, Esther stared at Ian.

Who the hell was this man?

She had expected him to come charging in, tearing Hank apart the way she'd imagined, even though she didn't want him to. Instead, he was standing there, calm and collected, watching it all unfold.

And it made her angry. Hank still held her, and she was weary of his grip. She twisted her wrist hard, trying with all her might to free herself.

"Let me go! I don't like ya, Hank!" she shouted, staring directly at him, desperate to make him believe her.

"I really don't think she likes you," Ian said, his smile never faltering as he glanced at Hank, while Esther shot him a scowl.

"Esther, all you have to do is ask me to free you from him, and I'll do it," Ian teased, his tone playful, as if he enjoyed the game of toying with her.

"But you told me not to hurt him," he said, his voice full of mock sweetness.

Hank, however, wasn't about to let his ego be shaken so easily by Ian's mental games.

"Like an old man like you could. Why don't ya go back to the field you're plowin'?" Hank shot back, trying to get under Ian's skin.

"Well, son…" Ian replied, still wearing a cool demeanor, "I think Esther likes her fields plowed properly—something you wouldn't know anything about."

"God, Ian," Esther muttered, her patience gone.

Hank, clearly catching the innuendo in Ian's words, turned to Esther, his voice edged with indignation.

"You let him talk to you like that? Not treat you like a lady?" he asked, his grip tightening as he held onto her.

Esther's eyes met Ian's, frustration etched into every feature of her face—but he just gave her a playful wink in return.

By now, Abram, seeing that Ian was having his fun with Hank, leaned casually against the truck, watching the exchange like it was some kind of sport.

Still hoping for a peaceful resolution, Esther tried the sweet approach, knowing it might provoke Ian just a bit, but growing more irritated with his cocky attitude.

"Listen, Hank," she said, her tone turning syrupy sweet. "It was nice of ya to come up here. And had I met you last year," she made sure Ian heard the "last year" part loud and clear, "well, who knows, I might've taken that walk with ya. But, despite that man over there bein' much too old fer me, I'm still gonna marry him. Now, let go of me. I'm askin' kindly. And go on home. Find yerself a nice little girl to sit on that back porch with ya." She flashed him a sweet smile, hoping to charm him into letting her go.

"I just can't, sorry, Esther. It's not too late, and I don't want no other girl sittin' on my porch but you. And you're right, he's way too old for you. Don't you want a man who can buy you nice things, maybe a piece of property you can call your own?"

Ian chuckled again, unfazed by the conversation unfolding.

"Hey, Hank," he called, gesturing toward the Blue Hollow Hills with a lazy sweep of his arm. "Esther already owns some property. That entire range is hers. You might want to offer her a little something more. I think she looks bored with you."

Esther had no idea what Ian was talking about, and her wrist was throbbing. It didn't seem to matter to either of the men—they both carried on without a care that she was in distress.

So, taking matters into her own hands, she turned sharply to Hank, stepping closer, her gaze fixed and steely-eyed.

"I said, let go. Now let go. I mean it—I'm done playin' with ya," she demanded, her voice low but firm.

But Hank didn't flinch. He just found it amusing—almost cute.

"You need help yet, Esther?" Ian called out, his tone relaxed, unbothered.

"NO!" she snapped back at him. "Hank's gonna let me go any second now," she added, the sharpness of her voice betraying her frustration.

"After our walk, I will," Hank smiled, undeterred. "Just take a walk with me."

"I ain't gonna walk with ya. I've already told ya that," she barked, her patience running thin.

"Aww, you should go on a nice little walk with him, Esther," Ian mused from where he stood.

She whipped her head around to face Ian. "Will ya shut up, Ian! Ya ain't makin' this any easier."

"I'm done," she added. And she was. She had tried every avenue, but still worried Ian might actually cause bodily harm to Hank. So, she decided to commit the violence herself, confronting Hank with a resurgence of strength.

She lifted her arm—the one Hank was gripping, her hand slightly pale from the lack of blood—and, without warning, leaned over and sank her teeth into his hand, biting down hard.

Abram couldn't help but laugh, watching the total scene unfold like some kind of circus.

"Fella, you should just let go," Abram said, chuckling loudly as he exchanged an amused glance with Ian.

But Hank was slow to release, like he needed to prove he could tame her.

"Ain't gonna hurt me," he muttered, though she was certainly doing just that—her teeth digging in, pushing him to the edge of letting go.

And the pain got the best of him. He grabbed her by the hair, trying to pry her off.

With that, Ian's voice rang out, firm and commanding.

"You're done!" He moved in. "Let go of her now!" His voice boomed, filled with authority.

But Esther didn't release her grip, her teeth still clenched tight because Hank refused to let go of her hand.

"She's still biting me," Hank said, almost perplexed by her aggressive behavior.

Hank noticed that Ian was moving in with prowess—his humor gone—and he began to falter.

"I said no more," Ian demanded, nearly within reach of them now. Finally, Hank forcefully released Esther's hand, letting her fall to the ground in an attempt to stop her from biting him.

"I'm so sorry," Hank muttered, as though he had no choice but to acknowledge that he was out of line.

But Ian was no longer amused. Seeing Esther on the ground stirred something in him. He was at her side in a second, offering his hand to help her up.

"Now leave, as she asked," Ian said, his voice edged with restraint, trying to keep his composure.

"I came up here for a walk, and I'm not going until I get one," Hank demanded, as stubborn as ever.

"Well, I'll tell you what," Ian replied, his humor slipping back in despite his sharp tone. "I'm kind of busy preparing for a wedding, but I'll go on one with you if you really want."

Esther, taking her chance to get away, moved quickly toward Abram by the truck, a cutting glance directed at both Ian and Hank.

"I'm not gonna let her marry you," Hank muttered, brushing against Ian like he was looking for a fight.

"You're a pesky fella, aren't you?" Ian shot back. "Can't get a hint to save your life. My girl literally bit you, and you're still standing here thinking she's got it bad for you. Let me tell you something—she's not that shy. If she liked you, I guarantee she would've let you know."

Hank's face twitched, the words sinking in, and for a brief moment, Ian almost felt bad for him. The truth was beginning to land.

"She did let me know," Hank replied, trying to hold onto his determination, though it was slipping.

"What—a smile or two? It was a smile, and a girl's smile can mean nothing more than she's happy," Ian said, his tone softening, like he was trying to teach him an important life lesson.

Ian's words didn't just land on Hank—they sank into Esther, too. Sometimes, a smile was just that—a smile. It didn't mean anything more, and it wasn't her fault, not now, not with Clive.

Hank stood there for a moment, pondering Ian's words. Finally, he sighed, his voice low. "Can I say goodbye to her?"

"Nope," Ian said firmly. "She's had enough."

Esther, still standing close to Abram, rubbed her wrist, refusing to look at either of them.

"I don't want to give up," Hank said, desperately trying to make eye contact with Esther. "I thought maybe I could change your mind, but I guess you've made it up. Miss Primm. I meant what I said." He sighed again, his voice heavy. "If I can't have you, I won't marry anyone else. If you ever change your mind, you know where to find me."

"Really?" Ian said, his tone steady but with an edge. "I'm trying to be nice, but don't be waiting around. I'm healthy, and despite being a few years older, I plan on sticking around for a long time."

"I can't leave," Hank muttered, shaking his head in resignation.

"Yes, you can. We just talked about this," Ian replied, his patience thinning.

"No," Hank pointed toward the truck. "You're parked behind me. How am I supposed to get out?"

"Oh, right," Ian said, glancing over at Abram. "Will you move the truck?"

"Sure thing," Abram answered, springing into action. He moved around the old Ford, jumping in and reversing just enough to give Hank room to pull out.

"Well, Hank, this has been nice, but we're kind of busy," Ian said, extending his hand as if to wrap things up.

Hank, almost by reflex, shook Ian's hand, still trying to hold onto whatever shred of dignity he had left.

Ian gave him a friendly pat on the shoulder, a gesture that left Esther even more perplexed. She couldn't understand it. Didn't Ian hate him? Now he was treating him like they were friends.

Hank gave Esther one last, sad, lingering look before climbing into his car.

Ian stood in the same spot, watching as Hank's car slowly backed up the driveway, his face still bearing that oddly pleasant look.

Once Hank was gone, Ian walked toward Esther, a playful glint in his eye.

"Much too old for me, really?" he teased, his voice light.

"I like my fields plowed?" she echoed, her voice flat. "That the best ya got?"

Ian broke into a loud laugh, stepping closer to her and lightly resting his arms over her shoulders.

"Esther, you bit him hard. I saw the mark on his hand. Might've even drawn a little blood. You're kind of mean."

"I was savin' his life," she insisted.

"Guess you're right. Better a wildcat bite than a bear swipe," Ian added with a wide grin.

"Really, a bear? I'm just a lil' wildcat, and yer a big bear?" she said, almost insulted.

"Yes, darling," he replied, grinning even wider as she smacked his chest hard.

"Ya just stood there, not doin' anything, lettin' him twist my arm," she said, still bothered by the whole altercation, if that was what you could even call it.

"Aww, you weren't hurt," Ian said confidently.

"How do ya know that? It did hurt," she said, adamant.

He leaned back, looking her in the eyes, but with a more thoughtful expression.

"Esther, you kicked the doctor when you got your blood drawn. You've changed. If Hank—whoever—had really hurt you, you would've let him have it. And the second I thought he got too rough, I stopped it."

He paused, glancing toward the porch where Rebecca and Benjamin sat on the last step, having witnessed the entire event.

"And Esther, they were watching," he added, a somber look crossing his face.

It was then that it dawned on Esther. The fighting Ian wasn't just strong—he was clever—always thinking ahead, controlling himself, even protecting the young eyes that had seen it all.

Not only was he physically tough, but his mind was far superior to Hank's.

Esther looked up at Ian. "Ya think he'll show up at the courthouse?" she mused.

"Probably," Ian said, teasing. "Maybe he'll bring you more flowers—though I'm not sure you like them." He pointed to the wilted roses, disheveled on the ground.

Esther raised an eyebrow. "You never brought me none, so how do I know?"

Ian chuckled. "You're right, Hank's got one on me there. But I still got the girl, so…" He shrugged, his grin widening. "My charm makes up for it."

But then a worried expression passed over him as he leaned down to look at her again.

"Do you want me to bring you flowers?" he asked, his voice uncertain, as if he had forgotten how to court a girl.

"Naw," she replied, resting her head against his chest. "Why'd I have ya do that? Aunt Clarissa got all these flowers in the world fer me to walk by every day."

"You sure?" Ian asked again, his brow furrowed. Clearly, Hank had been a threat, knowing how to woo a girl, though he struggled to take a hint. It made Ian pause, his thoughts turning to the fact that maybe he hadn't been doing his part—that he could've done more.

It reminded him he shouldn't take Esther's good nature for granted—that she deserved the flowers, or whatever that meant, even if she didn't ask for them or expect them.

Chapter 28: Peach Pie *

T he dress hung on the hook, a quiet promise in blue. Esther stood before it, her breath catching slightly as she traced its silhouette with her eyes. It wasn't just the fabric, the careful stitching, or the way it seemed to wait for her—it was what it meant. The day she'd wear it. The day she'd stand beside Ian as his wife.

To her surprise, the idea had grown inside her, not as something to brace herself for, but as something she wanted. Not just a future laid before her, but one she was eager to claim.

And despite Hank's precarious visit earlier, the rest of the day had gone smoothly as they made preparations. Ian had been unbothered, actually in good spirits, not rattled in the slightest by the morning's events.

He even made the occasional joke about how Esther had no choice but to marry him now—word would surely spread that she had a habit of biting potential suitors, which would inevitably tarnish her reputation.

She was quick to remind him that she'd bitten him at the lake the year before—yet he was still willing to marry her.

"Exactly. Case in point," he said, his grin widening. Then, with a chuckle, he added something about how Germans were used to mean women, and she luckily had one—a rarity in these parts.

Unable to resist a small laugh, Clarissa quickly chastised them, saying they didn't have time to fool around with so much still left to be done, pointing at the last of the ironing Esther needed to finish, making it clear there was no time for nonsense.

Ian mumbled under his breath that the same could be said for Clarissa—just as she came at him with a brisk step, hand raised slightly like she meant to give him a good spank.

"That's enough outta yer sassy mouth," she declared, grinning as she took a swipe at him.

He laughed, dodging at the last second and slipping out the back door before she could land it.

It was a good thing Clarissa had a firm handle on events like these, orchestrating the chaos as everyone hurried to check off the long list of tasks she'd assigned.

Supper that evening had been a rushed affair—at least, that's how it felt to Esther. They ate quickly, then got back to work. The regular chores of the estate still waited, and if it wasn't one thing, it was another. All of it was getting in the way of some much-needed alone time with Ian—the kind that didn't involve work, or company, or keeping their hands to themselves.

And though she had quietly excused herself from study time, eager to soak in the tub—much to Ian's annoyance—she hadn't seen him at all since he left for his house with Rebecca and Benjamin.

Now, after nightfall—with the dark settled in—Esther stood at her small bedroom window, gazing out at the old gray barn.

Her eyes followed Ian as he finished up his evening tasks, unable to resist watching him. He moved back and forth from the truck, carrying crates into the barn, disappearing inside only to return for more.

There was something magnetic about the way he moved—thick muscles flexing—and Esther found herself drawn to it, studying him intently as he worked, his movements seducing her senses.

She thought about how she would only spend one more evening in this room. No more watching him from this old, pained glass with longing, as she had done so many times. Soon, she would sleep at his house as his wife, living there with him and his children.

Clarissa, however, had assured her that this room would always be hers to do with as she wished, knowing she wanted to learn to sew—and that Ian's small clothing hutch was far too cramped for all her things.

Esther imagined keeping her nicer dresses here, treating it like a dressing room—the kind movie stars had in her favorite magazines. Or maybe just a quiet space, a place to slip away when she needed a moment to herself.

Disappointed that Ian had finished at the truck—her entertainment over—Esther wondered how many times last summer she had stolen glances at him. She had always been careful, turning off her lamp so he wouldn't catch her, but she had been more obsessed with him than she cared to admit.

Certain she'd never tire of the way he looked—his rugged body had filled her fantasies more than once.

Thinking about it made her breath catch in her throat.

Despite the distance of the yard between them, she could feel the heat of him, as if pulling her through the glass. It sparked that old, familiar feeling of pure, raw desire—the one the girl she used to be hadn't had a name for.

Just like then, the longing built deep inside her, aching to be released. All she could think about was the feel of his bare skin, the intimacy of being near him, his beautiful body pressing into her own.

Two days. Just two more days, and they'd be married. But the wait, the fake propriety they had to endure, felt unbearable. Pregnant with his child, but sleeping in another home—it was slowly unraveling her, the tension too much to bear. The feeling inside her had built to a precipice, and she didn't know if she could even lie in her own bed tonight, staring at the walls, restless.

They had shared some sweet kisses that day, a few playful touches, but it wasn't enough. Not nearly enough.

She needed to go to him, to feel his firm hands on her, to press herself against him and let the space between them disappear into nothing.

Would he just send her home like he did most nights? Remind her, with that maddening restraint of his, that there was a time for everything? Always promising that once they were married, he'd put her to bed proper-like every night. Maybe even wake her up the same way.

"Esther," Ian had said, his voice loaded with something that didn't need spelling out. "I'm a healthy man, and you have a lot to look forward to... that is, if you want that kind of thing."

And she did want that kind of thing—happily admitting it to herself.

Now, her mind was already plotting an escape, a way to steal just a little more time with him.

At the very least, she could kiss him a bit before he marched her right back to the back door.

Clarissa was already in her bedroom—most likely asleep, Esther reasoned, after a day that had worn her out more than most. She'd run around frantically until bedtime, barely sitting down for dinner. When she retreated to her room, the light had gone off almost immediately. Esther felt confident she was out cold.

So, with that, she quietly pulled off her shoes, taking each one off softly and setting them on the floor. She carefully opened her bedroom door, holding the knob, trying to stifle the squeak the best she could.

On her tiptoes, she crept down the stairs, shifting her weight ever so slightly, step by step. Once in the kitchen, she started toward the screen door, but the partially eaten peach pie she'd made fresh that day caught her eye, a cloth draped over the top.

Ian hadn't even had a chance to try it, having moved on from dinner quickly. Hours later, she was certain he wouldn't turn it down. She had wanted him to taste it, to get his approval, as she thought she'd improved the recipe—adding her own finesse.

With a fork in hand, she grabbed the metal pie dish and slipped outside. The back door clanked louder than she wanted, and she held her breath, hoping Clarissa wouldn't wake as she made her way to the barn.

Her bare feet were almost silent on the dirt path as she approached the large timber structure. It was dimly lit, warm lantern light spilling out from inside—calling her like a beacon. Its solid frame, towering outside, had been built to last, just as it had.

At the door, she paused for a moment. The smell of hay reminded her of the first time Ian and she had lain together there— how it had felt to release even a fraction of the pent-up desire she'd carried for so long, two bodies tangled in the straw, like a secret in the dark of night.

Esther leaned against the frame, watching Ian move around, organizing the crates he had brought in. His shirt hung open, baring his chest. The same body that had lain tightly behind her in the back of his truck bed for an entire night, with nothing between them but skin.

And she had never slept so soundly, never opening her eyes once, despite the coolness of the night. He had kept her warm with his arm tucked over her, as though he wouldn't even let her nightmares reach her while she rested.

Before she could even finish her thought, Ian spoke, breaking the silence.

"I saw you looking at me from the window."

Esther smiled, like she'd been caught, as he continued.

"I was about to throw a rock up at you, try to get you to come out here, but then you turned the light off. Thought maybe you had gone to sleep." His voice was light—glad she hadn't.

She held out the dish, extending it toward him, her smile deepening.

"Ya never tried the pie I made fer ya," she said, eager to see if he'd like it.

"You brought it out here for me?" he said as his eyes brightened. "Boy, you sure are trying to get me to marry you, aren't you?"

She rolled her eyes, handing him the dish as he quickly dug in, leaning against the short tack wall for support. Using it like a table, he took large bites, a smile on his face as he tasted it, pleasing Esther.

Not sure if he was just playing it up, she didn't care. She liked to watch him eat, especially if it was something he wanted, though she often wondered if he even tasted his food, eating so quickly.

Glancing down, Esther noticed a handful of hay scattered on the ground, just out of reach of the old mule. So, she bent down, picking it up, and held it out to the animal—the one that had been with her family for years in the hills.

Ian followed her every move, a glint of amusement in his eyes.

"Esther, I've never thought about this before, but does your old mule have a name?"

"Naw," she said. "I don't think we ever named him. Gran called him a useless beast most days, but I don't think that counts."

Ian's smile turned wry as he thought about it.

"I'll name him Hank, then," he said, his voice steeped in dry humor.

Esther laughed, looking over at him. "Hank? Well, ain't you just the cleverest thing." She shook her head. "Reckon I might could guess where ya done plucked that from."

"You're right, your old mule isn't enough of an ass to be named something like that. Too poor a name for such a fine animal," Ian continued, his smile widening.

He kept sifting through names in his mind as he worked on the pie. Then, his fork suspended mid-air, he proclaimed, "Thunderbolt." He was clearly proud of his choice, thinking it might impart some vigor to the old, weary animal.

Esther laughed. "Ya can't be serious, Ian. How 'bout somethin' like Gus or Buster?"

She tried to reason with him, but he looked far too pleased with himself.

"Nope, sorry, dear, you don't get to pick. You didn't give him a name for way too many years. Thunderbolt it shall be," he said, raising his fork again, as if knighting the animal from where he stood.

"I deem you, Sir Thunderbolt, mighty steed to Lady Esther," he finished, proud of his performance.

"I ain't gonna call him that," she resisted.

"Oh, yes, you are. The name's solid and will stick, just watch," he said, licking his fork.

"Ian?"

"Yes, darling?" he replied.

"You ain't gonna name our children." She wrinkled her nose.

"Hmm," he mused as she returned to picking up pieces of hay.

"Here ya go, Gus," she said with a smirk over her shoulder, as the mule tried to bite the handful she held out, missing most of it and dropping it to the ground.

"See," Ian said, a hint of triumph in his tone. "He doesn't like that name, doesn't respond to it."

Esther bent down again, gathering the fallen hay from the barn floor.

But Ian was no longer thinking about the old mule.

He was enjoying watching the way her body moved—her curves, her softness. And damn, he couldn't resist the way she looked tonight, the way her shapely bum moved as she leaned down—the roundness of it.

He found himself actively fighting the impulse to jump up, pin her against him, and give her a good couple of bumps from the rear.

"I like watching you pick up hay. You've got a nice backside, Esther," he said, not an ounce of bashfulness in him.

She hesitated, then turned to face him, playful indignation written all over her face.

"Well, don't stop," he teased, feigning disappointment.

"Now ya got me all nervous, thinkin' you're watchin' my every move," she said.

"But I am, so you'd be right," he said with a wink.

Returning to the pie dish, Ian shoveled the last scoop into his mouth, taking it in one big bite and swallowing it down with a gulp.

Then, noticing she was still looking at him, he purposefully licked his sticky thumb slowly, watching to see how she would react.

Never taking his eyes off her—locked in tight, his face controlled but charged with intent.

She just smiled nervously as his gaze turned sultry. His eyes were heavy with something as they raked over her—a lust in the way he held his mouth, breathing heavier than he had to.

It felt exciting as the working Ian and the silly Ian had left. Her favorite Ian was staring at her now—the one who liked to give his body to her.

There was a long pause, one that made her heart gallop in her chest, one that let the energy build between them as though he was taking her in, preparing himself.

He liked that she didn't look away, as though she wanted to be burned by the fire in his eyes, wrapped up in his power over her.

His muscular body looked relaxed, despite what was clearly rising in him as he leaned back against the tack wall. He seemed almost cocky, his elbows resting behind him, holding him steady.

"I bet you taste like peach pie," he said in a dark and husky voice.

There was a look in his eyes.

A rawness.

Ian wasn't a shy man, and whatever he was talking and thinking about, he was serious.

Esther laughed nervously.

"Ian, what does that even mean?"

He took his time answering her, smiling slyly, like he knew a secret she didn't.

He enjoyed making her wait a little longer, watching her squirm under his penetrating gaze.

Finally, after he thought he'd tortured her long enough, he said, "You know, darlin', that thing I promised you."

She squinted, still having no idea what that thing was exactly, but her face gave away that she was more than just a little curious.

Not liking her so far from him, he called her over to him with a small flick of a bent finger, not saying anything more.

Like he was pulling her strings, she took small steps toward him, eyeing him, trying to read his expression.

He was hot and hungry inside, and it radiated off him. He looked as though he would devour her, and it was intoxicating, exhilarating.

When she got close enough, he reached out for her waist and pulled her to him, making her fall against him, his steady body catching her.

Startled, she let out a small gasp.

Her body pressed tightly against his, his desire rock hard in his trousers, sending a sharp, almost electric sensation rippling from her core.

His voice came deep and confident, a promise in every syllable as he said, "I want to show you something."

She swallowed hard. He wasn't joking.

His eyes were shadowed in the barn's dim light, his breath growing heavier with each passing moment—anticipation rising through him. She felt it, thrumming between them.

Still leaning against his body, Ian let his rough fingers brush down her bare arm. His mouth hovered just above her ear, and he whispered, plain desire spilling from him, "Do you want me to show you?"

Her breath caught in her throat—her legs struggling to hold her. Nervous? Yes.

But the way Ian sounded, the way his heart slammed beneath his shirt, made it clear he was already struggling to hold back. And that only set her off, dragging her need to the surface, fast and consuming.

She leaned back, her face inches from his, giving him a small nod, yes, unable to resist his invitation.

He smiled—a slow, dangerously handsome grin as something danced in his eyes.

He wasted no time ushering her to stand, rising behind her without delay. His hands reached for an old picnic blanket, as though it had already been all planned in his mind. Next, the lantern, hanging from a hook on a post, was within his firm grip in seconds.

"Come with me," he said, the promise of mystery in his words.

He nodded toward the loft, dragging a hand through his hair— like he was trying to make himself even more irresistible.

"Climb up. Ladder's right there. I'll hand the light up to you."

The blanket was thrown over his shoulder, his eyes tracing her every movement now.

He stood directly behind her as she reached up to grab the side rails and placed her bare foot on a wooden rung. She struggled to balance as she climbed, finding another one with her other foot.

Reining himself in was going to require effort—just the thought of what they were about to do could ignite him instantly, burning too fast before he even had a chance to take his time.

He'd spent way too much time thinking about this, teasing Esther with it for weeks. He bit his lip, the rawness of it settling on his tongue. Ian hoped she would like it, as he was very motivated to offer it to her. Very.

She was a passionate girl—he knew this, hiding it behind her feminine shyness. He had seen it in the way she'd playfully grab his crotch when no one was looking, trying to provoke him, wanting to feel him harden for her. She was testing him, daring him to break. Not that he minded.

Truth was—he'd never had a girl like her before. Esther Primm, the girl from the hills, was wild in a way that kept him teetering at the brink of something thrilling and untamed, holding him there, pushing him further, stripping away his restraint piece by piece. And she did it all with a sweet smile and an innocent expression that only made it worse.

No, life with her—his marriage—would be nothing like what he'd known before.

That thought—her undiluted desire for him—had driven him to the edge most days. And when she walked into the barn, he had felt it again, emanating off her, seeping into his bones.

And this time, it shattered the last of his self-control. Nothing remained.

He was almost surprised he'd lasted this long, having already tasted what she had to offer—most nights left with nothing but his own hand for relief after sending her home.

But tonight, that wouldn't be the case—not with her mere feet from him.

As she reached the top and climbed into the loft, he handed her the lantern, his gaze trailing the way the flickering light danced over her skin, shifting shadows across her oval face. Her long, freshly washed dark hair framed it, spilling around her as if conjured from a dream.

She smiled at him, and the sight of it made his chest ache. God, he loved this beautiful girl, he thought to himself.

The loft was cramped, the low ceiling barely taller than Ian. A few hay bales lay stacked side by side, only one high—the perfect height for a makeshift bed.

He carefully spread the old blanket across them, the fabric rough beneath his fingers.

Esther looked at him, a soft smile forming on her lips. Ian knew she saw it—his quiet plan unfolding before her.

He reached out, grabbing her by the waist, wrapping himself around her—so close, yet not close enough to satisfy what had been building between them for a good long while.

"We're practically married, you know. It's only a technicality," he said, trying to convince himself.

"But not in Clarissa's eyes," Esther said as she shifted slightly.

Ian shook his head playfully before letting out a low growl-like sound as his lips found hers. He gave her a long kiss, his mouth moving hard as he pressed himself against her. When he broke away, he whispered just enough for her to hear, "I've wanted this… wanted you like this."

"Is it really gonna make me say things I don't want to say?" she said as she leaned back suspiciously.

"Maybe," he replied as his hands caressed her hips as if they belonged there.

"Lie down," he instructed in a low voice.

Esther hesitated for a breath, but only a breath, and then she moved, settling herself onto the blanket.

He watched, his eyes tracing the soft curve of her breasts, the way her breath caught as she lay back—like she was waiting for something to happen, unsure but trying to trust him.

He pushed her skirt up, his fingers brushing her thighs, the fabric shifting under his touch. Then, with calculated ease, he pulled her panties down, the coolness of the air grazing her skin.

His shirt came off next, the muscles of his chest flexing in the lantern light, rippling with each movement, every inch of him burning for her.

He stood above her for a moment, watching as she looked up at him, her eyes flickering between uncertainty and want.

"Put your knees up," he instructed, his voice gravelly like it was barely staying in control.

She let out a nervous giggle. There was a shift in her, a tension building as her knees came up slowly, hesitantly.

"You can tell me to stop if you don't like it," he said in a reassuring tone.

Ian leaned down over her body, giving her mouth one last passionate kiss, then moved back, kneeling before her, her legs bent in front of him.

He smiled as he eyed her bare feet, something she was so comfortable with after walking the hills that way most of her life. His hands rubbed over them lightly, examining how her small toes were shaped.

Lifting one of her pretty ankles toward him, he kissed the top of it. His heated breath lingered as he looked up, gauging the reaction on her face.

Ian could tell she was perplexed, wondering if this was what he'd been talking about. Smiling more to himself than to her, he continued.

He extended her leg in the air, keeping it straight with her foot pointed in a gentle arch. His lips moved, softly brushing against her skin, teasing her with a light tickle, slowly kissing up her leg as if it were the sweetest thing he'd ever tasted—trying to draw a response from her body.

But she was too quiet.

Wanting to win her desire, he found himself working harder, each action deliberate, an artistic reflection of the fire burning inside him.

It worked as he felt her shift under his touch, subtle movements that made his own pulse quicken.

With his tongue extended, he traced higher, moving toward her inner thigh, slow and drawn out, hoping to arouse her.

Not wanting to neglect her other leg, he smoothly switched. His eyes locked with hers, capturing her gaze, holding it as he let the passion-drunk want in him paint his face.

He was lost in the moment—Esther could sense it, as though he reveled in the essence of her skin, savoring it like the finest indulgence.

And she understood it. His musky scent, always so intoxicating, stirred something primal inside her, urging her to trace him with her tongue, too. To bite into him as though she were tasting the very core of him.

She felt his hands, his mouth following—roaming over her hip bone, pulling her closer. But he didn't stop.

It was a quiet hunger, each kiss an echo of something more, something fevered and aching.

As his lips traced the delicious curve of her thigh, a shiver ran through her—half enjoyment, half nervousness.

The kisses were slow and deliberate, as if he was painting her skin, claiming her in a silent promise between their bodies.

Her legs were restless, shifting away from him, only to return to the warmth of his tepid breath, her thoughts caught between hesitation and surrender.

Unsure, Esther let her imagination drift toward the place he kept edging toward, wondering if that was his true intention, though the thought seemed utterly absurd.

Did people really do that? she questioned.

She tried to rationalize it, though the sensations he was invoking in her made it hard to think clearly—the impulse strange, and yet undeniably strong.

It felt like the secret he had spoken of… and she couldn't ignore the way her body ached for it.

Her suspicions started to prove true as he inched closer, much closer than before.

His mouth was warm over the hair of her mound as he tried to tempt her.

He held his head there for a moment, just breathing, like he was weighing something in his mind.

But Ian wasn't thinking—he was taking a much-needed pause, letting the searing desire within him cool slightly. The inferno building in his body was growing too quickly, consuming him from the inside out.

And Esther's beautiful body lay wide before him, the body he adored, her unique feminine scent drifting toward his nose, penetrating his senses. He could smell her, the intoxicating wetness, and it made his mouth water—a carnal craving rising within him to taste her, to savor her essence.

Ian slowly lifted his head, waiting until her eyes met his.

With a glazed, almost intoxicated look, he muttered, "I'm going to make love to you with my mouth."

His voice was midnight-rich, heavy with the promise of what was to come—wanting to prepare her.

Esther gasped, holding her breath as his head moved downward, his hands now gripping her thighs in place.

He parted her hair with his nose as he extended the tip of his tongue, sliding it slowly between her lips, dividing them with precision.

She shuddered, her body trembling as he held her easily, his strength commanding.

His tongue moved deeper, working with a desperate urgency, tracing her, tasting her, ingesting her perfume into him with every heated stroke.

Each movement—a silent plea, as if her very scent, her very taste, was the only thing that could satiate him.

And that allure—the kind most gentlemen of his time wouldn't dare to admit they craved, though it pulsed beneath their thoughts like a forbidden dream—undeniable.

With Esther, he knew there would be no judgment, no shame, no scorn for giving in to the fierce hunger that burned between them. She wouldn't think less of him for wanting this, wanting her.

Beneath him, she was shaking, the newness of it, the surprise of it unfurling within her.

She quivered, and the more she did, the deeper his need grew—to devour her, to possess her with his mouth.

He moved closer, his tongue delving hungrily, savoring every velvet ripple, losing himself—drowning willingly in the sweet, wet paradise of her.

His hands gripped her hips firmly, lifting her, guiding her into his rhythm—inviting her to dance with him in a silent, feral language.

And she did. Her body moved in a shy response, self-consciousness fading beneath a rush of thrilling discovery—an excitement she'd never imagined. It carried her willingly into pure sensation.

The more she danced, the deeper he claimed her—his tongue exploring, thrusting with passionate urgency, loving her completely. Worshipping her until she surrendered, trembling beneath the fierce devotion of his mouth.

But the longer he lingered, the harder it became to hold back, his body fully overtaken by a ravenous need.

He wanted her to climax against his tongue, wanted to savor that rare, intoxicating moment.

Though it had been years, Ian remembered that finding release this way wasn't easy for a woman, and he wasn't sure how much longer he could resist the mounting pressure.

So, he returned to her soft, warm outer folds, sweeping his tongue across each delicate edge—gently, deliberately.

He explored, discovering her hidden bud—like a precious jewel placed only for those who truly seek—letting the sensitivity of his tongue guide him.

He drew it softly into his mouth, coaxing it, pulling it further, awakening it fully to him—to his command.

Esther's moans deepened as her hips pulled away from the overwhelming intensity. But her retreat only reassured him of his hold on her desire, now fully captured between his lips.

He stroked her faster, tongue firm and rhythmic, like a small flame from friction—the uninterrupted exactness a woman's body craved.

Her abundant fluid, sweet as ripe peach nectar, fueled him further, driving his passion and focus as he felt her body rise, ready to set her free into blissful ecstasy.

He would do this as long as it took.

Esther knew now—knew exactly what was coming, because he'd brought her there before.

Spark after spark, the flame grew, heat intensifying into a tight, focused beam.

She closed her eyes, lost in the inferno he built for her—pleasure rising so intense it burned through her, sweet and consuming, unlike anything she'd ever known.

Her body seized, the rush taking hold, heart pounding as it gripped her hard, merciless in its possession.

"Ian, I... I," she yelled out, gripping at the elusive words that danced at the edge of her tongue.

Ian refused to stray from the path—fanning the flame relentlessly, driving her higher until she was utterly spent. Until all the pleasure was wrung from her body, leaving nothing behind but the slow, aching aftershocks.

Which it was.

Yet in his mind, he was silently pleading for her to finish the two words she almost spoke. But she couldn't, even with the powerful blaze he had created, it wasn't enough—enough to loosen her tongue and make her say what he so desperately needed to hear.

Finally, Esther eased her grip, thighs relaxing their vise-like hold around his head, her breath heavy, ragged.

She lifted her arms above her head, then slowly lowered them, floating down from the heat that had lifted her higher than ever before, as her heavy eyelids fluttered open to reveal Ian's gaze still fixed on her.

Although his expression showed satisfaction—that he'd accomplished exactly what he'd intended—Ian's own hunger remained unsatisfied, and she could feel it radiating from him.

And Esther's own fire still burned hot, desire unabated, the need to be possessed by him now sharper, more focused.

She moved to sit up, his body still kneeling before her. Guided by an unseen force, her fingers began to undress him, determined to free that part of him she now craved the most.

He watched her, seeing she needed help—her fingers fumbling over a stubborn button.

Unable to wait any longer, he freed his hardness, his pants and boxers slipping to his knees as Esther's gaze settled on him—open, unflinching, stripped of shyness.

She smiled as she took in the sheer size of him, as if she meant to take him down to the root.

With a sweep of her hand, she moved her long hair to the side and sank onto the blanket again, arching slightly, her knees bent, clearly beckoning him closer, her eyes dreamy with anticipation.

But just as Ian moved to lower himself above her, he hesitated. His thoughts shifted, returning to the urge that had brought them here.

He paused, hovering just above her, then lifted himself back up, eyes darkening with intention.

"Turn over," he instructed, voice roughened by desire, guiding her gently. I want you this way. On your knees. Lean over the hay."

A small smile ghosted his lips.

Esther had trusted him thus far. So, she yielded, following his instruction.

As she lowered herself, she felt his rough hands guide her precisely where he wanted her. Once in position, Ian lifted her skirt higher, revealing the smooth, enticing curve of her round bottom, his hands resting on it as he admired the view.

Unable to wait any longer, he confessed sheepishly, "This isn't going to take long, darling."

With that, he eased his length inside her, sliding effortlessly into the smoky heat he'd created moments before. He pressed deeper, filling her completely, pushing farther than his tongue ever could.

She gasped, surrendering to him, feeling the hard expanse of him inside her body—exquisitely sensitive.

Ian tightened his grip on her hips, kneeling behind her as he began to move—slow at first, dragging out each thrust.

He loved watching her like this, loved every detail—her shape, her movement, her scent, her taste, the fire in her, the softness, the fight, the abandon.

He wanted the messy life. Imperfect.

Ian wanted it all. He wanted this woman more than he could have ever imagined.

Heat surged through his veins, his own fire racing higher, his pulse quickening as pleasure gripped him into its firm hold.

His thrusts quickened, friction tightening perfectly around him, drawing earthy groans from deep within his chest—primal sounds matching Esther's.

The beast within his core now unleashed as he surrendered to the pleasure, watching her fingers grip the blanket again, hips rising, dancing against him, a bellow to his furnace.

"What are you doing to me?" he mumbled.

Then, losing all control, he let the flames consume him completely.

He didn't have to hold back anymore, didn't need to hesitate.

Esther's body—already carrying his child—accepted him fully, swallowing him as he spilled himself freely, pouring like molten steel into her warm, willing vessel.

His muscles tightened, emptying himself with rhythmic thrusts, savoring every perfect moment. But even as the pleasure rippled through him, he could tell that this hunger for her would never be satisfied—never fed enough.

Gradually, Ian slowed, feeling a gentle exhaustion creeping over him. His firm grip lingered on her hips, reluctant to let her go, knowing she wanted more, always more.

Breath heavy, he withdrew, bringing Esther down from their shared high. He tapped the blanket as he said, "Let's rest here for a few."

She smiled as she climbed up, making room for him while he haphazardly pulled up his pants without fastening them and then let his long body down with a heavy thud.

"I don't have anything left in me," he said with a playful grin. "You took it all."

Esther cozied up to him, still feeling the hot smoke curling inside her, coaxing her body to continue the dance despite its end. She wasn't disappointed—not in the least, but he had built something else in her—a voracious hunger, knowing she could take more.

"Did you like it?" Ian asked bluntly as he turned to her. "The way I made love to you?" The practical side of him wanted to hear her honest opinion—to know she had enjoyed it.

But the shy girl returned, her face flushing, unwilling to speak about what they had just done. Words almost felt more intimate than the act.

"Ian, ya shouldn't ask me somethin' like that. It ain't proper and…" she chided as she searched for the right words.

He grinned, amused.

"Wait… I'm trying to understand something," he teased. "You'll let me do something like that, not stopping me once. And to be clear, darlin', I think you liked it—but you don't want to talk about it afterward?"

A laugh escaped him as he watched her retreat into modesty.

"Tell me just one thing," he went on. "You can even just nod your head if you'd like. Can I have you like that again?"

He watched her, unsure, trying to act confident. Had it been too much? Had he shocked her, despite the pleasure? Was this going to be a one-time thing?

"I ain't sayin' that, Ian. I just don't wanna talk about it. It makes me feel..." she started, struggling to put it into words.

"Shy?" he offered, trying to help her finish.

"Embarrassed," she corrected him, though even admitting that made her feel exposed.

The truth was, he had just buried his face in the most private part of her body—a place she had barely dared to touch herself. And yet, there he had been, seeing it all, consuming her with a hunger she hadn't known he possessed.

"Well, I'm going to take that as a soft yes," he said as he pulled her tighter to him. "We don't even have to talk about it next time," he added.

Esther smacked him on the arm, a small reassurance that she wasn't mad in the least.

She lay there a moment longer, staring up at the pitched roof, a question lingering in the back of her mind—one she almost wanted to ask, but couldn't quite bring herself to.

Had she actually tasted like peach pie, as he had hoped?

A small giggle slipped from her lips at the thought of it.

"What are you laughing about, darlin'?" he asked as he let out a yawn.

"Aww—nothin'," she said, hoping he wouldn't press for an answer. He didn't—his mind was already onto a new subject.

"Esther," he said in a resolute tone. "I want you to sleep in my bed tonight."

She smiled, liking the way it sounded—liking that he wasn't eager to send her home. But she knew she'd have to return to Clarissa's house. Her aunt was tolerant, but only to a point, and Esther knew better than to test where that line was drawn.

"Don't reckon I can, Ian."

"No, Esther," he quickly shot back firmly, as if he'd already made up his mind. "I'm done having you sleep up there, away from me."

He couldn't stand the thought of it. Not after something so intimate, so binding.

"I want you next to me as I sleep. You're done sleeping in that other room," he added.

She just smiled, hoping he was teasing her—but worried he wasn't.

Ian felt the need to make his point, so he leaned up, shifting onto his elbow, his gaze locking onto hers.

"I'll deal with Clarissa," he said, his expression solid, his intention clear. "She might have something to say, but she'll have to get over it."

"I've waited as long as I can." He went on. "And in my mind, my heart—you're already my wife. A little piece of paper isn't going to make that more real. Hell, the state of Tennessee didn't even recognize my marriage to Addie—acted like it never counted—and Clarissa didn't have a problem with it then."

He shook his head, as if sorting through his own reasoning, letting the words settle between them. "And you're carrying my child. You belong in my house."

"But you were the one always sendin' me home every night. Kickin' me out, marchin' me straight to Mama Clarissa's door like ya were afraid of me," Esther said.

Ian smiled, brushing a wild strand of hair from her face.

"Well, I was trying to get you to marry me. And unless you up and run away, I feel pretty confident you'll go ahead with it," he teased. "Plus, you've got that pretty dress just hanging there, waiting for you to wear it. And I know you can't resist a pretty dress."

"Oh, I'm gonna wear that dress, even if it means marryin' ya to do it," she said with a smile. "But if I stay, how we gonna walk into the kitchen in the mornin'? Lookin' like we got shame smeared all over our faces?"

He laughed at her description, as he literally wiped some of her scent from his face, thinking some of it had even made its way into his nose, permeating his brain.

"We'll walk in and act like we've done nothing wrong," he said, like he was done sneaking around.

"That ain't a good plan," she mumbled, as a tired sigh escaped her.

"I'll figure it out," he said, sitting up and glancing toward the lantern he still needed to retrieve, calling on the last of his energy. "Let's go home, my love. I'm tired."

Ian stood and reached for her, then bent down, picking up her discarded panties—almost handing them to her, but not before playfully bringing them to his face, inhaling deeply.

"Stop that," she said, reaching for them, clearly flustered again.

He just smiled, holding them out of reach as she stretched onto her tiptoes, swiping at them.

"You don't need them. We're sleeping naked tonight," he said as he sidestepped past her, tucking the undergarment deep into his pocket like a prize.

As they left the barn, Ian pulled the big door shut, locking it behind them—all the while keeping his eye on her, making sure she didn't make a beeline for Clarissa's back door.

"You better not run off toward that house," he warned, playfully. "I'll chase you in there and carry you out over my shoulder."

Esther took a few hesitant steps in that direction, just to test him as he cocked his head sharply, watching her like he was daring her to try.

"Are ya sure me goin' to yer house is such a good idea?" she asked, her voice quieter now.

She couldn't believe she was questioning him, but worry tugged at her, thinking about the consequences of her aunt's displeasure. Mama Clarissa would never be harsh or unkind, but her disappointment—now, that stung even worse.

But Ian Huggler had made his decision, and there wasn't a soul alive who could change it—Esther knew this about him.

Ian simply reached out his hand, waiting for her to take it before leading her toward his cottage.

They walked in silence, the night settling around them, until, as they neared the house, he spoke—his voice quiet but firm.

"I want my whole family under one roof. And if Clarissa asks, that's exactly what I'll tell her."

He pushed open the front door, guiding her inside.

As they made their way to his bedroom, Esther let the weight of it sink in.

This would be her life now.

Living with the German man.

She would be his wife—the mother of his children.

His companion.

Chapter 29: The Ring

Ian stood in front of the mirror in his bathroom, tying his tie, dressing for a date at the courthouse in Jasper. The day had come, and here he was, marrying the girl he loved.

He inspected himself in the small, hazy mirror that hung over a pedestal sink. A few wrinkles marked his copper-skinned brow—not a young groom, he thought to himself—but excited, nonetheless.

Grabbing a dab of pomade, he worked to style his newly trimmed hair back, thinking of how Esther liked the way movie star men wore theirs. His beard was neatly trimmed short, though he had offered to shave it.

Esther declined, telling him she was used to his face that way and wanted to marry that man, not some other fella.

He was almost ready—just one last thing before putting on his jacket.

It was time to do something he had been putting off—not out of reluctance, but because of what it meant.

The significance of it.

Esther had never mentioned it, and that had been enough for him to wait.

Until now.

Ian made his way into the living area of his cozy home. His eyes scanned a tall bookshelf until they landed on a box—the one that held small mementos of his life with his wife, Adeline.

A movie ticket.

The first letter he wrote her.

A dried corsage.

He pulled it down, fingers resting against the worn edges, almost feeling the energy of the memories contained within.

With a heavy sigh, he opened the lid and set the box on the edge of the fireplace mantel.

He then lifted his left hand and began pulling off the gold band—the wedding ring he thought he'd die with.

The one he swore he would never take off. The one that had carried the weight of every vow up until then that he'd made.

But that was a different life, a life he no longer had.

The ring didn't slip off easily, and he had to work at it, finally pulling it free. The round shape—lightly bent from years of hard work, the band scratched and worn.

But it didn't belong there anymore.

He was now going to be Esther's husband. She deserved his full and undivided commitment.

He slowly placed the ring into the box, a somberness on his face despite the joy he felt simultaneously.

"Addie, my love, thank you for sharing a large part of your precious life with me," he whispered, his voice cracking as he continued. "I promised you this day would never come, but that was when I could still see you standing before me."

As he looked down at the box, thumbing through the keepsakes, a smile touched his lips—memories flickering to life with each worn piece of the past.

"I would tell you, Addie, that you'd like the girl I'm marrying, but you knew her before I ever did," he said, a small, ironic laugh slipping out. "You loved her long before I could. I hope you're alright with that. Know she loves our children and keeps your beautiful memory alive in their minds."

As Ian closed the lid, a strangely familiar yet odd feeling swept over him—a warmth, a presence, as if he could feel Adeline's happiness wrapping around him.

"Thank you," he whispered.

With that, he set the box back on the top shelf and moved toward the door, grabbing his suit jacket.

Then he hesitated, suddenly remembering.

Hurrying back to his clothing hutch, he reached onto another shelf, fingers brushing against the small box he had nearly forgotten. He tucked it into his pocket, exhaling.

Then he made his way to the front door, knowing that when he returned, he would no longer be just a man—he would be a husband again.

A title he hadn't worn in years. The thought made him smile—it felt natural, like something he was always meant to reclaim, despite not knowing it.

Ian stepped lightly as he walked to Clarissa's house, careful not to dirty or scuff his freshly polished shoes. His dark gray suit—rarely worn—had been pressed by Clarissa, along with the new shirt he'd bought.

Clarissa had done it, despite her displeasure that he had overstepped her wishes by asking Esther to stay in her home until they were married.

The morning before, when they walked into the kitchen, Clarissa's expression showed both frustration and disapproval, even as he attempted to explain it privately.

He had insisted it was all his idea, that he simply hadn't been able to wait any longer.

To this, she had asked if he'd been a naughty boy as a child, the kind who couldn't wait for birthday or Christmas presents—sneaking them out early just to unwrap them and parade them around.

He had replied with a playful grin, "Yes, I'm almost certain I was." He'd hoped a lighthearted response would lessen the blow, but Clarissa just shook her head, knowing her wishes had fallen on deaf ears.

Then he had resorted to begging her not to be cross with them, saying he wanted his unborn baby to sleep in his house, next to him.

That had partially won her over. She knew how much his children meant to him.

She had rolled her eyes, muttering something about how Esther could've just snuck in and pretended nothing had happened—rather than acting proud of the shame.

Ian had reassured her that Esther had wanted to sneak in, but he hadn't let her. That seemed to make Clarissa feel better—at least her niece had held on to some decorum.

And the night before, as Ian and Esther left for evening studies—both knowing she wouldn't return and would stay at his place—Clarissa had pretended not to see them. But later, Esther told him she had heard her grumble something under her breath, something about spoiling their own surprises.

Ian took a deep breath as he stood before Clarissa's front door.

Despite already having "opened his present," as Clarissa had put it, he couldn't imagine feeling any more excited.

The anticipation of seeing Esther, driving to Jasper, and then returning for the party everyone had planned for them—it felt almost dreamlike, as if he were moving through something too good to be real.

He turned the doorknob and stepped inside, his wingtips tapping against the polished wooden floor as he walked down the hallway toward the kitchen.

Rebecca was the first to see him, running up with a smile.

"Papa, you look different," she said sweetly as he picked her up, her small hands wrapping around his face.

"You smell different, too," she added curiously.

"Do I look all right? You think Esther will marry me?" he teased.

Rebecca eyed him sideways, as if she were really sizing him up. Then, squinting, she said, "Yep."

He laughed, squeezing her and growling, "I thought you were going to say something else."

Rebecca giggled, but then quickly turned serious, like she had something important to say.

"I like Esther living with us," she said honestly.

"I do too, sweet girl," he replied with a grin, catching a sharp look from Clarissa as he set Rebecca down.

"Except, I think your aunt is going to miss her," he added, the warmth in his voice softening the words.

Benjamin, who had been polishing his shoes on the floor, stood up.

"Pa, why can't we go with you? I want to see you get married," the young boy asked.

The question broke Ian's heart, his expression revealing the injustice of it despite having already tried to explain.

Not wanting to complicate things further, he simply said, "They don't want to let other people share it with us, so you're going to stay here and help your aunt get ready for the party."

Ian's gaze shifted to Clarissa, who was fully aware of the reason—an ugly injustice, a dark aspect of life in the southern states for Black folk.

The courthouse was segregated.

Any guest they brought with a different skin color, including Ian's own children, would have been forced to sit in the back, in a far-sectioned corner of the building, if they were allowed in at all.

And Ian refused to ever put his children in that position. He avoided any such interactions, attempting to protect them from a society hell-bent on making them feel less than.

No. Absolutely not. He would guard them as long as he could, though he knew a day would come when he no longer would be able to.

When Ian had told Esther it would only be the two of them and explained why, she said she'd be happy shackin' up instead. But Ian knew that wasn't a good idea either.

"Benjamin," Clarissa said as she interrupted Ian's thoughts. "You go up there and be a gentleman and escort Esther down. Tell her her groom is waitin' on her."

With a proud smile, Benjamin stood up, wiping his hands clean. He always took tasks like this seriously, wanting to be the young man who represented his father.

Standing tall, he smiled at Ian before proceeding upstairs to Esther's room, where she was getting ready.

Inside, Esther stood before her mirror, a vanity Clarissa had moved from another room, saying Esther would get more use out of it.

Before her stood a woman dressed in the finest clothing. Ready.

Ready for what lay ahead—a life married to a tall, handsome blond man.

No longer the grubby girl in overalls.

Every hair was in place. Her lips, painted red, were perfectly shaped. Her beautiful Italian leather shoes had been restored to their former glory, polished and strapped securely to her ankles.

A pretty hat with a half veil covered her face, completing the look.

Margie Mae had outdone herself, and despite having invited her nephew for dinner, Esther couldn't hold anything against her friend.

The seams fit with precision, hugging her body like a glove. The darts were placed just right, accentuating her curves.

Esther sighed to herself, unsure of what else she could do. She only hoped Ian would find her attractive, not disappointed in how she looked.

A soft knock at the door drew her attention. She stilled, uncertain who it might be, steadying herself before answering.

"I'm coming," she said softly.

"It's me, Benjamin," a sweet voice called from the hallway. "They told me to come and walk ya down."

Esther's heart swelled at his words. He was such a little gentleman, just like his father—always opening doors for her whenever he had the chance, even after they'd just played rough in the yard and were covered in mud.

"Just a second," she said, grabbing a small matching handbag and stuffing her favorite lipstick inside. She scanned the room one last time before opening the door.

Benjamin stood a few steps back from the entrance, his skinny elbow extended, waiting for Esther to take it.

His eyes lit up when he saw her, a big grin spreading across his boyish face.

"Ya think I be lookin' alright?" she asked nervously, seeking a little reassurance.

The young boy shook his head excitedly. "My pa's gonna like it a lot," he said, his tone earnest.

Calmed by his words, Esther took his arm, letting him lead her to the top of the staircase.

As they came into view, Ian, waiting at the bottom, caught his first glimpse of her.

The early afternoon light settled around her like a halo, outlining her figure as she stepped forward, drawing his focus in an instant.

She was an angel, he thought.

Unreal. Beautiful in perfection.

His chest ached with something else—a father's pride—as he watched his curly-haired son lead her down the stairs, step by step.

And Esther felt it—Ian's powerful gaze lingering on them as they moved toward him.

She had never seen him dressed so fine. Having only seen him in a jacket and slacks, she was taken aback by the full suit and tie, struck by how much he looked like a movie star.

There was a brightness in his light blue eyes that held more than just happiness—it reflected something richer, undeniable, an endless devotion.

When she reached the last couple of steps, Ian extended his hand to her. He held her there for a moment, just looking at her, taking her in.

"My God, Esther," he said, his voice carrying an emotional undercurrent. "How did I get so lucky?"

She just smiled, mesmerized by his sharp appearance and charm.

"Let me see all of it," he said, gently spinning her around. He knew women liked to feel appreciated for their efforts, but selfishly, he wanted to see every detail.

"You are the most beautiful woman I have ever seen," he murmured, and in that moment, he meant every word.

She was.

Like she could have stepped right off the silver screen or out of one of the pricey magazines she liked to flip through.

"Are you sure you want to marry me?" Ian jested, though a small part of him wondered if he was marrying above himself—on beauty alone.

"I gotta wear the dress somewhere," she teased, and he let out a chuckle.

No, he was going to marry this woman.

Just had to get her to Jasper, he thought.

From the kitchen doorway, Clarissa watched, a tear rolling down her cheek as she thought back to the waif-thin girl who had shown up at her back door the year before.

Worn down, beaten thin, barely able to hold herself up—now standing tall, a polished lady.

A sapling grown strong, its canopy full and bearing fruit.

Esther, despite her challenges, had risen above them, earning Ian's affection and devotion.

Equally satisfied, Clarissa shifted her gaze to Ian—the best man she knew. She had watched him move past a grief most couldn't survive, finding purpose again in fatherhood and the land he tended.

She had witnessed him after Esther had been taken away last year—ripped not just from her and the children, but from him as well.

He hadn't taken it well, telling her that Sheriff Ronell was in the wrong, that he could drive right over and bring her back himself.

But Clarissa had begged him not to, not wanting to stir up trouble for her niece—though she knew now she should've let him.

And when the offer to go to New York came from his brother, Ian had left almost too quickly—like a man running from something.

When he returned, Clarissa had seen something different in him—a quiet resolve, like a wind in his sail, steadying him for the course ahead.

The evening that he came to ask if he could court Esther, his resolve had hardened into something else—a steel-edged determination—a man ready to fight for what he wanted. He had already made up his mind.

And what he wanted now stood before him—a pretty bride wanting to call him her husband.

"Well," Clarissa said aloud, thinking the two of them should get going.

But just then, the back kitchen door opened, and Abram and Mitzy walked in, Abram carrying Jeremiah in his arms. Mitzy, already seeing Esther and Ian together, had a disappointed look on her face.

"Y'all couldn't wait fer us? I wanted to see Ian's face when he saw ya, Esther," Mitzy said.

"I have the same expression on my face," Ian said, turning to the pretty Black woman dressed in a green dress.

And he did—the same raw excitement, boyish and charming, utterly endearing.

"Not the same," Mitzy teased.

"Ya want me to go back up, do it all over?" Esther asked, half-teasing, half-serious.

"Could ya?" Mitzy teased back.

Ian just smiled as he lifted Esther's hand to his mouth, pressing a gentlemanly kiss on the back of it. The gesture made Mitzy sigh just a little.

"Miss Primm, will you come with me and become my wife?" he asked, realizing he had never formally put the question before her.

Esther squinted, wrinkling her nose like she had to think about it.

"Ya actually askin' me, 'stead of tellin' me?" she said.

He nodded, feeling a flicker of nervousness, wondering if he'd pushed her into something she might not want. An insecurity crept in as the beautiful woman before him challenged him with her steady gaze.

"Well, like I told ya already, I wanna marry ya real bad, Ian Huggler. Guess ya should take me to the courthouse 'fore I change my mind."

Ian, still holding her hand, lifted it back to his mouth. For a moment, he just looked at her, then said loud enough for everyone to hear, "I'm going to love you for the rest of my life. I promise you this." He sealed the words with a kiss.

"Aww," Mitzy said loudly, as both she and Clarissa teared up. "Thank you for savin' that part fer me."

And with that, Ian led Esther toward the front door, with everyone following them out to send them off to their nuptials.

In the driveway next to the house, polished and cleaned by Abram, was Obadiah's car, waiting for them.

Abram had told Ian it wouldn't be a good omen to start off his married life driving the old work truck—that a lady needed a softer carriage, speaking Ian's language.

Esther gave one last hug to the children, then to Mitzy, even hugging Abram before turning to Clarissa.

"I love you, Mama Clarissa," she said, her smile faltering as she hugged the older woman tightly, tears welling in her eyes.

"Now don't ya go cryin' on yer way to yer weddin'," Clarissa said as tears rolled down her own cheeks. "I love ya, baby, and you is always my baby, even if ya don't live under my roof no more."

Esther pulled back from the hug, trying to put on a happy appearance, though her face betrayed her. Clarissa wiped at her eyes, steadying herself.

"I want ya to be there today," Esther said, unable to deny what truly pained her.

The woman who had done so much for her—sheltered her, shaped her, loved her unconditionally—now couldn't share one of the most important moments of her life.

Clarissa, seeing that she needed to once again put on her shield of strength despite her own heart breaking, said, "Girl, ya know I would if I could. God knows I'd fight hell if I could win, but I can't." Clarissa drew a strong breath, her voice steady as Esther's grief spilled from her eyes.

"I'm gonna be there, my spirit standin' next to y'all," she continued. "My love is strong. Don't pay no mind to those silly rules folks make. Listen here, don't ya shed one more tear."

With a hanky pulled from her apron, she began dabbing at Esther's cheek. "Baby, I can see ya gettin' married in my mind already, ya hear me? Don't even need to be there."

Clarissa looked to Ian, hoping to draw on him for support, only to find him mirroring the same sadness and bitter realization.

"Enough," Clarissa said firmly, shaking off her emotion. "This is a happy day. We got things to get ready fer y'all. People gonna be comin' lookin' fer some vittles."

Esther, trying to pull herself together, hugged Clarissa one last time before Ian opened the car door for her and closed it gently.

With a big grin directed at his children, he waved as he rounded the car and climbed into the driver's side.

"We'll see you all in a couple of hours." His voice echoed with excitement.

He started the engine, then, looking over his shoulder, slowly backed out of the narrow drive.

Inside, Esther watched him, trying to muster a smile as her big eyes still brimmed with emotion. The bittersweet ache of the moment clung to her—the joy of their union shadowed by the absence of those they loved.

Once out on the road, he looked over at her tenderly, gripping her hand with a squeeze.

"Smile, darling. You look too pretty to be sad today. Can't have my girl unhappy on the way to the courthouse—hurts my confidence, you know," he teased, making her smile.

No, despite not having those they cared about with them, he would make the best of it—and make sure she did too. This was their day more than anyone else's.

Chapter 30: The Courthouse

The courthouse sat at the edge of Jasper's square, its pale brick walls glowing faintly in the springtime sun, tall arched windows catching the light like watchful eyes. Built in the 1920s, its two-story classical design still spoke of grandeur, and its broad entrance, worn but proud, held a measured, imposing authority.

The faint scent of ink and old paper drifted from the open door as Ian held it wide for Esther, his other hand resting lightly on her lower back, guiding her in.

She stepped over the threshold cautiously, the soft tap of her polished shoes against the marble floor standing out against the quiet.

Looking around, she took in the hushed stillness of the courthouse, where only a handful of people lingered. Most were there for business—filing deeds, attending hearings—but their purpose felt entirely different from her own.

Her chest tightened as her eyes moved over the room, noting the faces of those seated on wooden benches or standing near the walls.

It didn't take long for those waiting to notice them. Dressed for a special occasion, they drew curious glances and hushed murmurs.

A woman in a faded gingham dress nudged the man beside her, her lips moving in a whisper as she took Esther in from head to toe.

A clerk behind the nearby counter stole a glance, his gaze lingering on Ian's polished shoes and neatly pressed suit.

Esther felt the weight of their stares, her hands fidgeting with the cinched belt at her waist.

Ian, standing tall beside her, seemed entirely unbothered by the attention. His hand stayed firm at her waist, a silent reassurance against the wild beat of her heart—certain he could feel it beneath his touch.

"They can't help but stare at you, darling," he murmured. "You're the prettiest bride they've ever seen."

She glanced up at him, trying to smile through her nerves.

With gentle pressure and a tilt of his head, he guided her to a door marked "Marriage Licenses and Certificates."

"After you, Mrs. Huggler," he said teasingly, as he opened the door.

Inside, the small room was orderly, lined with rows of filing cabinets. A single desk sat near the back, where a middle-aged woman was stationed behind a typewriter. Her glasses perched on the tip of her nose, her sharp eyes flicking up as they entered.

"Afternoon," Ian greeted, his voice polite but direct. "We're here for a marriage license and wedding. We have an appointment."

The clerk didn't respond immediately. Her gaze lingered on them, assessing, before she reached for a form and slid it across the desk along with a pen.

"Y'all need to fill this out and sign at the bottom. Both of ya."

Ian took the paper and pen, leaning over the desk as he began filling out the required information. His handwriting was neat, his pen strokes quick and confident. When he finished, he turned to Esther, sliding the paper toward her.

"Esther," he said, holding the pen out to her. "You just need to mark an X for your name."

Her brow furrowed, lips parting slightly. She could hear the understanding in his tone—the way he'd assumed this was all she could manage. He wasn't judging her—she knew that—but it still stung.

Taking a slow breath, she reached for the pen, her fingers brushing his hand.

"I reckon I can do more'n that," she whispered.

Ian blinked, surprised, his fingers stilled as he looked at her.

Her grip tightened around the pen, and she nodded with a raised brow, giving away just enough to feel clever.

Then she leaned forward, the paper steady beneath her hands, and began to write. Her letters were printed, not cursive—slow and deliberate—but they were hers. Esther Primm.

When she finished, she straightened, pulling her hands back as if to let him see.

His eyes lingered on her name, and a grin pulled at the corners of his mouth.

"You've been practicing," he said, clearly pleased.

She gave him a small shrug, not wanting to draw the clerk's attention. "Didn't wanna look like a fool."

He shook his head. "You've never looked like a fool, Esther. Ever."

Ian then picked up the signed paperwork from the counter, his thumb brushing over the edge of the document as if smoothing it. With one last reassuring look, he slid the papers across the desk toward the clerk.

"Here you go," he said.

The clerk adjusted her glasses and pulled the form closer to inspect it. Her sharp eyes scanned the lines, and after a moment, she gave a small, satisfied nod. Reaching for her stamp, she pressed it firmly against the paper, the sound echoing in the quiet office.

"Looks fine to me," she said, setting the document aside. Then she turned her gaze back to Ian.

"Now, that'll be two dollars for the fee."

Ian's hand went instinctively to his jacket pocket, pulling out his worn leather wallet. He thumbed through a few folded bills, plucking out two crisp ones, and placed them on the counter.

The clerk took the money, folded it, and slid it into a drawer. She jotted something in the ledger, her pen scratching the page.

"All right, you two," she said briskly, snapping the ledger shut. "Now, y'all need a witness to make it official."

Ian froze for a moment, realizing he hadn't planned for this part. His hand found the back of his neck, brushing the edge of his collar as he glanced at Esther, then back at the clerk.

"Witness," he repeated under his breath. "Right."

The clerk raised an eyebrow.

"Yes, sir. Might not be required, but I don't recommend goin' without. Better safe than sorry."

He exhaled sharply through his nose, a flicker of frustration crossing his face. He hadn't forgotten much about today—he'd ironed every detail flat in his mind—but this one thing had slipped through.

His gaze flicked toward the waiting area through the open door.

Seated on a wooden bench near the wall was an older man, his cane leaning against his knee. He had been watching them idly, his weathered face crinkling into a faint smile when Ian's eyes met his.

"Wait here," Ian said before quickly slipping back into the other room. He walked straight up to the man, his voice even but carrying a note of desperation.

"Excuse me, sir," he said. "Would you mind standing as a witness for us? I forgot we should have one, and, well, I want to marry that pretty girl over there today." He motioned to Esther, who stood looking confused.

The man chuckled, his voice raspy but kind.

"Ain't mind a bit. Got nowhere else to be today." He pushed himself up with the aid of his cane and nodded toward Esther. "Kinda looks like my ol' gal Helen on our day. Bet she's gonna be as fine a wife as she was."

Esther smiled, glancing over as Ian thanked the man, his own grin widening. "Much appreciated."

Together, they followed the clerk's instructions to go to the judge's chambers. They moved slowly, ensuring the older gentleman could keep up.

Esther's palm was damp in Ian's firm grasp, and for a moment, she thought she could hear him controlling his breath—like his nerves were creeping up on him, too.

When they arrived at the judge's chambers, they were as understated as the rest of the courthouse—a modest room with paneled walls and shelves crammed with law books. A large oak desk dominated the space, its surface covered with neatly stacked files and a bronze nameplate reading "Judge Matthew Curtis."

The judge, a stout man in his sixties with thinning gray hair and a no-nonsense demeanor, didn't rise as they entered.

Instead, he reached for the paperwork, his sharp eyes briefly scanning Ian and Esther before giving a short nod of approval.

"Ya here fer a weddin'?" he asked, his voice firm but not unkind.

"Yes, sir," Ian replied, handing over the license.

The judge examined the paperwork, lips pressing together in thought as he adjusted his glasses. His keen eyes flicked up toward Esther, lingering on her youthful features.

"Well, Miss Primm," he said, setting the papers down on his desk. "Ya sure you're old enough for this? Ya look like you oughta be in school, not standin' here gettin' married."

Esther stiffened slightly, opening her mouth to respond, but Ian spoke first, his voice calm but carrying an unmistakable edge.

"She's of age, Your Honor," Ian said firmly, his shoulders straightening. "She's twenty-four."

The judge lifted his glasses higher on his nose and leaned back in his chair, as if getting a real good look at them.

"Alright, then. Just makin' sure some pa ain't gonna be comin' after ya tonight, sayin' ya done took his daughter without permission. And I sure as hell ain't lookin' to catch flak for marryin' off a child bride."

A small laugh escaped Esther, imagining how Abram would've been rolling on the floor, unable to breathe after hearing the man.

Ian glanced over at her, catching the amusement dancing in her eyes. She was clearly unbothered by the question—in fact, she almost seemed to be enjoying it. He slid his hand lower along her back, giving it a light squeeze, and shot her a playful, mildly annoyed look in return.

"And you, young lady," the judge added, tilting his head. "Do ya even know this fella's age?"

Clearly, the man took his job seriously—making sure there'd be no wedding day regrets.

Esther blinked and glanced up at Ian, trying to keep her composure.

"He's... well, he's older," she said, not sure what else to say.

"Older," the judge echoed with a faint smirk. "I'll say. Mr. Huggler, how old are ya?"

Ian's mouth twitched, but he answered without hesitation. "Thirty-six."

With a low chuckle, the judge shook his head. "Guess that ain't too bad—still got some use in ya," he remarked. "But if ya both know what ya doin', who am I to judge—other than legally, of course."

Glancing his way, Esther caught a matching smile already painted across Ian's face as he leaned in, his voice low.

"Something tells me Abram's gonna get wind of this."

She nodded, her shoulders relaxing. "I was thinkin' 'bout it," she said.

The judge clapped his hands together, the sound breaking the quiet and drawing their attention.

"Alrighty, then! Let's get it done," he said, his tone lighter now. "Stand right here in front of me, and we'll make it legal."

Ian and Esther moved closer, standing side by side as the judge pushed himself up from his chair and adjusted his stance behind the desk. The older man who had agreed to witness leaned lightly on his cane, watching with a faint grin.

"Miss Primm," the judge began, his tone carrying a mix of formality and Southern charm. "Let's start with you, girlie. Take her by the hands, Mr. Huggler," he said, clearing his throat.

"Do you, Esther Primm, take Mr. Immanuel Wilhelm Huggler to be your lawfully wedded husband?"

Esther felt the power of his words as they settled over her, their weight sobering and real. Her breath caught slightly.

She glanced at Ian, who looked down at her with quiet affection.

"I do," she said, her hands tightening around his.

The judge nodded, satisfied, and continued. "Repeat after me, then. To have and to hold, from this day forward."

"To have-n-hold, from this day forward," Esther repeated, her voice a little shaky.

"For better or worse, for richer or poorer," the judge intoned.

She echoed his words, her gaze flickering to the old man standing witness, his expression knowing—like he understood what those words truly meant.

"In sickness and in health, to love, honor, and obey." The judge's voice slowed on the last words, his eyes flicking to Esther as if testing her resolve.

Esther hesitated, her lips parting, but no sound came. Obey. The word caught in her ears, stirring a flicker of resistance deep inside her.

She looked at Ian, her throat tightening as she caught the faint crease of concern on his brow.

Ian realized too late—he should've asked the judge to leave that part out, especially after seeing her displeased expression and remembering her earlier concerns.

The judge cleared his throat. "Go on now," he urged, though there was no malice in his tone.

Esther straightened, her chin lifting as she leveled Ian with a pointed glare. Her voice, when it came, carried a quiet defiance that surprised even her.

"I reckon most of that," she said, the words both a compromise and a declaration of her will.

The judge paused, his lips twitching into a faint smirk before he nodded. "Close enough."

Beside her, Ian let out a small sigh, not anticipating that hurdle.

The judge turned his attention to Ian, his tone once more taking on a formal weight.

"And now you, Mr. Huggler. Do you take Miss Esther Primm to be your lawfully wedded wife?"

"I do," Ian said without hesitation.

"Repeat after me," the judge said. "To have and to hold, from this day forward."

Ian repeated the words smoothly, his deep voice filling the room with quiet conviction.

"Fer better or worse, fer richer or poorer," the judge continued.

"For better or worse, for richer or poorer," Ian echoed, his gaze never leaving Esther's face.

"In sickness and in health, to love and to cherish," the judge recited, his words deliberate.

"To love and to cherish," Ian repeated, his tone softening.

The judge raised an eyebrow, a pleased smile forming on his lips. "Good enough for me." He cleared his throat. "Now, y'all wanna exchange rings?"

Esther flinched, her fingers twisting nervously. "We don't—"

"Yes, we do," Ian interrupted, pulling his hands away and reaching into his pocket.

A small blue box appeared in his palm.

With a flick of his thumb, he flipped the lid open, revealing two gold bands.

Esther's eyes widened. She hadn't expected a ring at all, let alone one like this.

The smaller band, meant for her, held a delicate diamond nestled in its center, catching the light in a subtle yet striking way.

Her breath caught in her throat, her hands twitching at her sides. "Ian... that's—"

He stepped closer, his voice low, meant only for her. "It's not much, but it's yours. Thought you deserved something a little special."

Her fingers brushed against the soft velvet of the box. The diamond wasn't large—it wasn't ostentatious—but it sparkled, understated yet perfect. Like him. Like them. Something she would have never dreamed of.

"When... when did ya...?" she stammered, her voice barely above a whisper.

Ian's lips curved into a small smile. "Last time we were in Jasper," he explained. "While you were at the diner."

Her eyes snapped up to his, her lips parting as realization washed over her. "But—"

"I'm not a rich man, but I wanted you to know I'll always give you whatever I can—everything I have," he said, his eyes steady on hers. "Figured it was this or some of those hairpins you like," he teased.

Her throat tightened. She pressed a hand against her chest, unable to speak, knowing he had most likely spent what little savings he had—his hard-earned money from New York.

He took her hand in his, fingers warm and strong as he eased the ring onto her delicate finger. The diamond sparkled against her skin, the gold band fitting perfectly.

"Looks even prettier on you than I imagined." There was a flicker of something vulnerable in his tone. "I compared the top of my pinky to your finger," he admitted. "Hoped it'd be the right size."

Esther couldn't take her eyes off it—happiness radiated from her.

"I believe you're supposed to put mine on now," Ian whispered, gently prodding her.

Her fingers trembled as she reached for the second ring.

A stark realization struck—he had removed his other ring. She hadn't wanted to ask him to take it off, thinking it was a part of the man she was marrying.

But here and now, she placed a new gold band on an empty finger.

It settled into place naturally, fitting the groove made by years of wearing another.

It nearly undid her, knowing what it meant for him to have taken off Adeline's promise.

The judge continued again, his tone sincere.

"Let's finish this up then."

He let them turn their focus back to him, Ian now clasping Esther's hands tightly in his.

"By the power vested in me by the state of Tennessee, I now pronounce you husband and wife. Sir—you may kiss your nice little bride," Judge Curtis said, clearly enjoying this part of the ceremony.

The tall German stood still for a moment, simply looking at her, taking in the reality of it. Slowly, he lifted her small half-veil out of the way.

Then, leaning down, he cradled her face in his hands, wanting to relish this moment but knowing they were being watched.

His lips met hers in a kiss that was slow and tender, a promise sealed with more than words.

When he pulled back, his voice was low, filled with quiet pride. "Hello, Mrs. Huggler," he said, the name rolling off his tongue easily.

She blinked up at him, an unexpected rush, akin to relief, as the realization dawned on her.

His name was hers now.

Primm was gone forever, a name that shouldn't have ever been hers in the first place, as it had belonged to her grandfather.

The judge let out a cheerful hum, breaking the moment.

"Congratulations to both of you." He extended his hand toward Ian, who shook it firmly, a large smile breaking across his face.

"Thank you, Judge Curtis," Ian said.

He turned to their witness—the old man still perched in the corner. "And to you, sir. I'm grateful."

The man tipped his head, a sly grin spreading across his face.

"Well, that was worth sittin' for. Y'all are a fine couple, I'll say that much."

He paused, his expression shifting, as if weighing whether to continue. After a moment, he spoke again, his voice shaky but laced with quiet wisdom.

"Hope ya don't mind takin' some advice from an ol' timer, but... always use kind words with yer little gal. Them womenfolk got tender hearts—bruise 'em too easy, and they take a long time to mend."

Ian gave a serious nod.

Esther, still holding Ian's hand, found her voice. "Thank ya kindly, sir."

The old man's grin deepened, her sweet tone warming his face.

The judge handed them a copy of their marriage certificate, folding it neatly before sliding it into an envelope.

"This here's yours. Keep it safe," he said.

Ian tucked it carefully into his jacket pocket, then turned to Esther and offered his arm.

"Well, Mrs. Huggler—ready to crash our own party?" he said with a smile.

Esther slipped her hand into the crook of his elbow, feeling the warmth of his body even through his suit jacket.

They walked back through the quiet halls, the muted sounds of the building falling away behind them as they stepped into the bright May afternoon.

Ian paused on the small steps, taking a deep breath, like a man who had just accomplished something long set in his heart—relieved it had gone as smoothly as it had.

With a sigh, he leaned down to kiss his new wife—a proper kiss, away from the eyes of others. Then, taking her hand once more, he directed her toward the car.

The courthouse was behind them now as they walked side by side down the narrow sidewalk.

"Y'know," she said thoughtfully, "I didn't reckon I'd ever be nobody's wife."

He glanced at her, his expression soft.

"Why's that?"

She hesitated, her words slow, careful.

"Didn't think anyone would want me like that. Gran always made sure I knew that." A truth slipping from her mouth, unintended.

Ian stopped walking and turned to face her fully. He reached for her shoulders, needing her to believe him.

"Esther," he said with conviction. "Those were Primm lies. But you're a Huggler now, and we don't believe such nonsense."

Noticing she needed more convincing, he went on.

"My love," he continued, his breath catching, "I don't know how a man like me gets to end up with someone like you. Maybe God decided to show me a little mercy for once—even though I don't deserve it—giving me the chance to spend my life loving you. But if He messed up… it's too late. I refuse to give you back."

Her breath hitched at the rawness in his voice, the truth of it fighting to settle.

Then he leaned down, tilting her chin so she had to look at him. "I'm gonna take my beautiful wife home now, all right? And, later tonight, I'm gonna show that beautiful woman just how much I like being married to her," he added with a charming grin, dimples and all.

Esther smiled back. "Ya ain't got any more of those secrets, right?" she mused, though part of her wondered if she was missing anything.

He chuckled as they walked toward the old car. "Some things, darlin', you're just gonna have to figure out on your own."

The long road back to Larkin stretched ahead, a dusty ribbon winding through the Tennessee fields. Ian drove with one hand on the wheel, his other resting warm and easy on Esther's leg. Her hand covered his, their fingers brushing lightly with each bump in the road.

Cracked just enough, the windows let in the scent of wildflowers and earth, lifting the edge of Esther's small half-veil—a detail she had insisted on with mock sternness, not wanting to undo the careful styling of her hair, which Ian had found impossible to resist.

For a while, they drove without speaking. The steady hum of the engine filled the space between them, the land slipping past in a gentle, sun-dappled blur.

Outside, the world looked the same.

Yet inside her, it felt as though someone had moved the sun—nothing was where it used to be.

Ian glanced sideways, catching the faraway look on her face.

"You're awfully quiet," he said in a relaxed voice.

"Just thinkin'," she said, readjusting herself on the seat and smoothing the back of her skirt.

"About what?"

She hesitated. "About… what comes next, I reckon."

The words slipped out, barer than she intended, leaving a rawness she couldn't quite tuck away.

Ian's fingers tightened around hers, a firm, steady anchor.

"Next is heading back to the house. Some supper, some cake, and maybe a little dancing—if you're up for it," he said.

She smiled at the idea as she admitted, "I ain't never danced with no one 'fore."

He blinked, surprised, before focusing back on the road.

Of course, she hadn't.

Not with a real man, not ever.

A flicker of anger stirred in him—thinking of what that bastard Clive had stolen, all the little firsts Esther should've had. At least that one remained. Ian gripped the wheel tighter for a beat, forcing the thought away.

Clive Jones didn't get to cast a shadow today. He refused.

"Well," he said lightly, letting warmth return to his tone, "I got a feeling you'll be good at it."

She shot him a suspicious look. "Why's that?"

His mouth curved into a grin. "You got a natural rhythm."

"Ian, I ain't exactly sure what ya mean—but it sounds dirty-like," she said, squinting at him.

He laughed, pure and unrepentant. "That's because it is."

She swatted his arm, laughing despite herself. "Why ya always gotta make things so naughty?"

"We're married now, darling," he said, flashing her a wink before turning his eyes back to the road. "It's only bound to get worse."

Chapter 31: Celebration

As they rounded the last bend, the Old Reed Estate came into view, stately and welcoming. Folks had already gathered, a line of old cars and trucks parked along the roadside near the painted wooden fence. The afternoon sun cast a bright glow over the property, catching the white clapboard of the house and fading the red of the roses climbing the porch.

Pulling into the long, flower-lined drive, Ian eased the car to a stop and shut off the engine.

Neither of them moved at first, savoring the last bit of privacy before joining the waiting crowd.

"Welcome home." Ian glanced at her, a teasing glint in his eye. "Should we just sneak over to our house first? Consummate our marriage?"

Esther huffed playfully, and Ian leaned back with a grin—though he knew he wouldn't have turned her down if she'd said yes.

"Ya think I don't know what that word means, but I do, Ian. And no, I ain't goin' to our party with my hair all messed up and red marks on my neck," she playfully chided.

Not dissuaded easily, he leaned over, his breath warm against her ear—not because anyone else could hear, but because he liked the way she reacted when he did.

"All right, but don't let the party tucker you out. The kids are staying with Clarissa, and I have plans for you."

Then, with a slow and deliberate motion, he slid his hand behind her head, drawing her lips to his, taking the kiss of the girl from the hills—now Mrs. Huggler.

His lips moved slowly, trying not to smear her red lipstick. But just as it started to build, the moment was shattered by the sharp clink of tapping against the window.

He sighed, resting his forehead against hers for a beat before turning to see Benjamin's grinning face pressed eagerly to the glass.

"Pa!" Benjamin shouted, barely containing his excitement. "Y'all are back! Aunt Clarissa says to come to the backyard, quick!"

Rebecca darted out from behind her brother, her tiny hands waving wildly as she bounced on her toes.

"Hurry! There's cake! And music! And people!" she squealed, nearly losing her balance in her excitement.

Ian chuckled, his hand finding its way to Esther's knee.

"Well, guess we've got a welcoming committee," he said.

"I reckon ya right," Esther murmured, pulling a small mirror from her purse to check her appearance.

Before either of them could step out, a crowd had already begun to form around the car. Clarissa stood on the porch, arms on her hips, a big smile on her face, flanked by Abram, Mitzy, and a mix of neighbors and friends.

Congratulations erupted as they stepped from the car, hands waving, voices lifting into the warm spring air.

"Look at that groom!" someone hollered. "Sharp as a tack!"

"And his bride!" another chimed in. "Prettiest thing we ever seen."

Esther smiled tightly, feeling the press of too many hands, too many faces she didn't know.

Clarissa made her way through the throng, her presence and voice commanding as always. She raised a hand, signaling for quiet when she caught the overwhelmed look on her niece's shy face.

"Now, y'all give them a little space! Poor girl just got married— don't smother her!"

The crowd parted slightly, allowing Clarissa to step forward. She carried a small bouquet of white roses tied with a simple ribbon and held it out to Esther.

"Here, baby. I meant to give ya this before y'all left, but I got caught up and done forgot."

Esther's hands shook slightly as she accepted the bouquet, her eyes softening as she looked at Clarissa.

"Thank ya, Mama Clarissa," she said.

Clarissa waved a hand, brushing off the sentiment, though her eyes shone with a motherly pride. "So proud of ya two. Now, Abram! Get that camera and take a nice picture of the happy couple on the front porch."

Abram grinned, the camera already in his hand. "All right, y'all. Miss Clarissa says y'all need a picture, so we better be quick about it," he said, motioning for Ian and Esther to step onto the porch.

Clarissa fussed over them, buttoning the top button of Ian's jacket, pinning a small boutonniere to his lapel, then adjusting Esther's veil.

"Stand up straight, Ian," she muttered, patting his shoulder. "And, Esther, hold that bouquet up proper-like. There ya go."

Ian smirked down at Esther, leaning in as Abram adjusted the camera.

"Have you ever had your picture taken before?" he asked.

Esther hesitated for a split second, then shook her head. "No," she lied, lips curving into a small smile—not counting the ones Clive had taken of her in a drunken stupor.

"Well, you're going to look beautiful in them. And your groom? Well, he's quite the dapper fellow," Ian teased.

Abram called out, "Alright now! Big smiles!" as he adjusted the camera, fingers steady on the controls. The flashbulb fired with a sharp pop, momentarily bathing the porch in bright light and leaving behind a faint metallic scent in the air.

The moment was captured—Esther's pretty smile, Ian's impressive grin, and the delicate bouquet nestled between her hands. The scene, frozen in time, was both modest and beautiful, a testament to the simple joy of their day.

"Perfect," Abram said, lowering the camera. "Now, y'all head around back before the food's gone."

As they made their way to the backyard, the sound of laughter and conversation swelled. Tables stood beneath the shade of towering oaks, draped in checkered cloths and laden with fried chicken, roasted vegetables, biscuits, pies, and cakes.

Children ran barefoot through the grass, and an old phonograph played a lively tune that wove itself into the hum of voices.

Ian's stomach growled audibly as he took in the spread.

"Now, that's a meal fit for a man who just nabbed himself a wife," he said, grinning down. "You hungry?"

Esther shook her head, fingers tightening around the bouquet. "Not really," she murmured.

"You must be kidding," he said, already reaching for her hand to guide her toward the food table. "You need to eat something. I haven't seen you eat much of anything for days."

She didn't argue—what was the use? Ian wouldn't let it go, so she nodded, though a flicker of annoyance passed over her face.

He was always watching, always keeping track of everything— like she was one of the orchard trees he expected to bear fruit.

"Fine," she said, though she wasn't sure he heard her, grabbing a plate and scooping small portions onto it before glancing up at him.

Satisfied, he gave her a quick smile and kissed the top of her head.

"Good girl," he said affectionately.

She sighed and carried her plate over to the table, setting it down just as Ian joined her, having piled his own plate a mile high with food.

He shrugged off his jacket with ease and draped it over the back of his chair. His eyes swept over the spread with obvious appreciation, joy playing across his face.

The air was thick with the rich scents of food, mingling with the fresh green of the grass.

But Esther, after taking longer than she should to remove her hat, only picked at her food. She nibbled the edge of a biscuit, her fork idly pushing vegetables around her plate in a pattern.

Ian, caught up in conversation with a neighbor, didn't notice. His deep laugh carried over the table as he told a story about his children, his voice warm and animated. Esther watched him. He was so calm, so at ease, even in a crowd. How did he make it look so effortless?

As his conversation continued, she quietly slid a piece of fried chicken onto his plate, then a spoonful of sweet potatoes. Her movements were small, deliberate—hoping he wouldn't notice.

He turned back to her after a moment, his plate noticeably fuller than it had been before. Not catching on, he flashed her a warm smile. "Clarissa outdid herself."

Esther hesitated, her fork resting against the table. "It's real nice," she said, barely audible over the surrounding chatter.

"Make sure you eat," he said, giving her knee a gentle squeeze under the table before quickly returning to the discussion he'd left.

Feeling out of place, her gaze flickered across the yard, nerves tightening as strangers approached. What was meant to be a gathering of no more than forty had swelled far beyond that—certain the promise of good food had drawn in more than expected.

Mitzy, noticing the look of distress on Esther's face, stepped in, slipping between her and a particularly chatty woman whose questions had started to feel too personal.

"Best wishes to ya both!" Mitzy said, her tone bright as she wedged herself into the conversation, nearly rude in her interruption. Then, leaning down, she pulled Esther into a hug, whispering in her ear, "Ya look like ya wanna run away somewhere."

"I was thinkin' 'bout it," Esther murmured. "Never met most of these folks 'fore."

"But they all know Clarissa," Mitzy said, laughing as she scanned the crowd, hands settling on her hips. "Somebody's walkin' 'round with Jeremiah, and I ain't seen him in a good long while."

Just then, an old farmer sauntered up to Ian, a wide grin spreading across his rustic face. Without warning, he smacked Ian hard on the back, nearly knocking him into his plate, a roar of laughter spilling out as he leaned in close, drawing a few curious glances.

"Ya better take good care of her, boy," the sly farmer said. "And if ya need advice on what to do wit' ya new bride, ya just let us know. One of us boys'll be happy to explain how all that works."

Ian chuckled, shaking his head with a dry smile.

"Think I've got it figured out, but I appreciate the offer," he said, brushing off the joke.

The old man ruffled Ian's hair like a boy, letting out a rough, booming laugh.

"Well, if ya change your mind, don't be shy! No sense makin' a fool of yaself," he hollered before ambling back into the crowd.

Ian turned back toward Esther, catching her watching the exchange. He combed his hair back into place, a faint smile tugging at his lips.

"Friendly folk, sorry, maybe not in good taste," he said.

She raised an eyebrow, clearly unimpressed with the exchange.

He chuckled, draping his arm over the back of her chair as he grinned down at her.

"Don't worry," he said. "I know exactly what to do. I don't need instructions."

Almost ignoring him, she glanced around again.

"I ain't seen Margie Mae," Esther said, a flicker of disappointment in her voice.

"I'm sure she'll be here," he assured her. "Despite her husband."

Esther frowned slightly. "What does that mean, Ian?"

He hesitated, then shook his head. "Aww, it's nothing." He kept it to himself, knowing Ralph had never seemed comfortable mixing with people who didn't look like him.

"Don't worry, just have a good time," Ian said, though his eyes drifted toward her lunch plate, a realization dawning on him.

"Esther, did you give me your food?" He shook his head, already knowing the answer.

"You did," he remarked, pointing to her plate. "Unless you suddenly eat chicken bones, you did."

"Ian... I just don't feel like eatin' right now. I'll eat somethin' later," she said, knowing she had been caught.

He exhaled, his lips pressing together. He didn't want to fight about it—not here, not today.

But just as he considered saying something more to her about it, his expression shifted, the ease in his face hardening into something serious.

His eyes were fixed on something in the distance.

His brows furrowed, and he stood abruptly, his chair scraping against the ground.

"Excuse me," he murmured, distracted, his hand brushing her shoulder before he moved off into the crowd.

Esther's gaze followed him, unease settling in her chest as she stood, searching for the familiar height of his head.

And then she saw what had drawn him away.

Sheriff Marty Ronell.

The lawman had followed the crowd into the backyard, his figure unmistakable in his dark-brown uniform.

His gait was steady, purposeful, his hat perched low over his face.

Ian was already moving toward him, his strides long and deliberate, intent on finding out the purpose of his visit—knowing it wasn't a social call.

The sheriff's presence always stood out in a crowd.

But it wasn't the sheriff that unsettled her—it was Ian. His easygoing demeanor had vanished, his frame now tense, shoulders squared, his body charged with a quiet intensity.

Her eyes stayed locked on him as he neared the sheriff. Ian wasn't a man who shied away from confrontation, preferring to face it head-on—almost charging at it like a bull.

Esther bit her lower lip as she watched.

When Ian reached him, Sheriff Ronell tipped his hat, a cool but serious demeanor emanating from him.

"Afternoon, Mr. Huggler," he said. "Looks like I'm interruptin' somethin' special."

"Sheriff Ronell. Didn't expect to see you out here. Everything good?"

The sheriff smiled politely, his eyes drifting over the tables and the crowd.

"Looks like congratulations are in order," he said, offering his hand. "Heard you were plannin' on gettin' hitched. Took a little longer than it should, but it's good to see it's done."

Ian shook his hand, his jaw relaxing as he nodded, still guarded.

"Thank you. It's been a good day so far," he said.

Before either could say more, Clarissa appeared, her sharp eyes scanning the two men.

"Well, hello, Sheriff," she greeted him with a welcoming tone. "Now, you best not tell me ya came all the way up here without havin' eaten lunch. Must've heard I was puttin' on a spread," she teased.

The sheriff hesitated, tipping his hat again.

"Can't say that I have, Miss Clarissa, though it smells mighty fine. But I'm actually here to speak to Mr. Huggler, and I see I caught him in the middle of somethin' pretty important," he admitted.

With a hand on her hip, Clarissa's smile widened.

"Then ya best not leave here hungry. Come on now, I'm gonna fix ya a plate. A fed man is always a more reasonable man," she said, casting a knowing glance at Ian, like she was doing him a favor.

The sheriff opened his mouth to protest but thought better of it, nodding instead. "Alright, Miss Clarissa. I won't argue with a good meal."

He turned back to Ian. "What I need to talk to ya about can wait a bit. No sense in turnin' down a determined woman."

Ian's expression lightened as he nodded. "Fair enough. Once Clarissa's offered food, best not test her by refusing."

The sheriff took off his hat, holding it in his hands with a knowing grin. "I reckon that's a battle I'd never win. And to be honest, my wife's got me on some kind of diet. Sent me to work with only a tuna salad sandwich, and this smells a whole heap better."

With that, he gave Ian a firm pat on the shoulder, his eyes following the direction Clarissa had gone.

Just as he was about to head that way, his gaze caught on Esther.

He paused as she walked toward them, her blue dress catching the light, a picture of perfection.

Marty Ronell's expression softened for a moment before he masked it behind his usual polished smile, tucked neatly under his heavy brows.

Esther approached cautiously, her steps slow and hesitant.

"Afternoon," she said politely.

The sheriff tipped his head, smoothing down his mustache as if suddenly aware of his own presence at such an occasion.

"Afternoon, miss—" He corrected himself with a small nod. "Or should I say Mrs. Huggler, that is. Ya are lookin' real pretty today. And congratulations." His words carried an unexpected generosity.

Esther's mouth softened into a hint of a smile, her cheeks lifting as she spoke.

"Kind of ya to say, sir."

Before anything else could be said, Clarissa returned, her voice cutting clean through the awkwardness.

"Found ya a nice spot under a tree. Let's get ya fed before it's all gone." She placed a firm hand on his shoulder, leading him away with a practiced ease.

As the sheriff walked away, Ian caught the fleeting glance he cast toward Esther.

There was something there—perhaps just fondness, maybe attraction—but something unspoken.

The thought sat uncomfortably with Ian, so he pushed it aside.

For now, he returned to Esther's side, draping an arm over her shoulder lazily as the festivities carried on.

Spying someone in the crowd, and knowing it would make her happy, he leaned in.

"I told you she would come," he murmured, directing his gaze toward Margie Mae, who had just arrived.

Esther's eyes lit instantly as she spotted her friend.

Margie Mae and her husband zigzagged toward them, the shopkeeper's hands full of prettily wrapped presents.

Ian was grateful they had come. He knew Margie Mae to be an insistent woman—one who wouldn't let Esther down. She held Esther in both affection and high esteem, something he respected, even if she had encouraged her nephew to pursue his girl.

As Margie Mae approached, her mouth fell open in an exaggerated gasp.

"My lord, girl, you're prettier than I could've imagined!" she declared, her voice carrying with its usual boldness.

Esther laughed, stepping forward to grab Margie Mae by the arm, leaving Ralph standing awkwardly off to the side.

Ian noticed the man's unease and considered offering a bit of hospitality, but paused when Abram stepped in, cutting off his path.

Abram's broad grin and easy stride made it clear he had his own plans for Ralph. Ian, curious about how the storekeeper would handle the situation, decided to hold back and watch.

Beneath his serious demeanor, Ralph seemed polite—stiffly so—but Ian figured a little discomfort might do him some good. Suppressing a big grin, Ian turned on his heel and headed in the opposite direction, leaving Abram to handle things in his own way, as he usually did.

As the afternoon wore on, Marty Ronell found himself on the other side of the yard, leaning casually against the food table, a hefty second plate in hand.

The sounds of the gathering swelled around him—laughter, the clinking of dishes, the occasional shriek of children at play.

He hadn't meant to stay this long, but something about the atmosphere held him. Folks wandered over to talk—some out of obligation, others with the easy warmth of good neighbors.

He didn't mind. It had been a long time since he'd let himself enjoy something as simple as a community gathering—talking to folks instead of warning them.

Still, every so often, his eyes drifted back to Esther as she moved through the crowd with quiet grace, accepting congratulations and warm words.

Marty's chest tightened every time he saw her.

It wasn't just her beauty—it was the undeniable resemblance to his daughter, Fannie Louise. The same eyes, the same delicate features.

But of course, they looked alike. Esther, now Huggler, was his daughter.

And his wife, Lavina, had been waiting for him that evening, the day she had gone to Margie Mae's and met the Primm girl.

It was a name Marty had never mentioned to her—but one his mother had, once.

And like most women, she had remembered it with clarity.

Lavina hadn't even let him step inside the house.

She had rushed him back out onto the hard driveway, her face set in a way that made Marty's stomach drop before she even opened her mouth.

With a bluntness that took even him by surprise, she demanded, "Ya'd tell me if ya had another daughter, right?"

Marty froze, the words hitting him like a freight train. His throat tightened as he stood there, silent and exposed. He didn't need to say a word—she could see the truth plain as day in his eyes.

"Marty," she said again, this time with a frustrated edge that cut deep. "Ya know that girl grew up dirt poor, barely eatin'." Lavina's voice broke, the anger rising as she stepped closer and smacked him hard on the arm.

"Why?" she spat, her words shaking with fury. "Why ya never went and got her? She's ya damn daughter—your blood!"

He couldn't answer. The words wouldn't come. The truth he had buried so deeply sat heavy between them, and all he could do was lower his gaze, his shame too great to face her wrathful, tear-filled eyes.

Lavina fumed, her breath coming fast and shallow as she turned her back on him for a moment, her hands clenched into fists at her sides. Then she turned back, her voice trembling.

"She could've had a life, Marty," she hissed. "A real life—with you. With us."

He had deserved every ounce of her anger, every word she threw at him. And yet, he couldn't find the courage to explain the decisions that had led to this moment. Not to her. Not to anyone.

"I'm sorry," he had said, unable to offer a proper explanation—because there wasn't one.

"I'm ashamed of ya, Marty," Lavina had snapped before storming off, the screen door slamming behind her.

He had wronged more than one person in his silence.

Later that evening, after the anger in her had cooled, Lavina had sat him down, her voice calmer but no less firm.

"I think she knows, Marty," she had said. "There's somethin' in her eyes. Like she's figured it out already. Are ya ever gonna give her the truth? Apologize to her like she deserves? Give her the right to turn ya down?"

Lavina's words had cut deep, and though he had nodded at the time, the idea of it had felt impossible.

In his mind, silence had been the only way to keep the waters calm. Saying anything to Esther would mean unearthing years of pain, years of decisions he had no way to justify.

But here he was now, standing among mostly acquaintances, some strangers, watching his daughter on her wedding day. The soft laughter of the gathering swirled around him, and for a brief moment, it felt... nice. Like he was part of something he had no right to be, but he couldn't bring himself to leave.

Just then, across the yard, he caught Esther looking at him. "It wasn't long—just a flicker—but the feeling of it lingered, knotting his stomach."

She knows.

The words repeated over and over in his mind, like a bell that wouldn't stop ringing.

He quickly looked away, focusing on the plate in his hands, willing himself to calm.

His mind churned, running through all the ways this moment could go wrong. He didn't want to have that kind of conversation with a bride on her day, least of all with his daughter.

The truth, now unspoken, lingered between them like a storm cloud on the horizon.

He let his eyes roam the gathering again, pausing when they landed on Ian, who had shed his jacket and was now running around with Benjamin, Rebecca, and what appeared to be a herd of wild children.

Their delighted squeals filled the air as he chased them, his tie askew, his shirt untucked, his laughter echoing across the yard.

Marty couldn't help but smile. The man was good with children—anyone could see that. And he knew the German man treated his daughter with kindness, protective in a way he should have been as a father. That was some comfort, at least.

When Ian finally stopped to catch his breath, Marty seized the moment. He set his plate aside and approached him, waving off a couple of neighbors who tried to catch his attention.

Ian noticed him coming and straightened, his playful expression fading into one of concern.

"Sheriff," Ian greeted, his voice steady. "Are you needing to leave?"

Marty nodded. "Yeah. Hate to pull ya away, but we need to speak before I go."

Ian glanced toward the crowd where Esther stood, watching them with a mix of curiosity and worry. He gave her a small nod of reassurance before turning back to Marty.

"Let's take a walk," Ian said.

The two men walked to the edge of the property, the sounds of the party fading as they approached the dirt road where Marty's patrol car was parked.

The sheriff walked slowly, his hands clasped behind his back, his tone measured as he began to speak.

"Don't mean to alarm you, especially on a day like today. Probably not the best timing," Marty said, glancing over. "But Mr. Huggler, we've got all sorts of trouble kickin' up. Ya may not have heard, but a large group of moonshiners—several outfits, actually— have banded together."

"They've been goin' around shootin' up houses, intimidating folks. I've got good reason to believe they've even killed a few people," Ronell added.

Ian sighed. "We had some trouble a few weeks back," he admitted. "Came by our place. Shot at the front window."

Marty stopped walking, his face tightening. "And ya didn't think of lettin' me know?"

Ian shook his head. He'd almost driven down to talk to the sheriff, but had changed his mind after Esther begged him not to.

"Meant to," he lied. "And, well… Esther went out to them. Exchanged a few words, and they left. Unfortunately, I wasn't home."

The sheriff's jaw tightened, his voice lowering. "What ya suppose she said?"

Ian gave a short laugh, leaning with his hand on the side of the sheriff's car. "Said it didn't matter, just that they weren't coming back. Gave me her word. Trust me, I tried to get her to tell me, but once she's made up her mind, she zips her mouth up tight as a sealed jar."

Marty's mouth twitched, hinting at a smile. "Sounds about right," he said, like he wasn't just talking about Esther. "Think she knew 'em?"

"Can't say," Ian said, hesitating. "Don't think she would. Doesn't make sense."

The sheriff let out a low hum, clearly unsettled. "I'll tell ya this, Ian—if I may call ya that—y'all lucky I didn't have to come up here to collect ya bodies. Those men ain't messin' around. They're fightin' like hell to hold on. And that ain't the only problem."

Ian's shoulders stiffened, his attention sharpening.

"What're you getting at?"

Marty sighed, pulling a folded piece of paper from his pocket and holding it out.

"This is a report from the ATU," he said. "They've delayed their full movement in the area, but they've already got an agent in the field. Name's James Hartford. He sent this to me—got it today. Your wife's name is in it."

Ian's jaw tightened as he read the paper, his grip firm. "Clive," he muttered, voice clipped.

Marty nodded grimly. "Yeah. They know about her connection to him. Don't know how deep, but they're sniffin' around. And I've got reason to believe someone local's feedin' them information. An informant."

Ian's gaze snapped up, sharp and hard. "Someone in Larkin?"

Marty held his stare. "I don't know. But whoever it is, they know Esther. They're tryin' to tie her to Clive's operation, and I don't have to tell you how bad that could get. If the ATU starts pressin' her, they'll use whatever they can—picking her up, putting her in a closed room, and threatening her with jail time. Maybe even get rough with her. These agents are a determined bunch. And if she says the wrong thing... the wrong name..."

Ian folded the paper tight, his knuckles whitening around it before he shoved it back at Marty. His face was taut as he exhaled hard through his nose.

"You think this fella—the one with the loose lips—would come up here just to menace the place? Not trying to get information, just making sure we know he's around?" Ian said, half-thinking aloud.

The sheriff paused, reflecting for a second, then shook his head.

"Someone's doin' that, huh? Maybe they're just tryin' to steal from ya but don't have the gumption. Truth is, I get called out at least a couple times a week—folks reportin' things missin'.'"

"Yeah, but it's odd. He's just lurking, not taking anything. Even drew in some damn bears. It just doesn't make sense," Ian said, shaking his head, still trying to figure it out.

"Well… yeah, that's definitely odd," Marty acknowledged. "But in my line of work, most of it is. I wouldn't give it too much mind. Crazy folks make their way through this county from time to time. Let me know if ya have somethin' like that happen again."

Frustrated, Ian snapped, "Maybe you can tell me what the hell I'm supposed to do about the damn ATU? Do I take my wife up into the hills—hide out?"

Marty slipped into that calm, measured way of his—something he'd used more than once to diffuse a tall man with a temper.

"For now, sit tight. Don't do anything rash. Give me time to dig into it more. But I'll say this—if you've got somewhere safe to take her for a couple of months, you might want to start thinkin' about it. July through late August, maybe. Have a plan ready, enough money stashed away. I'll let you know if it comes to that."

Ian's face darkened—it clearly wasn't working.

"August is our peach harvest. I can't just leave."

No longer bothering to hide his irritation, Ian planted his hands on his hips, staring the sheriff down.

"God, if I could've killed Clive, I would now. Will that bastard and all his dirty deeds ever be put to rest?"

Marty let out a short laugh and clapped a firm hand on Ian's shoulder to soften him.

"I'll pretend I didn't hear that," the sheriff said, his tone light, but his grip steady.

"I'm gonna do my best to keep her outta this, Ian. Ya wife don't need no over-eager agent comin' at her, and I know that."

The sheriff gave Ian a pointed look as he went on.

"I may not look it, but I'm pretty clever—and I know how to stick out my big foot just enough to trip up a pencil pusher from the ATU, even if it's only enough to buy you some extra time. Don't worry."

Wound tight, Ian exhaled hard. His mind spun, wondering how the hell he was supposed to shake this off—how he was supposed to enjoy the rest of the day knowing what the sheriff had just told him.

Marty's voice broke into his thoughts. "And... take care of her, alright? She's a sweet girl. Prettiest bride a fella like you could get."

With a tight nod, Ian said, "I plan to."

Marty stepped back, settling his hat on his head before giving it a slight tip. "Please don't let this ruin ya evenin'. I might just be overreactin'. I just want to be cautious—have y'all prepared if need be."

With that, Ian watched as the sheriff climbed into his patrol car.

The engine rumbled to life, sending a low vibration through the ground before he pulled onto the dusty road.

The sun had begun to sink lower, stretching long shadows across the estate. Ian stood there for a long moment, his mind churning with everything Marty had said.

When he returned, he found Esther in the crowd, sitting next to Margie Mae, chatting easily, her expression lively. He couldn't help but think that her friend was exactly what she'd needed today— someone who helped her navigate the chaos effortlessly. A cure he wasn't sure how to administer.

Esther's soft smile welcomed him back as she looked up at him cheerfully.

The rest of the evening unraveled in easy laughter, the gathering drifting on as guests lingered, reluctant to let the celebration end.

But as the night wore on, the crowd began to thin, guests slipping away before Ian and Esther even had the chance to cut the small, pretty cake Mitzy had made for them, adorned with fresh flowers.

Everything had been so nice, and Clarissa had surpassed every expectation. With the sun long since dipped below the horizon, only the soft glow of lanterns remained, casting golden light over the last of the guests as they pitched in to help clean up. Their voices carried easily in the night air, blending with the quiet sounds of the evening.

Margie Mae and Ralph stayed as well—Ralph even spent a good long while talking mechanics with Abram, gesturing animatedly as they spoke, like they had found something in common.

Ian caught bits of their conversation as he passed by.

"Had this old Triumph since '17," Ralph said, gripping one end of a table as he and Abram carried it toward the porch. "Damn thing's been sittin' near twenty years now. She won't turn over."

Abram let out a loud chuckle. "Well, hell, Ralph. Maybe she's just forgotten what it feels like to be turned on proper. Can't blame her after sittin' cold for twenty years."

Ralph snorted. "If that's the case, I'd need a miracle worker, 'cause I sure as hell ain't gettin' her to purr."

Abram grinned. "Reckon it ain't the first time a man's said that 'bout an old girl that's lost her spark."

They laughed, setting the table down with a heavy thud before moving on to the next task, their conversation carrying on between the last rustlings of the evening.

Ian hadn't thought Ralph would stick around and have an honest conversation with Abram, having pegged him as a bigot. Yet, here they were, laughing.

It wasn't much, but it gave him a sliver of faith in people—how sometimes, they surprised you.

Across the yard, Esther caught sight of Ian, his sleeves rolled up, lifting chairs and tables into the truck bed, still in his suit pants and dress shirt. His muscles flexed easily with the movement, and she watched as he worked without complaint, his smile coming easily when someone called out to him.

Esther had offered to help with the dishes, but Clarissa refused, telling her it was bad luck for a bride to do such a thing and waved her off, insisting that she and Ian take whatever alone time they could get.

"Keeping those young'uns away from their two favorite people ain't gonna be easy," Clarissa added with a grin.

With that, Clarissa stepped off the porch, crossing the yard to gather a pile of table linens that had fallen onto the grass.

Left alone, Esther took in the scene—a beautiful late May evening, the spring coolness drifting from the fruit orchards and rolling over the land, stirring a quiet urge to close her eyes and breathe it in.

It felt as close to perfect as any bride deserved, she thought, a small, reflective smile touching her lips.

She wrapped her arms around herself, her gaze drifting toward Ian as he walked toward her, his jacket slung over his shoulder.

A grin played on his lips as he locked eyes with her, crossing the yard with an easy confidence.

He climbed a couple of steps but stopped just short of the top, meeting her at eye level.

"I think you might have actually had a nice time," he mused, taking in the serene expression on her face.

Esther just smiled, not wanting to give him the satisfaction of knowing he was right.

"Can I take you home now?" he asked, his voice low and intimate. "I don't want to share you anymore."

"I just walked Margie Mae and Ralph out, so yeah, I guess ya don't have to share me no more," she said, wrapping her arms tightly around his neck.

She thought he might hug her, but Ian took her by surprise— pulling her flush against him before lifting her off the porch, sweeping her legs into his arms.

She let out a playful scream, shock melting into laughter as he held her effortlessly. Her hands instinctively tightened around his neck, clinging to him like she might fall.

It only seemed to encourage him, as he strode toward his house, carrying her as if she weighed nothing.

Ian called out loudly to everyone still helping clean up— Clarissa, Abram, Mitzy, and even the children—his voice carrying an easy humor, though he clearly meant every word.

"I'm taking Mrs. Huggler home now! You won't be seeing her for a couple of days."

Laughter rang out, even from the kids, who giggled at their father's boldness.

Clarissa smirked, shaking her head.

"Good Lord, Ian, put that girl down. She's yours now, no need to steal her twice."

He looked back over his shoulder, adding, "Don't come looking for us unless the barn's on fire or something equivalent."

He spun around dramatically, shooting the children a playful but stern look, as if daring them to challenge his words.

Esther, unsure what to do, just laughed, her face flushing as she waved back to Mitzy, who was grinning.

"If ya need a break, Esther," Mitzy called out. "Ya know where I live."

Ian chuckled, leaning in close to whisper just for her ears, his hot breath against her skin.

"Sweetheart, I don't know if you'll be able to walk there after I'm done with you."

A devilish smirk spread across his face as he tightened his hold on her, making her blush as she bit her lip.

Chapter 32: Honeymoon *

They had barely crossed the matrimonial threshold before Ian set Esther on the edge of the long oak table, her legs tightening around his waist as if she had no intention of releasing him.

Ian sighed, drinking her in—having thirsted for her all day—waiting patiently for his turn. His palms framed her face, firm but tender, keeping her close enough that her breath mingled with his.

They kissed gently, exploring, letting the intimacy unfold.

The table groaned beneath them, its surface scattered with wedding gifts—some wrapped in printed paper, others left plain, the practical ones no doubt from the more sensible farm folk. Ian's lips slowed, his gaze flicking down at the jumble of packages beneath them.

"We should've had them put these somewhere else," he remarked, his voice warm, low, as he shifted to clear a bit of space. Not noticing, he brushed his arm against a stack of neatly wrapped boxes, sending a couple sliding precariously toward the edge.

Esther leaned back on her elbows. Her dark hair, freed hours ago from its pins, spilled in loose waves across the polished surface.

"Don't you wanna open a present or two?" she asked, curiosity flickering in her gaze. She couldn't help but wonder what Margie Mae had gotten her.

"Umm, that's what I'm trying to do, darlin'," he teased, tugging on her belt as he pulled her closer. But just as he moved her, a few small packages tumbled to the floor with a soft thud.

"Damn it," he muttered, glancing down with a wince, hoping nothing fragile had broken.

Frustrated, he crouched to gather the fallen boxes, lifting them with an apologetic glance.

"Here, might as well open these—make sure I didn't get myself into trouble," he said, handing her the gifts as he helped her sit up.

"Who's this from?" she asked, squinting at the tiny tag, her fingers skimming the cursive letters.

Ian, now tugging his tie all the way off, leaned in for a closer look.

"Of course, it'd be from Margie Mae. Can I already say I'm sorry if it's not in one piece?" he teased.

Esther carefully peeled away the wrapping, conscious of her movements, savoring the moment. She paused, a small, almost girlish smile softening her features.

"I've never opened a wrapped gift before," she admitted, her voice quiet.

Ian stilled, his fingers going slack around the tie he was folding. "No one ever gave you one?" he asked, regret lacing his words. He should've thought to let her unwrap her ring earlier—or maybe something else. Something special, just for her.

Esther lifted the lid, and her face lit up, her delight unmistakable. "She got me a new pair of stockin's and my favorite lipstick!" Esther grinned, holding them up as if they were treasures.

He chuckled, shaking his head. "And how's that a gift for both of us?" he teased.

"Well, actually, there is somethin' in here fer ya," she said, handing him the box. He took it, curiosity flickering across his face as he pulled out a crisp blue necktie and a small can of premium shoe wax.

He held up the tie, turning it over with amusement. "You think Margie Mae's sending me a message? Like—you've married Esther, so now you'll be expected to dress up. Polish your shoes and look smart?"

He gave her a deliberately serious look, deadpan—just long enough to make her laugh—before glancing back down at the tie.

"I reckon she's got a way of sayin' it without really sayin' it," Esther leaned over to grab another small package, pausing when she noticed the matching wrapping paper. "Maybe this one's from her too," she murmured, easing it open.

Ian moved toward his favorite chair, slipping off his shoes with a sigh. Despite their earlier shine, they'd scuffed from playing with the children in the yard. Amused, he glanced at them briefly, thinking perhaps Margie Mae was actually onto something.

His eyes flicked to Esther, her hands stilling as she lifted the lid of a small box. Her expression shifted as curiosity gave way to something more uncertain, puzzled by the second gift.

"What's wrong?" he asked, setting his shoes aside.

She shook her head slowly, lifting a folded piece of stationery. "Not sure. Looks like a letter... but Margie Mae wouldn't write me one. She knows I don't read so well."

"Let me see it," he said as he rose and crossed the room in a few quick steps. He reached for the note, unfolding it carefully. The delicate script caught the lamplight as his eyes scanned the words.

His pleasant expression faded, his lips working into a tight, reluctant line. The tension in his shoulders was almost palpable.

"What's she sayin'?" Esther asked, worried.

Ian flipped the letter over, scanning the back, his jaw shifting.

He took a breath, pausing before answering.

"Well," he said, glancing at her, "I can tell you it's not from Margie Mae or Ralph."

Her stomach tightened. "Who's it from, then?"

Ian didn't answer right away. Instead, he reached into the box, brushing aside the tissue paper until his fingers curled around something small and solid.

He pulled it out—a single metal house key.

He just shook his head in disbelief.

It wasn't just a key.

It was an offer. A promise. Something unwelcome.

Esther slid off the table and reached for the discarded letter. She stared down at the neat handwriting, struggling to make out the words—recognizing only a few simple ones.

Ian's expression hardened with each passing second.

"That fucking little prick," he muttered under his breath.

Her head snapped up. "Can you just tell me what's goin' on?" she demanded, her voice rising.

He exhaled sharply, shaking his head like he was trying to shake it off.

"It's from Hank, Esther." Ian's voice was clipped, taut. "He wrote you a nice little letter. I guess you didn't tell him you couldn't read. Looks like you were supposed to read it all by yourself."

"Stop teasing me, Ian," she said, her voice almost pleading, hoping he was just riling her up. But the set of his features, the tightness around his eyes, told her otherwise.

"But why would he write me a letter? And what's that ya holdin'?" she asked as her voice wavered.

He turned the key over in his palm. "It's to your little garden out back," he said, voice flat, dripping with sarcasm.

"Good Lord, what's wrong with 'im?" Esther muttered, shaking her head. "I think his mama must've dropped him as a young'un."

She reached over, resting a hand on Ian's arm.

"Read me the letter, will ya," she asked, curious. She wanted to know what Hank had written.

Ian scoffed, irritated. "You want me to read your boyfriend's letter to you?"

"He ain't my damn boyfriend," she snapped.

"I don't really feel like reading it again," he said flatly as he dropped himself into a reading chair and reached for a shoe.

"Where are ya goin'?" she asked.

"Well, Esther, I'm planning on going outside and throwing his little promise as far as I can—that is, unless you want it?" Ian's mouth curved into a smile, but the sharpness in it made it clear he found nothing amusing.

"Ya bein' silly, Ian," she said, reaching to tug the shoe from his hand. "Don't go outside. Everyone'll think we can't even get along fer five minutes."

She coaxed him into setting the shoe down. Then, with a determined look, she sat on his lap, straddling his legs in a deliberate, provocative way. Her blue skirt hiked up, revealing the clips of her stockings—the sight she knew he liked.

And he did. Despite his irritation over Margie Mae's nephew and his damn gift, Ian's hands slid up her legs, his grip firm as he held her in place. She wrapped her arms around his neck, drawing him in.

"I don't really care what's in the letter," she murmured, her voice soft, hoping to pull him back to her, away from whatever had taken hold of him.

Ian took a slow, cleansing breath, trying to let it go.

"Well, dear, it pretty much says if you get tired of me, your pretty little garden's waiting on you. Along with Hank's undying devotion. Married or not."

Esther leaned back, brows drawn tight, insulted.

"That don't sound like somethin' ya ought to say to a married woman," she said sharply. Then the thought struck her—Margie Mae would've never brought that gift if she'd known what was inside.

"No, it's not," he agreed. For a moment, he reconsidered throwing the key. Maybe instead he'd take a nice ride to Jasper and wait for Hank in his kitchen. Bring some wilted flowers with him.

"What's goin' on in that mind of yers?" Esther asked, brushing her index finger over the crease in his brow. "Ian, give me the key. I'll throw it. I got my shoes on," she added, holding out her hand.

A slow, sly smile rose on his mouth as he pulled the metal key from his pocket and slipped it into her palm, clearly pleased she was taking charge of its riddance.

"Just don't throw it in the garden. You'll end up finding it when we plow," he said.

"Ya ain't got to worry—I got a strong arm and I'm gonna toss it clean across the road," she said, standing and smoothing the soft blue dress that hugged her frame, like a woman on a mission.

With key in hand, she strode toward the front door, pausing just long enough to glance back with a mischievous raised eyebrow, before stepping outside.

Ian moved to the open doorway, watching as she scurried across the dimly lit yard.

Bracing herself against the fence, Esther drew her arm back and hurled the key.

It sailed farther than Ian had expected, disappearing into the dark bramble on the other side of the road—if the sound of it was any indication.

She turned back quickly, catching him still standing in the doorway, her grin playful, triumphant. Sashaying toward the house, she carried the same lightness in her step as when he'd watched her dart through the orchard—carefree, full of life the year before.

As she reached the door, Ian caught her by the waist, pulling her inside, his powerful grip determined as he shut the door behind them.

"Ya think anyone saw me?" she asked, breathless, her cheeks flushed.

"Naw," he murmured, leaning down to press a kiss against her neck. His voice dipped low, serious. "Weren't you showing me something before you ran outside?"

"Well, I got somethin' cute on underneath this dress," she said, lifting her leg just enough to reveal a peek of the lacy step-in slip beneath.

"Ya might wanna see that, too," she added.

His gaze locked onto her, a slow grin spreading across his face, the frustration over Hank's letter already drifting away.

"You know we're not really married all the way yet," Ian said, his fingers grazing her skirt, inching it higher.

She caught his hand, playfully pulling it away.

"So ya've been tellin' me all day," she replied, a seductive smile resting on her pretty red lips. "Whisperin' it in my ear the entire party."

She pulled from his embrace and turned toward the bedroom door, glancing back over her shoulder. "Ya comin' with me, Mr. Huggler?"

Ian's lips parted slowly. All he could do was watch her, appreciate the way she moved, the way her sweet words curled around him like a promise.

"Yes, my love," he said finally, locking the front door behind him. But before he could follow, his eyes landed on the letter discarded on the table—the one Hank had written to another man's wife.

In a swift motion, he grabbed it, crushing the sweet nothin's into a tight little ball, and tossed it into the unlit potbelly stove. He thought about how satisfying it would be to burn it later that night—along with all those inappropriate promises Hank had made to a woman he clearly didn't even know.

Once in the bedroom, Ian shut the door behind him, becoming one more fortress of privacy.

His new bride now stood before him, bathed in the soft light of a small lamp on the nightstand, its golden hue brushing over her skin. And despite having made love to her the night before, this was different.

It had been growing, rising between them all day—like an invisible tether drawing him to her, binding his body, his mind.

He was hers to do with as she wished.

And today, this mysterious creature from the hills had stood beside him, had spoken the vows that bound them—had promised to cleave unto him.

A pledge for as long as they walked this earth.

A new band rested on his finger.

Esther's promise.

The only thing that could have made it feel more complete, more real, was hearing her say the words he longed for.

But she had married him, and for now, that would have to be enough. He would say the word *love* enough for both of them—to fill the empty space her fears wouldn't let her tread.

Ian stood before her, his tall frame filling the space of the small room. His presence seemed to wrap around her, yet it was his eyes—those deep, expressive eyes—that held her captive, as if he could see straight into her soul.

And for Esther, a girl who had spent so much of her life unseen, that was everything.

"Well," she said, her voice laced with a passionate intent. He'd earned the full show—the one that came with putting a diamond ring on her finger. A cool smile played at her lips as she pointed toward the chair Ian always used when dressing.

"Why don't ya sit over there."

"You want me to sit down?" he asked, his interest piqued. He liked this—letting her take the lead, giving him instructions.

Ian settled into the chair, his expectant gaze locked on her. Sitting forward with his arms loosely resting on his knees, he whispered, "Do you have any idea how downright breathtaking you are?"

She saw the way he leaned in, his hand lifting as if to reach for her—then hesitating, forcing himself to hold back.

Esther felt it then—the power she had over him. It was intoxicating, the way his desire belonged to her in that moment.

"No. I told ya to sit there. Now be good," she said, shaking her finger at him, then biting her lower lip.

"I've been good all day, though. And you're standing too far away," he said as he shifted in his chair.

"Now, Immanuel, ya gonna have to be patient. Took me a good long while to get dressed up this mornin'," she teased back.

He shook his head, tilting it back with an exaggerated sigh before looking at her again. "Immanuel, really? Are you being Mrs. Huggler now?"

She arched a brow. "Well, that's who I married today. Now ya sayin' it ain't your name?"

"Tell ya what, you can call me whatever you want… if you slip that dress off a little faster." His voice was edged with something raw—something that needed to be fed, and soon.

"Shh, ya ain't in charge right now." A playful lilt danced in her tone as she unfastened her belt, letting it fall to the floor.

Her fingers moved ever so slowly as she began unbuttoning the top of her suit dress, each button slipping free under his watchful gaze. Taking her time, she eased the fabric from her shoulders, letting it slide down to reveal the lace-trimmed undergarment beneath.

Ian's eyes darkened with approval. The sheer lace left little to the imagination, teasing at the firm curves of her body—her breasts now fuller, softer, tempting.

His jaw slackened, his breath coming shallow as he took her in.

Next, she reached behind her, undoing the button of her skirt. With a deliberate shimmy, she worked the snug fabric down her hips, letting it pool at her feet before stepping out of it—her heels still in place.

The effect was deliberate, and judging by his expression, devastatingly so as he drank her in.

She didn't stand there shyly, no. Her shoulders were back, her posture confident, like a model from one of those saucy magazine pages.

To him, she was the epitome of desire, the kind of woman who could make a man forget his own name. The slip hugged her in all the right places, its high cut teasing the curve of her thighs. Her stockings, clipped to a belt at her waist, framed her in a way that left him torn—did he want to rip them all off her, or just sit there and admire her a little longer?

"Ya like it?" she asked, wanting his approval.

Ian dragged a hand over his mouth, his voice thick and hoarse. "Aww—yes."

"Ya want me to keep goin'? Keep takin' it all off?" she continued, confidence blooming under the heat of his attention.

"Give me a minute," he replied. He leaned back in the chair, his eyes devouring her, wanting to savor every second.

But Esther had no interest in just standing there. She made her way over to him, nudging him to sit up straighter before lifting her leg over his, straddling him once more.

Her body molded to his, and his hands gripped her hips.

"What are you doing to me, Esther? You realize I'm not even gonna be able to satisfy you—you've got me panting for you."

She grabbed his face, her fingers firm against his jaw.

"Hush up," she murmured, before pressing her lips to his.

Her kiss was soft yet charged, a promise of the tenderness her body held for him. She enjoyed this—enjoyed the control—and rocked against his lap, feeling his body respond, ready and wanting beneath her.

He pulled back, his breathing uneven. "I think I'd like to see you finish taking it all off now."

"Sorry, but yer new missus says ya gonna have to wait a bit longer," she teased, making him grunt in playful frustration.

Leaning in, she kissed his neck, her lips trailing along his skin as her fingers worked to unbutton his shirt. Esther peeled it open, her hands gliding over his tan skin.

She slid the fabric off his shoulder, kissing along the curve of his collarbone. She lingered there, tickling his skin. This was one of her favorite parts of him, and, unable to resist, she gave him a little bite.

A pent-up moan escaped him as his hands tightened on her legs. Her every move was pushing him closer to the precipice.

Close to the brink, Ian stopped her, pulling her face close to his. His hot breath mingled with hers as he murmured, "If you keep moving on my lap like that, I'm gonna have one. I don't even need to be inside you—you know that?"

A pleased smile spread across Esther's face, her delight in his unraveling evident.

"Aww, I'm real sorry," she said, though there wasn't a hint of sincerity in her voice. She kept moving, slower this time, her arms lifting behind her head in a pose she'd seen women strike in suggestive magazines. Her eyes stayed locked on his, her lips parting slightly, letting her desire spill into her expression.

He groaned, his head dropping as he buried his face against her chest.

"Please, darlin', have a little pity on me," he whispered, half in jest but wholly overwhelmed.

Seeing him at his breaking point, Esther slid off his lap, giving him space to pull himself back from the edge.

His gaze was still fixed on her—intoxicated, undone, fighting the urge to throw her onto the bed and claim her body as his wife then and there.

"Take ya clothes off, Ian," she said with a smile, motioning toward the bed as she gave him her next instruction.

He nodded. Not hesitating, he rose from the chair, slipped off his already unbuttoned shirt, and tossed it onto the dresser. His hands moved to his suit pants, unfastening the button and sliding the zipper down. The fine fabric slipped down his legs, pooling at his feet as he stepped out of them.

He hesitated—just for a moment—his gaze locking onto hers, needing her to watch. Then, with slow, deliberate intent, his fingers hooked the waistband of his boxers. Holding her attention, he slowly slid them down, exposing himself bare before her.

It wasn't just about undressing—it was about showing her what she had done to him. The result of her teasing, her control, laid out before her. His body, aching, fueled by blood and steel, craving her beyond reason.

She was excited too—he could see it in her eyes—but she was holding back, performing. Her half-dressed, svelte figure moved toward him in slow, seductive strides, pointing to the bed once more. She waited, expectant, pausing until he obeyed.

Who was this girl? he wondered, marveling at how naturally she'd taken charge. Had she been holding back all this time? Had a ring and a promise freed her, peeling back another layer of herself— one he had never met before?

Not that he didn't like it—he loved it. But the thought crossed his mind—she might just wear him out.

And yet, the provocation thrilled him. And Ian wasn't the kind of man to back down from a challenge.

Esther watched as he climbed onto the bed, his hand extending toward her, beckoning her to join him.

But she wasn't ready to relinquish the reins yet. Lingering in the moment, she reveled in the final act of her performance.

His gaze didn't waver as she walked closer, the soft click of her heels on the floorboards stretching time, each step like the slow tick of a clock. Stopping just shy of the bed, she lingered, smiling.

A naked man—her husband—waiting and wanting her.

Then, slowly, she leaned down, unbuckling her shoes one by one, slipping them off before reaching for the garter belt. With deliberate care, she unclipped it, then slid her stockings down the length of her legs, letting him savor every inch.

Only then did she let the last of her lacy slip fall, the delicate fabric gliding down her body to settle in a soft circle at her feet. She stepped out of it—his unwrapped present standing before him.

Ian had reached his limit. His patience, stretched thin, gave way to the earthly desire of the man within him. She could feel it—see it in the way his muscles tensed, in the way his hand reached out for her. He'd been patient, let her set the tone, but now he was ready to make her his wife in every sense of the word.

He suddenly sprang to his knees, grabbing her tightly around the waist, as though catching a wild animal.

She let out a gasp, startled by his sudden movement, as he swept her beneath him onto the bed. His breath came fast, his chest heaving as he held her there.

The game was over. No more teasing.

Ian's body had taken over now, driven by unfiltered physical need. His mouth crashed onto hers, his kiss deep and consuming, his tongue warm and salty. His hands moved over her, taking her, knowing she belonged to him, just as he belonged to her.

"You're mine," he whispered, his voice rough, his tongue grazing her ear.

With that, he pulled her beneath him, entering her swiftly, his need too great for delay.

Esther didn't mind. She knew she'd earned this—teasing a wild beast like him until he finally gave in to his instincts. She loved their games, relishing the thrill of how different it felt every time.

He moved with urgency, his body powerful. The bedsprings squealed, a wild, clumsy music rising beneath their bodies. His thrusts were beautiful in purpose as he sealed their union.

His breath came faster, groaning as he neared the edge—louder than she'd ever heard before, his sounds animalistic and unrestrained. Her bare legs wrapped tightly around his torso, holding him close as he fought to keep his full weight from pressing down on her.

"I love you," he murmured, his voice breaking on a moan as he surrendered completely, his body spilling into hers. His grip tightened around her, muscles trembling as he pushed through the waves of pleasure, forcing himself to keep going—for her.

But he needed a moment—just a moment, he told himself—hoping she wouldn't feel let down as he carefully lifted himself off.

"Just let me catch my breath," he managed as he eased down next to her.

A small smirk curved her lips, as if she'd pushed him past his usual accommodating self.

"Ian?" Esther said.

"Yes, darling?" he said, still trying to reel himself back in.

"Did they bring any of that cake over here?" she asked, a flicker of delight in her eyes.

"Cake? Really?" he laughed, turning his head to look at her. "You're thinking about cake right now?"

"Yep," she said. "I ain't eaten anythin' all day."

"I can warm you something. There's enough here to feed us for days," he said, thinking she needed something with more sustenance.

"Naw, I just want some cake," she said, leaning back, her eyes drifting up to the ceiling.

"Well, darlin', after that, I'd say you earned it." He chuckled as he rose from the bed, striding confidently out the door—stark naked. She laughed as she watched him go, admiring the view. She knew this casual freedom wouldn't last once his children returned, grateful he'd fashioned a lock on their bedroom door for future privacy.

After a few minutes, Ian returned, carrying a tall glass of milk and what appeared to be the biggest slice of cake Esther had ever seen. She sat up straight, leaning a pillow behind her as he sat down and handed her the plate.

"This ain't all fer me, right?" she asked, eyeing the oversized portion.

"I figured I'd join you," he said, picking up the fork. He cut a generous piece of the frosted vanilla cake and held it out for her, feeding her the first bite.

"Ian, do ya think ya feedin' a giant?" she teased, trying to fit her mouth around the fork and the comically large piece he'd offered.

Smiling, he took a bite himself, following her lead—but the next piece he prepared for her was just as large. Esther shook her head, laughing, but still let him place it in her mouth. The frosting smeared at the corners of her lips, the bite too big to manage cleanly.

As she reached up to wipe it away, his hand caught hers, stopping her.

He leaned in, his gaze locking with hers before his mouth found her lips. His tongue grazed her skin, slowly licking the frosting away with care.

All Esther could think was that sometimes Ian was just plain different—doing strange things like this. She gave him a perplexed look, unsure what to make of it.

Seeing her reaction, he just laughed, handing her the glass of milk.

But she wasn't a fan—her nose wrinkled at the sight of it. Milk had never been part of her diet growing up, and he knew she didn't like it.

"Don't you want our baby to be strong and tall, like his father?" He asked.

"It ain't a boy, Ian," she replied, taking a reluctant sip before handing the glass back to him.

"I never said it was a boy," he said. "You've never seen some of the German women I've known. They're bigger and stronger than I am."

Her eyes widened, her imagination running wild, picturing tall daughters with their father's broad shoulders, as a concerned look crossed her face, making him chuckle.

"Don't worry," he murmured, his laughter low as he nuzzled her cheek. "I know how that mind of yours works. They'll take after you, sweetheart. Willowy and beautiful. Perfect."

But then, his grin turned wicked as he scooped up another bite of cake, holding it just shy of her lips. "Now, eat up," he said. "We've got unfinished business."

Chapter 33: Married Life

Ian wasn't sure what he thought marriage to Esther would be like, or if it might take some getting used to. She was a woman whose upbringing was as different as the hills she'd come from. But to his surprise, their life together had settled into a beautiful rhythm. Almost natural, despite the occasional butting of heads, which was to be expected.

And whatever had fooled him into thinking she was a passive woman, he couldn't say. The married Esther spoke with more confidence and ease, most times doing what she wanted, how she wanted. Or at least, more than she had before, when they were courting.

Esther was attentive and hardworking, slipping effortlessly into the role of mother to his children and woman of the house—something that had become more evident with each passing day.

That afternoon, Benjamin and Rebecca had eagerly pulled her outside to work on the treehouse they'd been planning for months.

The idea had taken root long ago and only grew wilder each time Ian reread *Swiss Family Robinson* to them—for the third, or maybe fourth time. His deep voice spun adventure into the quiet of their home as the children sat, spellbound.

Inspired by the story, Benjamin had insisted they needed a treehouse of their own, and Esther had joined the project. Ian had warned them he didn't have time to help with such frivolous activities—and not to just make a bigger mess for him to clean up.

Undeterred by his objection, Esther had just waved a hand at him on her way out the door.

Once outside, she said, "I like your ideas," as Rebecca proudly handed her the sketch they'd made together—a lopsided drawing of a two-story hut with a rope swing hanging from the tallest branch.

Benjamin tilted his head, studying the image.

"Not sure it's gonna look like that, but... Pa said we could use his tools long as we put 'em back. Ya know how to build it, right, Esther?"

Esther laughed as she crouched beside him.

"Benji, how hard can it be? No sense in waitin' any longer. Let's just give it a shot."

The three of them worked under the shade of the large oak at the edge of the yard, near the fence, dragging scrap wood from the old shed as Esther directed them.

Though with no real building knowledge, they mostly went in circles, cutting and hammering pieces without much progress.

The afternoon sun filtered through the branches, casting dappled shadows across the ground, while the scent of freshly sawn wood mingled with the faint sweetness of honeysuckle drifting from the hedgerow nearby.

When the children decided the hut needed more—extra planks for support and a long rope secured high for climbing—Esther kicked off her shoes and stepped forward, determined to reach the top.

"You can't climb up there, Esther!" Benjamin shouted, hands planted on his hips, standing like a miniature version of his father—too grown-up for his lean frame. "Yer gonna fall, and my Pa's gonna be mad!"

She just laughed, hooking her foot onto the first branch. 'I've been climbin' trees my whole life, Benji. Yer pa don't know everythin'."

His face scrunched with worry, hands balling into fists at his sides.

"But he's gonna yell at me for lettin' ya go that high!" he declared, his voice cracking under the weight of responsibility.

Before Esther could reassure him—or tease him further—Benjamin spun around and took off toward the barn, his bare feet kicking up little clouds of dust on the packed ground.

"Pa! Esther's doin' somethin' dumb!" he shouted as he ran, his voice carrying across the yard. He knew his words wouldn't stop her, and he needed backup.

Rebecca stood frozen, her hammer dangling from her hand as she looked from Esther to her retreating brother.
"He's really gonna tell on ya," she muttered, wide-eyed.

Esther laughed, waving a dismissive hand.

"Let him. I've been climbin' since before he was born. Your pa's just gonna grumble a bit, then leave us be."

Still, Rebecca didn't seem convinced, and her gaze darted nervously between the barn and the tree.

Meanwhile, Benjamin's shouts grew fainter as he disappeared into the open doors of the big building.

Inside, Ian was bent over the workbench, sharpening the blade of a pruning saw. The rhythmic rasp of metal on stone filled the space, drowning out the first few syllables of Benjamin's frantic call.

"Pa!" Benjamin hollered again, louder this time, skidding to a stop just short of him.

Startled, Ian straightened up, the saw still in his hand as he twisted toward his son.

"What's got you running in here like your tail's on fire?" he asked, his tone more curious than annoyed.

"It's Esther!" Benjamin panted, his chest heaving as he fought for breath. "She's climbin' a tree!"

Ian blinked, lowering the saw as his brows pulled together. "What tree?"

"The big one by the front yard!" Benjamin flung an arm toward the barn doors. "She's goin' to the top—and she won't listen to me!"

Ian exhaled sharply, setting the pruning saw down with a clank. "Of course she is," he muttered, dragging a rag across his hands. "Why would I expect anything less?"

Without another word, he strode past Benjamin, his long legs eating up the distance to the barn doors in seconds. Benjamin scrambled to keep up, his smaller frame darting alongside him.

By the time Ian crossed the yard and came into view of the oak tree, his jaw was set, his brows drawn low.

Sure enough, there was his wife, her bare feet gripping a lower branch, one hand reaching for a higher one as she prepared to lift herself.

Rebecca stood below, watching intently, her head tipped back as she tracked Esther's progress through the canopy of leaves.

"You gonna go all the way up, Esther?" she called out, pointing toward the highest branches.

Esther grinned, shifting her footing. "Not all the way—just close," she said, nodding toward a sturdy branch further up.

But before she could climb any higher, Ian's voice boomed across the yard.

"Esther Huggler! Have you lost your mind?"

She turned, spotting him striding toward her from the barn, his face a mix of disbelief and frustration. His sleeves were rolled to his elbows, sawdust still clinging to the hair on his forearms, his blond hair mussed from a morning of work.

"What are ya yellin' 'bout?" she shot back, though she knew full well.

Ian reached the base of the tree, looking up at her with an expression that made her feel both chastised and cared for all at once.

"You cannot be serious. And in your condition?" His hands were planted firmly on his hips, his head shaking in exasperation. "Get down. Right now."

Esther let out a slow breath, her fingers gripping the rough bark, bare feet firm against the branch. She wasn't some reckless child or delicate thing—and she sure as hell wasn't helpless.

She could get down just fine.

But Ian wasn't going to see it that way. Not with the way he was staring at her like he couldn't believe he was having this conversation. His hands now hovered at the bottom of the tree, fingers flexing, like he was already considering hauling himself up there after her.

She glanced at the limb below, judging the distance. It had felt a lot easier coming up.

Ian's fingers skimmed the bark. "Esther." His voice was unyielding. "Now."

A sharp huff left her lips, but she knew there was no winning this. Not today.

With careful movements, she inched down, not rushing, but not daring to test Ian's patience either.

"I wasn't gonna fall, ya worrywart," she muttered when his hands caught her waist, his grip solid as he lowered her the last few inches.

"Don't care," he shot back, keeping her steady even after her feet hit the ground. "I don't need my wife risking herself or our baby just to build a precarious tree hut. I'll help them build it later, but you—" he pointed at her firmly "—are done with this nonsense."

Rebecca held her hammer behind her back, muttering, "Esther is brave, though. She ain't afraid of climbin'. And I'm not either."

Ian leaned slightly, meeting Rebecca's gaze, his voice firm.

"Being brave is good, Rebecca, but being smart is better. Climbing too high isn't safe, no matter how brave you are." He paused, letting the words settle. "And when you see someone doing something silly, like Esther climbing too high, that's not something to copy. You understand me?"

Rebecca frowned, arms crossing tightly over her chest. "I ain't scared of climbin', and I'm real careful."

Ian let out a sharp breath, his gaze flicking to Esther, who stood nearby, an amused smirk tugging at her lips. "You see this?" he said, gesturing toward Rebecca. "She's watching you, taking after you."

"Rebecca, ya too young to climb up a tree," Esther said quickly, thinking it might satisfy him. But one glance at his expression told her it hadn't done the trick.

The young girl scowled at her father, her determined eyes locking on his with a defiance that felt all too familiar to Ian.

It wasn't easy for him to lay down the law with someone so sweet, but the stubbornness staring back at him made it clear she'd taken on Esther's battle.

"Daughter, if I see you climbing a tree without my permission, I'm gonna tan your back end. Have I made myself clear?" Ian's tone was firm, but his eyes still held a trace of kindness.

Rebecca's scowl deepened, her small fists tightening at her sides. "But ya ain't tannin' Esther's hide," she shot back, her logic as sharp as any child's.

He tilted his head, a faint grin tugging at his lips as he caught the look Esther gave him from the corner of his eye.

"Well, I just might," he replied, though his gaze slid toward his wife in mock warning.

Rebecca huffed, her little shoulders drooping in resignation.

"I need a yes, Papa, so I know you heard me," Ian pressed, not letting her off the hook.

With a small grunt, Rebecca dropped the hammer, her voice clipped as she muttered, "Fine." She spun away and marched toward the sanctuary of Clarissa's house, kicking dramatically at the ground as she went.

Ian watched her retreat, shaking his head with a sigh. "Why does every female I know have to be so difficult?" he muttered under his breath.

Turning back to his wife, he said, "You're coming to town with me. You can't get into trouble in the truck." His tone was firm— clearly, he didn't trust her to stay put without attempting to climb that tree again.

"I wasn't in trouble. I've climbed more trees than you can count," Esther replied, brushing dirt from her slacks with an air of defiance.

"Could have fooled me," Ian shot back, gesturing toward the thick branch she'd been standing on. "You see that split where it meets the trunk? That limb was only gonna hold you a little bit longer before crashing down with you."

Esther squinted at it, unsure if he was telling the truth or just trying to make his point stick. When her gaze returned to him, she caught the soft curl at the edge of his mouth, his blue eyes daring her to challenge him.

"Get your shoes on," he added.

She lifted her chin, meeting his gaze with a determination he recognized all too well.

"I ain't goin' unless you stop at Paulson Mercantile. I've been waitin' on some packages. They were supposed to be shipped there months ago."

Ian narrowed his eyes, irritation stirring at the mention of those packages. Things bought with Clive's money. He hated the thought of that man lingering in their lives, even in something as small as a box of goods Esther had ordered before she'd escaped him. He didn't blame her—how could he? But it still gnawed at him.

"What makes you think they've come in?" he asked, his voice edged with skepticism.

Esther shook her head. "I don't, but I wouldn't mind at least sayin' hello to Margie Mae. Ain't seen her since the weddin'."

He exhaled through his nose, rubbing the back of his neck as he considered her request. He was supposed to be keeping his wife out of trouble—keeping a low profile. But he also knew Esther wouldn't let this go. And the truth was, seeing her happy—settled—mattered more than his pride.

"You win," he muttered, the word half-swallowed by exasperation. "We'll stop by after the feed store. But don't get your hopes up too high, Esther."

Her lips curved into a satisfied smile, a gleam of triumph in her eyes. "I try not to most days."

"Hmm. If you say so." His response was laced with playful doubt as he motioned for her to follow.

Benjamin, who had been watching the exchange like it was a high-stakes negotiation, lit up with excitement.

"Can I come too, Pa? I wanna tell you about how we want the tree hut—if ya gonna help us."

Ian chuckled, ruffling the boy's hair as they made their way to the truck. "Sure, kid. You can keep me entertained while Esther figures out how to drive me crazy another way."

She shot him a look, but said nothing—the glint in her eye suggesting she was already scheming her next move in their ongoing battle of wills.

Benjamin stepped to his father's side and shot a grin at Esther. "See? I told ya Pa'd stop you!"

She huffed, nudging him playfully with her hip as she passed.

"Traitor," she muttered, making sure he heard her.

The old truck bounced along the dirt road, the cab cramped with the three of them squeezed inside. Benjamin sat in the middle, his skinny legs getting longer by the day, talking a mile a minute about the tree hut plans.

"It's gonna have two floors, Pa! And Esther says we can put a rope swing on it, like in Swiss Family Robinson!"

Ian cast a glance at his wife. "So that's where you got the idea. I don't remember Mrs. Robinson being pregnant and climbing trees."

Esther rolled her eyes, though a smile tugged at her lips. "Well, she didn't have ya hollerin' at her, did she?"

Ian laughed, shaking his head. "And I bet Mrs. Robinson knew how to be nice to Mr. Robinson, too. Not always trying to work under his skin just to see if she could."

Esther scoffed. "Well, if I didn't keep ya from gettin' rusty, life'd be awfully dull. Might even get bored."

Ian playfully huffed, shaking his head. "Trust me, sweetheart. Bored is the last thing I am."

Just then, the truck jolted hard, bouncing them in their seats and making Benjamin grab the dashboard. Startled but undeterred, he pressed on.

"Ya think we can make it strong enough to sleep in, Pa?"

"We'll see, Benji," Ian said, his tone indulgent. Ian shot Esther another look, catching her flirty expression and shaking his head again.

She laughed softly, leaning her head back against the seat, thinking maybe she should actually try to be a little nicer to him today. He'd brought her along, after all, and was letting her go see Margie Mae—even though he knew full well he'd have a hell of a time pulling her away once they got to talking.

When the truck finally rolled up to the feed store on the outskirts of Larkin, Ian eased it close to the entrance. A few cars and trucks were scattered across the lot, the smell of hay and feed thick in the early June air.

The old building stood weathered, its wooden exterior bearing the scars of decades of sun and storms. A faded sign hung above the door, its edges curled and paint nearly worn away, shifting slightly with the breeze.

Chickens clucked from wire pens near the entrance, and a few goats milled about in a makeshift enclosure to the side, their bleats mingling with the hum of flies.

Benjamin immediately perked up, his small hand reaching over Esther's lap for the door handle before Ian had even cut the engine.

"Pa, look! They got goats!" he exclaimed, his voice bursting with excitement.

Esther chuckled, glancing at Ian as she opened her door. "Reckon yer gonna lose him to the critters out there."

Ian sighed, stepping out and stretching his back. "As long as he doesn't come begging me for one to take home, I'll count myself lucky."

Benjamin tore off toward the pens, his excitement outpacing his coordination, skidding on the gravel as he caught himself against the wooden fence. Esther followed at a slower pace, pausing near a pen of rabbits nestled in the shade of the store's overhang.

"Aren't they somethin'?" she said softly, crouching near the fence, reaching out to pet one.

"They're something, all right," Ian muttered, distracted as he mentally ran through what he needed inside. He reached back through the open window, grabbed his wallet from the dashboard, and headed for the store, the jingle of a cowbell announcing his entrance.

The feed store was dim and cluttered, its wooden floorboards creaking beneath Ian's boots. Shelves lined with burlap sacks of grain, tools, and animal feed stretched along the walls, while the counter stood at the back. A ceiling fan turned lazily above, barely stirring the stale, warm air.

Behind the counter, a wiry man in overalls greeted Ian with a nod.

"Afternoon," he said, his voice gruff but friendly.

"Afternoon," Ian replied, stepping up to the counter. "I'm here for some chicken feed and corn feed. How's your stock?"

The storekeeper's eyes darted briefly to the side, and Ian noticed another figure standing nearby, half-obscured by a rack of harnesses. The man's clothes were simple, almost nondescript—not quite what Ian was used to seeing on the local farmers. His hat was pulled low over his brow, and his posture was too stiff to be casual.

"Got plenty," the storekeeper said, his voice strained. "How much ya be needin'?"

"Four sacks of each," Ian said, his tone brisk. He didn't like the way the storekeeper kept glancing at the stranger.

"Four sacks, huh?" the other man said suddenly, his tone light but edged with something probing. He stepped closer, taking off his hat to reveal sharp features and curious eyes. "That's a fair bit of corn. What you usin' it for?"

Ian stiffened, his brows drawing together. "To feed cows. Helps fatten up the cream," he answered, his gaze steady. "Why?"

The man shrugged, a small, unreadable smile tugging at his lips. "Just makin' conversation. Not everyone buys corn for cows these days."

Ian's jaw tightened. "Well, that's what I'm using it for," he said. "Anything else you're curious about?"

The man held his hands up. "Didn't mean to bother you, mister. Just seems folks've been buying more corn than usual lately."

Behind the counter, the storekeeper busied himself writing down Ian's order, his face neutral. Ian gave the stranger a curt nod and turned, heading back outside.

As he stepped out of the store, his expression remained unreadable. He passed Esther, who stood by the rabbit pen, a furry brown one cradled in her arms as Benjamin chattered excitedly about which one he'd pick if they could take one home.

Without pausing, Ian walked toward his truck, dropping the tailgate when the sound of footsteps crunching behind him caught his attention.

The man had followed him out.

"Esther," Ian called, his voice steady but sharp enough to carry. "He's bringing out the order. We're leaving."

At the sound of her name, the man's head tilted, curiosity sparking in his expression. "Esther?" he repeated, stepping closer. "That yer wife?"

Ian shot a look over his shoulder, his brow furrowing at the intrusion.

"That's right," he said curtly as he made room in the truck bed.

"What's the last name?" the man pressed, his tone light but probing.

"Huggler," Ian replied, his voice even but clipped. He straightened, turning to face the man fully, his eyes narrowing.

The man gave a faint smile, tipping his hat back just enough to reveal an inquisitive gaze. "Huggler. That ain't a name I've heard 'round these parts before. You folks new to the area?"

Ian's jaw tightened. He didn't like questions—especially not ones about his wife.

"Been here long enough," Ian replied flatly, brushing his hands on his trousers.

The man didn't back off. "And where're you from originally, if you don't mind me asking?"

"Germany," Ian said bluntly. He was used to the questions, but that didn't mean he liked them.

The man's eyebrows lifted, though his smile didn't falter. "Germany, huh? A long way from Larkin. Must've been quite a journey to end up here."

Ian didn't respond, his silence heavy, deliberate. He shifted his attention to the storekeeper, who had come outside with a hand cart stacked with feed sacks, carefully maneuvering it down the long wooden ramp.

"Do I need to sign for anything?" Ian asked, ignoring the stranger entirely as he hefted the heavy bags with ease.

The stranger, undeterred, angled his gaze toward the awning where Esther and Benjamin still stood. He rolled the name slowly off his tongue, as if testing how it felt in his mouth. "Esther Huggler," he mused. "She from Germany, too?

Ian's hands stilled on the edge of the truck bed. His voice was calm, but the edge was unmistakable.

"What's it to you?"

The man smiled faintly, extending a hand Ian didn't take.

"Name's James Hartford. Just curious, is all. A man in my line of work likes to know who's who in town."

Ian knew that name.

The realization struck him hard, but he didn't let it show.

No—he'd heard it from the sheriff. Spoken on his wedding day, a warning Ian hadn't taken lightly.

Agent Hartford. Alcohol Tax Unit.

A division of the damn IRS.

Ian's pulse kicked up, a steady drum against his chest, but outwardly, he didn't so much as blink.

He didn't bother with pleasantries.

"You finished being curious?" Ian's tone was level, unreadable.

Hartford chuckled, resting his hands on his hips.

"No harm meant. Just seems like a man can't ask simple questions these days. You and yer family have a fine afternoon."

Ian gave a single nod, turning away as if the conversation had already slipped from his mind. But inside, he was anything but calm.

He called again, louder this time.

"Let's go. Day's wasting."

Esther looked up, hearing the tension in his voice, and nudged Benjamin toward the truck.

"C'mon, ya pa's gonna leave without us," she said, grabbing his hand. But she didn't rush, walking at her own lazy pace, like she had all the time in the world.

As the tall German climbed into the driver's seat, Hartford remained on the wooden porch of the feed store, watching. His posture was casual, but Ian wasn't fooled for a second.

Once inside, Esther spoke softly as Ian started the engine. "Who is that man, and why's he starin' at us so funny?"

Ian didn't answer right away, his knuckles tightening on the wheel as he backed out of the lot.

"Nobody worth worrying about," he said, but the hard set of his jaw suggested otherwise.

As they drove down the dusty road toward Paulson Mercantile, the tension in the cab was palpable. Ian's whole body was rigid, his gaze fixed on the horizon.

Benjamin sat in the middle, picking at the seam of his shorts, sensing now wasn't the time to chatter. He stole a glance at his father, figuring he must be upset.

Finally, Ian turned to Esther.

"Can you brew with field corn? You know—feed corn?" he asked, his tone low but pointed, careful not to use the word *moonshine* with Benjamin present.

Esther blinked at the sudden question, her brows knitting together.

"Yeah, lots of folks prefer it," she said cautiously, her voice quiet. "It's cheaper than other grains, and it works just fine for... well, you know."

"Dammit," Ian muttered under his breath, his jaw tightening as he pulled on the steering wheel.

Benjamin's head snapped up, his curious eyes darting between his father and Esther.

"What's wrong, Pa?"

Ian forced a small, reassuring smile.

"Nothing, kiddo. Just thinking about something I need to handle. Don't worry about it." He glanced at Esther meaningfully. "I'll explain later."

Esther nodded subtly.

The small town of Larkin was nearly deserted as Ian pulled up in front of Paulson's Mercantile, the truck idling as a faint tune drifted from the open windows of the shop, the crackling sound of a radio filling the quiet afternoon.

Finally, he cut the engine and waited for Esther to look over at him. "I'm gonna drop you off here," Ian said. "Go see if your packages came in. Benjamin's staying in the truck with me."

"Why? Where ya goin'?" Esther hesitated.

"I need to talk to Sheriff Ronell about something," he replied.

Benjamin perked up. "The sheriff? Can I come, Pa?"

Ian shook his head, ruffling the boy's hair. "Not this time, Benji. You're gonna stay here and keep an eye on the truck, all right? Got it loaded up in the back—don't want anybody coming along and nabbing it. People are desperate right now."

Benjamin grunted but didn't argue, leaning back against the seat with a pout.

Esther opened her door and stepped out, but instead of heading straight inside, she circled around to Ian's window, tapping lightly on the glass.

He rolled it down, his brow lifting in question as she leaned against the frame, her tone curious at first.

"Ya sure everythin's alright?" she asked.

He nodded, though the tightness in his expression betrayed him.

"It's fine. You go on in. Don't waste your time with Margie Mae—catch up on whatever gossip you can. I'm sure someone's died or worn a hideous dress bordering on scandalous." His voice was steady but lacked its usual lightness.

She studied him for a moment longer.

"Ian," she began, drawing out his name slowly, like she was sweet-talking him, "I ain't got no money with me, and I wanna get Benjamin a treat."

She tilted her head, folding her hands innocently on the doorframe, her lashes fluttering just enough to be playful.

Without hesitation, Ian reached into his pocket, pulled out his wallet, and handed her a few bills. "Here," he muttered, barely paying attention, too distracted to question.

She took the money quickly, flashing a warm smile before leaning in to kiss him on the cheek. "Thank ya, Mr. Huggler," she teased, then turned and sauntered off toward the store—her hips swaying like she didn't have a care in the world.

He couldn't help but smile, watching her disappear inside—unsure how much money he'd even handed her, and certain she wouldn't be giving the change back. Not that it mattered. Ian enjoyed seeing her happy.

Her ease was contagious, and for a moment, it softened the tension in his shoulders.

Then, with a quiet sigh, he focused down the road toward the small brick police station. Shifting the truck into gear, he pulled out of the parking spot and drove the short distance, his mind already turning over the odd encounter at the feed store.

The building, its red brick facade weathered by years of sun and storms, appeared just as vacant as the store, the sheriff's cruiser the only vehicle out front.

Parking just outside, Ian stepped into the warm afternoon air. The faint scent of tobacco hit him as he approached the open front door, where Sheriff Ronell leaned against the frame, a cigarette dangling from his lips, his hat pushed back on his head.

"Afternoon, Ian," the lawman said, exhaling a curl of smoke as Ian climbed the short steps. His tone was casual, but his sharp eyes suggested he already knew this wasn't a social visit.

"Sheriff." Ian gave a small nod. "You got a minute?"

Ronell eyed the cigarette between his fingers, stubbing it out on the edge of the brick wall, then motioned for him to follow.

Inside, the station was dim and cool—a relief from the bright sun. The faint scent of residual smoke clung to Ronell's uniform as he sank into his chair.

Ian got straight to the point, standing across from the desk as he recounted the strange encounter at the feed lot.

"So, he just starts askin' questions, like what you're usin' the corn for?" Ronell asked, his brow furrowing as he leaned forward, elbows resting on the desk.

"That's right," Ian said, his voice low but edged with frustration. "Didn't even bother hiding it. Just came right out and asked. Like I'd be fool enough to say something incriminating—not that I am," he added.

Ronell sighed, rubbing a hand over his chin.

"James Hartford," he muttered. "Damn fool's been stirrin' up trouble since the day he got here. Ya ain't the first to complain. I've had half a dozen folks come to me sayin' he's been hangin' 'round, askin' after their business like he's got the right."

Ian crossed his arms, his jaw tight.

"He followed me outside. Even asked about Esther—because I used her name in front of him."

Ronell's eyes sharpened, his expression hardening.

"That weasel's got no limits. Ya know, he even had the gall to dig into me, too? Went talkin' to my neighbors like he was gonna uncover somethin' dark and mysterious 'bout me. Askin' the old granny next door if I was mixed up in moonshinin'—on account of my history with Frank."

The sheriff let out a dry laugh, shaking his head as he continued.

"And let me tell ya, that old woman drinks her own home brew. My wife said she was terrified. Almost in tears, worried he'd look in her cellar."

"Frank? Even now?" Ian frowned, his eyes narrowing.

Ronell nodded, the weight of the name settling between them.

"Yeah. Never mind the fact that I had to put that man down myself. You'd think that'd clear me of suspicion, but no. Hartford's convinced everybody's got something to hide."

"People around here don't take kindly to outsiders poking their noses where they don't belong," Ian said.

The sheriff's jaw tightened. "I agree with ya, but the man's got a badge, and that makes him think he's got the right to do whatever he pleases." He shook his head. "Tell ya what… I'll pay the feed store a visit, see if I can't rein him in. But I'll wait a day or two, so it doesn't tie back to you or Esther. Last thing either of ya need is Hartford makin' more of it than he already has."

Ian nodded, though irritation was still evident in his posture. "I'd appreciate that."

Leaning back in his chair, Sheriff Ronell folded his hands over his chest.

"Listen, Ian, my advice? Keep your head down, don't give him a reason to poke 'round. If he comes sniffin' again, send him my way. He don't scare me none, and right now, he's a one-man show."

Ian nodded again but didn't respond immediately.

After a beat, the sheriff's tone lightened.

"How's married life treatin' ya? Esther keepin' ya on your toes?"

"She's got her own ideas about how things ought to be, but yeah, she's keeping me honest," Ian said as he allowed a small smile to break through.

Ronell chuckled. "Sounds like you got your hands full, but in the best way."

Ian gave a soft laugh, the tension easing slightly. "Full's one way to put it."

With that, the sheriff extended his hand, and Ian shook it firmly. Then he headed back to the truck, his mind lighter knowing they weren't the only ones the agent had been questioning.

Parked outside Paulson Mercantile, Ian and Benjamin waited. The minutes stretched on, and Esther still hadn't come out—despite Ian laying on the horn in frustration, a loud "ahooga" belting from the old Ford.

Benjamin fidgeted in the seat beside him, the vehicle warm, his small legs kicking the air. "What's takin' her so long?" he muttered.

Ian tapped his fingers on the steering wheel, his patience wearing thin. "Good question. I know she heard me."

He glanced at his son, amusement clear in his eyes. "This is a good lesson to learn as a man," Ian added.

Benjamin blinked up at him. "I don't get it, Pa. What do you mean?"

"Exactly. You're never going to understand it." With a sigh, Ian pushed the door open. "Stay here. I'll go get her."

The bell above the mercantile door jingled as Ian stepped inside, his boots echoing faintly on the wooden floor. Void of other patrons, the place was unusually still.

Toward the back, he spotted Esther seated with Margie Mae, the two of them leaning over a stack of glossy magazines. Their heads were close together, laughter bubbling as they pointed to the latest fashions from the city—smart dresses with cinched waists and hats adorned with netting.

He strode toward them, stopping just shy of the counter, arms folding across his chest.

"Y'all havin' a good time?" he asked, his mock Southern tone tinged with playful irritation.

Margie Mae grinned up at him, unbothered by his presence.

"Poor Esther's been waitin' on these packages fer months. Least I can do is show her somethin' pretty I found to add to her wish list."

Ian shook his head, his exasperation melting into a resistant grin. "Well, Margie Mae, she's in trouble now. You've made me wait long enough. We're melting out there."

Esther laughed, lifting her head to look at him.

"Oh, yer alright. And I got everythin' I was waitin' fer—told ya it'd be here." She held up a small brown paper bag filled with candy, along with a couple of fresh-off-the-press magazines. "Got some sweets fer the kids, too."

Before Ian had time to say anything else, the front door jingled again.

His posture stiffened.

Caroline Suggs.

The red-haired woman who had shamelessly flirted with him at this very shop the year before—the same woman who had caused Esther so much grief.

Because, of course, his luck today wasn't bad enough.

Dressed in a figure-hugging dress and heels, Caroline scanned the room until her gaze landed squarely on Ian.

"Well, if it isn't the handsome Ian Huggler," Caroline drawled, her voice lilting. "Fancy seein' ya here."

Ian cast a quick glance at Esther.

Her laughter had stopped.

Her eyes narrowed.

Locked onto the red-haired woman.

The one she hated with a passion.

Margie Mae, seeing the sudden shift in Esther's expression, leaned in close and murmured,

"Don't do it, honey. She ain't worth the trouble."

Caroline sauntered toward Ian—too close—her painted smile widening.

"Still out at the Reed Estate? Must be nice. But I bet it gets awful lonely." Her eyes trailed over him boldly, her voice dipping into a sultry drawl. "A man like you—built like that—oughta have more to occupy his time than just a bunch of silly trees."

Ian knew he was in trouble, even though none of this was his fault. He cleared his throat awkwardly, forcing a polite tone.

"Have you met my wife, Es—"

But Esther cut him off, stepping forward, fire in her eyes, daggers aimed directly at the trollop.

"Sorry, but he ain't got time to talk to fake red-haired hussies." Esther's voice was sharp, dripping with sarcasm.

Caroline's smile faltered for only a second before she raised her chin, her lips curling into a wicked smirk.

"Oh, sweetie, no wonder yer so touchy. Must be hard keepin' a man like that interested in ya."

Esther's fists clenched at her sides. "I dare ya to spit those words outta yer mouth again," she hissed, her voice low and dangerous. "I'll skin ya alive and hang ya in a smokehouse. Leave ya gizzards for the peckin' birds."

Caroline let out a dramatic laugh, flipping a lock of curls over her shoulder.

"Like ya would? Ain't ya that sad little hillbilly girl who can't even read? Honey, a man like him… well, he's bound to get bored of a girl like you. Ain't nothin' soft on ya—just bones. Give it time." Caroline's words hit back hard.

From behind the counter, Margie Mae muttered under her breath, "Well, that didn't take long."

Esther's face turned red, her anger spiking.

"What happens when ya take off that corset?" Esther's voice was slow, deliberate, laced with venom. "Reckon ya just fall apart like melted butter?" Then she cocked her head sideways in disgust. "And at least I ain't gotta paint myself all up to get a man to look my way."

Caroline's eyes narrowed as she took a step closer.

"Oh, sweetie, yer so naïve, thinkin' he's with you for anything but keepin' his bed warm."

That was the last straw.

Esther lunged, arms swinging, ready for a fight—but Ian caught her around the waist, pulling her back just in time.

"Let me go!" Esther yelled, her voice shaking with rage. "I'm gonna rip those ugly curls straight outta her scalp!"

Ian sighed heavily, positioning himself between the two women.

"Caroline," he said, his voice calm but firm. "If I were you, I'd stop talking. Esther means every word she's saying, and I don't think you'd like how this ends—especially if you're fond of your hair."

For the first time, Caroline hesitated, her confidence wavering. Instinctively, she reached up, touching her hair protectively. She stole a look at Ian, then at Esther—who was still fighting against his hold, a wild, almost frightening look in her eyes.

Forcing a smug smile, Caroline's voice faltered slightly as she said, "Well, bless yer heart," before taking a careful step back.

Margie Mae—still leaning forward in shock—muttered, "I'd suggest you move along, Miss Suggs. Mrs. Huggler doesn't appear to be the sharin' kind, and I reckon you didn't come in here lookin' for trouble—least not the kind she's fixin' to give ya."

Caroline gave an exaggerated shrug and turned, moving into another room with what little dignity she could muster.

Ian exhaled, turning to Esther—who was still glaring daggers at the woman, her heart racing under his grip.

"That's enough," he said, shifting his hold to her wrist. "We're leaving."

Esther huffed, her voice still shaking with fury. "I've been waitin' a good long while to scratch her ugly face."

She shot one last glare toward the doorway. "If ya hadn't stopped me, I'd have knocked her right off them ridiculous heels."

Margie Mae stepped closer, shaking her head but smiling.

"Honey, you're the first woman I've seen with the gumption to stand up to that girl," Margie Mae said. "She's a shameless flirt, doesn't care if a man's married or not. 'Bout time someone told her off."

Ian sighed, steering Esther forcefully toward the door.

"Let's go," he said firmly. "You've made your point."

Once outside, he faced her, exasperation clear in his tone—but there was no hiding the faint trace of admiration that also lingered.

"Was that really necessary?" he asked.

Esther, still fuming, crossed her arms.

"I'm gonna go back inside," she snapped. "Actin' like she owned the place. That cunt."

Ian's eyes widened, his hand shooting up to cover her mouth. "Esther!" he snapped, glancing over his shoulder to make sure no one—especially Benjamin in the truck—had overheard. "Don't say that out loud."

Her muffled protest was short-lived as he removed his hand, shaking his head.

"Where did you ever hear such a word?" he demanded, though the wary look on his face suggested he wasn't sure he wanted to know.

Esther shrugged, her anger still simmering.

"I know plenty of words. Don't mean I use 'em all the time," she said.

"Well, don't use that one, please." He lowered his voice, rubbing his temple. "You can't go saying things like that in public. And you almost caused a scene in there."

Esther smirked, her temper giving way to mischief. "Almost? That ain't a scene, Ian. There ain't no blood."

Ian let out a deep sigh, pinching the bridge of his nose just as Margie Mae emerged from the store, balancing a stack of packages, Esther's fresh magazines on top.

Her laughter bubbled up as she handed them to Ian. "Lord, I don't think Caroline will ever dare look yer way again."

Esther tilted her head. "I just wanna give her one black eye, see if she could still snag any fellas lookin' like she done been in a rowdy brawl." She paused, then added with a wicked grin, "Maybe two—just to even her out."

Margie Mae let out a loud, full-bellied laugh, the sound echoing down the empty main street. "Oh, good Lord, girl, that would've been the talk of Larkin. And ya know I'm an awful gossip—I'd do my best to paint ya in a good light, but still... might not be the best idea."

"No, not at all," Ian muttered, seconding her advice.

But Esther just grinned, throwing her arms around her friend for a quick hug and kiss on the cheek before climbing into the truck.

Benjamin, already waiting inside, watched her with a mixture of confusion and curiosity.

Ian climbed in with a sigh, resting one arm on the steering wheel as he reached into the bag sitting in his lap, pulling out a piece of candy before tossing the rest of the brown bag to Benjamin.

"You're something else, woman." He spoke around the mint in his mouth, shaking his head—but the hint of a smile gave him away. "And here I thought bringing you along would keep you out of trouble."

Esther, unrepentant, settled back in her seat, her grin as wide as the sky. There was something deeply satisfying about putting Caroline Suggs in her place, and she couldn't deny it.

And maybe—just maybe—it hadn't been all the woman's fault. Ian was handsome, just like Caroline had said. But a girl ought to know better—look the wrong way at another woman's man, and she might just find herself clawed by a wildcat.

Benjamin's eyes widened as he ripped into the candy bag, glancing between his father and Esther with quiet wonder. He'd only caught bits and pieces of their conversation—and a new word he'd never heard before, though he already knew he'd get his mouth washed out with soap if he dared to use it.

One thing was certain—Esther was protective of his father, and he liked that. While Benjamin was shy to admit it, he loved Esther. She listened when others brushed him aside, when they thought what he had to say wasn't important. And earlier, when he had tattled on her, it wasn't because he was afraid of getting in trouble—it was because he didn't want her to get hurt.

With that thought, he plopped a hard candy into his mouth just as the truck rumbled to life, leaving Caroline and the mercantile behind.

Chapter 34: At the Bottom of a Box

All Ian had wanted was to sew the button back onto his favorite work shirt. It seemed a simple enough task to manage himself. He'd made his way up to Esther's small room at Clarissa's house, recalling a box of sewing supplies tucked away in the corner. His hands had searched carefully, pushing aside spools of thread and worn scraps of fabric until his fingers brushed against something unexpected—a small leather pouch with a zipper, hidden at the bottom. Curiosity whispered louder than caution, and he'd unzipped it.

What he found made his breath catch.

Now, the pouch and its damning contents lay open on the long oak table in his house.

Ian stood frozen, his broad hands pressed against the table's edge as if anchoring himself to reality.

The gray stone house around him was unnervingly quiet, save for the slow, deliberate ticking of the carved wooden clock perched on a nearby shelf. Each measured beat grated on his nerves, needling at him with every tick.

He was waiting.

Waiting for Esther to return from her walk with the children.

Waiting for an explanation, though he doubted there'd be one good enough to make him want to listen.

Clive's secret satchel lay open, its contents scattered across the table.

Two stacks of black-and-white photographs and a bundle of neatly arranged bills offered a stark window into Clive's hidden world.

One set of photographs captured powerful men caught in their indulgences—brothels, moonshine, and sins money couldn't erase.

But it was the other stack of pictures, the ones of his wife, Esther, that Ian couldn't look at without his stomach churning.

In them, Esther was almost unrecognizable, her eyes heavy-lidded and unfocused, her dress askew, unbuttoned, open—but worse, her vulnerability was stark against the backdrop of Clive's sordid intent.

Ian clenched his fists at his sides, his breath coming in sharp bursts as he fought to keep himself together.

He hated Clive for taking them, for reducing Esther to this... this.

But he was more than angry at just Clive.

He was furious at Esther.

The front door creaked open, breaking the tense silence with the sound of Benjamin and Rebecca's laughter. Their voices carried lightly across the floorboards, Esther's familiar steps following behind them, a handful of wildflowers hanging loosely in her grasp.

"Go wash up now, you two. Supper'll be ready soon."

Her voice had a soft lilt to it, a small warmth that Ian felt he no longer wanted to hear.

His tone, low and cold, cut through the room like a blade.

"Benjamin. Rebecca. Go to Clarissa's. Now."

The children froze in the doorway, their smiles fading as they looked between their father and Esther. Esther's eyes narrowed at Ian as she stepped forward.

"Why ya grumpy?" she asked, her voice cautious, catching the dangerous edge in his tone.

"I said go," Ian repeated, his gaze locked on hers, his jaw set so tight it might have shattered.

The children hesitated, looking at Esther for direction, but she nodded, forcing a small smile.

"Go on, babies. Do as your pa says," she said, her voice steady despite the growing knot of unease in her chest, still unaware of what lay before him on the table.

The children shuffled out reluctantly, their small footsteps fading as the front door closed behind them.

The silence returned, heavy and suffocating.

Ian's hands trembled as he reached for one of the photos and threw it onto the table in front of her.

The small snapshot slid across the wood, stopping inches from where she stood.

"Care to explain this?" His voice was cold, each word etched with a detachment that made her flinch.

Esther's stomach dropped as her eyes landed on the photo.

Blood drained from her face in an instant, her breath stalling in her throat as she took an involuntary step back.

Her hands trembled as she reached out, but Ian's hand slammed onto the table, covering the photo, stopping her cold.

"Don't," he growled. "Don't you dare touch them."

She swallowed hard, her mouth dry as sand.

"Where… where did you find those?"

"You know where." His voice was jagged, pointed. "In your sewing box," he spat. "Tucked away like some dirty little secret. Is this what you've been hiding from me?"

For a moment, his eyes flashed with something wounded, but just as quickly, they turned to steel.

"Clive's disgusting trophies? And these?"

He held up one of the photos of her, his voice breaking under the weight of his anger.

"How could you keep these? How could you let this even exist?"

Esther just stood frozen, desperate for some type of excuse, but the words refused to make it to her mouth.

Ian had seen everything.

Evidence of a shame she had carried alone, even if it hadn't been her fault.

Her breath hitched, and tears pricked her eyes as she shook her head.

"I didn't want to keep them. I—I was gonna burn them, Ian. I swear. I just… I couldn't look at them. I couldn't bring myself to…"

"You couldn't look at them?" he interrupted, his voice rising. "But you could keep them? You could let these things sit in Clarissa's house?"

His jaw clenched, his breath sharp.

"What the hell does that make you, Esther? Vulgar? Complicit?"

His voice dropped lower, but the venom remained.

"They are fucking disgusting. There's one with your legs wide open—nothing on."

His words were like daggers, cutting into her, leaving her raw and exposed.

Ian grabbed the other pile of photos, lifting them like brutal evidence.

"And men will kill for these—you know that, right? I saw the ones of Frank and Vic. And you just stuffed them in a box like they were a damn keepsake?"

Ian's rage simmered, sharp and unchecked, his breath coming faster as he fought to control it.

"They wouldn't think twice about killing you, Esther. Or anyone else here. You put everyone in danger!"

He glared at her, demanding something, anything.

"Speak," he ordered, but all she did was shake, his words rattling her to her core.

His voice dropped again, quieter now, but no less cruel.

"You lied when you said you'd never had a photo taken."

A bitter scoff.

"You let Clive take photos of you, Esther. You just laid there, posing for them."

The room felt too small, suffocating.

Finally, she spoke.

Her voice cracked and tears spilled as she tried to explain.

"I didn't pose for 'em, I... I didn't even know he was takin' them. I didn't know 'til it was too late. And when I found 'em, I—I couldn't even breathe. I was too scared to even look at them, let alone..."

"Stop," Ian said, his tone low and final. "I don't want your excuses. I don't want to hear it. All of your damn secrets—I am tired of them. I thought I knew you, Esther. I thought you were... someone else than this. But now?"

He shook his head in disbelief.

"I don't even know the woman standing before me."

She reached for him, her fingers trembling.

"Ian, please. It's not how ya think. I didn't ask fer it. I was so drunk, and I didn't—"

"Enough!" he shouted, slamming his hand onto the table. The sound echoed through the house, silencing her.

"You risked everything—everything—for this filth. For money. For what?"

"For you!" she cried, her voice splintering as the words spilled out. "Fer us! Ya needed a lawyer, Ian. I was tryin' to protect ya. I did it for you. Them pictures—not the ones of me, but the others—they got power. Power to keep y'all safe."

Ian stared at her, his expression hardening into something unrecognizable.

"I don't care," he said, his voice cold and detached as he snatched up the pile of photos—the ones of her—and threw them into the lit stove, discarding them forever.

"You've ruined us, Esther."

He grabbed his hat from the counter and moved toward the front door. She stepped in front of him, desperation in her voice.

"Where ya goin', Ian?"

"Away," he said flatly, pushing past her and slamming the door behind him.

The sound of his truck engine roared to life, the tires peeling out on the gravel as he sped down the road.

Esther stood in the middle of the small kitchen, her world falling apart, tears streaming down her face—her chest hollow and aching.

Her mind screamed at her for being so stupid, for shoving the leather pouch in a box of sewing supplies. Never thinking Ian would ever look there. Forgetting he needed a button sewn back on his favorite work shirt.

Damn it, why hadn't he just brought it to her instead of trying to sew it himself?

That evening, she prayed he'd calm down, come to his senses, and just talk to her—hear her out. She had planned exactly what she would say to him.

But he didn't come home.

She wondered if he'd gone to Abram's for the night or just slept in his truck. Either way, she hadn't slept a wink, tossing and turning in the emptiness of their bed.

Esther was terrified, utterly terrified that the words she had prepared wouldn't be enough.

Because she knew—deep down—it wasn't the photos of the compromised men that had truly angered him.

It was seeing the woman he'd grown to idealize brought to such utter shame—a common whore in his eyes.

Those photos had haunted her since the day she brought them back from Clive's.

And she had been lying to herself, telling herself she was only building the courage to sort through them. But deep down, she knew it wasn't true—she'd been running from them, avoiding them altogether.

She hated—despised—the girl in those photos. Though she'd only seen one snapshot, she knew there were more—each one tied to the blurred memory of Clive's camera flash, burned deep into her mind.

She remembered lying in his bed, too intoxicated to stop him, too far gone to fight as he positioned her like a lifeless doll for his wicked designs.

No, Ian—despite indirectly acknowledging that Clive had forced himself on her—hadn't wanted to hear another word. Just pretend your little pregnant wife was never tangled up with her bootlegging cousin, she thought bitterly. He wanted her flawless. Untouched by the cracks and scars of what she'd been through. Perfect. Not broken.

Not her, really. Some other girl who smiled pretty and laughed at his jokes.

The next morning, as the sun crept over the horizon, Esther heard the old, familiar rumble of his truck pulling in. She sat up, waiting, thinking he might come in for clean clothes.

But he didn't.

She knew he'd be working the lower fields today, with the men he'd hired from town set to arrive for the week. Maybe, just maybe, enough time had passed for him to stop and listen—to give her the chance to speak the things that felt so impossible to say.

But Ian wasn't in the mood to listen. His neck ached from sleeping in the cab of his truck, parked out where no one would think to look for him.

He'd spent hours pacing the dirt, trying to wrestle his thoughts into reason, but it was no use.

The images of Esther—her beautiful body laid bare on paper like some common woman of the night—seared into his mind, fueling his anger.

A few times, he'd nearly turned the truck around, torn between missing her and being consumed by frustration he couldn't untangle.

Addie would never have done such a thing. Too much of a lady for that, he told himself. She would have been appalled by such photos—let alone holding on to them.

Later that day, in the fields, Ian worked alongside the hired men, his body moving with the mechanical precision of someone trying to outrun his thoughts.

They dug ditches, the shovels biting into the earth in a rhythm neither calming nor distracting. His usual drive was gone, replaced by a heaviness that weighed down every movement of the tool.

The workers said nothing, sensing the storm in his silence. It didn't help that all he'd eaten was a couple of day-old biscuits grabbed hastily from Clarissa's kitchen, his hunger gnawing at him as much as his turmoil.

And Esther knew he most likely hadn't eaten. Praying he'd calmed down, she made her way past the lower orchard, toward the fields. Uncertain of what she'd find, the sting of his harsh words still lingered—but that didn't change the ache of missing him.

More than anything, she needed to know he was all right. That he was fed, taken care of.

Just seeing his face would be enough. She couldn't lie to herself. And maybe—just maybe—he wanted to see hers too.

When the working men came into view, her breath hitched. There Ian was, standing by his truck, his broad shoulders hunched as he talked to Abram. Her heart leaped at the sight of him, though her courage faltered just as quickly.

The hired men noticed her first, their conversation falling silent as she drew closer. One of them, a medium-built young man with sun-kissed skin named Toby, nodded politely.

"Afternoon, Esther," he said kindly.

Esther managed a faint smile. "Afternoon, Toby. How's ya momma doin'?"

"Aww, she's good. Don't care fer the new preacher that's taken up at the church, but she still goes," he said, grinning, clearly enjoying Esther's attention.

"Well, ya tell her hello," Esther said, though her mind was already distracted, her focus shifting toward Ian.

She could tell he had noticed her, but he didn't make any move to acknowledge her. Still, she took the opportunity, stepping closer to the truck, stopping just a few feet away.

"I brought yer lunch," she said softly, holding out the basket.

Ian didn't even turn his head.

"Take it back to the house," he barked.

"Ian, please," she began, but he cut her off, his voice sharp and unyielding.

"Go back to the house, Esther. I don't want to talk to you."

"Ya ain't eaten," she insisted, setting the basket on the tailgate of the truck.

Abruptly, he turned his back on her, on the food. His words had snapped like a whip, each one leaving an unseen bite. She fought to keep her shoulders from slumping beneath the force of them.

With a weak nod, she murmured, "I made ya a couple ham and cheese sandwiches. Put some of Clarissa's cookies in there, too. Please eat."

As she walked back up the dirt road toward the house, behind her, the men exchanged uneasy glances, their discomfort palpable after witnessing Ian's cold dismissal.

It had been humiliating.

That night, when Ian returned home, his expression was just as cold as it had been that morning. He walked past her without a word, heading straight for the bathroom. The pipes groaned as water rushed from the showerhead into the tub, the steady patter filling the quiet house.

Afterward, he went to the bedroom, disappearing inside for a moment before emerging in clean clothes.

Esther sat at the table, the children working on their studies nearby. Her hands were clasped firmly in her lap as she waited for him.

The tension between them was a living thing, filling the space until it was almost unbearable. It made her stomach turn—her body rejecting even the thought of food since the day before.

"Ian," she started, unable to bear the silence any longer. "Ya needa talk to me."

"I don't have anything to say to you," he replied, his tone flat.

She stood, her hands trembling.

"Ya ain't gonna let me explain?"

He turned to face her, his eyes hard and unyielding.

"There's nothing to explain, Esther. Go to Clarissa's. I'm staying here with the kids."

Her breath caught in her throat, his words hitting like a blow.

"Ian… ya sendin' me away?"

"I need to see my children, and they need my help," he said, his voice cracking slightly before he steeled himself.

"I don't want you here tonight," he added.

The floor seemed to drop out from under her.

He had cast her out, leaving her adrift.

Rejected her.

Unable to even speak, not wanting to alarm the children, whose wide, worried eyes were already searching her face—she turned and left.

Tears streamed down her face as she walked to Clarissa's. Ian had never been so harsh, and he wasn't softening. It felt like he hated her now. And even worse—she hated herself too, knowing she had caused this.

It had all been too good to be true, she thought bitterly. Being with him had felt like magic. And now she had ruined them—just as he had said.

Once inside, she brushed past Clarissa without a word, not trusting herself to speak.

Clarissa, respecting her privacy, let her go. She figured it was just a lovers' quarrel—newlyweds finding their way through the rough patches.

That night, as Esther lay in the dark, sleep never came. Her mind spun in delirium from exhaustion and hunger. Her body ached, but it was the ache in her heart that drove her to act.

Through a haze of tears, she made an impulsive decision, pulling out a small suitcase and packing what she could. Most of her belongings were still tucked away in the small bedroom—leftovers from when this place still felt like home.

"If he don't come by mornin'," she whispered to herself, her voice breaking through the stream of tears, "I'll just go."

He had cast her aside, leaving her feeling as though she no longer mattered.

Like she wasn't wanted.

Who was she to think she could outrun her past?

Clive's cruel grip still held her in those photographs—he owned her even now.

They weren't just photographs—they were chains. Shackles meant to control and manipulate.

She could almost hear Clive's ghost laughing, circling her, reveling in his power over her even in death.

It had driven Ian far from her, tainting whatever trust they'd built.

But what cut the deepest wasn't just his anger—it was that he'd taken the children from her. Used them to hurt her in ways Clive never had.

She couldn't bear the thought of being pushed aside, of becoming invisible to Ian again. His children felt like hers now. And the ease with which he could strip them away tore at the very fiber of her being.

Her hand drifted to her belly, and the fear settled even deeper.

And what if he did the same with the baby she carried?

What if this cold, closed-off version of Ian was all that remained of him?

What if the man who once loved her was gone for good?

Was he dead now?

No, she resolved.

She couldn't stay where she wasn't wanted.

Where she had become unseen.

She hadn't even wanted to get married in the first place, she told herself, clinging to the thought as if it might offer some comfort.

But the ugly lie did nothing to soothe her.

By morning, Esther's mind remained unchanged, though she had hardly slept.

She dressed in a pretty red dress, fixed her hair, and carefully applied lipstick, then sat on the edge of the small bed.

The sounds of the children arriving at Clarissa's reached her, faint but unmistakable.

She walked to the small window, the one she had watched for Ian from so many times before.

This time, she stood and watched him climb into his truck, his broad frame moving quickly as he shut the door and started the engine.

He never looked up.

Never checked her window.

Never hesitated.

He drove toward the fields without a second glance.

No, he hadn't come for her.

And in her mind, it was final.

He clearly no longer wanted her as his wife, she thought. She would have to find her courage and follow through with what she had planned, pride driving her forward.

The sun clung to the edge of the hills when she slipped out the front door unnoticed, the crisp morning air biting against her skin.

With her small suitcase gripped tightly in one hand, she moved purposefully toward Ian's house, where Clive's stash of money remained hidden.

She retrieved it quickly, stuffing the bundle into her case. Dirty money. But she would need it to carve out a new life.

The workers would be heading to the fields soon, and she needed to act fast.

If she could convince one of them to drive her to town, she'd be gone before Ian even realized she'd left.

Esther set her sights on the old barn where the workers parked their vehicles, lining up before heading down to the fields together. She focused her plan on Toby. He had always liked her, and she figured he would be the easiest to persuade.

The estate remained quiet, the early morning stillness broken only by the faint chirp of birds. She hesitated—lingering too long might risk running into Abram.

Her fingers held firm around the leather handle as she scanned the yard.

Then, she spotted him.

Toby's small, battered truck rumbled up the dirt path, dust swirling around its tires.

Esther drew a steadying breath and stepped forward, seizing her opportunity.

As his vehicle came to a halt, she marched straight to his driver's side window, catching him off guard before he even had the chance to kill the engine.

"Toby?" she said.

He smiled, rolling down his window.

"Mornin', Esther. Ya need somethin'?"

She took a deep breath, forcing herself to face him.

"Matter of fact, I be needin' a ride into Larkin. Would ya mind? I sure would appreciate it."

Her voice came out too sweet, almost unnatural.

Toby hesitated as he eyed the suitcase in her hands.

"That somethin' yer husband's all right with?" he asked carefully, knowing damn well how it would look.

Esther's heart clenched, but she straightened her shoulders.

"He ain't got time to drive me," she lied, keeping it simple, her voice steadier than she felt.

Toby studied her for a moment before nodding.

"Well, if he's alright with it, then—hop in," he said.

The truck's engine rumbled to life, its sound breaking the stillness of the morning. Esther climbed into the passenger seat, her suitcase resting on her lap. Toby glanced at her once, his expression unreadable, before steering the truck down the dirt road leading away from the estate.

Despite the pleasant expression she wore, her gut churned. She hadn't even said goodbye to Clarissa or the children—but she couldn't. If she had, she wouldn't have been able to leave. And the pain inside her was so raw, so intense, she felt like she was dying with each slow, passing mile.

She fought against the searing ache, forcing slow, steady breaths to hold back the tears, knowing she'd left her entire heart behind.

As the truck rolled down the road, Toby tried to make small talk. Esther offered polite answers, but it was clear she wasn't in the mood for conversation. He caught on quickly and gave her space.

She stared out the window, her hands gripping the edges of the suitcase as the familiar landscape blurred past.

Her thoughts tangled like briars, circling back to one thing—how she had slipped off her wedding ring that morning, leaving it on Ian's pillow.

She hadn't left him anything else. She couldn't.

No words.

And even if she had found the right ones, she had no way to write them down.

Ian had been in the lower fields for maybe half an hour, his boots already caked with damp soil as he worked alongside the other men, digging drainways to guide irrigation water.

The sharp rhythm of shovels hitting the earth filled the air, a steady cadence broken only by the occasional grunt of effort.

The morning sun had risen high enough to burn off the early mist, leaving the fields warm and thick with the scent of freshly turned dirt. His shirt clung to his back, soaked through with sweat as he drove his shovel deep into the earth, lifting out another heavy scoop.

He paused, leaning on the handle of his tool to wipe the sweat from his brow. The work was grueling, but it did little to drown out the thoughts plaguing his mind.

No matter how hard he tried, he couldn't push away the memory of Esther's expression as she left the house the night before—the pain in her eyes lingering like a ghost.

In the middle of the night, he had wanted nothing more than to reach for her, to pull her close and let it all go. But he'd been the one to send her away, and the weight of that choice pressed down on him like a stone.

When morning came, the images that'd been burned into his mind resurfaced, fresh and vivid. No amount of sleep could erase them.

He'd always known she wasn't untouched, but seeing her there, in Clive's bed, laid bare like she'd been his lover—it twisted something deep inside him, something he couldn't name.

It made him ill, a sickness he couldn't shake, despite how hard he drove himself into the earth.

The sound of approaching footsteps snapped his attention up. One of the hands was heading toward him, his steps hesitant, the shuffle of his boots louder than the steady rhythm of work around them.

The man's fingers fidgeted at his sleeve, pulling at the fabric nervously as he closed the distance. Ian straightened, his brow furrowing as he turned toward him.

"Mr. Huggler," the man began, his voice uneasy, his eyes darting between Ian and the others still digging.

"Reckon I oughta tell ya somethin'. Don't mean no trouble, but 'fore I came down here, I saw somethin'. Somethin' ya might want to know."

That got Ian's full attention.

"Sir, I saw yer wife... gettin' into Toby's truck."

Ian went still, his hand clamped like a vise around the wood handle in his grasp, the words washing over him like icy river water.

His chest tightened, and for a moment, all he could hear was the blood pounding in his ears.

When he spoke, his voice was low and razor-sharp, slicing through the still air.

"She did what?"

The man swallowed hard, raising a hand, like he could shield himself from the coming storm.

"Not sure, but I think they headed towards town, sir," he said quickly, his tone placating. "Just thought ya oughta know."

Ian's jaw clenched, his breath fast and shallow, eyes locked on the horizon. His mind was already racing.

Without a word, he drove the shovel into the ground, the blade slicing deep with a violent finality.

Then he strode away, his steps quick, unyielding, leaving the ditch half-finished.

He didn't wait for further explanation.

The blue Ford roared to life as soon as he climbed inside, the engine growling like a caged animal.

Ian tore down the road, dust billowing in his wake, his thoughts moving faster than the truck ever could.

In stark contrast, Toby's truck rumbled steadily along the dirt road. He drove with caution, easing into the bends with deliberate care—far slower than Esther would have liked.

Her focus drifted, somewhere past the cab where she sat—already planning ahead. She'd need to find a ride to Jasper, check the next bus schedule, and disappear.

It was a plan she'd once imagined with Clive—though now, it served an entirely different purpose.

Escaping with a broken heart.

Her fingers braced against the handle of her suitcase, thumb flicking over the tiny lock—the metallic click-click breaking the tension inside the cab.

Then, a low, familiar growl reached her ears.

A sound she knew too well.

A glance into the side mirror revealed Ian's truck barreling toward them, a cloud of red dirt billowing in its wake.

"Oh—no," she whispered.

Toby noticed too, his brow furrowing as he peered into the rearview mirror.

"That yer husband?" he asked, his hands tightening on the wheel.

She nodded, her pulse pounding.

Panic surged up her throat. "Toby, just stop the truck."

At first, Toby kept driving, his hesitation clear.

Then Ian's truck suddenly veered sharply ahead of them, cutting them off so abruptly that Toby had to slam the brakes—hard.

Toby's truck jerked violently, the tires skidding across the dirt. The soft edge of the road gave way beneath them, tilting the vehicle and nearly sending it into the ditch.

Dust exploded around them, thick and choking, filling the air in a gritty haze.

Esther flinched at the sharp slam of Ian's door—the sound like a gunshot splitting the air.

Ian stormed toward them, his long legs eating up the ground, his face dark, unforgiving.

His eyes locked on Toby through the windshield as he approached the driver's side.

His voice came low and sharp, carrying a mean bite.

"Get out."

Toby lifted his hands in surrender, a humble peace offering, still seated in the truck.

"Now, hold on, Mr. Huggler. Ain't nothin' goin' on here. She just asked me for a ride, that's all."

Ian didn't blink.

"Out."

His voice was quieter this time, more dangerous.

His calloused hands clenched at his sides, coiled like loaded springs.

"I'm gonna teach you a hard lesson."

Esther scrambled out of the truck, her feet barely hitting the ground as the suitcase slipped from her grasp, landing with a dull thud in the dirt.

She moved fast, darting toward Ian, wedging herself between him and the driver's side door before he could reach it.

Her hands pressed flat against his chest, her voice frantic, breathless, trying to halt his advance.

"Ian, stop! Please, he's just a boy—a nice boy! I ain't goin' nowhere with him. He was just givin' me a ride, that's all!"

Ian didn't look away, his eyes boring into the young man through the hazy truck window.

Toby shifted uneasily, leaning into the steering wheel as Ian's voice came low and hard, laced with more anger than the situation called for.

"Get the hell out of here. Step foot on my land again—or go near my wife—and it won't end well for you."

Toby hesitated, his eyes flicking to Esther.

"Ya sure you're alright, ma'am?" His voice carried a hint of worry, despite the intimidation radiating from Ian.

She nodded, her hands still bracing against Ian's chest, as if her small frame could hold him back.

"I'm fine. Just go, Toby. Please."

Toby lingered a second before giving her a reluctant nod. The engine sputtered to life, tires spitting gravel as he reversed, then turned, his truck disappearing down the road.

Ian's glare followed him, still posturing the way he always did when upset—jaw tight, shoulders squared.

But Esther's voice cut through the quiet—she was furious.

"Ya almost ran us off the road, Ian."

His head snapped toward her.

"Ya could've killed us—killed yerself!" she yelled.

Ready to fire back, he opened his mouth—

But the words fled.

The fight drained from his chest in an instant, his breath stalling, his world igniting as his eyes dropped to the small suitcase sitting in the dirt.

His expression shifted.

The anger hadn't vanished, but something else had taken its place—raw, unguarded hurt.

This had broken through his defenses—like a slap across the face. Sobering.

His voice was low—almost hoarse.

"Are... are you leaving me?"

Esther stepped toward the suitcase, her hands trembling as she bent down to pick it up.

Her throat closed, the words almost not making it past her lips.

"Does it matter?" she asked. "Ya don't want me 'round no more. Kicked me outta ya house."

Ian's posture slackened as he stared at her, struggling to make sense of what his rage had created.

"So... so you just decided to leave? My God, Esther, I wasn't going to end our marriage over this."

He took a deep breath, trying to steady himself.

"Where were you even planning on going? And with my child?" he asked.

Her voice was uncertain as she said the words, "New Mexico."

They hung in the air for a moment before Ian let out a sharp, bitter laugh, his frustration spilling over like a dam breaking.

"New Mexico? Do you even know where the hell that is, Esther?" He shook his head, disbelief and pain warring in his expression. "Were you planning to wander across the country with no plan? Give birth to our baby under a cactus?"

"Stop makin' fun of me," she snapped, insulted as her voice broke, tears welling in her eyes.

"I don't like ya anymore, Ian Huggler," she added, her words brittle. "Yer mean to me. So go ahead, make fun of me if ya want. I don't give a damn. Ain't gonna stop me."

He sighed with regret as he rubbed the back of his neck.

"I'm not making fun of you," he said. He knew laughing had been the wrong move, that it would only drive her further away.

And in that moment, realization struck with blunt force.

Ian Huggler found himself fighting again for something he hadn't fully grasped until now. Her.

She was on the verge of disappearing from his life.

But Esther was done.

She clenched the handle of the suitcase as she turned quickly and started down the dirt road, her steps hurried and uneven, her dress shoes catching on the ruts.

He stood frozen for a beat, watching her. Her posture was set—shoulders stiff with determination.

She was stubborn enough to walk the whole damn way to Larkin, and he knew it.

"Esther, stop!" he called out, his voice taut, almost pleading.

But she didn't stop.

Her tears fell freely now, the pain in her chest a dull throb that deepened with each step. She was used to pain, she told herself. It didn't matter how far she had to go—only that it would be far enough to escape this.

But Ian's own panic and frustration boiled over, spilling into desperation. On impulse and in a few swift steps, he caught up. His hand wrapped firmly around her wrist, stopping her in her tracks as easily as if she'd been standing still.

"Let go of me," she demanded, jerking against his grip, her suitcase dangling from her other hand.

"I never said I didn't want you!" he snapped, his voice rising. "I was angry, yes. Hurt. But running off to God knows where—you think that's the answer?"

He paused, taking a breath, trying to rein himself in.

"Esther, you're my wife. I was never gonna end this. Never. But damn it, you didn't even give me a chance to figure it out!"

His grip eased, but he didn't look away, the intensity in his eyes betraying just how much she meant to him—even if he hadn't said it outright.

"Yer hurt, Ian? How'd I really hurt ya?" she asked, her voice cracking under the force of his stare. "Have ya ever had anyone hold ya down? Make ya feel all torn inside? Make ya feel so small ya can't even breathe? No, ya ain't never been that person, not once."

He shook his head as if trying to unhear her.

"Esther, please don't."

"Ya never let me say it," she pushed, her voice filled with both defiance and sorrow. "'Cause ya don't wanna hear it. Now ya done seen it, and I'm sorry fer that."

"I don't want to hear it, I admit it," he said with more honesty than he intended. "That doesn't make me a bad person."

She took a shaky breath, steadying herself.

"It was me in those pictures, Ian. I'm the girl in 'em. And ya weren't there."

"I know that!" he let out, his voice cutting through the air. "And I can't get those goddamn pictures out of my head!" His voice rose to a yell as he turned away, running a hand through his hair, only to whip back around, his eyes blazing.

"Why did you let him take those photos, Esther? Why? Why?"

There it was—the real wound beneath his anger. The question that had been clawing at him.

He wasn't just furious about the images—he was angry at the idea that she hadn't fought harder, that she had gone along with it— even though, deep down, he knew how cruel that thought was.

Esther swayed, weighed down by hunger, exhaustion, and raw emotion.

Slowly, she set her suitcase down, her knees weakening as she lowered herself onto it. She didn't look at him right away, her hands bracing against her legs.

Ian just stared, hands resting on his hips—at an impasse.

She was tired. He could see it, and he didn't like it. It bothered him. There was a weariness in her eyes, and he wondered if she'd eaten, knowing how she often didn't when overwhelmed.

She inhaled slowly and tried to begin—not an emotional purge, just an open door, trying to get out of the way of the words.

"Ya know how I told Benjamin and Rebecca that Bones run off?" she said, her voice steady, but not rehearsed. She lifted her gaze to meet Ian's. A heavy sadness sat deep in her eyes.

He nodded, his fingers flexing, as if bracing for what was coming.

"Well... Clive killed him," she said as her lip quivered. She looked away briefly, the memory still fresh. "He was a fine dog, ya know, gentle heart and all. But Bones didn't like Clive—knew he was up to no good, comin' at me every damn day. So, Clive made sure my good dog couldn't stop him no more."

Not sure what to do with her hands, Esther smoothed the front of her skirt, the slow motion calming her.

She paused, risking a glance at Ian. His shoulders were slumped, his eyes still on her, absorbing every word.

"Ian, I want ya to know I fought him hard fer a good while," she said. "Even pulled a knife on 'im. But you may not know this—it hurts. Not just in the heart, but really hurts a body, too. I ain't strong like ya. I couldn't stop him, no matter how hard I tried."

Ian exhaled slowly through his nose as he absorbed the weight of her words.

"I know, Esther. That's not what I meant," he said, his voice still rough with emotion. "It's just... I don't know..."

She leaned forward, her hands gripping the sides of the suitcase tighter, her shoulders trembling as if refusing to keep her upright as she kept going.

"I was tryin' to survive. That's what someone like me does when they don't know what else they're supposed to do. I was half-dead inside—but still breathin'. And I know those pictures were ugly, dark. But all ya did was see a little photo of it. I lived it, Ian. It was me in them, even if I was just a ghost."

"Then why didn't ya just get rid of them?" he asked as he stepped forward, torn between reaching for her and holding back.

"I was fixin' to," she admitted with a thick drawl. "But I wasn't exactly in my right mind when I came back."

She took a breath and continued.

"Then the sheriff came 'round, makin' me think maybe they'd offer some kinda protection if Gran's moonshinin' came back to haunt me. The men in those photos... they's powerful."

"I know. I'm almost certain Judge Curtis—the man who married us—is in a couple of them," Ian said as a look of disgust crossed his face.

"Other than a few on top, Ian, I never looked through them," she confessed. "My head was soaked in whiskey most days, so I don't know if I can fault 'im. But I'm sorry ya had to see them. And ya burned the ones of me, so they're gone now. Gone forever."

Ian's posture sank as he tilted his head, as if he was biting back the next words—ones he knew would disturb her but needed to be said anyway.

"When you found these photos," he asked, his tone gentler now, "was there anything else with them? In a little envelope? Dark, but clear when you held them up to the light?"

Esther frowned. "No, just an old Bible left," she said.

Ian's eyes sharpened. "Do ya know of any other places where Clive might've stashed his things?"

She shook her head. "Naw. Other than maybe Pritchett Mill. But I don't reckon he'd hide somethin' like that out there." Her voice wavered.

"Pritchett Mill?" Ian questioned as his eyes widened. "Is that why they showed up by the lake last year? Clive and Frank? That mill is upstream from there, isn't it?"

Esther nodded. "There's a good half-dozen large stills up there— a big setup," she admitted, knowing there wasn't much point in holding back now. "But please don't tell the sheriff. If they raid that spot all of a sudden, the Wheelers'll know it was me. And I don't know if they're tied to that other group of shiners."

With a sharp exhale, Ian rubbed his jaw. "Lord, Esther, maybe you shouldn't tell me anything more."

"But yer the one askin' me about Clive's spot," she shot back, her voice edged with frustration as she pushed herself to her feet.

"Well, I was wondering where he might've kept the negatives," Ian said. "The ones used to print the photos."

Esther felt the words before she fully processed them. "I don't understand, Ian. Ya sayin' there's more pictures out there? Of me?"

His silence told her everything before he even nodded.

"Well, I reckon that's just another reason fer me to go," she said, her voice more resolute as she reached for the suitcase beside her feet.

"You're not leaving, Esther," he said firmly, stepping closer. His head tilted slightly, sharp eyes narrowing with a determination she'd seen before. What remained wasn't fury, but something raw— instinct, protection.

Even though her flawed logic frustrated him to no end, his anger had begun to soften beneath the truth of her intent.

She had done what she thought was right, even if it had been wrong.

And he would have to force himself to accept that.

But Esther had no plans of yielding.

"Ya told me I ruined everythin', Ian. Called me names. Called me vulgar."

"And I know what that means," she added as her voice trembled slightly, her eyes locked onto his.

The hurt he'd caused now carried its own weight. Laid bare in the way she stared at him, his words reflected back at him like a mirror.

"That was wrong of me, Esther," he said quietly.

But even as he said it, he knew—an apology wouldn't undo the damage.

She didn't soften.

She just stared past him, her expression unreadable, as if she had already gone somewhere he couldn't reach.

And it hit him like a punch to the gut.

Everything he had worked for, everything they had built—was now slipping through his fingers faster than he could hold on.

"Come home with me, please," he finally said.

"It ain't my home," she said, her voice resigned. "You made sure I knew that, Ian. They're yer children. Ya can't share 'em with me, then take 'em like that."

Her words cut deep, each syllable a brick in the wall she was building, her pride fortifying it higher and stronger.

He stepped closer, his voice firmer now.

"Esther, it's your home, and…" His words trailed off as his eyes fell to her hand.

He froze.

The ring—the one he'd placed there on their wedding day, the one meant to be a symbol of forever—was gone.

"You took your ring off?" he asked in a strained, disbelieving tone. His eyes searched hers, desperate to understand. "I gave that to you. Out of love."

"Well, ya words ain't been soundin' like that," she murmured, as she turned to glance down the road. "Will ya at least drive me to Larkin? Don't wanna ruin my shoes."

Ian just stood there, his hands braced against his waist.

It felt like standing in quicksand—every move sinking him deeper into a mess he didn't know how to fix.

Finally, he gave her a sharp nod.

"If you still want to go," he said in a clipped voice. "I'll drive you."

So, Esther followed him back to the truck, keeping a careful distance between them.

The silence was painful, filled only by the sound of shoes scuffing the dirt road.

When they reached the old Ford, Ian's attention went straight to it. The truck sat at an awkward angle, its front passenger-side tire deep in the shallow ditch.

Ian's fingers pressed into his lower back as a heavy breath left him slowly. He didn't need a closer look to know what had happened as he eyed the truck's sagging form.

Crouching down, he ran his hand along the rubber, his rough fingers brushing over the jagged edge of a timber nail lodged deep in the tire—a clean puncture, no fixing it. Just another goddamn thing to deal with. The gravel beneath his boots scraped against the dry ground as he shifted, muttering under his breath, "For the love of all that is holy."

The whole damn day had unraveled, and this was just one more knot in the mess. He stared at the flat for a long moment, the silence between him and Esther thick as the humid air.

Finally, he pushed to his feet, dusting off his hands as he looked at her.

"Well," he said, his tone dry. "Looks like you're walking to Larkin after all."

Esther stood still, her suitcase in hand.

The fight had drained her, leaving her legs unsteady beneath her. She stared at him, unsure if she should move or wait for his next decision, doubting she had it in her to make it that far now.

He shifted, catching the faint unease in her stance. His jaw worked as he continued studying her, frustration battling with something softer—something that wanted to reach for her, pull her close, and fix what he'd broken.

But her expression was still distant and cold, and he didn't know where to start.

Feeling her hesitancy, he decided to play the card he had up his sleeve, even if it wasn't nice.

He paced himself, wanting to sell it, really sell it, even if he was speaking God's honest truth.

Leaning his back against the truck, his arms crossed over his chest, he ignored the tension between them.

His eyes flicked to her suitcase, then back to her face as the faintest smile pulled at his mouth.

"Esther," he went on, "you might also want to know something if you're thinking about going to Jasper to catch a bus to… what was it? New Mexico."

Her eyes narrowed, unsure of what he was getting at.

"Well," he continued, letting the moment drag for just a second longer than necessary, "they only come on Monday and Friday. And, seeing that it's Tuesday, you're gonna have to wait around for a while. Might as well unpack that suitcase and stay a spell."

Esther's lips parted, her brows knitting together in a mix of frustration and disbelief.

He gave a slow shrug as if he was stating a simple fact.

"I know," he added, "'cause Freddie's coming in on Friday."

Esther's eyes darted to the road, as if expecting her escape to appear. But all she saw was the same stretch of dirt and trees, the same sky watching from above. The wind stirred the hem of her skirt as her grip on the suitcase faltered.

"Yer lyin'," she shot back, but there was no conviction in her tone, just defiance for defiance's sake.

Ian arched a brow, his gaze steady.

"Am I? You think I'd make that up just to keep you here?" His voice softened. "You think you'll find a bus at that station—one that isn't even coming? Or are you going to trust the man who's lived here long enough to know how things work?"

Her shoulders sagged, the fight in her dimming as the reality of what he said began to wash over her.

Her chest heaved and fell with a deep, unsteady breath as she looked away, refusing to meet his gaze. Why was he always right?

Unable to resist, Ian flashed her a smug smile.

"Look," he said, "I'm not saying you can't leave, Esther, if that's what you really want. But you might as well wait till Friday... and I'll drive you there myself, all the way to Jasper."

Her hold on the suitcase slackened.

She hadn't even considered bus schedules, assuming they came every day or so. Now Ian stood there, leaning against the truck with that maddening mix of confidence and aggravation, his arms crossed, as if he were the voice of reason.

And he was acting as though he was doing her a favor, like he'd actually give her the ride he claimed to be offering—such a gentleman.

Her stomach churned, frustration clawing up her throat. She shouldn't say it. She knew it would only make things worse. But the words slipped out—because she had nothing else left to fight with.

"Well, I reckon Hank wouldn't mind puttin' me up for a couple of days," she said, the name landing between them like a match struck in dry grass.

The change in Ian's expression was immediate, his posture snapping straight as he bolted upright, his sharp eyes narrowing. His finger came up, pointed directly at her like a warning.

"Not funny, Esther," he said, his tone hard and commanding, the gentleness from moments ago evaporating.

"I was trying to be soft with you, not fight with you, and you come at me with that bullshit." His voice cracked on the last word, but he didn't flinch, holding her gaze with an intensity that made her look away.

He turned sharply, needing to put his energy somewhere, and strode toward the driver's side of the truck. He got in, leaving the door open as he backed up just enough to fix the tire.

But not before muttering under his breath, loud enough for her to catch every word.

"I can guarantee it'd have to be a cold day in hell before I drop my wife off at some bloke's house."

Her jab had hit its mark, but it wasn't just what she had said that was wrong.

It was the lack of truth beneath it. Esther bit at the inside of her cheek.

She didn't want to go to Hank's—she never had. She'd said it to provoke Ian, to throw something back at him that might hurt as much as he'd hurt her.

But now, watching him, his movements sharp with irritation, she regretted it.

Ian said nothing as he got out of the truck, making his way around to the passenger side to remove the side-mounted tire.

He pulled it free, as though focusing on something else might cool his temper. His shoulders were tense, the muscles in his back visible through the damp fabric of his shirt as he grumbled a string of curse words.

She put her suitcase down, her fingers throbbing from holding it too long, her grip worn out. She fought the urge to apologize, but she didn't want to give him the satisfaction, even knowing her own words had been wrong.

Abruptly, Ian stood, wiping his hands on his pants before turning back to face her, his gaze still piercing but softer than it had been moments before.

"Do you think this is a joke, Esther?" He asked with all sincerity. "You throw Hank's name around like it doesn't mean anything, but you know damn well it does. Trust is fragile, and you're playing with it like it's a toy."

Her breath hitched as the truth in his words left her defenseless.

"I didn't mean it, Ian," she admitted in a small voice. "I just... I didn't know what else to say."

He exhaled, wiping the back of his hand against his neck as he glanced back toward the truck.

"Well, you sure know how to say the wrong thing." His voice dulled, laced with exhaustion.

"Yeah, I reckon that's true," she whispered, barely loud enough for him to catch.

The softness in her tone pulled at him. He turned, just staring at her, really seeing her—the woman standing in the middle of the dirt road. The woman he loved. His Esther.

His chest rose and fell with the effort to contain himself—seeing the cracks in her resolve, the warmth returning to her eyes, despite his own having been absent for far too long.

"I'm tired of fighting with you, Esther," he said, the words tumbling out of him.

That was it.

He couldn't take it anymore.

In one swift motion, he closed the distance between them.

His hands gripped her shoulders as he pulled her in, holding her tight against his chest, his arms wrapping around her as if he'd never let go.

"If you go to New Mexico," he said, "you know I'll just follow you there. You must know that. Damn you, Esther, I'd follow you anywhere. Even into the fiery pits of hell."

He paused, his breath shaking before he went on.

"Don't you get it? You're mine now. I don't care where you run—I'll be right behind you."

His voice dropped lower, the words softer.

"And you already made your choice—you made it when you married me."

She stood frozen in his arms, her own breath catching in her throat as the words washed over her. She didn't move, didn't speak.

"Hug me back, Esther," he pleaded. "Lift your hands and put them around me."

But she didn't. Her arms stayed pinned to her sides, her breathing uneven, betraying the storm inside her. He held on even tighter, feeling the slight shake in her body.

"Hold me back, my love," he whispered as he continued.

"I love you. And I know you won't say the words to me, but I think you love me too."

He paused, his tone shifting to something lighter, almost teasing. "And I think you'd miss me mighty bad in New Mexico. You may not know this, but it's really hot there, Esther. Being a girl from the hills, you'd miss all the green."

"I've seen pictures of it," she said, breaking her silence.

He smiled, relief flickering across his face at her reply, even if it wasn't much.

"Oh, good," he said, tilting his head down slightly to catch her eye. "Have you seen a picture of a scorpion? Big stinger on its back— it flips it forward to sting you when you walk by."

Her lips twitched, the faintest hint of a smile threatening to break her resolve.

"Yer tellin' me a story," she said as she gave him a skeptical look.

Out of habit, she gave him a light smack on the back. It wasn't hard, just a reflex, but her hand lingered afterward, her fingers clutching the fabric of his shirt, feeling the warmth of him.

"God, Ian," she choked out.

Her head fell against his chest, her tears breaking free—hot and burning as they soaked into him.

She leaned into his embrace fully, her defenses crumbling at last.

He cradled the back of her head as he drew her in close, resting his cheek against her hair, his own eyes closing as he felt the tension between them evaporate.

"I'm sorry," he whispered, his voice muffled against the top of her head. "For everything, Esther. I'm so sorry."

Her fingers tightened, and though she didn't say a word, the way she melted into him told him everything he needed to know.

For the first time in days, the distance between them disappeared, leaving only the two of them standing there on the road—not leading them away from home, but carrying them back.

Chapter 35: Forgiving

With the tire fixed, Ian drove his wife home. The road unspooled before them, the thread between them no longer drawn, no longer pulled to its limit, but slack— easing its way back into where it belonged.

When they reached the house, he stepped out first, hauling the blue suitcase from the truck bed. It wasn't heavy, not really, but as he held it, he felt the weight of what it could have meant.

That morning, Esther had packed this bag with the intention of leaving him.

She had carried it from Clarissa's house with that same resolve.

Planned her exit, even secured a ride—something he wouldn't have imagined her doing in a million years.

He glanced at the scuffed leather handle, then at her, trailing behind him, her steps quiet, measured.

Before they reached the door, he stopped. Turned. His hand found hers, his fingers curling firm around her palm.

He needed her to feel it—to know that he was done letting this thing poison at him from the inside out.

She had given him enough to quiet the fire that had consumed him, even if the embers still smoldered, waiting for the moment he could stamp them out completely.

And he was relieved, knowing that he could.

Navigating this part of married life, a relationship on the verge of ending, was foreign to him.

With Addie, things had never reached this point. There had been no rings taken off, no suitcases packed, no doors closing behind them for good. Maybe he'd taken it for granted, believing that Esther's obliging nature meant she never would.

But she had.

And he'd been wrong. Terribly wrong. The realization was a lesson he would never forget.

In the back of his mind, another truth gnawed at him—if the day laborer hadn't told him about Esther's departure, he wasn't sure he would have ever found her. Not knowing she was missing for hours— maybe longer.

Oh, he would've driven to Jasper, searching every dusty corner for her, but with no bus available, who knew what she might have done?

Taken a ride with a stranger, perhaps. And what if she'd made it to New Mexico?

A place so random, so far, he'd have never thought to look for her there.

She wouldn't have written to him in a weak moment, telling him where she was, as he hadn't taught her, insisting she learn.

No, she would have been gone—not dead, but no longer in his life just the same.

At the front door, Esther let go of his hand, heading straight for the bedroom.

She sat on the edge of their unmade bed before dropping to her side. Curled in on herself, knees drawn close, she looked tired— fragile. It pained Ian to think he was the cause. Whatever fight she'd held onto earlier had drained from her, leaving only the quiet collapse into the disheveled quilt beneath her.

It was then that his eye caught the flash of gold from her diamond ring. It lay perfectly centered on his pillow, staring back at him—accusing, full of meaning.

If he'd come home that night without speaking to her again, gone to bed, and found it there—all the while thinking she was at Clarissa's when she was halfway across the state—God, he didn't know what he would've done.

"My love?" he asked softly, sitting down beside her.

She turned her weary head to look at him, saying nothing.

"Have you eaten anything since I left?" he asked

She shook her head, too tired to lie.

"Nothing?" His concern deepened as he thought about the baby and how it had been nearly two days.

"I ate the lunch you brought me yesterday," he said, trying to lighten the mood. "Thank you for that, even if I didn't deserve it."

She gave him a faint smile and shifted, resting her head on its side.

"I'm going to bring you something now—something to eat, all right?" he added as he rubbed her back.

Before Esther could answer, the front door shut with a soft thud, the sound echoing through the house as Benjamin and Rebecca's voices drifted toward them.

Benjamin peeked his head through the bedroom door, but Ian waved him off with a flick of his hand. Unbothered, the boy just grinned and wandered away.

Not following her brother's lead, Rebecca pushed her way into the room, her big brown eyes filling with concern the moment they landed on Esther. Ian knew getting rid of her wouldn't be so easy.

"Esther, I couldn't find ya. I looked everywhere. Where'd ya go?" Rebecca asked, frustration laced in her small voice as she walked up to the bed.

"Yer not goin' anywhere, right?" she added, drawing a sigh from Ian.

Though he had seen it in the beginning, he noticed it more now—how his daughter had attached herself to his wife, as if she could sense the shift in her. That quiet distance Esther had created.

"No, baby," Esther murmured, reaching out for the girl. "Come here and let me squeeze ya."

With a relieved smile, Rebecca climbed onto the bed, curling into Esther's arms. Esther took a deep breath, holding her tight—drawing comfort from Ian's daughter.

Until that moment, Ian hadn't considered how much she might need his children, too, maybe just as much as they needed her. It was undeniable.

And he had cut her off from them so callously the night before, thinking they were his first and foremost. Yet now, he could see it wasn't just him they belonged to. They were hers, too.

She had adopted them in every way that mattered, her love for them woven into her being, body and mind.

"Esther, I'm hungry. My belly's grumblin'," Rebecca said with a pout.

"Yeah? Ya want some bread with jam and butter?" Esther asked, rubbing the little girl's tummy.

Rebecca nodded eagerly.

Ian started to speak, ready to offer Esther a chance to rest, but before he could get the words out, she sat up with surprising ease.

He watched her, saw the change in her posture, the quiet resolve in her movements. She seemed to draw strength from somewhere deep within—perhaps a mother's devotion, he thought.

Esther moved to the kitchen, her steps no longer dragging.

She opened the icebox, scanning the shelves until she pulled out a mason jar of strawberry preserves. At the small butcher board counter, she began assembling the simple snack.

Suddenly, Benjamin appeared behind her, wrapping his skinny arms tightly around her waist.

He'd told Rebecca that Esther wouldn't leave, but when they couldn't find her—and knowing his pa had been upset the night before—he'd been worried.

"Ya want one too?" she asked, giving him a reassuring pat on the back.

"Yes, ma'am," Benjamin replied. "I like yer jam better than Aunt Clarissa's. Hers is too sour."

Esther grinned. "That's 'cause I always sneak a little extra sugar in when Aunt Clarissa ain't lookin'."

Benjamin smiled back, satisfied with her explanation, as she handed both him and Rebecca their slices of bread.

Then Esther turned and saw Ian.

He stood a few feet away, leaning against the wall, watching her. His eyes were glossy—his mind still caught on how close he had come to losing her. The vulnerability in his features wasn't loud, but it lingered there, etched into the way he carried himself.

And as he stood there, he had a profound realization.

Esther had been wrong. And so had he.

Completely wrong.

She wasn't that girl, frozen in those soul-stealing pieces of photo paper.

She was the woman standing before him—good, beautifully wholesome, loving, and devoted.

There was nothing vulgar about her. Never had been.

He'd let himself fall into Clive's trap.

He had looked at her through an evil man's eyes, through the lens of a cruel camera.

And her purity—her goodness—wasn't something a wicked man like Clive could even comprehend, let alone see.

"I reckon you'll take one too," she said, a small smile on her lips, the jam spoon still in her hand.

"If you don't mind," he replied, his voice thick with emotion.

She turned back to the counter, going to work, but before she could finish, Ian moved behind her. His strong arms wrapped around her waist, pulling her into him, holding her close.

"I'm so sorry, my love," he whispered tenderly into her ear.

"Ya already done told me that, Ian," she said quietly.

"I know. But it's not enough, Esther," he said, his voice breaking.

With one arm still wrapped around her, he slid his hand out in front of her, stopping her from finishing her task.

On the tip of his smallest finger rested her wedding ring.

"Please, put it back on," he pleaded.

Esther stilled, her gaze falling to the delicate diamond ring and the way it shimmered in the dim kitchen light—small, but full of meaning.

"I don't know, Ian," she said. "It kinda looks nice on ya finger, but I don't think it's ya size."

He sighed as he removed the ring from his pinky.

"It doesn't belong there," he said, taking her hand softly in his, slipping the ring back onto her finger.

"And it definitely looks better on you," he added, watching as she admired it on her hand.

"Ya know how I like the stone. Ain't fair," she replied, playfully.

With that, she passed a piece of jam-covered bread back to him over her shoulder.

"Didn't put much butter on it, the way ya like," she said as he took a large bite, swallowing half of it whole.

Before taking another, he held it out in front of her, silently urging her to eat.

She knew he wouldn't back down, so she surrendered, opening her mouth and letting him press the thick slice between her teeth. She took a bite, chewing thoroughly, catching the pleased look he gave her.

"You'd better make a couple more. I'm starving, and Benjamin's right—your jam does taste better," he said, biting into the slice again.

Benjamin chimed in, grinning from the table. "We shouldn't tell Auntie, though."

"That's right, son. We don't want her rationing the sugar," Ian said, chuckling as he nudged another bite toward Esther's mouth. This time, she didn't resist.

As she chewed, she muttered, "Are ya just gonna stand here feedin' me ya food?"

"Yep," he replied without missing a beat.

She laughed, handing him another piece of bread, certain he was hungry, but liking the way this small game between them soothed the bruised places that still lingered.

"You know what I'm thinking?" Ian said with a full mouth.

"What's that?" she asked, tilting her head back.

"I think Abram's got enough men down in the field, and I need to help our children build that darn tree hut before you try to do it again."

Before Esther even had time to respond, animated cheers erupted from the small people in the room as they came running.

"Really, Pa?" Benjamin asked.

"Yes, but first, we've got to take down that death trap you were working on. I think I know a better tree out by the old cistern," Ian said, grinning as he pushed one more bite into Esther's mouth.

"Esther, ya gonna help us too, right? Pa might not make it like the drawin', and he listens to you," Rebecca begged, tugging on Esther's dress.

"I'll come on out with ya. Just let me put my other shoes on," Esther said as she moved toward the bedroom.

"We should take the rest of this loaf and jam out with us," Ian suggested, already moving to the counter to make more.

As the four of them made their way out past the upper orchard to the old cistern, Ian pointed out the large sycamore tree he had scouted earlier.

He was right—it was the perfect height, split down the middle, and tucked far enough away to keep it from being an eyesore in front of Clarissa's house, as the older woman had requested in private—a subtle suggestion he'd taken to heart.

With easy skill, Ian set to work, pulling old lumber from a pile by the barn. The children handed him whatever tool he requested. Benjamin, being his father's son, knew exactly what to fetch and did so eagerly, his boyish glee spilling over as his dream took shape. Each plank, each nail, brought it closer to what he had envisioned.

Noticing they needed more refreshments—and knowing Ian's appetite—Esther left to prepare lunch. She made a picnic of lemonade and sandwiches with bacon, lettuce, and the first of the early tomatoes just coming in.

Ian spread out an old blanket from the barn in the shade so she could sit and watch their masterpiece take shape—or at least, that's what he kept referring to it as.

Rebecca, however, had other ideas. With her little hands on her hips, she insisted it needed to be painted and have walls—because a platform wasn't enough and looked nothing like what the Robinsons had.

Abram, fresh from the field, wandered over to the project, shaking his head at Ian.

"Ya just abandoned me out there with a group of men who don't take instructions well," he grumbled.

Ian grinned as he hammered a nail into place.

"Well, neither do my kids nor Esther, so it's about the same job."

Somehow, Abram got roped into the construction, trading places with Ian for a while.

Ian took a break, walking over to the big blanket where Esther sat, a soft smile on her face.

Without warning, he nearly toppled her over, pinning her on the ground, his warm body pressing against hers.

"Ya all sweaty," she laughed as he leaned in to kiss her.

"Kiss me," he insisted, his grin wide and mischievous.

"Ya gonna leave me alone if I do?" she teased.

"Nope, never," he said, lowering his voice so only she could hear. "Darling, haven't ya heard of make-up love makin'?"

"Ya just makin' that up, Ian," she said, her tone skeptical but amused.

Ian, knowing he couldn't convince her on his own, hollered out, "Hey, Abram! What do you and Mitzy do after a big fight?"

Abram let out a hearty laugh as he sawed a piece of wood Benjamin held.

"I can't say it in front of your kids, Ian!"

"See?" Ian said with a triumphant grin. "It's almost as important as consummating your marriage."

"What's that?" Mitzy asked as she came up behind them, Jeremiah tucked in her arms.

"Make room, Ian. I'm sittin' with the two of ya—despite what looks like ya compromisin' my innocent friend out in the open," she said with a wide grin.

Ian rolled onto his elbow with a mock groan, dragging out the sound as if the effort was too much. Esther only laughed, shaking her head as Mitzy eased onto the blanket, claiming her spot without a second thought.

"Mitzy, I'm workin' on gettin' Esther to forgive me," Ian said, then leaned in, pressing another long, drawn-out kiss to Esther's lips.

"Aww, you mess up, Ian?" Mitzy teased. "Esther, don't let 'im trick ya into givin' him some lovin'. That ain't a punishment—it's a reward," she added with a smirk.

"Woman," Abram called out, loud enough for everyone to hear, "ya givin' them advice ya ain't followed yerself."

"What are ya talkin' about?" Rebecca asked as she wandered over, her cloth doll now sporting a crown of wildflowers.

"Nothing, Rebecca," Ian replied quickly, trying to steer the conversation onto safer ground.

But Rebecca wasn't finished. "Pa, why ya always holdin' Esther down like that? Layin' on top of her?" Rebecca frowned, her voice laced with concern, as if wondering whether Esther truly liked it.

Esther buried her face in Ian's chest, stifling her amusement.

Ian opened his mouth, searching for an explanation.

"Well…" he paused awkwardly, scrambling for an appropriate response.

From the shade of the tree, Abram chuckled.

"Yeah, Ian, what's the real reason ya always got Esther trapped under ya?"

Benjamin, ever the logical one, walked over to his sister, guiding her away as he said matter-of-factly, "That's 'cause girls like to be kissed that way."

"Benjamin," Ian said, trying to correct him—though he knew the boy was beginning to piece things together. Sooner or later, he'd have to have that talk with him.

Leaning down, he whispered against Esther's ear, "Any time you want to rescue me, darling, I'd be grateful."

Esther peeked up at him, eyes dancing. "Why would I do that? Benji's right. I do like bein' kissed this way."

Ian let out a low chuckle, shaking his head as he pressed a quick kiss to her temple.

"Well, now I know who not to count on when I'm in trouble," he said.

Rising to his feet, he dodged Rebecca's curious gaze and Abram's knowing grin before striding toward the tree.

"Let's finish this masterpiece," he called over his shoulder.

With both Abram and Ian working in tandem, the tree hut quickly took shape. Abram fashioned a sturdy ladder, securing it against the trunk, while Ian salvaged worn wood panels from an old, unused pen, piecing them together to form rough walls around the platform.

Nearby, Esther, Mitzy, and Rebecca busied themselves with a winding rock path, pressing stones into the soft earth and transplanting wildflowers to line the way—wildflowers Ian almost trampled as he passed, carrying another weathered plank for the roof.

Rebecca, eager for an audience, dashed off to the house and returned with Clarissa in tow, a plate of cookies balanced in her hands. Ian and Abram wasted no time, swiping more than their fair share while the children watched, giggling at their greed. But no one protested—the roof was nearly finished, and the afternoon hummed with the kind of easy warmth that made even hard work feel like play.

Mitzy leaned against Esther's shoulder, a slow smile spreading across her face.

"I bet our babies will come and play in this house."

"Ya think it'll still be standin'?" Esther teased.

"Excuse me?" Ian scoffed, straightening up from his work and gesturing toward the treehouse. "This thing's gonna outlast that old cistern—and that thing's ancient."

Mitzy rested a hand over the small swell of her belly. "Well, these babies ain't gonna be too far apart, I figure." She eyed Esther. "When's yours due?"

Esther hesitated, shifting. Truth was, she didn't know. Aside from the hushed talk she'd overheard about it taking nine months, she wouldn't even know how to figure it out.

Ian, listening nearby, set down his hammer and stepped closer, leaning in like he was sharing a secret.

"Christmas time," he said, wiping his hands on his trousers. "Baby's due right around Christmas."

Mitzy's brows lifted, her expression turning warm. "Well, ain't that a sweet little Christmas gift ya gave her, Ian."

"That was almost nice, Mitzy," Ian said sincerely.

Esther's breath caught as she processed his words. She lifted her eyes to him, uncertainty flickering beneath her quiet expression.

"Christmas, really?" she whispered.

"When did ya think it was?" Ian asked as he met her gaze.

She gave a small shrug. "I dunno… sometime next year, I guess. I hadn't thought about it."

He could already see the wheels spinning in her mind, the weight of it settling over her. So, he reached out, brushing a reassuring hand over her arm. "Don't worry, it's still a ways off. Plenty of time to get ready," he added.

Mitzy grinned and nudged Esther's other arm. "Well, maybe y'all can put a little bundle under the tree."

"Ain't had a Christmas tree since I was a young'un myself. Gran said it was a waste of good wood," Esther said, still taken aback by the other part of the conversation.

"Now that's just plain ridiculous," Ian said, giving the treehouse a once-over before shaking his head. "And now that we know we're not going to be shot on sight, we'll go up to the Blue Hollows and take some real nice trees—just to spite that old lady."

He smirked, shaking the hut to test its stability before hammering in a few final nails.

"It looks real nice, Ian," Esther said softly as she watched him work.

No sooner had she spoken than Benjamin and Rebecca scrambled up the ladder to test out their new hideaway, their excited voices filling the air.

"Pa, it needs a door—and it needs to go higher," Rebecca said, pointing far up into the tree.

"Like a crow's nest," Benjamin added.

"Well, I'll think about a door, but this is as high as you're going. Sorry. You don't want Esther climbing up there, looking for me, do you?" Ian said as he started gathering up his tools.

"Can we sleep out here tonight, Pa?" Benjamin asked, undeterred by his father's refusal to expand the project.

Ian lifted a shoulder, easy and unconcerned.

"You can sleep out here if you like, but I'm sleeping in my bed tonight—with my wife." He tossed Esther a cocky little half-smile, like a man offering a deal, though they both knew it wasn't up for negotiation.

Before Benjamin could argue, Esther cut in, hands settling on her hips.

"What ya gonna do if a bear comes fer ya? Naw, ya can play out here, but ya ain't sleepin' out here."

Benjamin's face fell, disappointment plain. He turned to his father, hoping for backup, but Ian only lifted a shoulder again, as if to say, *Sorry, kid.*

"That's between you and Esther. And since she's the resident bear expert, I'd say you might want to heed her advice," Ian said as he ruffled Benjamin's hair before nodding toward the scattered tools. "Now, help me pick these up before they rust."

The sun dipped lower, stretching long shadows across the hills. Abram, Mitzy, and Clarissa had already made their way back to the house, their laughter fading into the hush of the evening.

Ian and Esther followed, the children running ahead, Benjamin clutching an armful of tools as he hurried toward the barn.

"Don't run with that in your arms!" Ian called, watching as Benjamin sprinted through the grass, tools rattling against each other. The boy barely slowed, determined to reach the barn first.

Esther glanced over at Ian, catching the lingering smile on his lips, the way his gaze softened when it landed on her.

She shifted the blanket in her arms, her voice quiet, meant only for him. "That was nice, Ian. Thank ya."

He leaned in, temptation flickering in his eyes. "How nice are we talking?"

"I swear, how is it ya turn everythin' dirty?" Esther asked, giving him a pretty smile.

Lowering his voice, making sure the children were far enough ahead, he said, "Esther, I lived like a monk for almost six years."

She blinked. "What does that even mean? I know what a monk is, but..."

He cut her off with a smirk. "No sex, Esther. For six years. Nothin' but, well... myself." His sheepish smile only made her amusement grow.

She hummed, her eyes glinting.

"That's a mighty long time, poor boy." Then, after a beat, she glanced sideways at him. "And ya turned me down last year?"

He laughed, shaking his head at the thought. The man he was now wouldn't have even hesitated.

She studied him, with a hint of thoughtfulness behind the teasing as she asked, "Did ya even think I was cute back then?"

"You do realize you spent that whole day at that lake running around in those very short, cut-off shorts, right?" he answered as his lips twitched. "And yes, I had dirty thoughts about you back then— more than I care to admit."

Not wanting him to be alone in his honesty, she whispered, "Well... Ian, I had a lot of my own naughty thoughts 'bout ya too."

He stopped mid-step, his gaze flicking toward the children as they disappeared further into the distance. Then, turning back to her, his eyes sparked with curiosity.

"Like what?" he asked, leaning in. "Go on, I'm all ears, darlin'."

Esther wrinkled her nose as if she were shy. "Ya want me to tell ya the details?"

He pressed closer, unwilling to let it go, not caring that she was clearly embarrassed.

"Did you think about me when you... when you touched yourself?" His voice was low—laced with something darker, something wanting.

She swallowed a gasp, her hands curling tighter around the folded blanket.

"Why are ya askin' me things like this?" she said as the heat crept up her neck, his tall frame looming over hers.

Ian's gaze never wavered. "Is that a yes?"

She hesitated, her lips parting slightly before she finally gave him the answer he was waiting for.

"Sometimes... well, most times."

A slow, satisfied grin spread across his face.

"Most times?" he repeated, both pleased and surprised, and with obvious enjoyment. "You mean to tell me you were up in that little bedroom, satisfying yourself?" He paused, thinking about it, the thought alone sending a thrill through him.

Esther swallowed, knowing she should be mortified, yet for some reason she wasn't.

"I wasn't always in my bedroom, Ian," she corrected, indulging him.

He stilled, interest flashing in his eyes.

"Where, then?" His mind raced with possibilities. "The barn?"

"No," she said quickly.

A pause. Then, softly she uttered, "In the orchard."

Something shifted in his expression, his smirk fading slightly as he registered her words.

Only the trees had watched her. Only the wind had carried the quiet sounds of her longing.

She had gone there because she had wanted to be near him, to stand where he stood, to press her back against the same trees he had leaned against, their bark rough against her skin. His presence lingered there, even when he wasn't.

His shirtless torso burned into her memory. The sound of his voice drifted through the orchard. The sketches hidden in her hymn book, delicate lines of graphite tracing the shape of his arms, his hands, his face.

Ian exhaled, running a hand over his jaw.

"Wow, Esther." He studied her as if he were seeing her in a whole new light. "I'm never gonna walk through there now and not think about that."

"You could've been caught," he added, his tone caught between scolding and something dangerously close to admiration.

"Ya nearly did once," she admitted, embarrassment coloring her face as the memory surfaced.

It was late, and she thought he had gone in for the night. The orchard had been quiet, the air thick with summer, the scent of ripe fruit lingering on the breeze.

She'd slipped away to be alone, to let her thoughts drift where they weren't supposed to. Under the canopy of an older tree, her body had betrayed her, craving his touch, her imagination shaping his hands in the place of her own.

Ian's smile deepened, his curiosity piqued. He had no idea. He'd seen her there plenty of times, often wondering what drew her to that spot. Now, he found himself questioning which night it had been.

"What 'bout you, Ian?" she asked. She half-expected him to brush it off, to harass her instead.

But he didn't.

He held her gaze, enjoying the honesty between them. It emboldened him to match it.

"Well…" He hesitated, smirking slightly as the memory played out in his mind. "That time I saw your nightgown."

Esther's breath hitched.

"Remember?" he said in a hesitant tone. "I hadn't seen a woman like that in years. And, well… let's just say that memory—your nipples—kept me company many a lonely time."

He cleared his throat hastily, realizing how blunt he sounded. "Oh, I tried not to," he added, worried she might think him some kind of pervert.

But she only listened, quiet and unflinching, her expression unreadable except for the soft press of her lips, the way her breath had gone just a little shallow.

That alone urged him on.

His voice softened. "And New York." He exhaled, as if the admission alone was weighty. "Esther, I got so lonely. Don't think badly of me, but I thought about you a lot then and inappropriately."

She studied him, her eyes searching his. "Like what?" she pressed as if daring him to say it.

He leaned in, his lips grazing the shell of her ear as his breath warmed her skin.

"Of what I wanted to do to you," he murmured, his voice deep and deliberate. "Of how much I wanted your beautiful, naked body lying beneath me. Of you… you letting me take you again and again. Asking me too."

Esther gasped, her body going still, her mind reeling at the thought of him—miles away, aching for her the same way she had for him.

"Darling," Ian said, his voice low as his gaze flicked in the direction of the barn, "you might need to put these away for me."

She started to ask why, but then she followed his eyes, her breath hitching as she caught sight of the unmistakable strain against his trousers.

"I've got a problem," he added, his tone dry but laced with that familiar hunger.

She shook her head, but the corner of her mouth betrayed her, curving just as she took the tools from his arms.

"Ya've got that problem a lot," she said.

"I do. How about you meet me back at the house? I saw the kids heading to Clarissa's," he shot back as his eyes lingered on her, the space between them charged with a wordless understanding.

She turned toward the barn, but before disappearing inside, she glanced over her shoulder, her gaze dragging over him in a slow, deliberate sweep.

"Ian Huggler, you're so damn handsome it gets ya whatever ya want—ya know that?"

There was no mistaking the truth in her voice.

Ian stood there, watching her vanish into the barn, a slow, satisfied warmth settling in his chest.

As he walked back toward their little house, the late afternoon air hung thick with the scent of hay and dust, the distant hum of cicadas playing loud, as if bidding the long day goodbye.

Despite the events of the early morning, despite the tension of the past few days, something between them had returned.

They had mended things.

Rebuilt them—not haphazardly, but with the little things that truly mattered in a short life on this earth.

There was no regret in his mind for the unfinished work in the fields, for the tools left waiting.

Because today had mattered more.

His children had needed to see it—to see him and Esther not just standing together, but leaning into each other, stronger.

And Ian knew the shadows were still circling them—chasing her. And though he feared they could catch up, that made today all the more important.

Aware that his own childhood had been shaped by uncertainty and coldness, especially from his mother, he could still remember moments—fleeting, but real—when his parents had tried to do the same.

Watching them rebuild had made the world feel safer back then.

And now, as a husband and a father, he understood in a way he never had before.

Love wasn't just something spoken. It wasn't just something felt. It was built.

Piece by piece.

Chapter 36: Freddie

The road stretched ahead, empty but for the steady hum of Obadiah's old car beneath Ian's hands. Early Friday afternoon, Miller Highway rolled out before him, the world just waking as the blurred countryside rushed past.

It had been months since he'd seen his younger brother, Freddie—not since New York, when he'd left him to his playboy lifestyle, always in the company of some new beauty, with no intention of settling down.

Freddie was five years younger, Ian's opposite in more ways than not. Freddie had only spent a handful of years in Germany, just enough to remember the language but not enough to feel tied to it.

"I'm British, if anyone asks," he'd say, flashing a slick, good-looking smile. "And the broads like it."

But Ian had felt it was his responsibility to point out that anyone paying attention would piece it together, given they were brothers, but he left Freddie to his innocent games.

Just like Ian, Freddie had migrated to New York five years later, living with him and Adeline in their cramped flat until he found his own way in the sprawling city—and he had.

Now, for the first time, Freddie was coming to see the place Ian had made into a home. He had never met Rebecca—not once. And the last time he'd laid eyes on Benjamin, the boy had still been in diapers, clinging to Adeline's hip. So much had changed, and Freddie had missed all of it.

Pulled back to the road ahead, Ian took in the open fields, neat rows of corn framing the road on either side.

The drive had been fairly enjoyable, aside from a brief delay when cattle wandered onto the highway, herded by a lone rider on horseback.

Ian eased past without complaint, the road slipping by, Jasper rising in the distance.

And he was grateful to be driving alone—no passenger, especially not Esther, who had thankfully let go of her idea of New Mexico and leaving him behind. He had even gone so far as to show her pictures of the state, so that she'd know exactly what she'd be getting into if she went there—scorpions and all.

But just to spite him, Esther had said it still looked nice. She even added that she still planned to go there someday.

As Ian pulled up to the small Greyhound station—a rickety building with only an outhouse for the riders—he spotted the familiar figure of Freddie. His younger brother looked like a New Yorker lost in the sticks, clearly out of his element. Smoking a cigarette, Freddie's dark features stood out as he glanced around, suitcase in hand.

Ian stepped out of the car, his taller frame drawing Freddie's attention.

"So, this is it, Mannie?" Freddie said as he walked toward Ian.

"Ignatz, if you want me to call you Freddie, you'd better start calling me Ian," Ian teased as he stepped forward to hug his brother.

Freddie smiled, flicking his cigarette to the ground. "Well, Ian, I've got a nice little surprise for you," he said with a charming grin.

"That's funny, because I've got one for you too," Ian replied, thinking how he'd held off telling Freddie that he'd gotten married and was looking forward to surprising him with Esther.

"Well, I'll go first," Freddie said, nodding toward the small door of the bus station.

As Ian turned, a pretty blonde stepped out. She wore a green dress, her suitcase in hand, her eyes sparkling as they landed on him.

It was Dolores Donnelly, the Irish girl Ian had kissed and briefly dated in New York.

"Hello, Ian," she said, a sweet smile on her face as she walked toward him.

"Oh God," Ian muttered, his head snapping toward his brother's face.

The expression Freddie expected—a mix of delight and gratitude—was nowhere to be found. Instead, Ian looked somewhere between horrified and exasperated.

Freddie had convinced Dolores to come along for the visit, thinking his brother needed to see a pretty girl. He'd seen Ian miserable and lonely in New York without a woman, and in Freddie's mind, this was a surefire way to cheer him up.

Ian, managing a strained but polite smile at Dolores, quickly excused himself. "Hiya, Dolores. Just give us a moment," he said, his tone betraying his nerves as he grabbed Freddie's arm and dragged him toward the car.

Once they were out of earshot, Freddie spoke first. "You're bein' rude, Mannie. She came all the way across the country to see you," he said, glancing back at Dolores and offering her a reassuring smile as if everything was fine. "She's got it bad for you, and I had to convince her to come with me."

Ian ran a hand through his hair, his mind turning over the problem.

"While I'm sure your gesture had some kind of annoying goodness to it, why don't you ask me what my surprise for you is?" he said, staring blankly at his brother.

Freddie blinked, confused, before venturing a guess.

"What? Did you get married or somethin'?" he asked.

"Um, yes, Freddie. I did. And my wife is at home right now, waiting to meet you—not you and Dolores." Ian's tone was sharp, but not without guilt, as he glanced back at Dolores, her smile faltering slightly.

Freddie's jaw dropped open, holding it for a beat before a boyish grin spread across his face. "Well… that's awkward."

"Shit, this isn't good," Freddie muttered, swallowing hard. "Who the hell did you go off and marry so fast?" His curiosity piqued—it was second nature to him, gathering quick scoops, polished from years of managing a popular nightclub in New York's bustling nightlife scene.

"You remember the girl from the hills I told you about?" Ian replied, already formulating a plan to explain this mess to Esther. His stomach churned as he thought about how he'd described his loneliness in New York but had conveniently left out Dolores, the girl who lived just two floors above Freddie in a small high-rise.

"Clarissa's other niece?" Freddie asked, raising an eyebrow as Ian nodded.

"Boy, you sure like that family," Freddie added, straightening his tie as he prepared himself to face Dolores. "You wanna tell her, or should I?" he offered, clearly in no hurry to break the bad news himself.

"Will you just do it, Freddie?" Ian asked, his voice strained. He wasn't ready to confront the emotional fallout.

"And when you talk to her, tell her that while she's at the estate, she needs to pretend she's with you. You know what I mean," Ian added, his tone verging on desperation.

Freddie sighed, shaking his head. "I could just take her back to New York, but we're beat—it took two damn days to get here," he replied, waving at Dolores, who was beginning to look visibly worried.

"The next bus that way isn't until next week," Ian said, thinking briefly about driving them to a bigger city but realizing they'd most likely have to make do by bringing Dolores back with them.

"Well, here goes nothin'," Freddie muttered, steeling himself as he headed toward the waiting girl.

Her expression was pleasant at first, her eyes darting to Ian as Freddie began explaining the uncomfortable truth.

Ian saw the shift instantly—despite his lack of feelings for her, Dolores had clearly liked him more than he'd thought.

Her eyes filled with tears as Freddie tried to comfort her, rubbing her arm and attempting to pull her into a reluctant hug.

Ian watched as Freddie delivered the second part of the message, the part about pretending they were together. Dolores didn't take kindly to the suggestion, shaking her head and resisting as Freddie seemed to plead with her.

"Please, Lord," Ian muttered under his breath, his thoughts turning to Esther. He could only imagine her reaction if she caught wind of the girl. Esther wasn't the type to exchange pleasantries with a woman she felt threatened by.

He'd seen her sharp edge with Caroline, and while that situation had amused him, this one was different. Dolores was a sweet girl—a department store worker who'd turned down plenty of suitors—yet for some reason, she'd set her sights on him.

After what felt like ten excruciating minutes, Freddie finally walked back to Ian, his face a tangle of worry and frustration.

"I explained everything. She agrees not to say anything, but she doesn't like the idea of pretending she and I are together. So, if you can make do with that, she'll keep her mouth shut," Freddie said.

Irritated and just wanting the ordeal over with, Ian motioned toward the car. "Put her in the backseat," he said, grabbing his brother's suitcase and making his way around to the rear.

As Ian opened the trunk, Dolores walked up, handing him her luggage as well.

"Ian," she said shortly, her eyes still red with embarrassment.

"Dolores," he replied, his tone even. He thought briefly about apologizing but decided against it, not wanting to ignite a conversation—or worse, stir up any lingering feelings.

The drive back to the estate wasn't painful, but it wasn't what Ian had hoped for either. He'd imagined bonding with just his brother, not navigating the awkward tension of an uninvited guest.

Unfazed by the strain, Freddie—ever the entertainer—kept the conversation going. Switching to German once Dolores had settled in the backseat, he began filling Ian in on every scrap of family news, knowing full well she wouldn't understand.

"Got a letter from Papa," Freddie started, his voice lively. "You'll love this. They're trying to make it to New York—with Liesel in tow. Can you believe that?"

Ian glanced at his brother, the road twisting gently before him. "Liesel? She's... what, almost twenty now?"

Freddie nodded. "Yeah, nineteen going on twenty. And guess what? England's not working out for them anymore. War's creeping in, and our last name isn't doing them any favors."

Ian's grip tightened on the wheel. He didn't need to ask what Freddie meant—he already knew.

"And," Freddie continued with dramatic flair, "our dear maternal grandparents are still waving their Der Führer flags high. Can you imagine the scandal if that ever got out? The old man—what's his name, Leopold?—probably keeps a framed picture of Hitler on his nightstand."

Ian grimaced. "You're exaggerating."

"Am I?" Freddie asked, unbothered by the gravity of the topic. "You know Papa's pulling his hair out over it. A progressive married to... well, a dyed-in-the-wool Nazi."

Ian sighed, his focus remaining on the road. "Do you think they'll make it?"

Freddie shrugged, settling back into his seat. "Maybe. Papa says they're trying. But can you picture the circus once they're here? I'm not going to play host to them. Let's just say, I wouldn't book the room next to theirs."

The Huggler family was complicated—one of the reasons Ian had left England for New York at the young age of eighteen, never looking back. He hadn't seen his parents since.

His mother had almost outright denied his marriage to Adeline and refused to acknowledge his children as true Hugglers, claiming they weren't pure Germans. That bigotry and her poisonous beliefs had driven a permanent wedge between them.

When Adeline died, Ian had received a heartfelt letter from his father—but nothing from his mother. The silence hadn't surprised him. He hadn't even thought to tell his father about his second marriage, knowing it would only be shared with a woman who had no right to know such private, intimate details about the life she had criticized so harshly.

Ian tightened his grip on the wheel, his thoughts darkening. Beside him, Freddie flipped effortlessly back into English, as if sensing Ian's mood and deciding to ease the tension.

"So, this is your Tennessee," Freddie commented, his tone curious as he peered out the window. The dirt road twisted upward, thick trees parting now and then to reveal distant mountains.

"Oh, it gets prettier the farther up you go," Ian replied, steadying the car as the incline grew steeper. Dust swirled behind them, the old car rumbling with effort.

Not trying to, but out of habit, Ian glanced into the rearview mirror. Dolores still had a sulky expression, arms crossed tightly, with her displeasure visible in every line of her face. If she walked into Clarissa's house like that, it wouldn't go over well—and he knew it.

Hoping to smooth things over, he tried to draw her into conversation.

"How's your job, Dolores? Did you get that position at the front counter like you wanted?" Ian asked, his voice measured and sincere.

Dolores squinted, her eyes narrowing slightly as if deciding whether to engage.

"No. I didn't have nice enough clothes, I think," she replied curtly, her accent sharp.

"I'm sorry to hear that. Their loss," Ian said, flashing one of his effortless smiles, the kind that had softened many moods before.

To his relief, it worked. Her expression eased, and a faint smile moved to her lips.

As the car crested the hill, the sprawling estate came into view. Ian took a breath, preparing himself as he pulled into Clarissa's driveway, his eyes scanning for any sign of life. The aged, elegant house, with its wide porch and climbing ivy, loomed ahead, but the yard remained still.

"Wow, Ian," Freddie said, leaning forward to get a better look at the large home. "This your place?"

"No, Freddie. This is Clarissa's. My family lives over there," Ian said, pointing toward the modest stone cottage nestled nearby.

Freddie nodded, still impressed, but Ian could see the questions brewing in his eyes. The contrast between the two homes seemed to spark his curiosity, but for now, he held his tongue.

For some reason—perhaps vanity, or maybe the presence of a former love interest in the backseat—Ian found himself adding, "Well, someday it will be. Clarissa plans on leaving it to my wife and me."

He wasn't lying. Clarissa had mentioned it shortly after his marriage to Esther, telling him it solved a complex problem in her mind. She'd wanted to leave half the property to Ian and half to Esther, but had worried about how to divide it fairly. Their marriage had made the decision easy. She'd also been clear about her plans to leave Abram and his wife the small parcel of land and house they lived in, insisting they were as much kin as anyone else could be.

Ian climbed out of the car, pulling the suitcases from the trunk as the noontime sun warmed the gravel driveway. He considered where Dolores might stay, thinking Esther would likely give up her small dressing room for the next couple of nights. Clarissa had already turned Adeline's old bedroom into a guest room, prepared for Freddie's arrival.

Ian glanced at the house, thinking of how an outsider might see it, its stately frame imposing. He caught Dolores's curious gaze lingering on the structure and sighed inwardly. He knew the truth of his modest life, but a part of him still wrestled with the idea of being judged by a woman whom he had once wanted to like him.

With a silent prayer, Ian stepped into the big house, ushering his brother and the blonde girl inside. Thinking Esther would be waiting, he braced himself for when introductions would have to be made.

The house was quiet except for the faint clatter of movement in the kitchen. Ian called out, "We're back," his voice carrying down the hall.

Small feet pattered in response almost immediately.

Benjamin and Rebecca came tumbling out of the kitchen, their excitement slowing to a halt as they stopped shyly in the hallway, eyeing Freddie curiously.

Freddie, ever the natural charmer, broke into a wide Huggler smile. "It's your favorite uncle!" he proclaimed grandly, crouching slightly to their level.

Rebecca tilted her head, and Benjamin glanced up at Ian, unsure.

"Ya don't look like my pa," Benjamin observed with a shy grin.

"That's because not everyone can be as handsome as me, Benjamin," Freddie replied with exaggerated flair, glancing at Ian mischievously. The playful jab drew a small laugh from Benjamin, who looked a little more at ease now that his uncle knew his name.

"And is this Rebecca or Bitsy?" Freddie asked, turning his attention to the little girl. He reached out his hand to shake hers, leaning down to kiss it like a proper gentleman. "My lady," he said with a grand bow, earning a delighted giggle from Rebecca.

Ian watched the exchange with equal parts amusement and playful exasperation.

"Freddie, you've been here all of two minutes, and you're already trying to steal my kids," he teased.

Freddie stood back up, winking at Ian. "What can I say? Charm runs in the family."

"Ya sound funny," Rebecca said, her big brown eyes twinkling as she wrapped him around her little finger.

"So do you," Freddie shot back with a fun grin, making her giggle.

The ruckus carried into the kitchen, and Clarissa soon appeared in the hallway, wiping her hands on her apron. She'd clearly been preparing food for later, the faint scent of something savory trailing behind her.

"Well, this must be Freddie," she said warmly, her smile lighting up her face as her eyes shifted to the girl standing slightly behind him. "And who is this?" she asked, her tone kind and welcoming.

"Oh, this is my friend Dolores," Freddie said smoothly, his polished voice practically gliding off his words. "I hope you don't mind, but she was as curious about the rural South as I was. She couldn't resist seeing your beautiful home."

Ian stayed quiet, letting his brother's charisma work its magic, though he couldn't help but glance at Dolores, who still looked slightly uncomfortable.

"How are you, ma'am?" Dolores said as she stepped forward, shaking Clarissa's hand with a polite, practiced smile and adding a small curtsy.

"Well, honey, it's mighty fine to meet ya," Clarissa replied, her voice warm and steady. "Welcome to the Reed Estate."

Clarissa then reached out for a handshake from Freddie, but he waved it off with a grin and pulled her into a big, affectionate hug. "I think we're far past formalities, as I hear we're family once again," he said, gripping her tightly.

Clarissa laughed, taken aback by his exuberance but instantly recognizing the warmth and generosity that mirrored Ian's, despite their differences in appearance.

"Oh, goodness," she chuckled as Freddie planted a playful kiss on her cheek.

"And speaking of that," Ian interrupted, "where is my wife?"

"She's upstairs, gettin' all pretty fer ya—and your guest," Clarissa said, still laughing as she adjusted her apron.

Ian made his way to the base of the stairs, calling up, "Esther, please come down. We're back."

Esther stood in front of her mirror, adding the final touches to her outfit—a pricey dress she had ordered during her time with Clive. It had taken almost six months to arrive, the wait stretching longer than she had expected.

The gown was everything she had hoped for—delicate stitching along the bodice, fabric that draped perfectly over her frame, and a rich color that made her feel like someone far removed from the struggles of her past.

Despite the excitement she felt now, guilt lingered in her chest. She had assured Ian the packages were "nothing important," brushing off his curiosity when they had picked them up. But the truth was, she had spent an exorbitant amount on the custom-made dress, rationalizing that the money was already spent—and wasn't even hers. The process required meticulous measurements and time for custom creation and shipping, which only heightened anticipation.

As she smoothed the yellow fabric over her hips one last time, her hands trembled slightly. The dress was perfect, but she worried Ian would recognize the truth—that she hadn't just pulled it out of her closet.

Esther had only heard stories about Freddie and his antics in New York—tales of his undeniable flair for mischief, of a life so far removed from her own.

She took a steadying breath, dusted her red lips with powder, and set them with care. She glanced sideways in the mirror, smoothing the dress over her frame once more. Her body still didn't show the faintest sign of pregnancy, save for her fuller bosom. Even Mitzy had commented that Esther only seemed to look more unpregnant every day—whatever that was supposed to mean.

"I'm comin'," she called, her voice steadying as she opened the door.

The dress seemed to take on a personality of its own as she stepped into the hallway, its fabric flowing with every movement. Esther felt its power, its elegance wrapping her in newfound confidence. She approached the staircase, realizing what a grand impression it would make—and it did.

Ian was the first to see her. His eyes locked onto her, his expression shifting into something unmistakably pleased. He drew his brows together slightly, his lips parting as he exhaled slowly. For a moment, he thought about whistling but decided Esther might give him a talkin' to later if he did.

"Wow, darling. Just… wow," Ian said, his voice low, almost reverent.

Freddie, hearing Ian's words, turned and followed his brother's gaze.

The moment his eyes landed on Esther, his reaction was instant and visible.

Shock flickered across his face.

She was nothing like Freddie had imagined.

He had expected someone plain, someone quiet and small-town. But the woman before him was elegant and striking, her presence magnetic. His eyes widened, nearly popping out of his head as he stared, unable to look away.

"She's divine," Freddie muttered, more to himself than anyone else. Then, louder, as his admiration spilled over, "My God, Mannie. Well done, well done."

Esther smiled softly, amused by Freddie's use of "Mannie." She hadn't heard anyone call Ian that before, and Freddie's accent was distinct—British, not as Americanized as Ian's.

Ian watched as Freddie moved to meet Esther at the last few steps. Without hesitation, Freddie reached out his hand, playfully cutting in front of his older brother.

"Don't hog her," Freddie teased, taking Esther's hand and leaning over to kiss it with exaggerated form.

Ian smiled and just shook his head. He knew Freddie too well—his brother was a natural flirt, someone who enjoyed winning affection from women.

Slightly taken aback, Esther glanced at Ian for reassurance. He was leaning casually on the banister, rolling his eyes with a grin that seemed to say, That's just Freddie.

Her attention shifted, however, to Dolores, who stood off to the side, near a table lined with framed family photos. The girl's timid expression tugged at Esther's memory, reminding her of her own unease the first time she'd stepped into Clarissa's home.

Dolores's gaze lingered on Esther, hesitant and appraising, as if she expected her to be presumptuous or snobbish like many of her customers in New York.

But Esther, noticing the retreat in her body language, felt a pang of empathy.

With a warm smile, Esther stepped toward her, closing the gap.

"I'm sorry," Esther began kindly, extending her hand. "I didn't know Freddie was bringin' someone with him."

Dolores blinked, surprised, then reached out, her hand a little unsteady.

Esther's voice was warm and soft as she welcomed her.

Dolores managed a small smile in return, introducing herself as well. Despite the awkwardness of the situation, the two women began to converse. To Ian's relief, they seemed to find common ground quickly.

Freddie and Ian exchanged a glance, the unspoken tension easing.

The group settled into the front sitting room, the warm light streaming through the tall windows.

Freddie, ever the showman, set his suitcase down and flipped it open with a flourish.

"Now remember," he began, addressing Ian's children with a grand air, "your uncle—referring to myself, of course—expects ya both to call him Uncle from now on, as I am officially the best one ever."

Benjamin and Rebecca giggled, curiosity pulling them closer. Freddie paused for dramatic effect, his mischievous gaze shifting to Esther. "You don't have a brother, do you?" he asked with a grin.

Esther shook her head, smiling at his antics.

"Well, that's good," he said, nodding sagely. "No competition then."

As the children bounced with excitement, Freddie carefully moved some of his clothes aside in the suitcase, revealing two neatly wrapped presents beneath. Pure anticipation lit their faces as they stood on tiptoes, craning for a better glimpse.

He held the presents out to them, savoring the joy as Benjamin and Rebecca eagerly took the packages, their small hands fumbling to unwrap the surprises.

Rebecca squealed with delight as she showed Esther the tin tea set, complete with tiny plates and cups nestled inside a woven carrying case.

Benjamin proudly held up a shiny cap gun and a small metal sheriff's badge, turning them over in his hands, as if they were treasures from another world.

Without much coaxing, the children wrapped their arms around their uncle, their hugs enthusiastic and warm. There was something familiar about him—his effortless charm, perhaps, or the way his smile mirrored their father's.

Ian watched the scene unfold with quiet satisfaction, his arms crossed. He knew Freddie would adore his children. Back in New York, Freddie had often held Benjamin as a baby during his visits with Ian and Adeline, always eager to play the doting uncle.

Esther glanced over at Dolores, who sat off to the side, her expression distant and uneasy. Determined to put her at ease, Esther scooted a little closer, recalling how Margie Mae often diffused awkwardness with gentle conversation.

"So, how do ya know Freddie?" Esther asked with a smile.

Dolores hesitated, her hands clasping nervously in her lap. "I— uh," she started, her eyes flicking toward Ian and Freddie as if seeking their permission. "I live in the same building as Freddie," she finally said.

"Oh," Esther said, piecing it together quickly. "Then I reckon ya've met Ian before? Ya know he lived there," she added, glancing at Ian with a smile.

Ian stiffened slightly, a strange look flashing across his face as he forced a nod, feigning ease.

"We've met a couple of times," Dolores admitted, her voice soft as she adjusted the shoulder of her dress, shifting uncomfortably.

Ian, eager to steer the conversation in another direction, stood up abruptly. "I guess you've been looking forward to seeing the orchard," he said, his tone slightly forced. His eyes darted toward Freddie, silently asking for help.

Freddie, quick to catch on, stood up, clapping his hands together. "Absolutely. Let's go take a look," he said with a grin, motioning toward the door as Ian gave him a grateful nod. "I do love a thrilling tour of... botany."

"You coming, Dolores?" Freddie added, extending his hand toward her. "Let's see if you've got what it takes to be a real country girl."

Dolores managed a polite smile as she stood, though her reluctance was clear. She looked as though she were being nudged into joining rather than stepping forward willingly.

"And you, Mrs. Huggler?" Ian said, his tone teasing. "Have you spent enough time in the orchard?"

Esther caught the meaning behind his words, the private joke they'd been sharing for the past couple of days, bringing a small, embarrassed smile to her face.

"I'll come with ya," Esther replied, moving to join them.

The group started down the main road, the hum of nature settling around them.

Ian and Freddie, their strides naturally quicker, eased ahead. Confident the women were only talking about fashion, they slipped into German, their conversation animated and punctuated with laughter.

"I ain't got no idea what they're even talkin' 'bout," Esther said as she walked alongside Dolores, her tone light but curious.

"Yeah, it's kind of annoying," Dolores admitted quietly. Back in New York, she'd often wondered the same thing—whether their conversations in German were about her. The thought still nagged at her.

Up ahead, the two men were indeed discussing the women behind them. Freddie leaned closer to Ian. "You always did have a knack for picking the forbidden fruit," Freddie murmured, voice low and teasing.

"You're a jackass," Ian replied with a playful shove, though he knew Freddie meant no harm.

Freddie grinned, glancing back briefly at Esther. "God, Mannie—I mean, Ian—you just took a wild creature and tamed her. She's too pretty—and way too young for you."

Ian rolled his eyes, sighing. "What is it with everyone thinking I'm too old for her? I swear, I get an earful almost every day. It's a popular observation."

Freddie didn't let up. "What is she, twelve? Fourteen?" he teased.

Ian shot him a warning look, though his tone was laced with humor. "I can still put you in a headlock, you know that?"

"Why didn't you wait for me?" Freddie asked, his voice sincere. "I would've liked to see you get married."

"I mean, you knew I was coming," Freddie added with a smile, though it was clear he wanted a genuine answer.

Ian turned to Freddie, his serious expression and brief look back at Esther saying everything. It was subtle but clear enough for his brother, who easily read the unspoken truth.

Freddie smirked, knowing better than to judge. After all, plenty of women had spent the night at his place in New York.

Still, Ian had always prided himself on being more of a gentleman, though that confidence had wavered after his mishap with Esther.

"Oh... another little Huggler," Freddie said in a hushed voice. "Record time, I might add."

"Freddie, that's not the reason I married her," Ian replied firmly. "Just to be clear."

"Well, I guess knocking her up ruined your chance of adopting her," Freddie shot back, pushing the joke further.

He laughed as he stepped quickly to the side, anticipating Ian's reaction.

But Freddie wasn't quick enough. Ian grabbed the pocket of his jacket, yanking him back and slipping an arm tightly around his neck in a playful grip.

"Listen here, little Ignatz," Ian said, grinning. "You're not in the city anymore. Out here, we hide bodies where no one ever finds them."

Freddie laughed, struggling to break free.

"Christ, Ian! You're built like some Bavarian strongman from the circus." He wheezed, his tone mock-serious as his brother finally let him go.

Later that evening, the house was alive with the warmth of a shared supper.

Clarissa's dining room was steeped in post-supper satisfaction. The table, long and well-worn, bore the remnants of a meal that could only be described as a feast—what remained of a pot roast soaking in its gravy, mashed potatoes, green beans cooked with bacon, fresh rolls still fragrant from the oven, and a peach cobbler so sweet and rich the scent alone had everyone murmuring in anticipation.

Conversation buzzed through the air, a pleasant hum of voices punctuated by the occasional clink of forks against plates and bursts of laughter.

The children leaned forward on their elbows, relishing the rare opportunity to sit at a table filled with so many lively adults.

Abram leaned back in his chair, fishing a toothpick from his shirt pocket and slipping it between his teeth. "Ian," he began, his voice low, "ya think you could get those cows milked any faster if Freddie here lent ya a hand?"

Ian grinned, not missing a beat. "Abram, the cows are your responsibility. And you've got those gentle and soft hands they like." He paused, shifting in his chair, arms behind his neck. "It's only two cows. Don't go making it sound like we're running a dairy farm."

Abram shook his head slowly, like he couldn't help but disagree. "Two's still too many if it's left to me."

Freddie snorted, swirling the last sip of sweet tea in his glass. "Well, I'd help, but I'd just slow you all down. I'm not much for farm life, Abram. Truth be told, these paws are more accustomed to the company of dames than dairy cows."

"No surprise there," Ian said, his tone dry as his eyes flashed with a warning for his brother to watch his language. Ian went on, hoping the others—especially Clarissa—had missed his comment. "Freddie's more of a pretty city boy. Had to teach him which side of the cow to climb up on."

Rebecca giggled, the sound bubbling out of her as she clutched her spoon. Benjamin, sitting straighter, joined in with wide-eyed enthusiasm.

"You rode a cow, Uncle Freddie?" Rebecca said, so excited she almost fell off her chair.

Ian grinned, leaning forward like he was about to share a deep secret. "Oh, I might've mentioned a certain incident with Old Matilda back when we were kids."

Freddie's brows shot up, and he gave Ian a pointed look. "You're making things up again, aren't you?"

Ian shrugged, all false innocence. "All I'm saying is you were closer to riding that cow than milking it."

"You really sat on a cow, Uncle Freddie? Like a horse? What was it like?" Benjamin's eyes lit up with excitement.

"Terrifying," Freddie admitted with a dramatic shudder, earning a fresh round of giggles from the children. "Cows aren't made for riding, Benjamin. Don't let anyone tell you otherwise."

Freddie leaned forward to Rebecca, his tone dramatic. "I didn't ride the cow. I fell on the cow. There's a big difference."

Rebecca's curiosity was etched across her face. "But how do ya fall on a cow? Did ya climb a tree first?"

The entire table erupted in laughter as Freddie groaned, rubbing his forehead. "No, Bitsy, I didn't climb a tree. Your Pa set me up for failure, that's all."

Ian chuckled, shaking his head. "Don't go blaming me. You were the one who thought Matilda would stand still for you. Didn't even make it five seconds before she tossed ya."

Abram slapped the table, tears of laughter glinting in his eyes. "You mean to tell me you thought you could ride ya old milk cow like a bronco? Freddie, that's the best thing I've heard all week."

"I didn't think anything. Ian dared me, and you know how he is." Freddie pointed at his brother accusingly. "He gets that smug look on his face like he already knows you'll fail, and next thing you know, you're sitting on a cow's back wondering what went wrong."

Too excited to sit still, Benjamin sprang up and darted toward his father. "Can I try, Pa? I bet I'd last longer than Uncle Freddie," he said, bouncing on his toes.

Ian shook his head firmly, though his smile hadn't faded. "Absolutely not. I don't need another story like this making its way to the dinner table."

Clarissa, standing by the kitchen door with her hands on her hips, chimed in with a knowing smile. "Y'all are worse than the children. Leave them barn animals alone, Freddie, and let's see if you're brave enough to wash some dishes instead."

Freddie leaned back with a theatrical sigh, throwing his hands up. "Well, I guess my work here is done."

Across the table, Esther laughed softly, her hand smoothing the napkin. But as her gaze lifted, it collided with Freddie's.

He was watching her again, his dark eyes lingering just a beat too long, like he was seeing something no one else could. She smiled politely, inspiring a roguish grin from him—one that held just long enough to make her uneasy.

Dolores, seated beside Freddie, caught the exchange. Her posture stiffened, her fingers tightening around her fork, but she remained silent. She had no interest in Freddie—he was a ladies' man, after all, and trouble followed him like a shadow.

There had been points on the trip when Freddie had even teased her, saying he wanted to kiss her—just to see what Ian was getting himself into. But no, he was, without a doubt, vying for Esther's attention, even if it meant nothing. Freddie had a habit of picking the prettiest girl in the room and trying to catch her eye.

"Pass the rolls, would you?" Ian's voice broke through, his tone light and unaware of the undercurrent running through the table.

Freddie blinked, the request pulling him back to the present. "Sure thing, Mannie," he said, the old nickname slipping out again as he handed the basket across to him.

Ian's eyebrow quirked at the slip, but he said nothing, choosing instead to focus on slathering peach preserves onto a roll.

Esther's gaze flicked to Dolores, their eyes meeting for just a moment. It was brief, almost accidental, but it felt odd, like something Esther couldn't put her finger on.

Abram clapped his hands together, breaking the lull. "Alright, enough about cows, that story's been milked dry. Who's ready for cobbler?"

Benjamin and Rebecca's hands shot into the air simultaneously, their eyes lighting up at the prospect of dessert.

In the kitchen, the bustle of cleaning up carried the same lively energy as the meal had.

Pots clanged, dishwater sloshed, and laughter echoed against the walls. Clarissa, ever the matriarch, moved with purpose, barking orders with the efficiency of a seasoned general.

"Mitzy, you and Abram handle the leftovers," Clarissa instructed, pointing toward the dining room. "Freddie, get those plates off the table and bring 'em here. Dolores, you wipe down the counters."

Ian stood at the sink, sleeves rolled up, forearms damp, passing clean plates to Esther. She dried them with practiced ease, their movements fluid and synchronized. It was clear they had fallen into this routine before.

"Don't go thinking this means I'm helping every night," Ian said, smirking as he handed her another plate.

Esther shot him a playful look over her shoulder. "That's funny 'cause ya always do when I ask ya," she teased, her drawl lilting.

Abram, scooping some mashed potatoes into a smaller bowl, chimed in. "Clarissa, next time you'd better make extra cobbler. Ian eats like Esther don't feed him."

"I work hard, but you're right," Ian retorted, though the grin on his face gave him away.

Esther scoffed, reaching down into the water-filled sink and splashing him.

Without warning, Ian snatched the dish towel from her hand and twisted it tight. A second later, the sharp crack of fabric landed squarely on Esther's backside. She jumped, startled, and turned to swat at him.

"Ian Huggler, ya better stop!" she said, though her laughter betrayed her outrage. "Don't get my new dress dirty."

"New?" Ian paused, his grin fading. Esther had given herself away. "We'll talk about that later," he said in a flat voice—one Esther tried to laugh off.

Freddie rested a shoulder against the doorway. "It's a very nice dress, Esther. Fits you extremely well," he said, his voice low and serious, smoke curling around his words.

"Yes, it is. Thank you for pointing that out, Freddie," Ian shot back, grabbing a nearby glass and thrusting it toward him. "Why don't you help me instead of puffing away like a chimney?"

Freddie stepped forward, unapologetic. "Don't get your little apron all twisted up." He took the glass with exaggerated care, rinsing it under the water. "You happy now?"

Ian smiled, reaching for another dish. "Ecstatic."

Clarissa reappeared from the hallway, undoing the strings of her apron. "Well, that's enough outta y'all. I'm takin' the young'uns over to Ian's. I'll keep 'em occupied so the rest of ya can enjoy yourselves."

The room went still for a moment, the offer unexpected but appreciated.

"Are ya sure, Mama Clarissa?" Esther asked, drying her hands.

"Of course I'm sure," Clarissa replied, ushering Benjamin, Rebecca, and little Jeremiah toward the door. "I've got a book they've been wantin' me to read, and I ain't afraid of a few rascals for a night."

The children scrambled after her, Rebecca clutching her doll as she looked back at her father. "Don't let Uncle Freddie ride any cows while we're gone!"

Freddie barked a laugh, raising his hands in a solemn cross. "No promises, Bitsy."

With the children gone, the kitchen quieted just slightly. The remaining six adults relaxed into the newfound freedom, the tension of a full house easing into something softer.

"Now that the kids are outta earshot," Freddie began, looking around, "how about we liven this place up? Got a record player?"

Mitzy brightened. "We do! It's in the parlor, but it's too hot in here. Let's go out on the front porch."

"Fair warning, Freddie, Clarissa's records date back to a time when you were still in short pants," Ian said as he started making his way out of the room.

"Aw, my favorite. And I've been told I have nice knees," Freddie replied, grinning as he followed him to retrieve it.

Moments later, Ian emerged from the house, lugging the heavy machine while Freddie followed with a stack of dusty records. Abram fetched a small table from the hallway and carried it out onto the porch.

As Ian fiddled with the record player, Abram brought out extra chairs, their wooden legs scraping against the floorboards.

The warm summer air wrapped around them like a blanket, the hum of crickets blending with the scratchy music that spilled from the machine.

Freddie disappeared briefly, returning with a bottle of scotch from his suitcase and a set of glasses. "Thought we might need this," he said, winking.

Ian hesitated, his eyes darting to Esther. She caught the concerned look in his expression and leaned in close, her voice low but firm. "I'm fine, Ian," she said with a small smile. "Let 'em have their fun."

The men poured themselves drinks, Abram raising his glass in a silent toast before taking a long sip.

The conversation drifted to the war and the reality of the young male population missing from the country.

Freddie recounted stories from New York—how intolerance toward those of German heritage had only grown worse.

Abram shared the local perspective and his concern about being drafted and leaving his family behind.

Ian tipped his chair back slightly, stretching out his long legs, chiming in now and then but mostly listening, his arm draped lazily over the back of Esther's seat.

After a while, Freddie jumped to his feet, the scotch clearly fueling his enthusiasm.

"All right, enough talk. Dolores, let's dance," Freddie declared, holding out a hand with a handsome grin.

Though hesitant, Dolores allowed herself to be pulled to her feet. "I'm not much of a dancer, Freddie," she said.

Freddie spun her around the porch with effortless flair, her laughter ringing out as she tried to keep up. "You're better than you think," Freddie teased as he dipped her slightly, earning a squeal.

Abram, always one to join in the fun, stood and offered Mitzy his hand. "C'mon, sweetheart. Let's show 'em how it's done."

Mitzy rolled her eyes but stood, swaying gently to the upbeat tune. Abram moved deliberately slow, his large frame careful with hers, even as the music urged them to pick up the pace.

"Abram, you're gonna break her feet creeping along like you're counting your steps," Ian said.

"Better slow n' sure than steppin' on 'em," Abram shot back, drawing a soft laugh from Mitzy as she rested lightly against his chest.

When Dolores finally sat down, her cheeks flushed, Freddie turned his attention to Esther. His smile widened, mischief sparking in his eyes. "Your turn," he said, holding out a hand toward her.

Esther hesitated, glancing at Ian, unsure if she should take it. "I ain't never danced with a man before," she admitted, her voice soft.

Freddie's grin only grew. "Then there's no time like the present. Don't worry—I'll take good care of ya." He extended his hand further, and with a shy nod, she took it.

Ian seemed unbothered, even relaxed, as Freddie guided his wife to the center of the porch.

Freddie's hand rested lightly on Esther's waist, his steps confident as he led her through a series of easy movements. She stumbled at first, her nervousness showing, but Freddie was patient, his voice low as he guided her. "Relax. You've got natural rhythm. Just follow me."

Her laughter bubbled up as she found her footing, the tension easing from her frame.

Freddie spun her out and back in, his eyes never leaving her face.

The sound of her laughter, the brightness in her expression—at first, it was nice. But as Ian watched his brother and Esther dance, something possessive stirred in him, reminding him he hadn't danced with her on their wedding day, as he'd promised.

His chest tightened, jaw flexing as he watched his younger brother hold her hand, his arm brushing her waist.

Freddie swung her wide again, her skirt fanning out as she laughed.

Ian stood abruptly, the chair scratching the wooden boards of the painted porch.

"Mind if I cut in?" Ian said, his tone blunt.

Freddie gave a playful bow, relinquishing Esther's grasp with a wink. "If I must."

Ian stepped forward, taking Esther's hand firmly in his. Pulling her against his body, he murmured, "Freddie doesn't count as your first dance."

She smiled up at him, her cheeks warm.

"So, ya sayin' this is my first dance?" she questioned.

"Yep. It's not who you start the dance with, but who you end it with," he said, holding her close.

Ian's movements were slower, less polished than Freddie's, but there was a sincerity in the way he held her, his arms steady. He leaned down, his lips close to her ear. "And we've danced without music, haven't we?"

Esther gave him a smack, her eyes drifting briefly toward Freddie as she hoped the others hadn't overheard him.

Freddie was leaning casually against the porch railing, his stare—sharpened by liquor—fixed on her.

Dolores, seated nearby, sipped her drink quietly, her gaze darting between Ian and Esther. Her own expression was unreadable, but the way her fingers traced the rim of her glass—a silent gesture of longing—spoke volumes.

As the evening wore on, Freddie poured another generous round for himself, Ian, and Abram, the scotch catching the soft light of the porch.

The liquor had loosened their tongues, laughter spilling easily among the group as Freddie relived stories from his nightlife. He spoke with his usual flair, spinning tales of famous people he'd met in the nightclub scene, his lively wit keeping everyone hanging on his words.

Abram, not to be outdone, leaned forward in his chair, letting his hand rest casually on Mitzy's leg. "Freddie," he began, "you might have met some fancy folks, but I betcha ain't met a bear killer like Esther here."

Freddie paused mid-sip, raising an intrigued brow as he turned to Esther. "A bear killer?" he repeated, a smirk tugging at his lips. "Are you telling me she actually took down a bear?"

"Two bears," Abram corrected, his grin widening as he leaned forward, his storytelling energy mounting. "Biggest ones ever seen in these parts. Ain't that right, Ian?"

Ian chuckled, his gaze soft as he glanced at Esther. "It's mostly true," he said, his voice laced with amusement.

Freddie leaned in, his eyes gleaming with intrigue. "What's it like to slay such powerful beasts by yourself, darlin'? You're not much bigger than a bird."

Esther waved a dismissive hand. "Please don't tell this story, Abram," she said, her Southern drawl soft and modest.

"Don't let her fool ya," Abram said, ignoring her protests. "She walked right up to those bears like they weren't nothin'. Shot 'em dead."

Freddie sat back, shaking his head in amazement. "Well, I'll be damned. A fearless bear killer maiden with a keen fashion sense," he said, his gaze lingering on Esther a moment longer than necessary.

Dolores, sitting beside him, shifted in her seat, her expression caught somewhere between shock and annoyance.

"Good Lord, Abram," Esther said, trying to nudge the conversation away from herself. "Ya makin' it into a tall tale."

"Ain't no tall tale about it. Got the pelt on our floor," Abram said as he laughed.

"The way ya tell it, Abram," Mitzy interrupted, "ya'd think ya done it yerself. Now I got a heap of fur sprawled in the middle of my front room. Damn thing scares me in the middle of the night," she added, pulling the whiskey glass from his hand.

The group laughed, the warmth of the moment stretching out under the clear night sky. But even as the chatter moved on, Freddie's gaze drifted back to Esther, drawn like a bad habit.

The music slowed, and Freddie once again took to the porch, pulling Dolores to her feet. "One more dance, doll," he said.

Dolores nodded, letting him twirl her, but her movements lacked the ease of earlier. She was clearly worn out, and Freddie—despite his attempts to hide it—kept glancing toward the beautiful and alluring girl from the hills.

There was something about her. Something that unsettled him.

At first, he had thought she was just a pretty girl, considering his brother lucky—but now, the more he looked, the harder it became to look away.

Ian noticed this time. His grip tightened around his glass, irritation flickering across his face as his brother's gaze lingered a moment too long.

Esther, sensing Ian's shift in mood, placed a hand lightly on his arm. "Ian," she said softly. "It's time to get ya home."

Ian, his cheeks flushed from the alcohol, resisted at first. "I'm fine," he said, though his unsteady footing betrayed him.

Mitzy, now cradling Jeremiah, stood and tugged at Abram's arm. "We're walkin' back. Ain't no way you're drivin' like this," she said, her tone firm despite the warmth in her eyes.

With a firm push from Esther, Ian finally relented, and together they headed back to the stone cottage, the cool night air settling around them.

Still in a playful mood, he twirled her one last time on the path, when he stopped suddenly—as though he needed to tell her something important.

"Freddie's just a flirt," he blurted out, almost too loud. "Don't pay him any mind."

Esther smiled faintly but said nothing. She replayed the way Freddie had stared at her—his compliments too easy, his gaze too intense. The alcohol had loosened his tongue, but it hadn't dulled his interest.

When they reached their front door, she gave Ian a knowing smirk as she tucked a loose strand of hair behind her ear.

"Hope ya enjoy yer headache tomorrow," she said.

Ian slouched against the frame, his grin boyish—nowhere near repentant.

"Only if you take care of me, darling," he mumbled, his eyes raking over her for a moment.

"Right? You're gonna take care of me?" he asked again, his hand reaching out to trace a finger down her neckline.

"Don't I always?" she said, letting herself be drawn into his play.

Esther could tell Ian was quite drunk—his eyes glazed, leaning in almost too close. He looked sweet, a little endearing. She'd never seen him like this before.

"You can say no—you know?" he added.

"I know that, Ian. Let's go inside," she said as she tried to steer him through the door, but he refused to move, not even budging.

Suddenly, he was set on having a serious discussion, his inebriation fueling whatever thoughts had taken root in his mind.

His words slurred as he continued. "Meine Liebe, I… I just don't want you to think you can't. You haven't turned me down once." He held up a finger, swaying slightly. "And I ask a hell of a lot."

She laughed, shaking her head. Practical Ian and drunk Ian weren't all that different.

"Ya bein' silly. I ain't turned ya down yet 'cause I didn't want to. I like it. Now, can we go in?" she said, slightly impatient.

"Really? Is that true?" He mumbled as he held his spot in the middle of the doorway. "'Cause I've been thinking about how I was gonna get that new—dress off you all day."

She stepped inside without him and held out her hand. "Well, come on then—I need help with the zipper."

He just stood there, blinking in slow realization. That's when Esther knew—he was going to need help getting to their bedroom.

With a sigh, she turned back, grabbed his hand, and dragged him inside with all the force she could muster.

"You're really gonna feel it tomorrow," she mumbled as she led him across the main room toward their bedroom door, thinking it felt a whole lot like leading a horse into a barn.

Chapter 37: Mata Hari

Esther had been wrong, as Ian was up at the crack of dawn, moving like he'd never touched a drop of liquor the night before. He kissed her forehead as he slipped from their bed, eager to work in the coolness of the morning before the summer heat settled in.

"Will you bring me some breakfast when you get up?" he whispered as he pulled on his old denim trousers.

"I can make ya somethin' now, if you want," Esther mumbled, groggy, pulling off the thin quilt as if that alone might wake her up.

"Naw, darlin', you sleep longer. I'm fine for now." He leaned over the bed and kissed her again, softer this time. "I'm planning on getting Freddie up, too, so bring him something as well."

Esther just laughed, thinking of how Freddie had mentioned in a drunk challenge that he could keep up with Ian and wanted to really see what he did in a day.

"Poor Freddie," she said as she turned over, stealing Ian's pillow to put over her head to block out the light.

"Where ya gonna be at?" she asked, realizing she had no idea what Ian's plans were.

"Need to tighten up the fence line," he said, rolling out his shoulders stiffly before snapping the suspenders into place. "Some of the posts are leaning, and the corn's knee-high. Damn deer keep making their way in. And the ditches? Full of weeds again."

"Didn't ya already put a scarecrow out?" Esther asked as she turned back to him.

"Yeah, but it's not enough. Maybe I'll tell Freddie he needs to stand out there with his arms outstretched like this," Ian said, extending his arms and sticking his tongue out. "Make him stand like that for a couple of hours, as punishment for encouraging Abram and me to drink scotch with him."

"I'm going back to sleep," Esther said, smiling, but not before she asked, "I suppose ya be wantin' coffee?"

"Please," he replied.

By the time Esther made her way to the fields, the summer sun had already climbed higher in the sky, turning the morning coolness into a slow, simmering heat.

Ian had already stripped his shirt, his skin slick with sweat as he drove a fence post deep into the ground. Nearby, Abram worked to untangle barbed wire, making Freddie help him.

Freddie looked pitiful—squinting against the sunlight, his whole face twisted in regret. The sorry man belonged in smoky parlors and city nights, not out here under an open sky.

The men were so focused on their work that they didn't notice Esther. Light blue calico fabric brushed against her legs as she walked. Nothing like the dress she'd worn the day before—looser, easier for moving through the day's work. Her long dark hair, still wild from sleep, spilled across her back with every step. Unbothered, she hadn't taken the time to set it yet, making sure Ian was fed first.

"Ya boys hungry?" she called as she neared them.

Abram was the first to look up. "Did ya bring any extra?"

"Of course," she said with a smile, knowing Abram had an appetite like her husband's.

She made her way around the back of the old blue truck. The tailgate was already down, so she set down the heavy basket and arranged a thermos of coffee, some tin-handled cups, and plates.

"Ian," she called out, "Ya want me to make you a plate?"

"Give me just a minute," he replied, finishing up the task at hand, the sledgehammer still gripped in his sweaty hand.

Abram and Freddie, however, were already making their way over to her, appreciative smiles on their faces.

"Is that coffee?" Freddie asked, perking up.

Esther nodded as she poured him a cup and handed it to him.

He took it gratefully, like it was a tender mercy for the torture his brother was putting him through.

"Ya doin' okay, Freddie?" she asked, wondering if Ian might have been too hard on him.

Freddie just laughed, glancing over at Ian, who was still hammering away. "I think ya took down the wrong animal, Esther. My brother's got some strange idea that I can actually do these things."

She shook her head, a knowing smile on her lips. She understood Ian's high expectations—he put them on everyone around him, including himself.

Abram nodded his thanks as she handed him a cup of coffee, knowing he'd want it as much as Freddie had.

"Freddie, ya like biscuits and gravy? I've got some boiled eggs and fried potatoes too," Esther offered warmly, a light breeze brushing her long hair across her face as she looked at him.

And just like the day before, Freddie was mesmerized. He wondered why his brother had taken so long to realize he liked this divine creature. She wasn't pretentious—she was down-to-earth, softly feminine, but strong in a way her upbringing had shaped her. She was exciting, and the way she spoke—her drawl had the lilt of untamed poetry.

"Is that a yes?" Esther asked, noticing Freddie's distraction.

"I would very much appreciate it," he replied, watching as she served him food. Fresh biscuits, kept warm by a cloth, and a mason jar filled with warm gravy. She carefully assembled the plate and handed it to him with a cloth napkin and a fork.

"Well, I like—" Abram began, but Esther turned her attention to him with a knowing smirk.

"I know what ya like, Abram. Ya ain't got a picky bone in yer body," she teased, piling a large amount of food on a plate and giving it to him.

The two men found a cool spot to sit on the ground in the shade of the truck, their conversation a low murmur as Esther's eyes drifted back to Ian, who was finally making his way toward her.

"It's gonna get cold," she said, noticing the irritated look on his face as he picked at something on his palm.

"Before you make me a plate, will you get this damn sliver out of me?" he asked, resting his arm on the edge of the truck bed.

She leaned in to inspect it, his calloused hands rough beneath her touch. "I can barely see it," she said, motioning for his handkerchief.

"It's in there pretty deep," he added, wincing as she pinched the skin, her brow furrowed in concentration.

With a little spit on the hanky, she set about cleaning his palm, spotting the splinter he was complaining about. She pulled a safety pin from the front of her dress—where she'd used it to make the neckline a little more appropriate for daytime—and opened it, preparing to remove the splinter.

"Are you going to stab me with that?" he asked, eyeing the pin warily.

"Stop bein' such a big baby," she said, stabbing the point in.

"God, you're mean, Esther." He pulled his hand away protectively.

She grabbed it back, determination flashing in her eyes as Abram chuckled from the other side of the truck.

"Aww... I think the ol' bear's got a little thorn in its paw," Abram teased, Freddie laughing along with him.

"I've got it, Ian. Just hold still and stop hollerin'," she insisted as she jabbed the pin in again.

"My hell, woman, are you mad at me?" he exclaimed, bringing his palm to his mouth instinctively.

"It's over, Ian," she said, holding up a small sliver of wood triumphantly. "Yer gonna live." She smiled as she turned to pour him a drink.

"Here I thought you'd be all gentle-like, sweet about it. Next time, I'll think twice about asking for your help," he said, though he didn't look upset. An almost-forgiving smile crept across his face as she passed him a warm cup of coffee.

"Are those biscuits fresh?" he asked, his eyes lighting up as she served him a plate big enough for a goliath.

"Yes, and I even made you fried potatoes, like ya like," she said, watching him quickly dive into his food.

"I'm still mad at you," he added playfully as he stepped around the truck to sit with the other men.

She followed him, finding a large rock on the side of the road to sunbathe on as she watched the men eat.

Something was clearly on Freddie's mind as he ate, eyeing his brother. "You know, Ian, the company you worked for in New York— what's his name? Otto something?"

"Langendorf, Otto Langendorf," Ian supplied.

"Yes, that's him. He was at the Midnight Canary a couple of weeks ago and asked me if you'd be able to do some more work for him. Said you had a knack for translation and simplifying the paperwork. Says he can even pay you more than last time. Sure beats breakin' your back out here," Freddie added.

"Naw," Ian replied, glancing over at Esther as she tilted her face to the sun, her eyes closed, soaking in the light.

"I don't want to be away from my family," Ian added.

Freddie, seeing Ian's hesitation as he looked at his wife, thought he had the perfect solution. "Bring her with you. She'd love it there."

Ian just shook his head with a smile. "I don't think so," he said, taking another big bite of food.

"What is it y'all talkin' 'bout?" Esther asked, her ears tuning into the conversation.

Thinking this was his chance to win her over, Freddie grinned as he said, "Ian doesn't want to bring you to New York."

He turned to see Ian shooting him a displeased look.

"But I think you'd love it. All the pretty clothes—you'd fit in perfectly," Freddie added, his charm turned up a notch.

His comment only drew a low laugh from Ian. She might look the part, he thought, but she most certainly didn't have the temperament for a place like that.

Esther tilted her head, her curiosity piqued.

"It's somethin' I've only dreamed of. All those shops—I can't imagine the things ya'd find in them," she said, her tone carrying a wistful note.

Ian, ever the realist, added a touch of practicality.

"Esther, we can't afford anything in those shops," he said firmly. "Unlike your previous budget, you married a poor farmer, must I remind you?" he added, his gaze blank but pointed.

Esther gave him a sharp look, undeterred.

"Ian, I don't need to buy those dresses. I just wanna see 'em in person, so I can get some ideas in my mind. I'm plannin' on learnin' to sew. Clarissa said I can have her old sewin' machine, and Margie Mae's been teachin' me," she explained, clearly having thought about this before and finding unexpected support in Freddie's suggestion.

"Well, we're not going," Ian said in a clipped tone, dismissing the idea as he focused on his plate.

He glanced up, catching a look from Abram, who leaned back slightly, his expression hinting that Ian's quick dismissal was far from the end of this conversation.

Esther waited patiently for Ian's eyes to drift her way again as she had a nice little scowl waiting for him—her lips pressed tightly.

Seeing this only fueled the fire as Ian muttered back, "And you already have a new dress—a magical one that just appeared in your closet yesterday."

Freddie snorted, unable to contain his laughter. "Ian, you think you understand women so well, but you don't know a damn thing," he said, shaking his head. "Dresses aren't just bought and done with. They're curated. Part of a collection that's always growing."

Esther smiled faintly, not fully grasping the elegance of Freddie's point, but understanding enough to feel validated. It was nice, having someone in her corner, even if it was Ian's own brother.

"Well, I wanna go to New York," Esther proclaimed, her voice carrying a note of determination.

"Kind of like how you want to go to New Mexico," Ian quipped, a slow, smug grin breaking through as Esther shot daggers at him with her eyes.

"I shoulda poked ya harder with that pin," she shot back, trying to look serious, though the hint of a smile betrayed her.

Unbothered, Ian bit a biscuit in half.

"Your biscuits are getting better," he said, chewing slowly. "Not burnt anymore."

She scoffed, shaking her head. She knew he was just trying to rile her up, avoiding the topic of New York altogether.

Abram, no longer distracted by their banter, leaned forward, his mind returning to the task ahead.

"Thinkin' we should hang some empty tin cans with rocks in 'em on the fence," he said. "Those pesky bastards'll jump this damn fence in an instant if they're hungry enough, and the hills are startin' to dry out." He punctuated his thought with another mouthful of food.

"Clarissa's got a big box full of cans. That's a good idea," Ian agreed, nodding as he weighed the idea. He turned to Esther. "If I punch some holes in them, you could string them up?"

She nodded reluctantly, wondering if he thought she did nothing but burn biscuits and wait for him to assign her tasks.

Her thoughts shifted, however, when her eyes caught a subtle movement by the tire near where Freddie was sitting.

Years spent in the hills had sharpened her instincts, and she didn't hesitate.

"Freddie," Esther said cautiously, her tone measured—controlled. "Don't jump up real quick," she added, already scanning for a stick nearby.

Freddie's head snapped up, his face tightening with alarm. "Why? What's wrong?" His eyes darted around, searching for whatever had her on edge.

Ian and Abram's attention followed hers, their gazes locking on the same spot. Ian's jaw tightened as Esther's calm voice broke the tension.

"There's a copperhead sittin' about a foot from ya, near the tire," she said, steady as a stone.

Ian sprang to his feet, his body taut with urgency. "Move very slowly away," he instructed, his eyes not leaving the snake.

Freddie placed his plate carefully on the ground, his hands trembling slightly as he began crawling away on all fours.

Abram, who had been sitting nearby, quickly stood, stepping back cautiously before reaching down to help Freddie up. Despite the danger, Abram still clung protectively to his plate, refusing to let go of his meal.

Ian rushed toward the fence line, muttering something under his breath, heading to grab a tool to deal with the problem.

Before he could return, Esther moved in, a thick stick clutched tightly in her hand.

She approached with careful, slow precision, pinning the snake's head to the ground in one fluid motion.

"Esther, get the hell away from it!" Abram barked, his voice rising as alarm bled through. His foot shifted forward, as though he might intervene, but he held back, unwilling to risk startling the snake.

"Ian's gonna kill it, and he doesn't need to," Esther replied, her voice calm and resolute. She crouched low, her fingers steady as she reached down and grabbed the snake firmly behind the head.

Abram groaned audibly, running a hand down his face. "If the snake don't get ya, yer husband will," he muttered, exasperation dripping from his tone.

Freddie, now standing at a safe distance, watched the scene unfold, his face frozen in astonishment. "You've got to be kidding me," he muttered under his breath, though his admiration for her was unmistakable.

Esther slowly stood up, dangling the snake in the air, its tan head clasped in her outstretched arm, just as Ian rounded the truck with a shovel in hand. The expression on his face—equal parts terror and fury—said it all.

"God, Esther! Are you trying to kill yourself?!" Ian shouted, his voice sharp and unsteady.

Esther, unfazed, started walking down the road, carefully moving to an area farther from where the men were working.

Ian followed closely behind her, a shovel gripped tightly in his hand, his tension palpable. His anger boiled over as steam seemed to rise from him with each step.

When she reached a safe distance, Esther swung her arm once and released the snake in a smooth, swift motion. It landed in the tall grass, slithering off into the brush.

"I can't believe you fucking did that!" he barked, his voice taut as he caught her wrist, pulling her back toward the truck. "Why do you do such damn stupid things?" His tone was sharp, the weight of his worry etched into every word.

Abram, who had returned to his food, avoided the awkward exchange, slipping around to the far end of the truck with his plate. Freddie, however, didn't share Abram's discomfort. His shock wasn't over the snake but over Esther herself—her audacity, her poise.

As they neared the truck, Ian finally let go of her hand, exhaling sharply, his frustration still thick in the air.

Freddie couldn't hold it in any longer. "She's a goddamn snake charmer," he said, his voice tinged with awe and a grin spreading wide across his face. He couldn't take his eyes off her, marveling at how this dark-haired, wild, fearless woman had treated a venomous snake like it was nothing more than a garden worm.

"Snake charmer," Ian echoed, his tone sharp as he glared at his brother, still fuming.

"Ian, there was no need in ya killin' it. It just curled up to the truck to get warm," Esther said, her voice steady as she tried to reason with him. But Ian wasn't in the mood for reasoning.

"Can we add this to the list of things I prefer you not to do?" Ian said, his serious tone unrelenting.

"I ain't ya child," she snapped, the bite in her voice making him huff.

Her retort made Freddie burst out laughing. He leaned casually against the truck, egging on the same mischief he'd started with Ian the night before.

"Don't say it, Ignatz," Ian warned, pointing at his brother. Then, turning his gaze to Esther, he muttered in a low tone, "Ich werde dir den Hintern versohlen wie einem."

Freddie, understanding every word, laughed harder, delighted by his brother's slip into German. The phrase—roughly translating to "I'm going to spank your bottom like one"—was not something Ian would want Esther to hear.

"What'd he say to ya?" Esther demanded, her sharp eyes turning to Freddie.

"I would love to tell you, but I'm kind of afraid of your husband," Freddie said.

"I think we all are a little," Abram added, his serious look suggesting he wasn't entirely joking.

Esther, certain Ian was waiting for her reply, planted her hands on her hips and narrowed her eyes at him.

"Well, he ain't scare me none," she declared, her voice full of defiance. The determination in her gaze chipped away at Ian's irritation, and despite himself, a small smile crept onto his face.

Damn if he didn't admire her for it. Even though she'd risked her life for a snake, she had a way of making her point with unwavering resolve. He thought she looked downright adorable when she was trying to prove her mettle.

"Esther, you're not just a bear killer," Freddie added with a grin. "You're a pretty little bear tamer too."

Ian turned to his brother. "Freddie, that's at least the tenth time you've called my wife beautiful. Don't you think that's a few times too many?"

Freddie merely shrugged, knowing he was needling his brother. As he wandered toward Abram, he said over his shoulder, "Better get used to it when you bring her to the city."

Though Freddie thought he was just teasing, Ian's face tensed at the mention of New York. The city had been on Ian's mind more than he liked to admit. If the ATU or Agent Hartford became too aggressive, New York was his backup plan—his only plan.

He had even mentioned it to Clarissa in private. She had agreed, saying the children could stay with her again if it came to that. But Ian had decided not to alarm Esther, thinking she might become too aware of the danger and act suspiciously. And now, Freddie's offer from Otto Langendorf could work as a plausible cover if they had to leave in a hurry.

Still, the idea of abandoning the estate didn't sit well with him. He trusted Abram completely, but leaving him to face the challenges alone had its own issues.

The South, despite its undeniable beauty, was not a hospitable place for Black folk. Ian knew that everything Abram accomplished came with an added burden of prejudice—systemic and deeply ingrained. There were those in the region who sought to maintain control through fear, perpetuating an oppressive environment for a significant portion of the population.

Ian was grateful for Sheriff Ronell, who had become an ally over time. The sheriff was widely regarded as a fair and responsible man who refused to tolerate blatant acts of abuse. But even Ronell's influence had its limits; no single man could stem the tide of quiet intolerance and the unspoken barriers that remained rooted in the land and its people.

But New York would only be an option if there was no other choice. The last thing Ian wanted was for Esther to get her heart set on going there.

"Ian... Ian! Are you listening to me?" Esther's voice pulled him out of his thoughts, her fingers tapping on his arm.

"Hmm?" he said, shaking off his thoughts.

"I'm headin' back. You want any more of this food?"

With a lopsided smile, he said, "Give me one more of those biscuits."

"The burnt ones?" she teased, already handing him one.

"I like them that way," he replied, biting into it as she pretended not to hear him.

"Give me a kiss before you go, my love," he said, pulling her closer despite her protests as she packed up the basket.

Holding her tightly, he added, "Please, no more snakes. I won't kill them if I don't have to, but don't pick them up anymore." He tilted his head, trying to catch her eye. "What good am I if I can't at least offer you a snake removal service? I let you handle the bears—can't I at least deal with the snakes?"

Esther could see the sincerity in his eyes, and, giving in, she reluctantly nodded, letting him give her a soft kiss.

Freddie leaned down to put some leather gloves on—the ember of his cigarette flared briefly as he drew in a breath. He watched his brother. He watched his brother's wife. Freddie's expression teetered between amusement and something else.

While he often teased Ian about the allure of city life and all its supposed sophistication, a quiet craving lived in Freddie's heart—a longing for something he'd never even tried to name.

Immanuel Huggler, the brother he often harassed for his steadfastness and simple ways, had managed to find something money couldn't buy—a life worth living.

Freddie couldn't deny the admiration growing in him as he observed Ian and Esther together—something close to jealousy.

Despite the tragedy of losing one wonderful wife, Ian had chosen to keep going, to find love again. And Freddie saw the way Esther looked at his brother—not just with affection, but with something deeper, a fierce loyalty that seemed unshakable.

It was a bond Freddie, for all his charm and escapades, had never come close to experiencing. And with a woman like her—magnetic, challenging, undeniably beautiful, and unpredictable.

An Appalachian Mata Hari, he thought to himself.

He exhaled slowly, the smoke curling upward as he turned his gaze back to the horizon, the illusive Blue Hollow Hills. Maybe the city had its glamour and its endless distractions, but Ian had found something far more valuable in this quiet corner of Tennessee.

Something Freddie hadn't known he had wanted until that moment.

Chapter 38: The Hounds

The week had passed quietly, almost deceptively so. Dolores's arrival had slipped by without stirring the waters, and Ian remained tight-lipped about her connection to his life in New York. Esther, blissfully unaware, had found an unlikely companion in the blond Irish girl.

The two spent their afternoons flipping through Esther's magazines, Dolores's polished city air contrasting with Esther's organic charm. Their friendship bloomed despite its backward beginning.

Late Thursday evening, the warm summer air seeped through the open windows of Clarissa's house, carrying the faint hum of cicadas.

Ian and Freddie sat on the rug in the sitting room, an old box of photos spread out before them. A metal fan perched on a small table, its slow rotation stirring the air just enough to keep the room comfortable, its low, winding hum rising and falling in a steady rhythm.

"That's me at fourteen, with that awful haircut Mama gave us." Ian breathed out a small laugh, brushing his fingers over the edges of the photo. "Remember how we hid in the woods for hours so no one would see us?"

Freddie howled with laughter, his eyes watering. "Ian, you looked like a sheep that got sheared by dull clippers. I can't believe she thought those bangs were a good idea."

Freddie leaned back, laughing so hard he nearly spilled his drink. "And then when we finally came out, everyone at school called us 'the mushroom brothers' for a week!"

Esther glanced over from the couch as Ian flashed her the photo. Dolores sat beside her, a magazine spread open between them.

"Y'all were still cute," Esther teased.

"Cute?" Ian replied, raising an eyebrow. "We looked utterly ridiculous. I almost think my mother did it on purpose."

"Trying to make us look like little German boys, despite trying to fit into English schools," Freddie said, flipping through another stack of photos.

"She wouldn't even let us speak English at home, making it uncomfortable if we ever tried to bring anyone over," Ian added, his tone sobering.

Freddie stopped on a picture, grinning before holding it up. "Like your first girlfriend?" he said, quickly passing the photo to Esther before Ian could stop him.

"What was the Romani girl's name?" Freddie asked, a mischievous gleam in his eye.

Esther smiled as she looked at the small school photo of a pretty girl with darker features, big brown eyes, and wavy hair.

"She's beautiful," Esther remarked, holding it.

"Her name was Zora," Ian said, the name rolling off his tongue like a memory from another life. He reached out for the photo, pausing to look at it before setting it down.

"What happened to her?" Esther asked.

"It didn't end well. Her parents didn't like that I was German, and my mother... well, she was cold as ice to her," he said, placing the picture in a pile with the others.

"You left out the part where you ran off to try and get married," Freddie interjected, his grin widening. "Got caught just out of town after you borrowed Uncle's car without asking. Didn't even have enough money for gas."

"You almost married her?" Esther asked, her brows furrowing. She'd never heard a word about this girl.

Ian laughed, though he shot Freddie a look of mild irritation.

"We didn't know what we were doing," he said. "I'd spent all my money on a new pair of shoes, thinking they'd impress her, not the fact that we had to walk back home with our tails between our legs. I had blisters on my feet for a week. Her parents sent her away afterwards to live with an aunt."

"That's a mighty sad story, Ian. Poor boy, limpin' l' home in them shiny shoes," Esther said, giving him a quick wink. "So, ya got any other girlfriends I oughta know about?" Her tone was playful but probing.

He quickly shook his head, carefully avoiding Dolores's direction. Ian had never considered her a girlfriend—just someone he went on a few dates with.

"What about you, Freddie?" Esther asked, turning her attention to Ian's brother. "How come ya ain't got a girlfriend? With all them pretty city girls."

"Maybe if you had a sister," Freddie said, with a flicker of a smile, though his expression was surprisingly sincere.

Esther just smiled back, but the thought of Marty Ronell's daughter, Fannie Louise, crossed her mind. Of course, no one here knew about her, and it wasn't worth bringing up. She hadn't even let Ian in on her suspicions, and besides, the girl was entirely too young.

"Oh, Esther, that dress!" Dolores exclaimed, pulling her attention as she pointed to a page. "That's the one Lana Turner wore to a premiere last month. You'd look stunning in something like that."

"Lana Turner? Oh, I can't even imagine wearin' somethin' so fancy," Esther replied, her tone tinged with awe. "Do ya really think she's as pretty as she looks in the pictures?"

Dolores smiled knowingly. "She's breathtaking, but they do a lot of work to make them look perfect. Makeup, lighting, the works."

Esther's fingers lingered on the page. "I just like to dream a little, ya know? About what it'd be like to be dressed up like that."

"I get it," Dolores said softly. "When I was younger, I'd stare at these pictures for hours, imagining myself walking into one of those grand theaters."

Esther glanced up at the sound of small footsteps in the hall.

"Uncle Freddie," Rebecca's small voice piped up as she and Benjamin peeked around the corner of the doorway. "Are you really leavin' tomorrow?"

"I thought you both already went to bed," Ian said sternly.

Freddie sighed, smiling at the children as they crept closer, despite their father's scolding. "I am, Bitsy darling."

"But you said two weeks and ya only stayed one," Benjamin protested, crossing his arms. "It's not fair."

Freddie leaned back on his hands, looking at them both with a playful smile. "Now, now, don't start plannin' my funeral just yet. I'll be back before you know it."

Rebecca climbed onto the arm of a chair, her big eyes pleading. "But Christmas is so far away. Can't ya stay a little longer?"

Freddie glanced at Dolores, knowing she had been patient but wanted to return to New York as it hadn't gone as they had planned.

"I'm sorry, kiddo," Freddie said as he reached out to tousle Benjamin's hair. "Listen, I'll make you a deal. When I come back for Christmas, I'll bring presents. Big ones."

Rebecca's face brightened, though she tried to hide it. "Ya pinky promise?"

Freddie crossed his heart solemnly, then stuck out his pinky. "Promise. And maybe, if you're extra good, I'll bring something special."

"What kind of special?" Benjamin asked, skeptical but intrigued.

"That's a surprise," Freddie said with a wink. "You tryin' to trick me into tellin'? I know that game, Benny-boy."

Climbing down from the chair, Rebecca threw her arms around Freddie. "We like you, Uncle. Yer our most favorite uncle ever!"

The words caught Freddie off guard—tugging at his heart. He hadn't expected to get so attached to them, and so quickly.

"Thank you for that," Freddie said, patting her back gently. "Uncle's gonna miss you—especially all the nice pictures you drew for me. I adore the one with me riding the cow. I'm gonna frame that one as soon as I get home."

Rebecca leaned back with a grin. "I made sure to make ya look scared."

"You did a fabulous job. I looked like I had seen a snake," he said, clearly pleasing her.

Clarissa came into the room and eventually coaxed the children upstairs, promising them they could sleep on a cot by her bed, their excitement giving way to yawns.

"Come on now, up you go," she said gently, ushering them toward the stairs.

Rebecca pouted as she climbed, her brother trailing behind. "But Uncle Freddie's leavin' tomorrow," she protested, her words dragging with sleepiness.

"And he'll still be here to say goodbye," Clarissa reassured her. "Now, get on up there. You can help me make him a send-off breakfast."

Their footsteps faded, their chatter slipping away into the distant murmur of tired voices.

Just as the conversation picked back up, a loud, hollow thump hit the front door, echoing through the sitting room.

Knock—knock! It came again.

"Who the hell's that?" Ian said as he sprang up from the floor, his body tense. "Stay here," he said over his shoulder, already crossing the room.

Freddie set his cigarette down in an ashtray, his carefree expression replaced by a bewildered look. "Country people come around this late?" he asked.

"No," Esther said as she rose to follow Ian.

Not knowing who to expect, Ian opened the door cautiously.

Sheriff Ronell stood in the dark of the front porch, his hat clutched in his hands and his face rock-hard serious.

"Ian," the sheriff said, his tone tense. "I went by your house first, but when you weren't there, I came here."

"What's goin' on?" Esther asked as she made her way up behind her husband.

Ronell hesitated, his eyes darting between them.

"Just need to speak to yer husband. Alone. Sorry fer the late-night visit."

Ian glanced at her, giving her a reassuring smile, then stepped outside and closed the door tightly behind him.

But Esther didn't sit down. Instead, she moved to the window, peering out into the darkness. Whispering under her breath, she muttered, "What the hell is goin' on?"

The sheriff motioned for Ian to step off the porch, gesturing toward the driveway where the tall rose bushes cast faint shadows under the moonlight. His face was grim, his usual steady demeanor clouded with concern.

"The ATU's here, Ian. They came earlier than expected, rolled in without even givin' me a warnin'. The whole lot of them," the sheriff began, his voice low but urgent.

Ian stiffened, his hands moving to his hips as he listened.

"They're hell-bent on findin' every moonshiner and bootlegger who's ever so much as touched a bottle in the last decade. And I'm damn certain they know who Esther Huggler is," Ronell continued, his eyes darting toward the house. "For some reason, they're convinced she's a sizeable piece of the puzzle—even if she don't know a damn thing. And I'm gonna let you in on somethin'—and it's disturbing, Ian. They're gonna try to pull that information one way or another. And they have their ways, and it ain't gentle. I'm afraid they'll do whatever it takes."

Ian's jaw tightened, disbelief sharpening each word. "Marty... are you saying they'd rough her up? What kind of men would do something like that?" Ian shook his head. "That can't be what you meant."

Ronell exhaled, nodding toward the darkened fields beyond the house. "Take her somewhere. Anywhere. Until this blows over. They've got a limited budget, and eventually, they'll run outta money and leave. But until then..." He hesitated before saying, "They're not even pretendin' to follow the law. I can't stop 'em. I'm just a little county sheriff—not someone important."

The sheriff's voice dropped even lower, laced with righteous anger. "I just came from Leroy Wheeler's place. They roughed him up, bloodied him pretty bad. Questioned him for hours, left him so swollen I couldn't even recognize him." Ronell gripped his hat tight in his hands, like he might tear the brim clean off. "The boy could hardly walk himself home—he'll be in bed for weeks. He's lucky they didn't just kill him and dump his body." The sheriff's words hit with the same blunt force as his expression. "And he's not the only one."

Ian felt his chest tighten, desperation creeping in. "God, Marty— she's just a woman. She's pregnant."

The sheriff looked Ian square in the eyes. "Hear me good," he said, his voice weighted with regret. "They don't care."

Sheriff Ronell paused as her pregnancy registered, a small, fleeting smile crossing his lips. "A baby, huh?" he said softly, then continued in a more serious tone. "The ATU is unpredictable. That's why I got in my cruiser and drove up here, despite the hour."

"If I take Esther away for a while, what happens to my family here? Clarissa, the kids?" Ian asked, the strain clear in his tone.

"Don't see any reason they'd bother with them. They're not on any list. They're not important—not worth their time," Ronell said. "But Esther... she's tied to Clive in a big way. The agents are callin' her his girl, and they won't let that go."

"She was never his goddamn girl, Marty," Ian growled. "If you knew what that man did to her..." He stopped himself, reining it in.

Marty Ronell already had his suspicions. "I know that. But right now, we gotta be smart. She needs to be gone when they drive up that hill to come fer her."

Ian looked out into the vacant night, his resolve steeled. "We'll go. Tomorrow."

"Please take her somewhere safe," Sheriff Ronell added, his expression heavy. "Somewhere you can get lost fer a while."

"I have an idea of where to go," Ian said, already planning the escape.

"I'm sorry for all of this trouble," the sheriff said as he shifted his gaze to his patrol car.

"Don't see how this is your fault. We're beyond grateful for your help," Ian said as he gripped the man's shoulder.

"I shouldn't have dropped that girl off at that bastard's house," the sheriff continued, the pain echoing through his voice. "I should have left her here, where she was safe. I thought I was doin' the right thing by her, ya know. It kills me—makes me sick what I've done."

"Well, I let you take her, and I've had to own that as well," Ian added, finding himself offering comfort to the man standing before him.

The sheriff straightened, trying to pull himself together despite the tightness in his throat. "Let me know that ya both got there safely, wherever it is yer goin'. Don't use your name on the phone, though— just say yer my cousin Bert from Alabama or somethin'."

Despite the worry clouding Ian's mind, he met the sheriff's gaze head-on. "How will I know if it's safe to bring her back?"

"Well, most of the arrests will have happened—it'll be in the paper, I suppose," the sheriff replied. "If you give me a call—and I tell you it's hog huntin' season here, don't come back."

As Ian walked the sheriff to his car, the man turned, something lighter flickering across his face as he thought of the news Ian had shared.

"Congratulations to you and your wife on what the stork is bringin' ya. That's a little piece of cheerful news on a dreary night."

Ian gave a small nod, thanking him again.

He didn't move. Couldn't. He just stood there, watching as the patrol cruiser's lights faded into the night.

Life had just taken a drastic turn. Ian had been bracing for it— preparing mentally for some time—but the reality still felt unreal.

Esther was getting her wish. He would take her to New York. Not because she wanted it, but because he had no other choice.

His world bent around her now—every choice tied to her safety.

To shield her from the ripple of Clive's sins.

Esther, seeing the sheriff had left, made her way outside. The warm night air wrapped around her as she walked barefoot up to Ian, the soft grass beneath her toes.

He turned as she approached, his face unreadable in the low light.

Once close enough, he reached for her. Taking a deep breath, his mind made up, he said, "We're leaving, you and I. Going... with Freddie and Dolores to New York tomorrow."

"New York? Tomorrow?" Esther repeated, her words faint, unbelieving. "Why? What's happenin'?"

His face searched hers in the dark, the weight of the truth hanging on his tongue.

"They're going to come looking for you here, darling. The Alcohol Tax Unit—their agents are here now, in the county. Remember the man at the feed store?"

Her breath hitched, stomach twisting.

"What does that mean? I ain't said nothin' to no one," she whispered.

"They'll make you talk, my love," he said softly. "They'll pull it from you any way they can." He wrapped his arms around her, holding her as if his embrace could hide her from the world that was trying to take her from him.

Esther shook against him, her mind racing.

"But what about the children and Clarissa?" Her eyes were wide with desperation. "Shouldn't we take 'em with us?"

"They'll be fine," he said firmly. "The ATU's not after them. It's you they want."

Her breath caught as her body tensed.

"I changed my mind, Ian," she blurted. "I ain't goin'. I can't leave Benjamin and Rebecca."

Ian tilted her face to his. "Where Freddie lives... well, Esther, it isn't a place that's very welcoming for my children. Do you understand?"

Tears welled in her eyes as her lips trembled.

"Then we'll stay somewhere else, Ian," she insisted, clinging to any solution.

He exhaled slowly as his words came out measured.

"Esther, you've got a German last name now. And folks aren't gonna rent to us once they see it on paper—or hear me speak. Doesn't matter how well I speak English. I slip now and then, and people catch on quick—especially in New York."

She was silent, her heart pounding against her ribs—he could feel it.

He took her hands again, giving her his strength.

"It's only for a couple of months. We'll come back, I promise. But right now, I need you to trust me. I need you to be safe until the hounds stop circling. I won't let you bleed for a fight that was never yours. My love, I'd die before I let that happen."

Chapter 39: Goodbye

Luggage sat perched on Clarissa's front porch, prepared for the trip ahead. The summer heat was already beating down on the ground, the air heavy and oppressive. It was a warm, rushed day. Not a happy day.

With his own suitcase in hand, Ian walked up from the cottage. He plopped it down by the back of Obadiah's old car, parked haphazardly in the driveway. His eyes swept over the landscape, lingering on the undone projects scattered across the property—the fence posts he hadn't finished reinforcing, the ditches needing attention. Tasks now left in Abram's capable hands.

It felt uncomfortably familiar—too much like when he'd tried to make himself disappear in New York. And yet, it was completely different. Now, the weight of responsibility stretched far beyond crops and fences. He wasn't just running from himself and a stubborn heart—he was running from the law with the woman he loved.

Earlier that morning, he had brought Benjamin and Rebecca's belongings to Clarissa's house. The plan was to have them stay once again in their mother's old room—Adeline's room. The space had remained untouched for the most part, preserved almost like a shrine since she'd left home as a young woman, long before he'd entered the picture.

But no matter how comfortable the room might be, the children were inconsolable.

Rebecca and Benjamin had cried when Ian and Esther sat them down to explain, their tearful protests breaking Esther's resolve.

Esther had fled to the bathroom, the sound of water running from the faucet masking her muffled sobs.

Ian had knocked on the door, speaking softly through the wood, but she hadn't let him in.

Leaving the children went against every instinct she had, and no amount of reassurance from Ian could give her peace.

"It'll be all right, my love," he had whispered through the doorjamb, his voice steady, though he felt ripped open too. "Abram and Mitzy will stay at the cottage while we're gone. They'll be closer to our children, just in case. He will defend them with his life, Esther. You know that. He loves them—and Clarissa."

When that didn't ease her worry, Ian added, "He can be intimidating if someone gives him a reason."

Abram had told him the same thing earlier—reassuring Ian with that quiet conviction of his. He'd also promised to spread the word around town, say they'd gone to help an ailing family member in Minneapolis, a place he knew well.

It was a plausible story, and they'd devised a way to communicate without drawing suspicion—sending mail through Mitzy's mother, who lived just past Jasper, instead of directly to the Old Reed Estate.

Despite all the careful planning, it did nothing to calm the storm inside Esther.

Standing in the small bedroom at Clarissa's house, she stared blankly at the few belongings she'd chosen to take.

The second suitcase Ian had given her sat open on the bed, half-filled with a chaotic assortment of items. She couldn't bring herself to care. She tossed in a few more random things—a hairbrush, a scarf, the ribbon Rebecca had once tied around her wrist—her mind too clouded to decide what mattered.

Ian had urged her to pack her nice dresses, insisting they'd find a way to make the trip enjoyable, despite the reason. But the idea felt impossible.

Rebecca had refused to help her. When Esther asked her to sit with her in the room, Rebecca had glared at her, her small hands clenched into fists.

"I thought ya said you weren't gonna go anywhere," Rebecca snapped. "Ya lied to me."

The words struck Esther like a blow. She had reached out for Rebecca, but the girl stormed off, leaving her alone with the echo of her accusation.

They tore into her heart, leaving it raw—aching with no place to go.

Ian, trying to console Rebecca, had scolded her for calling Esther a liar, telling her it was his decision to take Esther with him.

But Rebecca's reply was sharp and tearful. "Stop sending her away!" she had said, and it cut him deep. It wasn't a happy goodbye for anyone.

The obstacles of a rushed morning continued to bear down on him as he stood by the car. His eyes traced the orchard stretched out before him—vibrant green in the sunlight, the trees swaying slightly in the breeze.

The summer sun warmed his shoulders, but it wasn't enough to shake the chill building in his chest.

The sheriff's late-night visit—his urgency—kept replaying in Ian's mind. He couldn't help but worry that the ATU could show up at any moment, and he wanted Esther long gone before they did.

Abram's footsteps broke the quiet, gravel crackling beneath his boots. He came up and gave his friend a solid smack on the shoulder, his usual jovial demeanor masking the concern etched into his features.

"I know ya gonna miss me, but Lord, I already told ya I was taken," Abram teased with a grin. "And Mitzy and I are gonna enjoy tryin' that cottage on for size."

Ian turned to him, his face tight with worry. "I hate leaving all of this mess in your hands," he admitted.

Abram waved him off with a chuckle. "Ya didn't have a problem runnin' off 'fore," he said, his grin widening.

But his gaze told the truth as it settled on the orchard, knowing full well the worries plaguing Ian's mind. The dry summer had left the crop struggling, and this year's harvest wouldn't be as abundant as the last.

"I left all my ledgers on the table in my house. Please use them, Abram," Ian urged, his tone quiet but firm.

Abram snorted, amused. "Good Lord, Ian, we'll be fine. Stop frettin'. Miss Clarissa knows this place through and through."

Ian smiled, though he knew Abram didn't realize the full extent of the challenges ahead.

Clarissa might know the trees, but she had never handled the logistics of the harvest—the pickers, the deliveries, or the buyers. Obadiah had always taken care of that, and Ian had stepped into his shoes when the time came.

Abram, on the other hand, had arrived after Adeline and Obadiah had passed.

Ian had hired him to fix a tractor, and within months, Abram had become indispensable to the estate.

One day, Abram showed up with Mitzy, a not-so-shy but charming young woman, and announced that he intended to marry her. Clarissa, unwilling to lose a hard worker, had offered them the bunkhouse down the road, despite it needing repairs. Abram and Mitzy had accepted, grateful for the opportunity, and had carved out a life for themselves on the estate.

"I've got this, Ian," Abram said firmly, snapping Ian out of his thoughts. "But y'all really need to get goin' if ya gonna make that bus."

Ian sighed and nodded. "You're right."

Together, the men loaded the last of the suitcases into the car. Ian stepped back inside the house, calling out into the hallway.

"Time to go," he announced, his voice carrying through the rooms.

He glanced around, seeing Clarissa, Freddie, Dolores, Benjamin, and Mitzy gathered near the front room.

"Where are my wife and daughter?" Ian asked, a hint of impatience in his voice.

"Esther said she couldn't find Rebecca, so she went looking," Freddie replied, standing casually, though his eyes were laced with concern.

"I think she said she was gonna check the tree hut," Mitzy added, her voice soft as she jostled her cranky toddler on her hip, her expression mirroring the mood of the morning.

"I'll go get 'em," Benjamin offered, his small voice trying to sound brave.

Despite his father's instruction to be the man of the house while he was gone, the responsibility weighed on him. Ian had said he expected Benjamin to act like a Huggler—taking care of the womenfolk and the other children. The boy had taken the words to heart—his father's opinion of him was a matter of utmost importance.

"Naw, why don't you all head outside," Ian replied, resting a hand on Benjamin's shoulder. "Those of you going can start loading up. I'll run out there."

Ian's long strides carried him toward the old cistern and tree house. He pushed past the fruit-bearing trees of the upper orchard, squinting against the brightness of the sun, hoping Rebecca and Esther were actually there. He didn't want any more delays.

As the small clearing came into view, a breeze stirred the yellowing grass, making a soft shh-ing sound that made Ian pause— like the land itself was saying goodbye. Then he spotted the large sycamore, the wooden hut nestled in its bosom.

Relieved, he saw Esther's foot dangling just over the edge as he stepped closer. Through the wooden doorway of the tree hut, he saw his wife sitting, rocking Rebecca gently in her arms.

The little girl's face was blotchy from crying, her small chest hiccupping against Esther's. Tear stains traced down Esther's face as well, though her movements remained soothing.

Ian rested his arms on the frame of the open doorway, watching silently for a moment. Esther glanced up, their eyes meeting, and he gave her a small nod, letting her take her time.

"Found her out here cryin' by herself," Esther said, brushing Rebecca's hair back before leaning down to kiss the top of her head.

"Aww, sweet girl," Ian murmured. "Come here," he said, holding out his arms.

Rebecca lifted her tear-streaked face, hesitating before crawling toward him.

She melted into his embrace as Ian scooped her up, the warmth of her father's arms settling her trembling body.

With one arm still around Rebecca, Ian reached out to help Esther down from the treehouse.

"Let's head back to the house," he said quietly, rubbing Rebecca's back as they began walking.

Rebecca's small voice broke the silence. "I don't wanna stay without y'all," she said, her words muffled against his shoulder.

"I know, daughter," Ian replied. "We're gonna miss you, too. But there's a lot to look forward to when we get back."

"Like what?" she asked, her tone skeptical, challenging him in the way only a child could.

Ian smiled at her, then glanced at Esther walking beside him. "Well, for one, when we get back, Esther's belly's gonna be round with a baby. And before you know it, you'll have a little brother or sister. That's something to be excited about."

"It's gonna be a girl, Pa," Rebecca said firmly, pulling back to look him in the eyes. Her little hands grabbed his face with the conviction of a prophet.

"She's my sister. And she's gonna look like you," Rebecca added firmly.

Ian chuckled, his heart softening as he held her gaze. "Maybe."

But Rebecca shook her head, insistent. "Pa, it's my sister. She's got your hair," she said, tugging at a piece of his as if to prove her point. The certainty on her small face was something he couldn't argue with.

Glancing at Esther, Ian was surprised to find her wearing the same calm, knowing expression. She didn't disagree. In fact, she looked as if she believed Rebecca without question.

Rebecca continued, her voice quieter now. "I talk to her sometimes, Pa."

Ian frowned slightly, curiosity and concern mixing. "You talk to her?"

"Mm-hmm," Rebecca said, her tone serious and matter-of-fact.

"I talk to her sometimes, too," Esther added.

Ian raised an eyebrow, his practical mind balking. "That would be nice," he said. "But we can't really talk to the baby until it's born. And that won't be for a long time, Rebecca."

He worried their shared fantasy was setting the little girl up for disappointment if it turned out to be a boy.

But as he glanced between Esther and Rebecca, their shared conviction made him pause. For a moment, he wondered if there was something he was missing—a connection between them that defied reason.

He decided to let it rest, holding his daughter a little tighter as they walked back toward the house.

But Rebecca doubled down, her small voice unyielding. "Pa, you don't know everythin'. My sister is gonna be born on Christmas."

Ian paused, his brows furrowing. "Rebecca, you heard me talking a couple of days ago. That's how you know that," he said, his tone firm but gentle.

Esther cut in, shaking her head as they walked, the house and driveway now coming into view. "Ian, no, she didn't. She wasn't anywhere near us."

Ian glanced at her, his expression skeptical. "Well, she must've heard it somewhere, Esther."

Rebecca stopped in his arms, her small hands clinging to his collar. "Pa, my little sister told me in a dream," she said, her voice wavering—almost hurt that he didn't believe her.

Ian sighed and rubbed his large hand over his daughter's hair. He didn't want to argue with her, not now—not when this might be the last memory of him for the next couple of months. "If you say so," he said, his tone soft with resignation.

As they walked up to the waiting car, Ian set her down. He crouched to meet her eyes, a big smile spreading across his face. He hoped his charm might smooth things over.

It worked—at least as much as it could. Rebecca's lips quivered before she gave him a reluctant smile in return.

There were more embraces, more tears. Clarissa held each of them tightly, her whispered prayers almost audible as she told them to take care. The children clung to Esther and Ian, their small voices laced with sadness as they repeated, "I love you."

With a final, heartfelt goodbye and a quiet wish that time would pass quickly, they left.

The car rattled down the long dirt road, the view of the Old Reed Estate fading in the rearview mirror.

Ian sat in the passenger seat, his face unreadable as he glanced over at Esther, who sat in the middle.

She turned and looked back one last time.

Behind them, the Blue Hollow Hills seemed to whisper her name.

Its voice was tangled with all the others—Rebecca and Benjamin, the ones who laid claim to her love—asking her not to leave.

As if he heard it too—the hush of the hills, the ache in her silence—Ian reached over and squeezed her hand, his silent vow that they would return clear in the gesture, a reply to her sorrow.

Thank You for Reading!

If you enjoyed *Where the River Settles – The Lost Pages – Hymns of Blue Hollow*, I would be grateful if you took a moment to leave a review on **Amazon** or **Goodreads**. Your words help more readers discover Esther and Ian's story, and I appreciate every single one.

But the story doesn't end here—

Book 3: *Held in the Rising Smoke* (available)

Book 4: *Forged by Wind and Song* (available)

Book 5: To be announced.

To stay connected and be the first to hear about new releases, exclusive content, and behind-the-scenes updates, you can find me here:

Website: HymnsofBlueHollow.com

Facebook: Hymns of Blue Hollow

TikTok: @kemma_indie_author

Instagram: @KemmaMarShall

YouTube: @HymnsofBlueHollowBookTrailer

Thank you for being part of this journey, for making the Blue Hollow Hills your home, and for hearing its call.

www.ingramcontent.com/pod-product-compliance
Lightning Source LLC
Chambersburg PA
CBHW021940110726
47901CB00003B/914